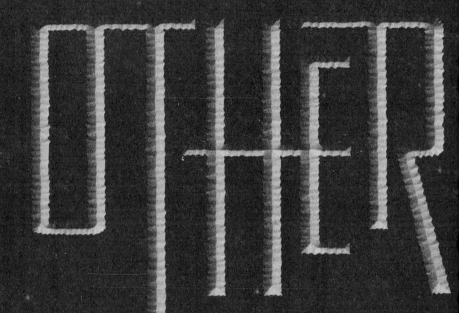

OTHER

AMULET BOOKS
NEW YORK

# BOUND

CORINNE DUYVIS

Library of Congress Cataloging-in-Publication Data
Duyvis, Corinne.
    Otherbound / by Corinne Duyvis.
        pages cm
    Summary: A seventeen-year-old boy finds that every time he closes his eyes,
he is drawn into the body of a mute servant girl from another world—a
world that is growing increasingly more dangerous, and where many things
are not as they seem.
    ISBN 978-1-4197-0928-9 (alk. paper)
    [1. Fantasy.]  I. Title.
    PZ7.D95850t 2014
    [Fic]—dc23
2013029536

Text copyright © 2014 Corinne Duyvis
Book design by Sara Corbett

Printed and bound in U.S.A.
10 9 8 7 6 5 4 3 2

THE ART OF BOOKS SINCE 1949

115 West 18th Street
New York, NY 10011
www.abramsbooks.com

For my four grandparents, who have
always encouraged me—
even when they weren't entirely clear
on what I was doing, exactly.

Voor mijn vier
grootouders, die
me altijd hebben
aangemoedigd—zelfs
wanneer het ze niet
helemaal duidelijk was
waarin precies.

Alinean Islands

GRAY SEA

★Maessen

DUNELANDS

Bedam★

★Roerte

★Teschel

GREA+ER OCEAN

N
W    E
S

Elig Islands

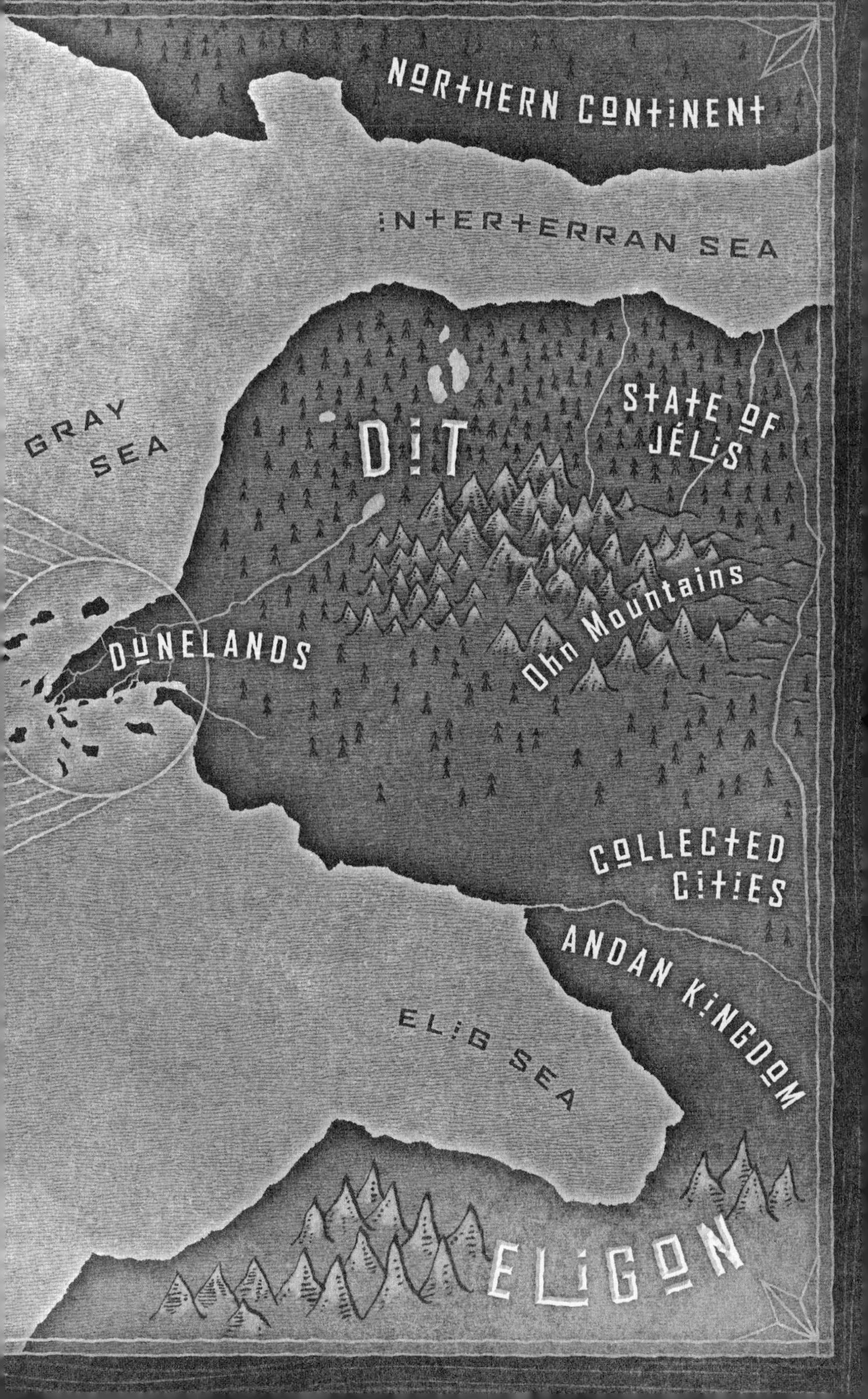
NORTHERN CONTINENT
INTERTERRAN SEA
GRAY SEA
DIT
STATE OF JÉLIS
Ohn Mountains
DUNELANDS
COLLECTED CITIES
ANDAN KINGDOM
ELIG SEA
ELIGON

n the world of the Dunelands, Amara was sleeping.

Striding through the Walgreens aisles, Nolan wished he could do the same—just curl up in bed, shut his eyes, and see nothing but the insides of his eyelids.

No: see nothing but the insides of Amara's eyelids. He hadn't seen his own in years.

If he hurried, he could buy the notebooks and get home before Amara woke up. He stopped by the office supplies, adjusted his backpack, and hunted the shelves for the right kind: hard-backed, easy to stack, and with thick enough paper that his ink wouldn't bleed through when his pen paused at the same spot too long.

"Can I help you find anything?" A perky salesclerk appeared to his right.

Nolan offered a smile. Not quite his teacher-smile, but close—he didn't visit stores often enough to have a salesclerk-smile. All these fluorescent lights and shoppers made him uneasy. If something happened in Amara's world, he had nowhere here to hide. At least his school had bathrooms. Sometimes he even got to use a teacher's office. When the disabled kid said he felt a seizure coming, teachers listened, if only out of fear that Dad would threaten to sue them again.

"No, thank you." Nolan drew back from the salesclerk. Another smile. He fingered the straps of his backpack. "I'm doing fine. But thank you."

He turned back to the notebooks. Amara would give everything she owned for a single one of these. He ignored that thought—with Amara asleep, this was the one time of day he could focus on his own world. Once she woke, or when she started dreaming, all his inner peace and quiet would fade.

Maybe he should pick up some pens, as well. He couldn't risk running out of ink.

The salesclerk crouched to rearrange some mixed-up kids' sketchbooks. Nolan zeroed in on the shelves, on the recent pop cover blaring from the store's speakers. Easier said than done. The music cut out every time he blinked, replaced with Amara's slow breaths and the quiet rustling of sleepers in her inn room.

There. They'd moved his brand of notebooks to another spot. Nolan raised his—

**—get up!—**

—it was just a snatch of a voice. Male. At first, Nolan thought it was another shopper, maybe the radio.

It wasn't. Amara had woken up. Nolan turned away from the salesclerk. He needed to shut his eyes without the clerk worrying, get a second's glimpse of Amara's world to see what was happening. The fluorescent glow of the Walgreens faded into nothing—

"—this?" It was Jorn's voice, as Nolan knew it would be. Long fingers dug into Amara's wrist. They were cold to her sleep-warm skin, and strong, squeezing too tightly.

Jorn yanked her out of the alcove bed. Her blanket slid off, caught by the hatch, and Amara stumbled on all fours onto the inn floor. Splinters stabbed her knees and feet.

Jorn shoved beige squares of paper at Amara. Scratches of ink covered every inch, forming slashes and loops and dots Amara recognized as letters. "I know these are yours," Jorn growled. "You're learning to write. What do you think you need that for?"

Amara didn't answer. Even when she could, when he wasn't dragging her by the arm like this, she never answered. Jorn would only get worse. She scrambled for balance, but her every muscle held stiff from fear and sleep.

Through the panic, Nolan tried to yank Amara's arm free. It didn't respond. Never did. He only got to watch and feel.

*Cilla,* Amara was thinking, *maybe Cilla can stop him, she could tell him that teaching me to write was her idea, that it wasn't just me*—but Jorn wouldn't care. He couldn't punish Cilla. He *could* punish Amara—

"—Nolan?"

His eyes flew open at the feel of the salesclerk's hand on his back. Her perfume wafted into his nose, sharp and Jélisse fruity—no, the Jélisse people were from Amara's world, not here. The clerk's perfume was just plain fruit. End of story. This world: perfume and office supplies, the inconstant whir of the AC. Forget the Dunelands. Forget the splintery wood of the inn floors, the musty smell of Amara's mattress, the salt coming in from the dunes.

He must've been in Amara's head for longer than a second. At least he'd stayed upright, though he'd slouched against the store's racks and knocked a pack of notebooks to the floor.

"Are you all right?" The clerk squinted. Caked makeup around her eyes wrinkled into crow's-feet. "You're Nolan, aren't you? Nolan Santiago? Should I call Dr. Campbell?"

"No. I think I'm all right." He forced a smile. She not only knew his name, but his doctor's, too? Small-town gossip would be the death of him. "Sorry for dropping those."

"No problem at all!"

Nolan took a pack of pens from the rack, then bent to help pick up the fallen notebooks. His eyes started to ache, but he couldn't allow himself to blink. He knew what Amara was facing; blinking meant he would have to face it, too. He needed to hide. "Could you point me to a bathroom?"

He couldn't keep his eyes open any longer. They burned. He blinked, and for that fraction of a second Amara sucked him in—**flames crackled in the room's fire pit, and Amara made a sound that barely escaped her lips**—then Nolan was back. He blinked a couple more times, too rapidly to get anything but flashes of heat and fear. The fire was getting closer.

Something had happened to Jorn. Nolan hadn't seen him this outraged in years. He'd hit Amara often enough, and writing and reading were off-limits for servants like her—but *this*? No.

Nolan held the plastic-wrapped notebooks so firmly they shook. The salesclerk was staring at him. If she'd answered his bathroom question, he'd missed it. "I'll get your mother," she said.

His mother? How would she find his mother? But the clerk was gone before he could respond, and Nolan gritted his teeth, spinning around. Finding a bathroom would take too long. He'd find a place to hide in the parking lot, instead. He couldn't break down in the store. Couldn't make a scene.

Another blink. Nolan went from stalking through the aisles to—**dragged along, legs tangled and kicking**—and when his eyes opened and he snapped back to his own world, he stumbled. His prosthetic foot slid out from under him before he could get a grip. Nolan caught himself on the nearest rack, sending metal rattling against metal.

"Nolan?" Mom's voice. He stiffened. There she stood, short and thin, wearing an ill-fitting Walgreens uniform and a name tag that proclaimed her MARÍA.

Despite everything, that caught Nolan's eye. Mom was a child-care professional. She had training, certificates, her own business. What was she doing here?

"Are you OK?" Mom asked.

"I need a—a space." Nolan tried a Mom-smile and failed.

"Is he going to have a seizure?" The salesclerk stood behind

Mom, her eyes as wide as Nolan's own probably were but for entirely different reasons. She dug around in her pockets for her cell. "I'll call 911!"

"No," Mom bit out. "They can't help. Is the back room free?"

The next time Nolan blinked, flames licked at Amara's hands. He muffled a scream. He found himself bent over, the notebooks in his hands creasing. Let me go, he thought at Amara, though she didn't hear him and never would. This was a one-way street. She didn't know Nolan existed, let alone what her magic did to him. Please. Stop pulling me in. I don't want to feel this.

He wanted to tune her out. Even with his eyelids spread wide, the aftertaste of her pain clung to his hands, and more than anything, he wanted to tune her out. On their own, the images he got through blinking were chaos, like switching between TV channels and only catching a half word here, a bright shape there—enough to wreak havoc on his concentration but nothing more. Get enough of them, though, and he had two movies playing alongside each other and no way of pressing pause.

A group of curious shoppers watched from a distance. Not that many, given that it was a Sunday morning, but enough to make him wish for the parking lot, despite the risk. He'd lost one foot already. If Amara made him stumble onto the road, who knew what'd come next? He should've stayed home. He should've asked Mom or Dad to pick up the notebooks while getting groceries. Served him right for thinking he could handle anything on his own.

Mom wrapped her arm around his shoulders and guided him to the back room, where he slammed his ass to the floor and pressed himself against a wall. He managed a tight nod in thanks as Mom clicked on a table fan, which whirred and stuttered into action. She pushed aside chairs and boxes, anything he might hurt himself on. Standard seizure procedure. Even though there was nothing standard about his seizures.

Nolan managed to open the zipper of his backpack, then grabbed his current notebook and the pen clipped to its cover. He should write down what he saw. Writing always helped.

"I'm here, all right?" Mom said, in Spanish now, her voice soothing. "I'm taking an early lunch break. We'll go home the moment you can. I'm right here."

Every time he blinked: the sear of pain, the smell of burning flesh. Already, sweat was beading on his forehead. The pain lingered after he opened his eyes, his brain still shouting panicked messages of fire! fire! fire! before catching up. Nolan's hands were intact, Nolan's world safe.

Until he blinked again.

He couldn't hold on to the pen. His hands squeezed to his chest until they were all that remained.

Amara's skin curled away, then healed in fits and starts before burning anew. Jorn held Amara's arms still. Fighting was no use, but the rest of her thrashed, anyway. She couldn't help it.

"One task," Jorn said. His voice filled her head, thumping with every breath. "You have one task. Keep Princess Cilla safe. That's your duty. Instead . . ."

Cilla and Maart were awake now. Cilla murmured something, her voice barely audible over the crackle of the fire. Was she crying? Was that why her hands were pressed to her mouth, or was it because of the smell? Amara tried to focus on Maart instead. Across the room, beyond angry flames, his callused hands signed support, love—things she couldn't do anything with.

Amara tried to focus on him.

Instead her head whipped back, and she screamed, wordlessly, until Jorn slammed his hand against her mouth to smother even that.

⌒〰️〇〰️〜

"I'm sorry," Cilla said.

After he'd finished punishing Amara, Jorn had snapped at

Maart to go get water for laundry and left for the bathhouse, leaving Amara and Cilla alone in the inn room.

"I'll talk to him." Cilla stood with her back straight and spoke as primly and carefully as ever. Only the fingers clutching one another by her stomach gave away her unease. "I'll tell Jorn it was my idea to teach you and Maart to read and write."

What good would that do? Would that draw back the flames from Amara's hands? Amara couldn't bring herself to answer yet. Jorn had been like this before, years ago. He'd drink too much and get too angry, and of their group—Jorn and Princess Cilla and the two servants—Amara was the only one he could take it out on without repercussions.

She'd need to be careful not to give him another excuse.

For now, she sat against a wall, her fingers outstretched on her knees, and studied her unmarred, sand-colored skin. Fresh hair sprouted along the backs of her hands, the strands orange as they caught flickers from surrounding gas lamps. Long fingers. Pale, barely there nails. They hadn't had time to regrow fully.

She'd taken a long time to heal, minutes and minutes, when other healing mages would've taken seconds. Only the fragile pink tinge of freshly grown skin remained, along with the smell, which had nested in her hair and clothes and the walls pressing in on them. The scent of the fire pit's coals wasn't strong enough to mask it.

"I doubt talking to Jorn will make any difference, Princess," Amara signed finally. She chose her words with care. She couldn't afford one wrong sign, one too-angry flick of her fingers. "Servants are not allowed to speak, read, or write. Those are the rules."

It was easier to stop someone from speaking than anything else; the scars in her mouth testified to that. If she'd learned to heal a couple of months earlier than she had, she might still have a tongue.

She was wasting time. Visiting the baths might calm Jorn, but if not, he couldn't return to see her sitting uselessly. She ought to start on her work. She pushed herself up and off the wall. Maybe she could clean the food—no, she'd better start by checking the floors. Jorn prioritized Cilla's safety. He'd made that clear. Amara's hands shook from rising anger, but she forced them flat and ran them over the floorboards. Pebbles, sharp pieces of bark, pine needles—anything that might injure Cilla and activate her curse. Splinters had to be rubbed off carefully, and the floor generated plenty of those. She'd already dug two from her knees.

She avoided the fire pit for now, sticking close to the walls. A nearby gas lamp illuminated the floor. Bit by bit, she felt her pulse slow.

"You're reading faster every day, though," Cilla said. "If you want, we can keep studying. I'm sure we can hide it better from Jorn."

Amara turned her hands over. The pink had faded, settling into the standard beige of her palms. Her jaw set. At least Cilla had waited for her to heal before suggesting they continue.

How had Jorn found out she'd been learning letters in the first place? Amara had let nothing slip, and Maart knew better. As a mage, Jorn had plenty of ways to discover things on his own, but what if Cilla had told him? It wouldn't have been on purpose—she and Amara had known each other too long for that, since they were little kids adjusting to life on the run—but Cilla might've mentioned it offhandedly, or maybe hadn't taken enough care to hide their papers. They weren't her consequences to bear, after all.

Amara ought to respond. "Perhaps," she signed. The wood was fusty so close to her nose, and a splinter stabbed her palm. She held her hand to the light to wiggle it free.

"Is that necessary? It's not as though I ever take off my boots," Cilla said.

Amara dropped the splinter into the fire pit. "Jorn's orders."

"Well . . . I found a news sheet for us to study."

Amara hesitated. She signed slowly, "Is that a request?"

"It's a . . ." Cilla looked down, towering over her. Cilla was younger and only a fingerwidth taller, but from this angle the difference between them seemed monumental. "It's a do-whatever-you-want."

Amara curled her hands into loose fists. The skin on her knuckles stretched but stayed even and whole. She didn't want to anger Jorn further, but she hated the thought of giving up on her words now that she'd come so far. She knew how to write most letters and recognized them almost always, from

Cilla's neat, instructive slashes to stallkeepers' shortened loops on signs advertising bread and grains and kommer leaves. Reading made every trip outside into something *more*, like strangers talking to her, words and connections wherever she looked. The world had been so empty before.

But she couldn't anger Jorn. And she couldn't trust Cilla.

"Here." With a flourish, Cilla retrieved a crumpled broadsheet from her topscarf. She placed the paper on the floor and moved to smooth it out. A formless sound escaped Amara's throat. She shot forward to still Cilla's hands before they reached the page.

Cilla started. Then, after a moment, she said, "I . . . wasn't planning to touch the floor."

Slowly, once Amara was sure Cilla wouldn't make another move for the paper, she let go. She couldn't risk the bareness of Cilla's skin so close to the splintered wood. Cilla shouldn't even come near the edges of the paper. Even one small, spilled drop of blood would activate her curse, and then Amara would need to lure the harm her way, and she'd already hurt enough for today.

"I really wouldn't have touched it," Cilla reiterated, but for all her care, one misstep could mean her death, and Amara's task was to not let that happen.

Even if—too often—she wanted to. No Cilla, no curse. No pain. Then she'd see that restrained smile on Cilla's face, or they'd sit hunched over a book, thigh by thigh, and Amara didn't know what she wanted.

It didn't matter. If Cilla died, Jorn would make certain Amara did, as well.

"It's colder every day," Amara ended up signing. She couldn't tell the princess what to do outside of emergencies, but this was within bounds. "Shall I find your gloves?"

A smile wavered on Cilla's face. "I'll fetch them myself. Thank you."

Amara watched her rise and move for her bag. The curse meant Cilla needed to be fully aware of her every movement, which made her graceful and cautious at the same time. People would say it was simply her Alinean arrogance, but it went further than that: Cilla owned every step she took. Even when she ate, she did it gently to avoid biting her cheeks or tongue. That kind of thoughtfulness—the barely there sway of her hip, the deliberate way she crouched and her fingers plucked open her bag—drew the eye.

It shouldn't. Amara averted her gaze and smoothed out the news sheet. She shouldn't be reading, either, should do as she ought and search the floors, but she started with the far-right headline, anyway: Developments—In— She didn't recognize the next word and read it slowly, mentally sounding the letters. Am—Ma—Lor—Ruh. Ammelore, the town. A tiny thrill ran through her. The next headline: Ruudde—Celebrates—Capture—

A lock of hair fell past her shoulder into her face. She recoiled at the scent of her own burned flesh trapped in the strands. Pressing her hand to her mouth, she kept going—

Ruudde was the minister closest to the island they were hiding on, and that made him a threat, and that made him worth reading about—but the letters came slowly, far too slowly, and by the time Cilla sank down by Amara's side with her hands safely gloved, Amara had only made it past the first few words.

"Bedam's minister made a rare public appearance," Cilla read, her index finger moving down the page, "to celebrate . . . Oh."

"What does it say?" Urgency showed in every twitch of Amara's fingers. Shouldn't read this. Shouldn't trust Cilla. If there was news on their enemy, though, they ought to know.

Cilla scanned the rest of the column. She read so fast, her dark eyes moving up and down, right and left—Amara couldn't imagine what that was like. "They captured the Alinean loyalists—'rebels'—who attacked Ruudde's palace the other day. Ruudde's palace?"

Amara doubted Cilla remembered the palace where she was born; Ruudde and the other ministers had slaughtered the Alinean royals and taken over the Dunelands when Cilla was only a toddler. Cilla scoffed, anyway. "Ruudde made an appearance to celebrate on the Bedam town square . . . a woman threw a stone . . . Ruudde retaliated . . ."

"Who'd be stupid enough to throw a stone at a minister? It wouldn't hurt them." Ministers didn't have to be mages, and mages didn't necessarily heal, but the current ministers were masters at both. They were trained mages, like Jorn, who drew on the spirits of the seas and winds for their spells in a way Amara had never been able to mimic. The spirits let her do nothing but heal herself, and slowly at that, with jerks and stutters and long pauses.

"I imagine it's satisfying," Cilla said humorlessly. "But no. Not smart. The article doesn't mention the woman's name." That said enough. Nobody, least of all an official news sheet, would disturb the dead by calling on them.

Cilla stared at the page, her eyes unmoving, no longer reading. Amara understood. Ruudde had killed Cilla's parents and siblings in the coup. He would've killed Cilla, too, had one of the palace mages—Jorn—not smuggled her out in time.

When Ruudde and the other ministers had discovered Cilla's escape, they'd cursed her. And while that curse was active, she was too fragile to make her survival public. Anyone could kill her with a scratch. Plenty of hired mages had tried over the years. The only way to stay alive was to duck her head and run from town to town, which gave Cilla no chance of reclaiming her throne. That throne was in the Dunelands' capital, Bedam, only hours away from where they were hiding now. They hadn't been this close in years.

Amara wondered if that weighed on Cilla the same way it did on her.

Footsteps approached the inn room. Cilla stuffed the news sheet back into her topscarf. Amara crouched and pressed her hands to the floor. Her heart slammed. Jorn wasn't supposed to return yet. He took long, slow baths, and given the mood he'd been in, he'd be in no rush to get back, and—

The door creaked open. Maart stood in the doorway, his waves of hair tangled from the wind. Amara's breath hissed in relief. Not Jorn. He and Maart might have the same splotch of freckles and the same blocky jaw, the same splayed Dit nose and shallow Dit eyes, and both let their hair spill to their elbows in the old way, but the resemblance people always remarked on was lost on Amara. It had nothing to do with the hint of Alinean features on Maart's face or even the age difference; Maart could simply never be like Jorn.

Maart could never scare her.

He hurriedly put down his bucket so he could sign. "Are you OK? Your hands?"

Amara showed the backs and palms—not a trace of her injuries left but her too-short nails—then glanced past him. Cilla had sat down in her alcove, leaning forward to keep her head in the light.

Maart turned to follow Amara's gaze. "Princess." His hands moved rigidly.

"I was just showing Amara a news sheet. Do you want to take a look, too? We've decided to keep up her studies."

Had they?

"I'm meant to wash our clothes." Maart took his eyes off Cilla the second he finished signing. He had to be more careful. Cilla would pick up on his reticence. A warning hovered on Amara's fingertips, but she saved it for later, when they were alone.

"I'm . . . not certain I should keep studying," Amara signed instead. She didn't dare look away as Cilla's eyes darkened, hope fading. "Thank you, though."

The gratitude felt like a betrayal. At least Maart was so busy plucking the used clothes from their bags that he might not see her hands.

Cilla nodded. The heels of her boots brushed past the wood paneling under and beside the bed as she swung her legs left and right, as if she was trying to keep busy. It made her look younger. Cilla didn't move like that often, but right now, her legs were swinging the same way any normal girl's might, and that caught Amara's attention just as much as Cilla's self-possession did.

It shouldn't, Amara reminded herself.

Maart sat by the bucket he'd carried in and worked stubbornly on. His breaths still came heavily. He must've rushed back to the inn, lugging that heavy bucket with him, worried sick. But with Cilla here, they couldn't talk. Amara lowered her head and continued her work, dust and dirt tickling her nose. She held in a sneeze. For too long, the only sounds in the room were Maart's scrubbing, the swishing of Cilla's legs, Amara's hands brushing the ground.

Finally, Jorn returned, his hair still wet, a bag of supplies in his arms. He put them away, ignoring Amara and Maart, and went back out. Cilla eagerly followed him to the pub downstairs. Amara waited for the door to shut behind them and sat upright. "That wasn't smart. You can't ignore Cilla like that."

A leg of one of Amara's winterwears flopped over the edge of the laundry bucket as Maart shoved it away, freeing his hands to sign. "I don't care. What she did—"

"We don't know if she told Jorn! And learning to read and write was my choice to make. Our choice. You're lucky Jorn didn't recognize your handwriting."

"You shouldn't thank her. You shouldn't even be checking that floor! Let those splinters stab her instead of you. Let her die. Why do you even care about putting her on the throne?"

"I don't." Her hands moved snappishly. Any fool knew the Alineans should have the Dunelands throne back—they had never abused magic the way the ministers did—but what did it matter to her and Maart? Servants would stay servants. "I—no. Maart, I don't want to fight. Let's play a game," she signed, but even as she did, she wasn't sure what kind of game. Jorn had burned her practice papers along with her hands, and the only paper left sat in his bag. He'd notice if they took any. They'd once had a game board and pieces and a set of dice, but they'd abandoned those weeks ago when they'd fled a farm. "No, no game. Stories. Tell me about . . ."

"It still smells," Maart said. A dripping wet topscarf rested on his lap. The soap reached to his elbows, and he flicked water and suds around with every word he signed. "The room still smells. Amara, I can't . . . I should've done something. I should've fought."

"We could hum," Amara said, thinking back to the day

before, when they'd started out with a tune and ended up pitching their hums higher and higher, until Amara could no longer match his and ended up laughing so hard her stomach hurt. They used to do that all the time, and that was the Maart she wanted right now.

He didn't respond. Didn't smile, either. His lips stayed in that same, by now too familiar, straight line.

Amara relented. "What could you have done? What's your great plan? Look at me: I'm fine. You wouldn't be."

Maart's skinny eyebrows sank and knitted together. This seriousness didn't suit him. His signs slowed down with intention. "We can run."

"He'd find us." He'd kill them.

"We can run fast."

"That's not a plan." Amara scoffed. "You'll get us killed by talking like that, you idiot."

Last month Maart might've grinned at that. Now, he simply drew back, stone-faced.

Amara hadn't meant . . . She sighed. Her eyes shut. Maart was the only person in the world on her side. The only person she could talk to—and the only one she could shout at freely. And she needed to shout. Sometimes she didn't think she could keep it all in. It simmered under her skin, pushing outward until her body no longer felt like her own.

She'd need to keep it there. Maart wasn't the right person to shout at.

"I'm sorry." Amara walked over and lowered herself to her haunches. She reached for the side of Maart's neck. Her fingers ran over the raised skin of his servant tattoo, identical to hers but for the different palace sigil in the center. That was her answer. People would recognize those tattoos anywhere they ran, if they didn't recognize their signing first. They'd deliver her and Maart to the nearest minister, who would punish or kill them for abandoning their duties—and if anyone realized Amara and Maart had betrayed the new regime by protecting the princess, they'd be just as dead, but their executioners would put a lot more thought into how.

Given Amara's healing, they'd need to put thought into it.

Jorn had enchanted some of their possessions to act as anchors to let him track them. Even if they ran fast enough to escape the anchors' reach, they'd have no food and no shelter and no way to get the money needed for either.

"It's not right." Maart's hands moved reluctantly. "Standing there, doing nothing, while Jorn—while you—" He stopped at that, jabbing at Amara's chest.

"It's hard to watch. I know." Amara bet it was harder to feel. She didn't say that, instead inching closer, balancing on the balls of her feet. "Don't talk about running."

"Jorn can't see."

"Doesn't matter." Even this felt dangerous. They were too open here, too visible, with this entire wide room around them. Jorn would know. Somehow, he'd know. Maart was wide-shouldered and strong, but going up against a mage—even a mage like Jorn, who couldn't heal—never made for a fair fight. Amara didn't know what Jorn would do to Maart. Or Jorn might remember that he needed Maart functioning and he'd take out his anger on Amara, instead, and she didn't—she didn't want—

She sucked in a breath that stuck in her throat. She didn't want to anger Jorn. That was all.

"You can't ignore—" Maart started.

That only made her want to shout again. She chose the better option, rising and leaning in to smother Maart's words with her torso. His hands stilled, turning into flat palms, still slick from the laundry water, against her ribs. As they slid across her skin, she kissed him. His lips were sticky-sweet from breakfast fruits. The older kind, overripe and dented, because that was all people like them got. They squeezed the fruits, anyway. Juice and pulp went down easier in hollow mouths.

Her teeth nibbled Maart's lips, Alinean-full like Cilla's. Bless his grandfather for passing those on. Amara hid a moan as Maart's fingers crept higher on her chest. This close, the scent of him drowned out all others.

He smiled against her lips, and she smiled back, knotting her fingers into his topscarf. These were all the words she wanted right now.

The good thing was, when you puked often enough, you learned where in the toilet bowl to aim in order to minimize splatter.

The bad thing was, you automatically shut your eyes in the process. In Nolan's case, that meant switching between feeling his knees on cool tiles and acid in his throat to witnessing Amara and Maart in the alcove bed, leaving him with mental whiplash and voyeur guilt and—in short—terrible aim.

"Nolan?" Pat thumped a fist on the bathroom door. "You, uh, need anything?"

Nolan wiped his mouth with too-thin toilet paper. Then he yanked off some extra sheets, slammed his hand to the roll to keep it from spinning endlessly, and wiped the toilet seat, too. "Did Mom send you up?" He sounded pathetic. If it'd been Mom out there, he'd have cleared his throat and aimed for a laugh, but he didn't need to with Pat—

**—Maart was kissing Amara, slick lips on her neck, the dip of her collarbone—**

"—texted me to check on you." Nolan could almost hear Pat frown. "But if I can help . . ."

"Probably not." He crawled upright. His legs tingled with

numbness from the knees down. He barely kept his balance as he leaned in to flush, then half stumbled, half hopped to the sink, using a single, sleeping foot and no crutches. They were still downstairs. Idiot. At least the bathroom was small. He ended up crash-landing on the sink with both elbows. Stuck between dry-heaving and panting, he stared at the mirror. He looked pale. Not pale-pale, like Mom, but paler than his normal, even brown, which made those bags under his eyes stand out even more.

Another surge of nausea hit. He pressed a fist to his sternum to quell it. The movement reminded him of before, in the Walgreens back room, and a phantom burn flared in his hands and faded straightaway. He ought to just shut his eyes until the nausea passed. If he had to deal with Amara's pain, shouldn't he be allowed the good parts, as well, no matter the guilt—

**—Amara's hand ran down Maart's side, heat spreading across his skin and hers, and she hardly felt the wall patterns pressing into her back or—**

—Pat shoved open the door. Probably a good thing. Whenever Nolan *wanted* to get sucked into Amara's world, it took forever to wake up.

"I heard you flush," Pat said by way of justification.

"I hate these pills." Nolan stuck his head under the tap. Cold water. For more reasons than just cleaning up. Puking and sex—two surefire ways of feeling awkward around your thirteen-year-old sister. Not that she looked thirteen. Pat took after Dad, tall and unapologetic and dark, and with Nolan bent over like this, they were almost the same height.

"Weren't you feeling better?" she said. "I thought you got used to those pills weeks ago." She fiddled with her gloves. Summer in Arizona, and she wore gloves. Leather ones, with cut-off fingers and metal spikes across the back. Nolan didn't know how she managed.

"I messed up the timing. Took two doses too close together." The taste of acid coated the back of his throat. He rinsed his mouth again.

"Are these pills better than the old ones, at least?"

"Which old ones? There's plenty to choose from." Nolan managed a laugh—a little-sister laugh, a big-brother laugh—but not much of one, and apparently he wasn't the only one feeling awkward, since Pat was still twisting the spikes on her gloves one by one. Pat didn't hesitate often. Then again, they didn't talk about his condition often, either. Nolan preferred it that way. She shouldn't have to worry about her screwed-up brother's supposed epilepsy.

That was the diagnosis: epilepsy. To be specific, a rare type of photosensitive epilepsy that triggered absence seizures on blinking. Seizures that came with hallucinations. The EEGs were works of art, the symptoms didn't add up, and the so-called seizures never responded to medication—but it explained everything, from the overstimulation to the flares of pain and the worthless attention span. It had also explained why a five-year-old Nolan would mention flashes of noise, people who didn't exist, visuals he couldn't explain. He claimed those had gone away years ago, but the pain was harder to hide.

The numbness from kneeling so long had now shifted into full-on pins and needles, assaulting his leg with every twitch of movement. *Eyes open*, he told himself. He was almost relieved when Pat pointed at the inside of his arm. "What's that?"

He glanced at the faded ballpoint scribbles that stretched across his flesh. Dit letters. He'd practiced writing them the other night at the same time Amara had, and he'd forgotten to scrub them off. The letters along his arm aligned in a firm grid. His ballpoint couldn't vary line thickness properly, so the lines weren't as neat as Cilla's or even Amara's meticulous attempts and ended up looking cheap, almost fake.

Nolan didn't want to linger on them, though. Pat should be more important than some distant girl he'd never meet, no matter how much that distant girl slathered herself across his eyelids and pushed between this thought and that. "Nothing. Doodles."

"Huh. Didn't you draw those in your journals, too?"

Nolan froze. He tried not to sound upset: "You—read my journals?"

"How could I? I can't open your cabinet." Pat shrugged. "I walked past once while you were writing. I don't want to read about your sexcapades, anyway."

Pat had that fake casual air, as though she said the word

every day and it wasn't just something she'd read online and thought was funny, but Nolan didn't call her on it. If she'd read his notebooks, she'd be asking different questions entirely. *Who's Amara? And Who's Cilla? And How come you're not more heavily medicated, Nolan?*

"OK," he said, still leaning against the sink, the counter pressing a straight line into his elbows. He cleared his throat. "OK. Sorry."

"Anyway, Mom said she'd be home by five, so we'll eat early. We're having leftovers."

"I thought we finished those yesterday."

"That was Grandma Pérez's carnitas. We're having the Thai now."

*From three days ago?* Nolan swallowed the words. The rule was that you didn't toss out food until it turned suspicious colors. "Sounds good," he replied, and managed a halfway genuine smile.

"Patli, do you really need those gloves during dinner?" Mom said wearily.

"Yeah?" Pat shoveled more rice into her mouth. "If I only wore them at school, it wouldn't be *authentic*. And I take them off during rehearsals for the play. Sometimes. My drama teacher said we need volunteers, by the way."

Nolan rolled a piece of corn around the rim of his plate. As long as he played with it, he didn't have to consider the horrifying notion of actually eating it. His stomach rebelled at the thought. The spicy smell from Mom's beef was bad enough already—

—Amara rushed to clean up after lunch, scrubbing the plates, the cups. Next to her, Maart's legs stuck out from the nearest alcove as he made Cilla's bed. Amara was doing fine, Nolan thought, Nolan hoped—

—throughout Mom and Pat's conversation, Dad's wide grin stretched even wider. All Pat's weird choices in fashion and music and friends just seemed to amuse him. When his eyes fell on Nolan, all he said was, "Don't forget to mention that nausea to Dr. Campbell tomorrow."

"Do you feel up to swimming yet?" Mom asked. "I'm working tonight. I'm leaving in twenty minutes, if you need a ride."

Nolan had almost forgotten: Sunday was his standard swimming day. He'd missed going that afternoon, but the pool closed late. He smiled a Mom-smile. "I'm much better"—such a lie—"but I think I'll skip today." Swimming would take his mind off things, but after what he'd found out about Mom, he had other plans. "I appreciate the offer, though."

Pat gave a roll of her eyes and—

—downstairs, the nonstop raucousness of the inn's pub increased. Jorn was down there, which meant Cilla was, too. They never left her alone—

"—he's just being polite, Patli." Mom tucked some hair from Nolan's forehead behind his ear. He flinched at her hand entering his view unannounced. He was seventeen, and still she did this—she'd even check the gel in his hair before school, and some mornings she barged into his room to wake him up, and, before he knew it, she'd be rummaging through his closet and tossing slacks and a shirt onto his bed as if he was five years old. She wouldn't dare do that to Pat.

Mom probably felt she needed to take care of him. Nolan didn't know if it was his leg or his seizures or something else. He'd complained about it once, two years ago. Then he'd seen the look on her face. Ever since, he'd let her baby him. If she needed this, he refused to cause more hurt—

**—a sharp noise—**

—Nolan closed his eyes. Noise meant bad things. Jorn's temper. Cilla getting hurt—

**—Amara and Maart went dead still, alert for further sounds. "I should check on Cilla," Amara signed. A second later, the pub crowd downstairs burst into cheers. Relief washed over her—**

"—Nolan? Polite? I'm shocked." Pat laughed.

Nolan took a second to replay her words. His parents would be waiting—hoping—for a smart-ass big-brother response. Pat knew better. Her eyes only met his briefly before she gave her plate her full attention again.

It wasn't as if he didn't try. He laughed, which seemed to please Dad, but when he racked his brain for a response, nothing came.

This act used to be easier. He'd always been the good big

brother and the ideal son, who might be aloof but at least didn't do drugs or smoke or hang with the wrong crowd. At least he didn't splurge on video games or stay out all night. At least he no longer had those hallucinations.

But lately, people wanted more than tailor-made smiles, and he didn't know what to give them.

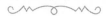

Whenever Nolan read, he lost his spot on the page, every page. Music interrupted and paused but was low-key enough to be bearable, unlike TV, which had him zoning out within minutes.

Homework? Out of the damn question.

What Nolan could do was this: open his journals and report on every blink without thinking. The Dunelands took up five dozen notebooks and counting.

He wanted more than that. Something that was his.

Without the money for a running leg, sports were out, whether it was disabled sports two hours away in Mesa or regular sports here in tiny Farview, Arizona. He'd get too distracted, anyway, and anything involving running or jumping was too dangerous with the Dunelands catching him off guard at any moment. What'd happened ten years ago proved that: Cilla had tripped and skinned her palms. Blood welled up in tiny drops. The curse awoke, sending ripples through the earth; they had only seconds before it would strike.

By then, Amara had been with Jorn and Cilla for a year.

She'd lost track of how often she'd had to cheat the curse, but she knew her script and everyone else's.

It didn't make her shake any less when Jorn grabbed his knife. He slashed open Cilla's skin further, then thrust Amara's hand into the cut and dragged her arm along it. Then, pushing her out of reach, he helped Cilla wrap up, shielding her palms from the air so her blood couldn't call louder than the fresh smears on Amara's skin.

The earth drew open. Roots wrapped around Amara's ankles. They dragged her down, slicing her legs through the thick fabric of her winterwear. When she stumbled to all fours, the next root coiled around her arms, up to her throat. One wormed its way between her lips. Pushed into an empty mouth, past the remains of a sliced-up tongue, and beyond.

All in all, it might've taken five minutes. When the roots drew enough of Amara's blood to block out the final whispers of Cilla's dried streaks, the curse backed off, leaving Amara to cough and choke and claw and heal.

She must've been seven. She was thinking: I don't want to heal anymore I don't I don't

Nolan was seven, too. Five minutes was more than enough for him to lurch off his bike on his way to school and fall to the street, groping to free himself from roots that weren't there. He barely saw the Jeep in time. Adrenaline flooded him. He crab-walked out of reach, but too slowly, leaving his left foot and a child-sized bicycle for the Jeep's tire to crush.

The good part was that Nolan passed out from the pain. The bad part was that Amara's world offered him just as much pain as his.

So he avoided sports. Even a regular fall with only half a leg was a pain in the neck.

Just as Nolan's family couldn't afford a running leg, they couldn't afford a swimming leg. What they could afford—or would make sacrifices for, anyway—was a season's membership to the nearest pool and an adjusted flipper. It wrapped around the stump of his shin, allowing him to push off and keep afloat.

So he swam under the lifeguard's watchful eye, reducing the world to kids' screams and the kick of his legs and chlorine in his nose. Swimming meant moving on autopilot, making it ten times easier to deal with the back-and-forth between worlds. It made his parents happy, too. They thought he had a hobby.

Right now, Nolan really wished he was swimming.

Instead, he'd gone upstairs after abandoning his meal, leaving Pat to her Nahuatl studies and Dad to sort through bills and write angry letters about banned books at Nolan's school. Nolan made a beeline for the bathroom, where dirty laundry was stacked knee-high in one corner despite the quick load Dad had run yesterday. Mom normally handled the laundry. Working two jobs probably explained the size of the pile.

How had Nolan not noticed? When had she started at the Walgreens anyway—and *why*?

Nolan suspected he knew. Dad's insurance from his hospital administrator job covered only part of the cost of the latest pills. Nolan had known they were in a bad situation, just not how bad.

Three jobs to pay for anti-seizure meds when he didn't even *have* seizures, and all Nolan did was fill up one notebook after another and go swimming three times a week. If Amara wouldn't leave him be long enough for him to help himself, he should at least help others.

"How difficult can a washing machine be, right?" The words came out angrily. He lowered himself to the ground and started sorting through the pile.

B y late afternoon, Amara had decided that, as dangerous as sneaking downstairs was, she'd do it anyway.

She hovered at the top of the inn stairs, listening to the noise from the ground-floor pub. The clinking of glasses, shouts and laughter, a flute player's screech. She smelled greasy bread and alcohol—Jélisse ports and wines, and beers from all over the Continent. She'd never liked the taste but wished for a sip anyway; at least she had enough of a stump in the back of her throat to notice that taste, or any taste at all. Maart rarely did.

Amara moved down a stair, then two, until she had a sliver of a view of the crowd. Most were Dit workers, sun-freckled, flat-faced, broad-shouldered. Jorn fit right in, sitting at a booth near the bar and shouting for another beer. He'd drunk more in the past few weeks than he had in years. He hadn't punished Amara so badly in just as long.

In the deepest end of the booth, with her back safely to the wall, Cilla nursed her own drink—her first and last. They couldn't risk her losing her coordination. Cilla took a tiny sip and glanced up as a gangly boy leaned into their table with a lopsided smile. His words were lost in the noise.

Jorn said two words of his own, and the boy stumbled back before Cilla even had a chance to return his smile. Amara relaxed marginally. Jorn was still alert enough to be cautious. No one should come near Cilla, especially after drinking.

Amara looked for the news sheet pinned to the wall downstairs, in a weakly lit niche. The innkeeper refreshed it every three days. She moved down another stair, keeping a close eye on Cilla and Jorn as she went—part caution, part habit. Most people in the bar gave Cilla a wide berth. Amara didn't know if that had anything to do with Jorn telling off her last suitor, or just her being Alinean in a predominantly Dit bar; most Alineans had returned to the Alinean Islands after the coup, but the ones who remained in the Dunelands still made all the money, still had the best jobs, and still walked with their heads held high, and that was starting to bother even those who'd supported the monarchy.

And Cilla—she might not wear her hair the proper way, but she was Alinean through and through, from the way her dark skin blended into the shade of the booth to the way her nose pinched between her eyes, then flared wide. The candle glow accentuated the full curve of her cheeks, her dark, narrow eyes. Her tongue darted out to wash the wine from her lips, then she leaned toward Jorn to ask him something.

Amara used the distraction to sneak down the most open part of the stairs. She'd be seen if she went too slowly. In this dimness, her skin—though dark for an Elig like her—practically glowed. She dashed into the niche, then waited for a moment. No one came. She put her finger on the broadsheet, following along with the words just as Cilla had. Amara knew she shouldn't be reading. She especially shouldn't do it within spitting distance of Jorn. She couldn't give up, though—and if she was going to do this, she'd do it because *she* wanted to. Not because Cilla urged her on. Not because Maart liked their futile rebellions.

Knowing roughly what the article said made it easier to follow. Cilla had summed up the main points. What must not have occurred to Cilla was why Amara would care. Had she forgotten that Amara had lived at Ruudde's palace, as well?

Amara had served in Bedam for barely a year, half of that working for Cilla's family, the other half for Ruudde once he'd taken over. She'd still been a child when Jorn had stolen her away from Ruudde. A healing servant came in handy when protecting a fragile, on-the-run princess.

If Amara were ever caught, though, her tattoo marked her as belonging to the Bedam palace. She'd be returned to Ruudde, so she ought to know of him what she could.

—suspect—Alinean—loyalties, Amara read about the woman who'd tossed the stone, but—no—family—members—have—

"Amara!" a voice whispered. Amara spun. If Jorn saw her reading—or realized how careless she was, getting so caught up—

Cilla stood across from her. She gripped the sides of the

niche. Normally her eyes were narrowed, hidden in the shade of her lids, but now they spread wide, and under her wrap, her chest heaved from exertion or panic or both. Cilla never rushed unless it was important.

Amara's heart sped up, a thump-thump-thump with no pauses in between. With practiced speed, she scanned Cilla's face and the arms exposed by her loose topscarf; she checked the winterwear that went from right below Cilla's arms to her horse-fuzz-lined boots. No scratches, tears, scrapes, nothing.

"Where?" Amara signed, and automatically reached for the knife in her boot pocket. Shit. She'd left it upstairs. If Cilla's injury was small enough that Amara missed it, Cilla's blood might not yet have tasted enough air to activate the curse, but when it did, it could bring down the entire inn. Normally Cilla was faster about alerting her where she'd been injured. They had enough experience to know all the moves.

"We need to leave," Cilla hissed.

No injury, then. Mages working for the ministers instead.

Amara ran up the stairs after Cilla and dove into their room, searching for her knife. Using her voice, she pushed out the single syllable of his name, "Mar!"

Cilla thumped the closed hatch of Maart's bunk. "They're close," she said, talking fast. "Jorn went out to hold them off. He's dissolved his detection spell. We can pass safely."

Amara slipped her knife into the side pocket of her horse-fuzz boots. "How many?"

Cilla was helping Maart from his bunk; with her head turned away, she missed Amara's signs. Didn't matter. They'd need to run fast no matter what.

They hadn't encountered hired mages in months. Jorn normally sensed them coming once they passed his boundary spell, giving him the chance to take the group out of range. He must've been distracted. Or drinking. Amara swallowed an oath.

Maart stumbled on the floor and made for his boots. His shoulders were bare. No time to wrap a topscarf. "Go," he said, and the pleading in both his hands and eyes told Amara things she didn't want to know: to be careful, to run, to let whatever happened to Cilla happen. "Go!"

She pretended not to see, and he grabbed his boots and yanked them on as he scanned the room. They all had their tasks. Jorn fought. Amara fled with Cilla. Maart safeguarded their essentials.

The mages wanted Cilla, but if they couldn't trigger her curse, they'd hinder the group any way they could. They'd steal the herbs that stopped Cilla's bleeds, their money, Jorn's enchantments. They'd kill the group's servants.

They had before.

"Hide when you can," Amara told Maart, and ran.

Cilla followed footlengths behind. Their boots pounded narrow, steep stairs. "They're coming from the direction of the mill," Cilla said, a whisper of wine on her breath.

The nearest mill was two houses south, close enough that they heard the wings creak during quiet moments, the wind fluttering through the fabric. They'd go north, then. The mages could track Cilla by the curse, but only when close enough. All Amara needed to do was get Cilla out of reach and hide.

Amara paused on the third step from the bottom to look over the pub. If the mages had arrived, they were lying low. She squinted at the smell of fungi, penetrating enough to stab at her eyes. To reach the exit, they'd need to slip past a good ten people in various stages of drunkenness. If Cilla was grabbed, that'd be bad. If Cilla was grabbed a little too roughly, that'd be worse. Amara didn't want anyone finishing the mages' job for them.

A touch on her neck. Her hands flew up to guard herself, but the look on Cilla's face stopped her. Calm. How could Cilla be calm? There were mages on the street—who knew how close, who knew how many.

"Your tattoo." Cilla's voice cut through the pub-goers' shouts.

Amara flattened her hair against her neck. If it didn't cover her tattoo, they'd be sure to get held up. She dipped her head in thanks and took Cilla's wrist. After regrowing only that morning, Amara's nails were in no state to cut skin, but she was cautious, anyway, even with her eyes fixed on the entrance.

She held her breath when the door opened and people stepped through. The first thing Amara searched for—always—

was the knife-wielding mage. Tall and Alinean, she carried that same curved knife every time.

Instead, the first person to enter was male, and Amara recognized him instantly. He always stood out among the mages who chased them. Elig people like he and Amara stood out in any crowd, no matter how silently they spoke or furtively they walked. And, unlike Amara, this mage was pink-skinned and pale-eyed, with hair like fire—exactly what everyone north of Eligon expected them to look like.

The second mage was a Dit woman, just as familiar. The last time Amara had seen her, the mage had been side by side with the knifewielder. Amara's cheek ached with a long-ago memory: encountering the hired mages for the first time, that blade hooking into her cheek—

Focus. Amara double-checked the entrance to make sure the knifewielder wasn't with them.

She wasn't. Just the two mages. It should've calmed Amara, should've made her grab Cilla and flee.

But what Amara wanted—needed—was to burst through the crowd and kill these mages, knifewielder or not. Killing a mage ended their spells. A curse like Cilla's would've required tens of mages working in unison, but in the end, a single person channeled the magic. A single mage responsible. It could've been a minister. Could've been someone they hired. Could've been one of these two.

Without the curse, Cilla would still need to stay on the

run, but life would be infinitely easier. The mages wouldn't be able to track her. She wouldn't need endless drugs to stop her monthly bleeds. She wouldn't have to worry about stray paper cuts.

She wouldn't need Amara to get hurt in her stead.

Amara wanted the mages dead. These two. The knife-wielder. All of them.

But that was Jorn's task. She reined herself in, focused on her own. Were the mages tracking Cilla? She checked the lamps suspended to the walls and the beers in people's hands for any immediate reactions to nearby magic. Nothing.

Magic backlash wasn't always visible, though.

They needed another exit. Amara nodded at the door to the dumphouse and didn't wait for approval to pull Cilla along toward it. She'd grown up protecting Cilla, and Jorn let her do that however she saw fit.

The dumphouse's shit-stink grew thick as they neared it, streaking past rented rooms. Amara chanced a look over her shoulder. Someone waltzed into the dark behind them. Too big to be the woman, too dark to be the man. Too drunk to be either of them. Good, so—

—Amara barely corrected her stumble. Cilla's grip kept her upright. Her hand squeezed Amara's in reassurance, or a word-less *Careful!*

What had she stumbled on? No time to check. The dump-house door stood ajar. They barged inside. Shuddering gas lamps lit the hut, illuminating men leaning into walls to piss into ditches, two other shapes sitting in crouches. Amara ran straight through, Cilla's hand safe in hers.

"You girls in a hurry?" a woman shouted, her voice thick with alcohol. Too loud. If the mages heard, it'd point them right at Cilla.

Amara reached the doors on the other side of the dump-house, the ones that led to the street, and stood aside so the light hit the lock. Often, inns locked their dumphouses, unlocking them only for back-street cleaning. No one wanted to drag shit through the inn, and no one wanted a dumphouse on a respectable street front.

Amara really missed the mainland's sewage system. For all you could say about the ministers, they'd still come up with a decent invention or two.

If the doors were locked, she could manage the mecha-nism with her knife, but if she was lucky she could—

—Amara's hand rested loosely around the handles. She blinked a couple of times fast. Cilla stood awfully close all of a sudden, close enough for Amara to smell the wine on her breath despite the dumphouse stink.

There'd been a full footlength between them a second ago. What'd happened?

"What is it?" Cilla asked, tension visible in the hunch of her shoulders, the press of her lips, the balls of her hands. Both hands. Just a moment ago, Amara had been gripping Cilla's fingers tightly. Why hadn't Amara noticed them slip away? She should've noticed.

Shaking her head to clear the fuzz, she pressed the handles together. The doors opened wide, fresh air and light bursting in. Amara shielded her eyes. The inn was all low ceilings, black wood, shimmering gaslight, and flickering fire pits. She'd almost forgotten it was daytime.

Amara checked behind her. A woman stumbled in and hunkered by the door. Another two shapes approached. Their steady, sober gait told Amara enough.

This time, Amara probably did grab Cilla's arm too tightly. They turned north and ran.

Nolan had separated the whites and darks just like he'd always seen Mom do, keeping the patterns he wasn't sure about to one side, and tossed the whites into the washing machine. While that ran, he'd pulled up yesterday's laundry from the clothesline in the stairwell. Still moist. That couldn't hurt, could it?

He sat on his parents' bed—better AC in this room—and tried to fold carefully, like Mom, but his movements came anxious and fast, resulting in uneven folds and sleeves that stuck out the wrong way. The faster Nolan moved, maybe the faster Amara would run through the inn, too. The faster she'd be safe.

Downstairs, Dad talked on the phone—

—**Amara disappeared. From one moment to the next, she was gone, and**—

—Nolan grasped an undershirt tightly. This was the second time Amara had blacked out in the space of a few minutes. First in the hallway, now here, by the outhouse doors—

—**Nolan always got more of Amara's thoughts the longer he stayed, until he forgot there was a Nolan at all. But even when he was there for just a blink, kept his eyes shut for under half a second, he sensed her.**

Not now.

Nolan still saw the outhouse doors through her eyes, still felt the chilly, rusted metal of the door handles. Still smelled the stench. Still saw Cilla moving closer. Her hand fell from Amara's, leaving behind cool air on clammy skin.

But Amara wasn't there. Her mind was empty.

*Move!* he wanted to shout.

For three full seconds, she stayed at the doors, thoughts beyond reach. Then, as quickly as she'd left, she blossomed back into the vacuum at the edge of Nolan's mind.

Amara blinked rapidly, looked at Cilla, then at her now-empty hand. Her confusion didn't last long. She threw open the doors, and they fled, cold blasting inside—

—Nolan stared at the crumpled undershirt in his hands. Shakily, he spread it on the sheets. He could do nothing for Amara, anyway. He watched. He dealt. End of story.

Fold the sides in. Fold it double. He pressed the fabric flat, hoping to get out the wrinkles as he watched flashes of Amara running through the streets, dragging Cilla along, their boots slamming into painted cobblestones—

—*we can go inland*, Amara was thinking, *lose them in the streets like Jorn always says, hope he finds us soon.* But if she led the mages west, toward the dunes, Cilla could flee into the local carecenter. A carecenter meant healing spells. The mages might lose track of Cilla's curse in all the magic swarming around the area.

Amara tugged at Cilla's arm. A moment later, they dove into an alley on their left, narrow enough that no one had bothered painting the pavement. Laundry hung from beams suspended between high-up windows. Sheets flapped in the wind and blocked the afternoon sun, choking the alley in darkness, as if night had fallen in the space of a second.

They hadn't ducked into the alley in time. Pain flared in Amara's shoulder—

—Nolan jerked back. He reached for his shoulder, intact under his shirt. The pain faded into a memory. It wouldn't stay that way. Already, his eyes were dry enough to sting.

He dropped flat on the bed until he could reach his backpack, fishing out the notebook and pen he carried with him no matter where he went. He blinked. Kept in a scream. But he had to see what happened—

—Amara ran, clutching her shoulder. Blood seeped through her topscarf and into the gaps between her fingers. The arrow had only scraped her. Could've been worse. If it'd hit her spine, she'd be down for the count. But the cut was *deep*. It'd take at least twenty seconds to heal—twenty more than she could afford, especially with no other alleys in sight, nowhere to escape.

"Get—in front—" Amara tried to sign, hoping Cilla could see her hands. Cilla didn't run fast enough. She lagged behind. Amara needed to shield her in case the mages let loose another arrow.

Normally, they'd simply fire raw magic they drew from the spirits, as the ministers had when they took over Cilla's palace all those years ago. These mages couldn't afford to. You didn't enchant something—or someone—twice. Ever. That was why Jorn deactivated his boundary detection spell whenever they needed to cross it—it might interact with Cilla's curse or Amara's healing.

Sometimes, mixed magic flared tenfold. A single bolt could destroy the whole street. Other times, spells canceled each other out. Hitting Cilla with a bolt could mean the mages sabotaged their own curse and the bolt fizzled into nothing before even breaking her skin.

The wind slapped the laundry overhead into brick walls. Not far ahead, a girl Amara's age reached out the window to adjust her clothes. She shouted something in a language Amara didn't recognize. Before that, Amara hadn't even noticed the silence. The alley was locked away from the world. Just the wind and too-shallow breaths and endless footslams that reverberated throughout her body.

The carecenter was another minute away. Exhaustion in her legs and lungs joined the pain in her shoulder, which bored deep and sharp and hot, even as she felt her skin stitching up—

—Nolan favored his shoulder without thinking as he wrote. About the news sheet. Amara's resolve to keep reading. Jorn's drinking. Cilla in the niche, the mages in the doorway. His handwriting turned crooked. He checked his shoulder again, knowing he wouldn't find anything.

Breathe. In, out. He was fine. Amara's pain was not his. Still, her exhaustion seeped into him, weighing heavier with each blink. He focused on keeping his writing legible, and took his pen off the paper whenever he closed his eyes, wanting to avoid ink blotches. That was a good thing—

—because when the next arrow hit, it wasn't Amara's shoulder, and it wasn't a scrape. It hit her low, between pelvis and spine. The arrow didn't feel sharp. It felt blunt, like a punch. Amara's legs gave out. She went flying to the pavement, shredding her palms on the stones. She gave it a second, two seconds, three, unable to do anything but lie there and wheeze. The world shrank to that spot in her back.

*Get up!* Nolan wanted to scream. *Get up! Get up!*

The mages were coming closer. Nolan heard their footsteps and saw Cilla's boots scrape to a halt and turn to Amara, limp on the stones. Blood trickled down her back, and for one bewildering moment, Amara mistook the laundry flapping overhead for birds, great big herons bearing down on her, a fish splashing on dry land. She even heard squawking, not far off now.

No, not herons. Seagulls. They were close to the dunes.

With a shaky hand, Amara reached back for the arrow. She pulled, swallowed a scream, and let the arrow clatter to the stones. The sound was light. Harmless. Something that made a sound so harmless shouldn't be able to hurt so much. She pushed herself up, and in the corner of Amara's eye, Nolan saw the shapes of the mages approaching and people pulling in their laundry and shutting their windows.

Then—Amara disappeared. For the third time, blackness

**swept over her, pulling her out of reach. Her body thumped back
to the ground, lifeless—**

—Nolan's eyes shot open. He looked around in a daze, at
the glow coming in through thick curtains, at stacks of laundry
surrounding him in blacks and browns, at the old-school TV
set bolted to the wall. Through the wall came the muffled rattle
of the washing machine.

Amara had a theory about how she could die: hit fast, hit
hard. The mages following her through that alley would be
eager to oblige. Taking out Amara would mean taking out the
princess's last defense.

And then? Maybe whatever magic of Amara's that pulled
Nolan into her world would disappear. He'd live out his life
in his own world and his own body, a concept he could barely
grasp.

Or he'd die, too. Nolan's life was secondary to Amara's. That
much he'd always known. He was the hanger-on, the badly
made copy, the hazy mirror image in this alter-ego life they led
together. Maybe whatever connection Amara had forged with
him was strong enough that he'd experience her death along
with her pain.

He couldn't stop it, either way. And either way, Amara
would die. On cold, unpainted cobblestones with fingernails
that hadn't grown back all the way.

He hated her. Amara had taken his life and locked it into

hers, and he hated her more than anything in the world for that. But he didn't want her to die. Nolan closed his eyes—

—and felt the wound healing, despite Amara's absence. If she'd just come back as she had before, if her mind was just *here*, she'd be running again in seconds. It'd hurt, but she'd have no choice. They'd been in worse situations, and—all she needed to do was come back like before, crawl upright and run, and—

Her arms convulsed as if a pulse went through them.

"Come on!" Fear made Cilla's voice crack. She grabbed Amara's hands to pull her up, but Amara's mind was still absent. Nolan had never felt her mind this far gone, not even when she slept. *Run*, he pleaded. *Run.*

Amara's hands tightened around Cilla's. She let herself be pulled onto unsteady feet, then away, in a stumble that turned into a run. An arrow slashed past her ear.

Amara moved, yes, but where were her *thoughts?*

The hospital still lay—what?—half a minute off? Nolan needed to know how far behind the mages were and if Amara and Cilla had any chance of making it. Amara's head turned. Enough to catch a glimpse of the Elig mage rearming himself, the Dit mage still running. Nolan looked back in front of him, at Cilla dashing around a corner—

He looked back in front of him. He. *He.*

He exploded into a sprint, but his legs moved on autopilot. He clenched his hands—Amara's hands—and guided her eyes, and opened her mouth, and pursed her lips. His breath—Amara's breath?—came in too-short spurts.

He was doing this. These movements couldn't be a coincidence. Couldn't be. "Nolan," he tried to say with unfamiliar lips. The *n*'s were lost, and so was the *l*, his name unrecognizable except to him. *Owwa*, it sounded like. But it was close enough.

"What?" Cilla shouted. The wind turned her voice frail.

Nolan was steering Amara's body. He could—he was really doing this—

Amara lay in the alleyway, the clatter of the arrow still echoing—

—then she was running. Stumbling. The alley no longer choked her, the world having opened back up. Storefronts and pubs lined one side. On the other, dunes blocked any view of the ocean but not its salt on the air. She crashed to the ground before she could take in the image properly. Her palms scraped open, just like—just like a moment ago, she wanted to think, but more than a moment had passed. She'd blacked out again.

The mages couldn't be far behind. She had to keep moving. She couldn't let whatever was happening cost Cilla's life, but—how had she been able to get here while blacked out?

Amara scrambled to her feet. She'd almost finished healing, but that didn't stop her lungs from burning or her mouth from tasting of metal. Cilla was still running in that way she did, at once precise and raw, unpracticed. Cilla looked over her shoulder. The wind tugged at her chin-length hair.

All right. Focus on Cilla. Focus on the stinging of her own healing palms. On the now. Everything else came later.

"Into the carecenter." Amara signed as broadly as she could. Servant signs weren't suited to speaking across distances. "I'll delay them."

Cilla looked as if she'd object but whipped her head back anyway.

Another arrow flew. Amara ducked instinctively into its path. The arrow clipped her arm, and she hissed, slapping her palm against the cut. Sweat pasted her hair to her face, smoky strands obscuring her vision.

She couldn't afford another blackout, but right now, she couldn't prevent one, either. What she could do was slow down the mages. She had her knife and one advantage: not worrying about getting hurt. She'd go for the Elig mage first. Wrestle away the bow.

Then, on her right, blocky shoulders came into view, thick black curls, things she recognized in a heartbeat. "Keep going!" Jorn snapped, and faced the mages. "Find her!"

Amara ran before fully processing his order. Jorn told her to run. So she ran.

Up ahead, Cilla was sprinting up the carecenter steps. Once under the archway she went left, and Amara followed. The sting in her arm had already faded. Up two steps. Two more. She didn't like having Cilla out of her sight like this. At least no one would stop them: island carecenters were poorly staffed, simply places for the sick and injured to gather as they waited for volunteer doctors or the mages on duty to stop by—and for those already enchanted to avoid any magic that'd interact with their healing spells. Mages weren't supposed to cast spells out in the open that might affect passersby. Not all mages cared.

Amara found Cilla rubbing her ankle in the second-floor hall, by a tall window overlooking the boardwalk. "Jorn is holding them off," Cilla said, breathing a sigh of relief.

"We still need to go." Amara's hands were urgent. That window made them too visible. Something else worried her more, though. "Your ankle?" She jogged past patient rooms to close the distance between them. A girl's sticky coughs leaked out through hardwood doors.

"I twisted it going up the stairs," Cilla said. "It's fine. It's all internal."

Amara crouched and loosened the tie that bound Cilla's boot and removed it gently, prompting a stifled grunt of pain. She needed to be sure, though.

Cilla's skin was the near-black of soaked bark, which made contusions hard to see. Blood stood out better. She scanned the back of Cilla's ankle and the warm curve of her calf, and ignored the jump of her own heart. She rarely came this close to the princess.

She ignored the coarse hairs and the imprints from Cilla's winterwear, too, and the stink of sweat-drenched horse-fuzz that drifted from the boot lying next to her. Cilla had to wear her boots all hours of the day, taking them off only to sleep. Otherwise, her toes might stub or her toenails might tear.

Splinters, rocks, or grass might cut her open. Bugs could sting her too easily. Cilla's winterwear was extra thick, too, and they'd sewn pads to the knees, and when the weather chilled further, she wore long Jélis-made gloves.

Amara leaned away. No blood.

"See? It's fine. Look outside. Jorn . . ." Cilla smiled feebly despite the strain in her jaw.

Amara's own jaw clenched for different reasons. She knew what she'd see. Jorn, fighting the mages, risking his life for Cilla's, using magic the spirits had never let Amara access. She understood Cilla's gratitude and what Jorn's dedication to the Alinean crown must mean to her. Cilla had nothing else left of her family.

Amara also understood what Jorn's dedication would mean to her. He couldn't afford to have her blacking out while protecting the princess. She was a liability.

She moved automatically as she thought, taking Cilla's boot and widening the opening, then taking her toes to guide them back in. Cilla pulled her foot away and tried that same smile again. Tentative. It lit up her face regardless. Amara wished she didn't notice those things.

"You don't have to," Cilla said.

"I do." Amara kept her gestures direct. "Can you run?"

Experimentally, Cilla leaned on her still-bare foot. Her eyebrows pulled together. "I doubt it. What I mean is, I'd appreciate it if you weren't so—if you could act normally around me."

"This isn't the time." Amara shouldn't talk to the princess like that. Ever. But surviving took priority. She stood and looked out the window. In the distance, a gust of wind spiraled around Jorn, then swept out and knocked down both mages. The Elig rolled over and clasped a pale, blood-smeared hand with the other mage. The air around them glimmered.

Amara had meant to simply assess the situation but found herself drinking in the sight. The only time she could see magic was like this, when it was raw and fleeting. Once a mage used a spell to bond that magic to something physical, an object or a person, it became invisible to non-mages.

And to Amara.

It was said that spirits favored some people, and that made them mages; that the spirits favored some mages in particular, watching over their health without even making them pay the price of backlash. The thought of Amara being favored made her smile wryly. Not favored enough, apparently, if she couldn't even detect other mages' spells, let alone cast her own. All she could do was wait out her healing.

Maybe she was simply doing magic wrong. It was hard to tell, when no one would explain how to do it right.

Jorn turned to run toward the carecenter. Amara watched the glossy magic of the Elig mage's shield, and his upheld arm, which even from this distance she could see was shaking with exertion. Spirits provided the raw energy. Mages were responsible for the rest.

Amara's knowledge of the process started and ended there. She wondered what it felt like.

Cilla's arm brushed past hers and snapped her from her thoughts. "Amara?"

Amara made a questioning sound.

"Do you hate me?" Cilla spoke with an oddly clear voice for such a loaded question.

Amara shook her head automatically. "Of course not." Jorn was coming up the stairs. Dull bricks muted his footsteps. They shouldn't be talking about this now. Or ever.

"You've saved my life so often. I owe you."

"May I speak honestly?" Amara's signs came awkwardly. Cilla leaned on her shoulder as they moved away from the window and the display of magic. Cilla had put her boot back on but still walked slowly.

"Yes! That's what I'm trying to say."

Amara darted another glance outside but couldn't see anything. "It's not that simple. You're the princess. You *can't* owe me."

"I . . ."

Cilla's voice and Amara's hands dropped the second Jorn came into sight. He didn't even look tired. "You should've been gone by now."

Amara gestured at the way Cilla favored her foot; she couldn't run like this. Did they still need to? Amara had no place asking those questions.

Cilla, on the other hand— "Are we safe?"

"No," Jorn snapped, then checked himself. He smiled thinly. "Apologies, Princess. No. Dissolving the mage's shield would have cost too much time. Others might be coming." Only now did Amara notice the red stains spreading across his topscarf. Small. She'd expected worse. At least Jorn focused on Cilla, not Amara. He didn't know about the blackouts. When he did find out—

She couldn't let that happen. If the blackouts were another ability the spirits had given her, she'd need to learn more, put a stop to them before she got Cilla—and herself—killed.

"I think the mages are too weak to follow," Jorn said. "Let's find Maart and go."

N olan had moved Amara's body.

He'd run.

He buzzed with energy and felt it building into a headache at the back of his skull, but his pen practically flew across his notebook's pages, and he couldn't stop now. Amara's magic was shifting. She'd gone from letting him witness her world from the backseat to offering him the wheel and gas pedal, and that meant—

Nolan couldn't begin to understand what that meant.

Amara's blackouts gave Nolan control.

He didn't realize he wasn't alone until Dad stood right in front of him.

"You look better." English. That didn't bode well. Nolan and Pat always spoke English together, but their parents stuck to Spanish around the house, or simple Nahuatl between Dad and Pat as practice. Dad saved English for his rare Talks, capital T. "That explains the noise."

Oh: the washer was banging on the bathroom tiles and whining high. Nolan slapped his notebook shut, though he wasn't worried about Dad peeking. As much as Pat took after Dad, she hadn't inherited his respect for privacy. "Sorry—"

—and Cilla was still leaning on Amara's shoulder as they trailed after Jorn—

—Dad shoved open the curtains to let the evening sun roll in. Slow, wide beams caught dust swirling around the room. "Don't apologize," he said. "Your mother told me you saw her at the Walgreens. You're trying to help out?"

Nolan wanted to listen, but his mind was stuck on the word he'd just written down. Control. The ink burned through the pages of the book, right into his hands and head.

"I. Yeah. I wanted to . . ." He gestured at abandoned, knocked-over piles of laundry. Some of his euphoria ebbed away. He'd meant to refold the messier stacks now that Amara's world was calmer, but how long had it taken him to get even this far? Some help he was.

"I figured. It's a good thing." Dad pulled up an old chair that mainly served as a mannequin for his business jacket. "An odd thing for a teenage boy, but a good thing."

Nolan found it hard to care about what a teenage boy was supposed to do. He spent half his life as a girl. As Amara, he'd done laundry a hundred times.

"I'm glad you're showing initiative. But if I had to choose, I wish you'd take the initiative to do homework or sneak out for a date. Wouldn't you like that better than laundry?" Dad eyed a pair of Pat's skinny jeans.

Nolan took care not to shut his eyes for too long, but he couldn't tune out Amara entirely. By now, Jorn had locked on to Maart's anchor. Nolan tried to ignore that, replaying Dad's words instead. Did he want those things? They sounded nice in the abstract, but it seemed safer to care about what he could actually accomplish. Writing in his notebooks. Swimming.

Laundry.

"Listen, when your mother gets home and sees this . . . she'll feel touched. Then guilty."

"She's working two jobs," Nolan protested. "I'm the one who feels guilty."

"You shouldn't, which is why she didn't tell you. You need that medication, Nolan."

"I don't! All it does is make me nauseous. I know Dr. Campbell said to give it a couple of months, but . . ." But no pills would ever work, was the truth. Every time, Nolan tried to refuse them.

"We won't give up," Dad said sharply. "As long as you keep trying, we'll keep trying."

And every time, his parents insisted. Nolan would take the pills for a few months, deal with the side effects, and stop once people realized his seizures weren't going away.

"Can I keep trying while doing laundry?" Nolan wanted to smile, but it rarely worked when Dad paid him such close attention. He had this way of scrutinizing people, level and unflinching, that made Nolan's smiles feel transparent.

"Just know your mother will struggle with it."

Nolan averted his eyes. He'd meant to help. Not add to guilt Mom shouldn't feel, anyway.

"I should finish up some work. There was a system crash at the hospital that set us back a few days . . ." Dad waved it off. "But I have five minutes." He looked over the bed—the collection of Nolan's stump socks dotting the sheets, the crookedly folded tops. He reverted to Spanish. "You, uh, want a lesson in folding?"

By the time Nolan finished folding and hanging the newly washed clothes, the buzz he'd felt over affecting Amara's world had transformed into a full-on headache and the early stir of nausea. As he headed to his room, Pat called something to him.

Nolan hopped back. Her door was ajar. He could just catch a glimpse of Pat's reflection in the crescent-shaped mirror Grandma Pérez had given her on her eighth birthday, when she'd spent every waking moment reading about astronomy. She gave the mirror a wounded look, which included her eyebrows going comically high and her lower lip jutting out. "I can't stop you," she declared. "But, oh, it's *dangerous!*"

Apparently she hadn't been calling to him, after all. Nolan shifted, allowing him to see more of her face. She wasn't holding a phone to either ear. Her eyebrows shot up again. "It's dangerous!" she repeated. Her eyes caught his in the mirror. She squeaked. In a single step, she yanked her door open. "Nole? Are you spying on me?"

"Your door was open."

She plucked at her T-shirt's neckline. "The AC's acting up."

"Were you practicing for that school play?" He vaguely recalled it coming up at dinner.

"What? No." She shifted her weight and scoffed. Pat's scoffs had as wide a range as Nolan's smiles. At the bottom rung was *Seriously?* followed by *I'm really too cool for this but, whatever, I'll play along.* Somewhere at the top sat *This is the most important thing in the world, but OMG I'll die if anyone knows.* This scoff had seemed closest to that last one. He should talk to her about it, but his head hurt. He craved sleep. It'd make his parents happy—proper sleep meant less chance of seizures—and it'd let him keep track of Amara. She was following Jorn around the harbor now, keeping her head low and waiting for another blackout.

He'd controlled her. The memory made a smile twitch at his lips, headache or no, but he curbed it. Watching Amara was the last thing he should do. The last thing he should want to do.

He couldn't get sucked back in. He'd ended up in a coma twice before.

"What's your role?" he made himself say.

She sighed. "I'm this nurse solving a mystery. There's singing. And I have to be vulnerable."

The disgust in her voice almost made him laugh. "Do you need help rehearsing? Or feedback?"

He couldn't help Mom without her feeling guilty, but maybe he could help Pat. Using Pat this way might not be fair, but the more he had going on in this world, the less he'd think about Amara's.

Pat looked confused. "Um. Are you sure you can?"

"I'm feeling pretty good on these pills," he lied.

"If you say so, but . . . I need someone objective. You lie. You lie to make people feel better."

Nolan considered lying about that, too, but it wouldn't be much use. "I'll be honest. I swear."

Pat laughed. "All right. Nolan with opinions. This, I gotta see."

8

They'd arrived on Teschel the night before. Another island. They hadn't been to the mainland in weeks. This time Jorn hadn't bothered with an inn. Instead, he'd set up camp in an unused granary across from a run-down farm. The storehouse was blocky and stained from age and weather and had long windows so filthy, they bordered on opaque. Pale trees—the very edge of a forest—pressed up against one side of the building, and abandoned fields stretched out on the others. Weeds sprouted upward, some tall enough to reach past Amara's hips.

Amara didn't know what had happened for people to abandon the farm, but Jorn was right about one thing: no one would expect to find a princess here.

Maart was inside, tending to Cilla and preparing their lunch. Amara ought to help. Instead, she sat crouched by the entrance. The low sun cast everything in the pink shade of morning, from the dew on the grass to Jorn's shape as he crossed the fields. After every determined step, he paused, leaned in to brush his hands over the ground, then took his next step. He kept his head down. A distant whine accompanied his spell.

Shimmery air—as if from heat—trailed behind him, coiling around too-tall weeds and dipping with every dried-out ditch he crossed. Slowly, the tail end of the trail sank and faded as it settled into blades of grass and thick-leaved autumn flowers.

*It shouldn't fade,* Amara thought. *I'm a mage. I should still be able to see a simple boundary spell.*

Amara concentrated, squinted, willed with all her might: nothing.

Frustrated, she glanced back at Maart, who was muttering from inside the granary. He'd been rinsing their kommer leaves in a bowl of cold water, but right now, the water frothed and bubbled.

Backlash. Harmless backlash, maybe, but it added up. That was exactly why she sat in this crouch whenever Jorn cast his detection wards. With her legs getting stiffer by the second, she'd draw a crude temple in the cold-as-water dirt before her, place her hand in its center, and ask the spirits to forgive Jorn for demanding so much of them.

This time, instead of a temple, she drew three lines. Three blackouts. They had one thing in common. She'd been in danger each time. She might've called on the spirits without realizing it, like a defense mechanism, instinct.

But why? Danger was exactly when she couldn't afford to black out.

Movement. Jorn was pulling away from his spell. Quickly,

Amara rubbed out the lines in the dirt and backed into the storehouse, but Jorn wasn't coming their way. He crossed the field toward the forest's edge. He'd already completed the part of the spell that extended into the forest, though, and he never left without telling them.

Right before he disappeared behind an abandoned shed, Amara saw a piece of glass flicker in his hand, and her eyes widened. Mages used enchanted glass or mirrors to communicate. She knew Jorn and Cilla had people working alongside them. That was how they'd recruited Maart when the servant before him died; that was how Jorn kept their funds up. Amara had never found out who, and she'd stopped asking long ago. If those people included mages, though . . . mages on their side, without Jorn's temper, who she might be able to ask about the blackouts . . .

Following Jorn was stupid under normal circumstances. Jorn's mood lately made it even stupider.

Amara did it, anyway.

"I'll get firewood," she signed to Maart, and ran lightly across the field. A heron stood watch on the shed's roof, overseeing a ditch below. She slowed the closer she came. She heard Jorn's voice but couldn't make out the words. She heard another voice, too. Male.

She pressed herself against the shed and sneaked around one corner, then peeked past the next. Jorn looked as if he was praying, head bowed, one hand to the ground. His fingers rested on the edges of the glass, which flickered in the watery morning light.

A breeze carried his voice with it. ". . . I can track Cilla if she runs. No, I'm worried about Amara. I can handle her, but these blackouts . . ."

The wind brushed stray nettles past Amara's hand, and she flinched at the sting but stayed dead silent. Her heart crept upward and beat in her throat. Jorn knew about the blackouts? She needed to hear every word of this.

"Blackouts? Plural?" The other man swore.

"According to Cilla, yes. She told me out of concern. But it's not just that the blackouts might put Cilla in danger—"

"Yeah. It's about what happens if they get worse." Amara knew the voice but couldn't place it. She inched back around the corner. Nettles rustled by her ankles. "Whoever's causing this will catch on and try again. Keep an eye on Amara. If it continues, bring her to Drudo palace. In the meantime, I'll send one of us to help. I'd go myself, but I don't know how much Amara remembers. Bracha's new, though. Those kids won't recognize her. Maessen is a ghost town, anyway—they don't need her there."

Maessen—a Dit-founded mainland city, Amara knew, on the north side of the Dunelands. The servant before Maart had died near there. Jorn then took Maart from the Maessen palace, told him his duty was to the crown, not the ministers, and proceeded to forget all about the servant who'd come before.

Up until a minute ago, that was all Amara had known of Maessen.

Now, she remembered another detail: the name of Maessen's new minister, Bracha.

One of us, the man had said, and I don't know how much Amara remembers, and Drudo palace, and—acutely—Amara realized why she knew his voice.

Jorn hesitated. "Let's wait. I'll handle it for now."

"But if—"

"Better than recognizing Bracha." Jorn's sudden rise in volume startled a nearby hare. It bolted to safety, diving into the thicket at the edge of the field. "I need to go. How's Ammelore?"

"She's a big city—she's doing fine without you," the man said. "Hey, I'll contact the harbor and tell them you need more silver. Keep me informed—and in the names of the dead, stay away from the pubs. We don't need to clean up more of your messes."

Amara turned, sidestepping nettles and twigs that might give her away. Behind her, she heard the crack of glass.

She walked faster, disappearing into the trees, far away, farther, as far as she could without crossing Jorn's detection ward, kneeling to pick up dried branches here and there for firewood. Thorns tore open her skin.

Jorn would know she'd listened in on him. He knew about the blackouts and he probably knew a million more things she didn't and never would, and *that voice*, and—and she needed to calm down. Work on collecting firewood. When she returned, Jorn had to believe she'd collected firewood and nothing else.

He couldn't find out Amara had listened in.

He couldn't find out Amara had recognized that man's voice.

He couldn't find out Amara knew where she recognized it from.

Between the ministers' coup and being plucked away to protect Cilla, Amara had spent months at the Bedam palace learning its new name and serving its new owner. She'd been a kid with all her early teeth still, used to getting ordered around. The person behind those orders didn't matter. She'd been more concerned about her friends who'd died in the takeover and the way her elbow had healed after she'd cut it on a rusted nail in the barn.

Still, she'd seen her new boss around. Ruudde was a short man, thickset and draped in Dit gemstones. His voice had been kind but direct and had sounded almost—not quite, but almost—the same coming through a broken pane of glass.

Jorn was working with the ministers.

olan had been fading in and out during his history test, worried about Amara, squirming at all the names of dead people listed on the quiz, and—

*Whoever's causing this will catch on and try again.*

Nolan sat near the back of the classroom, by the window, and stared uncomprehendingly at the road stretching away from the school. A breeze swept sand across the blazing asphalt.

Jorn knew about the blackouts. Was working with the ministers. And—

*Whoever's causing this will catch on and try again.*

They were talking about Nolan. Had to be. He'd thought he was dependent on Amara's blackouts to take control, but did Ruudde's words mean it was the other way around? What if the blackouts were his doing—Nolan piggybacking on whatever connection Amara's faulty magic had established and using it instead of letting it use him? She'd suspected her panic had activated the blackouts, but Nolan had panicked just as much as she had.

All around him, pencils scratched on paper. Chairs scraped against the floor. Nolan looked at the classroom, dazed, then at the near-blank quiz on his desk.

"I have to—go," he blurted. Before Ms. Suarez could answer, he was on his feet, weaving between desks.

You OK? Luisa mouthed as he passed. They'd done a project together that winter. She either liked him or felt sorry for him—Nolan couldn't tell which—but they hadn't talked in weeks, so it wasn't as if he could find out. He didn't answer, his mind stuck on Ruudde's words. If he could control Amara, he could talk to Maart and leave a message. She'd finally know he existed.

"Nolan," Ms. Suarez said sharply. "I thought your doctor's appointment wasn't until later. This is not how—"

"I'm sorry. I'll be right outside. I just need to . . ." He stumbled into the hallway and shut the door behind him, muffling Ms. Suarez's voice. She wouldn't follow him. She'd tell the principal, who'd contact his parents, who'd say he had a seizure, and that was that. He walked straight to the lockers across the hall, then lowered himself to the ground, the movement flaking off rusty metal behind him—

—Amara was still gathering firewood. Her thoughts raced as much as his, repeating the conversation she'd heard over and over. She didn't understand half of it. She honed in on what she did understand: that Jorn knew about her blackouts, and that if they continued, he'd bring her back to Bedam. They were close by. It'd only take hours.

And what would happen there?

For all Amara's thoughts, at least her world was quiet, and her only pain came from splinters and bark scrapes that healed straightaway. That made it easier for Nolan to concentrate.

*Move,* he thought, staring at her hands searching the forest ground. *I need to do this. I did before. If you'll just—move—*

—over one of the classroom doors hung a clock, and Nolan couldn't help measuring time. Ten minutes. Twenty. He hadn't moved Amara even an inch. He brushed off a passing teacher's concern, ignored two juniors staring at his exposed prosthesis.

It wasn't working.

The door to Ms. Suarez's classroom opened, and Sarah Schneider stepped out. Her eyes flitted to the bathrooms down the hall, then to him. "You all right? You were in kind of a hurry."

"Sick." Nolan had been in a hurry. He hadn't even stopped to think of an excuse.

"Sick as in, *bwaagh, meet my lunch?* Or sick as in . . ." Sarah gestured vaguely. "Seizure?"

"I'm always having seizures," Nolan said, suddenly tight-voiced. Too tight. Sarah didn't deserve that. By now, it'd been thirty minutes of nothing but sitting and pushing his way into the Dunelands. Nothing was happening. Slowly, he let his lungs deflate. "Sorry. I'm fine. Thank you."

"Huh." Sarah shuffled her feet, as if she wanted to leave but wasn't sure how. "Those small ones . . . Luisa said they happen every time you blink?"

"Not every blink," Nolan lied. "But often."

"Freaky."

"People can have hundreds of seizures a day. It's on Wikipedia." Nolan couldn't have people disbelieving him. If anyone realized he didn't have epilepsy, they'd want to put him through testing that Dad's insurance didn't cover, and his parents would pay for it, anyway, no matter how far in debt they already were after all the prostheses and custom shoes and those damn pills.

"And Wikipedia never lies, right?" Sarah looked slightly more at ease.

"Never." Nolan smiled wanly, his mind still on Amara— **who was headed back to the granary as thunderclouds met overhead. Magic backlash, she was sure of it**—and tried to pay attention to Sarah, instead. He wasn't used to this. Whenever people made rare, awkward attempts at small talk, they avoided mentioning the seizures or his leg. Sarah didn't seem bothered. She didn't even seem curious, like some of the freshmen who sometimes walked up and gaped; she seemed interested. Nolan went on despite himself. "The small seizures happen most of the time. The big ones come every few weeks or months." Whenever Cilla hurt herself. Whenever Jorn got angry.

"Wow. Sucks."

"I can't complain. I'm safe as long as I'm careful." He hesitated. "Other people have it much worse."

"Safe," she repeated. It had to be an odd choice of words. "And you feel them coming?"

"Yeah. It's called an aura."

"Cool. I'll definitely check out that Wiki page." Sarah gave a half-assed salute. "Gotta go, or Suarez will bite my head off." She jogged off before Nolan could answer. He watched her leave, and only when she disappeared into the girls' bathroom did he realize this was the longest conversation he'd had with a classmate in weeks.

The thought should excite him or bother him—he didn't know which. He felt neither. That bothered him. He grimaced, rubbed a hand across his face, and returned to the Dunelands.

"The pills aren't working." The sooner he stopped wasting his parents' money, the better.

"It's a little early to determine that. This medication can take months to take effect." Dr. Campbell was used to Nolan by now. He'd told her the same thing a dozen times in the past few years. Next, she'd tell him not to give up hope, that all these medications were different and who knew what he'd end up responding to, and he'd sit in that plush chair in her office and try not to let his doctor-smiles turn into doctor-grimaces. He'd heard the exact same thing from Dad the day before, and he was tired beyond anything—

**—by now the storm was in full swing, thunder tearing through the skies—**

"—a positive attitude. You'd be surprised how much difference it makes."

"Of course." Smile. Don't forget to smile. "You're right."

"Any side effects?" Dr. Campbell studied something on her bulky iMac, then wiped at a smudge with her thumb. "We can adjust the dosage if they're bothering you. Your blood levels came back within therapeutic ranges, but there's wiggle room."

"Headaches. Tired. The usual."

"Any behavioral changes? Nausea? You've always been prone to that."

"It's fine." Nolan hesitated. Yesterday's tryst with the toilet had been his own damn fault, but Dad had said to tell her. "I threw up yesterday. I'm OK now. I just messed up on the dosage, and . . ." His breath caught.

Sarah Schneider had been right: he'd been in too much of a hurry. Throwing himself into the Dunelands wouldn't do any good. He'd just figured he could finally do something—but he should've paused, should've thought.

Why the blackouts now? What had changed?

Two doses too close together. That was what had changed.

This time nothing about Nolan's smile was faked. "I think," he said, his voice sounding foreign to his own ears, high-pitched and unusually fast, "yes, thinking back, maybe I had less seizures after that. After I took the extra dose." He kept his eyes wide open. He didn't want Amara to yank him back in now. He studied Dr. Campbell's face for a reaction, something in her eyes, her mouth, to show she believed him.

He had to sound convincing. He licked his too-dry lips. "I might be wrong. I'm probably imagining it. I don't want to . . ."

"No, this is good, Nolan. This is great! It's the first time we're seeing a difference."

Nolan had swallowed a pill at lunch, just an hour ago. The moment he stepped out of the doctor's office, a grin growing on his face, he slung his backpack around to his front and hunted for another.

A mara had to tell Maart what she'd heard.

Maart was gathering water, and Amara had asked Jorn for permission to wash her clothes, which were crusted from blood where the arrows had hit her. "Just stay near enough that I can call you," he'd said, and she'd bolted outside, down the road leading into the woods. Under torn branches and dirt and leaves everywhere she looked, tree roots had burst through, displacing slabs of stone. She couldn't tell how much of the mess was from the storm and how much from neglect. No one took this path, Jorn had said, not now that Teschel was one of the few islands with an airtrain.

Amara jogged around a fallen tree blocking the path. Enough earth clung to the roots to fill half the granary. The storm had been brief but intense, as backlash always was.

A punishment from the spirits, some people said, for abusing their power. Others said the spirits simply put the world back in balance after mages knocked it down and drained it dry.

The end result was the same: storms and quakes and a hundred things more. If those were punishments, all the smaller, immediate instances of backlash—water frothing, flames flickering, bugs spasming, and plants wilting—must be warnings. The ministers didn't care to listen.

"Mar?" she called aloud once near the creek. Despite the post-storm chill, sweat pricked at the base of her skull and pooled by her hip, where her sidesling rested. Overturned earth warned her of boar, and when bushes nearby rustled, she tensed, relaxing only when a tall shape stepped out.

"We need to talk," she signed.

Maart lowered the buckets he'd been filling to the ground and ran his fingers over her arm, spreading a tingly-hot feeling. He kissed her forehead, then stepped back. They needed room to sign. "About your blackouts?"

She told him what she'd overheard. What it meant. "We have to find out what they're doing," she said, her hands fluttering. "How long they've been working together. We have to tell Cilla."

"Cilla is your priority?" The way he signed the name bordered on revulsion even as his face stayed stony.

"I didn't say that."

"It doesn't matter what Jorn's doing or why. All right?"

She shook her head and looked past him at the forest—leaves dripping with rain, the sky still dark overhead. Early winterbugs scurried in solid clouds between the trees. Storm-damaged mushrooms the size of Amara's head bulged from the ground and bark.

"You can't stay for her," he signed.

"We've talked about this." She stepped away. Her boots sank in the mud. "It's not about putting her on the throne. There's nowhere we can go."

"Is that all it is?"

"Just say it," Amara said. Then she wouldn't be the one to bring it up. She could deny it and be done with it.

"I see how Cilla looks at you."

How—how Cilla looked at her? She breathed deeply, the warm scent of moss filling her nostrils, and moved her hands carefully. "How's that?"

"Why?" Maart asked. "Does it matter to you?"

"Don't be like this. Don't play games."

He twisted his lips into a smile. "We used to talk about her. We used to hate her."

"It's not that simple. Before you came, Cilla and I played games together. The servant before you was older; Cilla was the only person close to my age I knew. The only friend I had."

"And now?"

"Now I have you. Is that what you want to hear? Now I understand that Cilla and I *can't* be friends."

"Do you want to be?"

"It would not end well," Amara said.

"But do you want it to?" Normally at this point Maart grew frustrated. Now, his signs only became smaller, turning his question into a plea.

"I care about you. All right?" Amara stepped in and pressed her lips to his. They lingered in the kiss, staving away the chill, which rolled back in the moment they separated. Amara wanted to wrap her arms around herself, rub away that goose-flesh, but couldn't while they still talked. "That's what I want," she said once there was enough room between them. It was true. She wanted Maart. She wanted his teasing and his wide grins and his full lips and the way he'd squirm and laugh when she trailed kisses along his hipbone.

She didn't want these endless arguments.

"I want you, too." Maart pressed his forehead to hers, and she bowed her head to see his signing, pressed close and awkward between their bodies. "You and me, away from them. That's *all* I want."

Amara wished she could say the same thing back.

Leaves rustled. She jolted away, turning toward the noise. Jorn stood near an oak, one hand on its wet bark. If he'd seen her and Maart together, he didn't show it. "Amara. I felt an intrusion. It's probably just a mage dealing with damage from the backlash, but we should be sure. Go check."

"Cilla—" Amara started to sign.

"Maart and I will look after her. If there's danger, I'll take them into the woods." He pointed to the path. "Come back the second you know more."

This wasn't right. They each had their tasks, and this wasn't hers.

"You said Cilla should avoid forests in emergencies," she said. "There's a beach nearby. It's safer." She should listen, not dumbly sign objections—but this was about Cilla. This was her task.

"That's stupid." Jorn sniffed. "With open ground like the beach, hired mages would have a field day shooting at her. And they'd have the full Gray Sea at their bidding for power. No. We'll go inland."

If Cilla ran, the branches would tear open her skin within seconds. Why would Jorn change his mind?

"I have to go back to Cilla. I've already lowered the boundary spell. Go!" Jorn shoved her toward the road.

She wasn't supposed to leave Cilla.

It had to be the blackouts. Jorn no longer trusted her.

Before Jorn could see her dawdling, Amara tossed her sidesling at Maart and took off, boots slapping muddy leaves. The forest smelled of moldy mushrooms and wet soil, mixed with pine and the occasional, almost-gone scent of chrysanths, bursts of white flowers fighting to be seen in the few sunlit gaps between trees. The layer of leaves under her feet—deep reds and burned yellows and faded browns—was so thick and moist that she almost slipped. She dashed around trees, slowing only when she reached the road. Her boots were too loud on the stones. She stopped, silent, listening. They'd never had mages tracking them so soon after moving. They'd only been on Teschel since last night.

She didn't hear anything. She moved farther in the direction Jorn had indicated, but she stayed close to the side of the road, ready to dive to safety—then she did hear something, a woman's voice, to her left. Amara peered through the trees. After a second, she saw movement. A flash of thick curls. Dit? "—give me—" the woman murmured.

Amara came closer, careful to avoid branches. Leaves were harder to dodge. At least they were wet, less noisy than usual when they crumpled underfoot. If the woman heard her, she didn't seem to care.

"I have to help. Please forgive me."

Peering past a tree, Amara spotted the woman. She was leaning forward, both hands on a slab of polished stone held up by blocks of rock on each side. Underneath the rock lay a small, still pond, perhaps the size of a table.

A temple. An old one, judging by the dirt-brown moss creeping across the rocks, but a temple nonetheless.

The Dit mage stood still, as if listening. Amara pressed her hands to her hair to keep it from wafting out past the tree. The wind had picked up again. The woman wasn't listening for her, though. Jorn had told her this, years ago. Mages would draw on the spirits for spells, then read their response in the rustling of trees, the rush of water rubbing against the shore.

Amara had almost forgotten that the topic of magic hadn't always been off-limits.

She tried to listen, too. All she heard was the wind.

The mage pulled her hands brusquely off the rock and turned back to the path. Behind her tree, Amara stood as still as the dead, listening as the woman's footsteps broke into a run, moving away from the granary.

The mage wasn't after Cilla. Backlash cleanup, just as Jorn had said. Amara should go back and tell him. But . . . she'd been searching for a plan. She could ask this mage—a stranger, someone who wouldn't tell Jorn—about the blackouts.

Amara ran. For the next minute she followed the woman through the woods, diving behind this tree and that, until a pair of silver rails sitting on raised earth abruptly bisected the road.

A moment later, Amara smelled something burning. Carefully, she moved closer to the rails. The trees thinned, robbing her of cover. The smell strengthened. Her own hands had stunk the same way yesterday.

She shivered. The sensation ran down her spine again and again. She pressed clammy hands together and made herself step through the trees so she could see down the rails in both directions.

The airtrain stood a stone's throw away, gleaming metal except for a massive black stain on one side. That explained why it had stopped. Amara saw movement through the windows. She sneaked closer, until the voices drifting through the windows formed words.

"Lightning," someone was whispering. "Lightning."

"Just stay calm," the Dit mage said. Amara saw the back of her head through the windows now, moving around, then dipping out of sight. "I'll help you. All right?"

The voice kept whispering. A different voice said, "My father. How's my father?" When the mage didn't respond, a sob tore through the man's words. "The weather was fine before— when—how is he?"

"It wasn't me," the mage said. Even from this distance, without seeing her face, Amara felt her irritation. "I haven't used magic in months. I'm oath-bound. But I'll get you to the carecenter, all right? Just let me put my hands here . . . This'll hurt, but I need to . . ."

"Your magic will make it worse," the man said.

"I've already prayed. The spirits might allow it. I'll need a moment. Oh, curse the ministers!"

The breeze carried more of the burning-flesh stink. Amara fought back a gag. She approached, anyway, climbing over a fallen tree, hiding behind another one. If the mage was against the ministers, maybe she'd be safe to talk to. Amara hadn't been sure. The Dunelands ministers had roots in every corner of the world, but the Dit were their strongest supporters—more out of spite against the Alineans than anything else. Jorn was an exception.

She'd always thought so, anyway.

The Dit mage disappeared from the windows. Amara peeked around the tree. A moment later, the mage stood in the pried-open train doors, stunned, looking exactly at where Amara hid.

"A spirit. You're a spirit." The mage stepped from the train. The earth squelched underfoot.

Amara should pull back. Run. Anything but stand here, half-hidden behind a tree, watching that mage with a single eye. If Jorn knew . . .

The mage went on. "No. You used to be? Were you possessed by one? But there's still . . . There's a presence . . ."

A presence. Ruudde's words echoed: *Whoever's causing this will catch on and try again.*

"Can we talk?"

A passenger stumbling from the train drew the mage's attention, but only for a moment, as if afraid Amara would disappear if she looked away for too long.

Amara's signing would give her away. If the mage didn't rat her out, the airtrain's passengers might. This had been a stupid idea, stupid and dangerous.

And that stink of flesh was so, so intense.

She pressed a hand to her mouth, turned, ran, left the mage's shouts behind, forgot all about stealth and silence. The mage wouldn't follow—she wouldn't abandon the injured passengers—but Amara couldn't slow. The smell stuck to her hands. Stuck to everything.

She only had to return to Jorn and pretend nothing happened, and . . .

That'd get her nowhere.

She stopped. Took a quarter turn. Stormed through a layer of wet leaves. Thorns and burrs clung to her winterwear. She found the temple within a minute, spotting faded stone that blended perfectly into the colorless, storm-drenched woods; if she hadn't known it was there, she'd have looked right past it.

She'd always thought that if she prayed at a true temple, perhaps the spirits would forgive Jorn's magic use and prevent accidents like the airtrain's. He never prayed, to the point that Amara wondered if he'd ever sworn a mage's oath in the first place. She'd asked him about it, back when he'd allowed questions, when sometimes he'd even smiled and indulged her. He didn't pray at temples, he'd explained, because hired mages like the knifewielder might set a trap for him. He didn't need to pray, besides: temple or no temple, the spirits understood why he called on them so often.

Amara always suspected it was nonsense, but that hadn't stopped her from hoping that, if the spirits listened no matter what, sketching misshapen buildings in the dirt still stood a chance of catching their attention.

She crouched, steadying herself with one hand on the temple's stone. She'd never touched a temple before. It felt icy cold. *Let this work*, she thought. *Let the mage come back.*

She searched around half-rotted leaves for a chalky piece of stone, and slowly, carefully, drew it against the temple. Even with ink she struggled to mimic Cilla's letters, let alone with a rock this blunt, but she remembered the basics.

Mage, she wrote blockily, the chalk cold in her hands. Then, Spirit airtrain. Need talk. She'd probably misspelled it. The mage would understand, though, wouldn't she? Market, she wrote next. Maart had a trip scheduled tomorrow. Market stallkeepers were so busy that you could get away with pointing and never speaking a word.

She'd find a way to go in his stead.

Amara stared at her letters with a mixture of pride and fear.

**H**ow come you're not rehearsing with your friends?" Nolan asked, perched in Pat's desk chair. The extra pill would need time to kick in. He had a hard time sitting still, though. He kept pushing the notebook on her desk back and forth and tapping his foot and spending a second too long in Amara's world—

—Cilla was reading on one side of the room while Amara finished up lunch at the fire pit with Jorn and Maart, rootpatties in hand, acting as if nothing was wrong. Jorn was looking at her with prying dark eyes, but he hadn't said a word about how long she'd taken to find the mage—

"—I am." Pat frowned. "Our drama teacher makes us rehearse together in the gym, but we don't have a lot of time since we also have to build the set. That's why we need volunteers. I asked Mom, but she's too busy working."

Nolan held back a cringe. "Rehearsing with your friends at home, I mean."

"I just don't want to make a big deal out of it. What if I screw up?"

"You won't. I promise."

Pat fought a tiny surprised smile. Straight teeth pushed

into her bottom lip to keep it in line. Nolan couldn't recall the last time she'd taken anything he said so seriously. For a moment he wasn't sure what to do with himself.

"Thanks. Um—so I'm in the ER, and a girl just went missing from her room . . ." Pat stood by her bed, chest puffed out, ignoring schoolbooks and bags scattered around her feet. "No!" she bellowed. "I have to know where she went—"

—Maart stood to clean up the mess, leaving Jorn and Amara at the fire pit. She should be calm. Jorn couldn't know she'd contacted the mage. But if he did . . . Already, tension was locking up her spine; already, she was crushing her rootpatty between her fingers. Jorn had burned her simply for daring to read. He'd do so, so much worse for this.

A clap shook the granary. She jerked. Thunder?

"Again? This *must* be backlash." Cilla kept one finger in her book.

"Yes. I sense it." Jorn smelled clean, a whiff of fish on his breath as he spoke—

"—know I'm a nurse! Don't tell me what my job is!" Pat took a threatening step forward—

—Jorn's and Amara's eyes kept meeting without a reason, and every time it held Amara still. She wanted to suck the patty's remains off her fingers, just so she wouldn't be stuck like this, but any movement might make Jorn snap.

*Just say it!* Amara wanted to shout. *Say what you want to say!* She tried to slow her breathing, and her frustration alongside it.

She felt too loud. Too present. She needed to be invisible. Nolan fought off her fear, because he couldn't let it crawl into him, he had to stay an observer, shouldn't even be here—

"—you awake?" Pat was gathering thick bunches of hair into a ponytail, her movements irritated. Nolan found himself staring somewhere over her shoulder, swallowing as he tried to get a grip. Why was his throat so dry? He shouldn't let Amara get to him.

"Right. Sorry." In his absence, his hands had pressed onto the notebook enough to warp the paper. Ink dotted his fingers. He flattened the pages, the familiar paper grain a comfort. He'd meant to jot down notes to show Pat he took her seriously, but he hadn't written a word. "You're doing great."

"Really?" Her hands dropped to her sides. She sounded at once suspicious and hopeful. Did she care that much about his opinion? Why did that thought make him so damn uncomfortable? "I'm trying for a Michelle Rodriguez vibe, you know."

Was he supposed to know that name? Dad had Rodriguez family down in Mexico, but Nolan guessed Pat meant an actress rather than that great-aunt they'd met as kids.

"Would you . . . if you saw me in a movie . . . Never mind. You don't have to do this if you don't care."

"I do care," he said immediately. That wasn't true. But he wanted to care. He was trying to care.

He shoved Amara from his mind. Her fear wasn't his. He wanted to stay here, in the safety of Pat's tiny room with its dusty shelves and dorky mirror and neon gym bag dumped in one corner. He didn't want to go back, but—

"—when I'm queen," Cilla was saying, "I won't let any ministers abuse magic like this. We'll keep the world in balance."

"It's repulsive how they've treated this country," Jorn said in a clipped voice.

*But you're working with them*, Amara thought. Was all this an act? Or were he and Ruudde working *against* the other ministers?

All Nolan could think was, *You know I'm here, Jorn, don't you?*—

—he needed to say something, and fast, because the way Pat looked at him, he knew he'd blown it. Their second practice session and he'd spent half of it with Amara. He wiped sweat from his hairline and stared at the notebook as though studying his earlier, nonexistent notes. "You might be overplaying this scene. You're shouting a lot."

"But I'm talking to my boss. I'm supposed to hate him. I told you: my character thinks he knows something about the missing patients. Oh, and she's scared because he might've left those voice mails."

"I'm not seeing fear." He focused on Pat with all his might, to the point where his staring would probably creep out anyone else. "You're just shouting."

"You said I was doing fine!"

"You are. I'm impressed," Nolan rushed to assure her. He'd promised to be critical, though. "I just think you can play that fear more convincingly. Fear, true fear—you can't cover that up. There's always this voice at the back of your mind: What if I'm not safe? It changes everything." He didn't know what he was saying. He rubbed his thighs while he talked, hoping to avoid blinking. He didn't want to mess up again—

**—Amara was eating her rootpatty, stuffing it into her mouth faster than she ought to. She couldn't swallow all this, not without her tongue, not without sauce to help it down, but she needed something to do and no, *no*, Nolan didn't want to know any of this—**

"—true fear?" Pat didn't move. Nolan wasn't used to her so still. Normally she'd fiddle with her hair or cross her arms, or her eyebrows would move weirdly across her forehead. Now, her eyes drifted to his stump. He scratched it self-consciously. Pat should be blowing him off by now—he got plenty of concern from their parents already. He'd liked seeing Pat this way, as far removed from his issues or Amara's panic as possible: making over-the-top proclamations, waltzing around her room with a fake stethoscope around her neck . . .

But Amara still—always—won out. It wasn't fair to Pat. Nolan rubbed his face. "True fear is the kind you can't reason away. It makes you want to puke. To do anything, anything, except face—whatever it is you fear. And every time you think of it, even for a flash, part of you panics."

Pat still didn't move. "But if you're really angry?"

Nolan thought of Amara, who pushed her anger down so deep it couldn't escape. He thought of Maart, who let it burst out in pieces. He thought of Jorn, who gripped Amara's hands and— "It depends, I guess." When he talked next, the words came more easily. This was about a school play, nothing more. "You could make your character shout, then step back, like she realizes what kind of trouble she's getting into."

"OK. Thanks." Nolan didn't recognize Pat's high-pitched, nervous laugh. He'd freaked her out, hadn't he? He breathed deeply, then let the air escape. He should go to his own room, see if the extra medication was working the way he'd hoped.

"I'm nauseous," he lied, and hated himself for it. "I should go."

12

Amara's legs trembled with energy. So did her hands. She couldn't afford them to. A seam of Cilla's topscarf had torn, and putting a needle into Cilla's hands was asking for trouble, so it was up to Amara to carefully push gold thread through the scarf's patterned maroon surface. She bit down hard in concentration.

Putting a toothbrush into Cilla's mouth was asking for trouble, too, but Jorn insisted. Nearby, Cilla boredly ran the brush past her teeth, her shoulders bare to avoid stains on her topscarf. Her winterwear was just as chic as the scarf Amara was repairing, with finely stitched cuffs at the ankles and golden satin lacing running down the thighs and back and sides. A lace pattern adorned the very top where it sat snugly around her breasts, even though that part would be hidden under a topscarf most of the time. Now, though, her sternum and arms were bare, revealing muscle flexing under the skin of her arms and that faintly glowing palace tattoo above her breasts. It was the same as Amara's—the shape of an Alinean volcano surrounded by a star's spikes—but Cilla's tattoo was larger, and it sat free while Amara's was encircled. And if Amara were looking at Cilla at all—which she shouldn't—she should look at that tattoo and not the softness of the flesh underneath.

She cleared her throat, both to distract herself and to get Cilla's attention. There was something she needed to ask. She chose her gestures with care, though tension showed in every flick of her fingers, and said, "If those blackouts happen again, Jorn will punish me."

Anything more explicit was too dangerous.

Amara stared right into Cilla's eyes. Looking away meant disrespect; it meant fear. Fear meant distrusting your betters. That was unacceptable. She'd already taken a risk saying this much without a lead-in or a specific request for Cilla's time.

Cilla lowered the brush, looking surprised. "I . . . understand." She bit her lip, then caught herself. Teeth and skin were a risky combination. "Well, I'm certain you won't black out again."

Promise? Amara wanted to ask. Promise you won't tell him if I do?

It didn't matter. Cilla could swear up and down that she'd keep quiet, but she'd already told on Amara once, and she was still her better. She remained a danger.

"Let's hope," Amara said, and checked the bowl near Cilla for pinkened spit. Clean. She picked up her needle again.

Cilla lowered her head, her expression hidden behind pointy locks of hair that Amara could never make sense of. Most Alineans wore their hair shorter than Cilla's chin-length locks, even shaving the sides; since they tattooed their servants' necks, long hair meant you had something to hide. When the Alineans had crossed the Greater Ocean and founded the Dunelands as a trading outpost, they'd taken both their servants and hairstyles with them. The shorter hairstyles had rubbed off on some settlers from the Continent, but most of them wore it long, especially given the Dunelands' persistent, wet chill.

Amara didn't know whether it was a statement or vanity, but Cilla had opted for the middle road: short enough to reveal her neck, long enough to run her fingers through. Amara's hands twitched wanting to do just that. Her feet twitched, too. She couldn't sit still. She had all this pent-up worry and anger and nothing to do with it, nothing but pricking this stupid needle into Cilla's scarf, studying patterns that reminded her of flames—nothing at all like her own scarf, which was drab and thin.

Her legs wouldn't stop moving. Muscles pulling, her feet wrenching back and forth. Amara held them down, but then her head shook, too, tiny tugs in all directions. Her sight faded for a second without her ever shutting her eyes. She willed her neck still.

It didn't work.

She wanted to raise her hands to press them to her cheeks, but they hung unresponsive by her sides, as though she'd slept in the wrong position and a million needleseeds were about to stab her skin with every movement. Those pricks refused to come. Her arms simply didn't listen.

Her head stopped moving. It came to a halt with her face turned right, looking at Maart still cleaning the fish on an old grain cart across the room.

"Amara?" Cilla made a sound of hesitation.

Amara's lips moved. But she didn't move them.

It wasn't just her head or her arms she couldn't use. She tried to wiggle her toes. To direct her eyes back to Cilla, who was getting up from her seat, based on the sound of her chair scraping against the floor. None of it worked. This wasn't like needleseeds. This was worse.

Amara felt her heart speed up—so maybe she could control that, at least, her heart was still hers, still listened to her panic—and then her hands rose, and her head turned back to Cilla, all of it without her say-so.

Amara stumbled, and for that split second she was falling to the floor and couldn't stop herself, couldn't move her feet forward or extend her arms or cover her face—

She caught herself. That unseen something tugged at her lips again. Like fingers playing with her face, pulling her muscles left and up without her consent. She was trapped.

And this time, she was aware of every second of it.

"Eh worrgee," her mouth said, pushing air from her lungs past her lips. What did that mean? The sounds came from her own mouth, but they sounded alien, foreign—Jélis, maybe, or some language from the northern continents.

Her hands still hovered by her chest, then spread apart.

They signed, unfinished and too quickly and nothing like her normal gestures, "It's working. I'm here. This is me I'm doing this I'm using her hands, this is working, it's working—"

"Amara, what are you—what do you mean?" Cilla's voice caught.

Behind Amara came footsteps. Maart. Her body turned to face him a second later than she would have. "Anything wrong?" Maart asked.

*Yes,* she wanted to say. *This isn't me. I'm trapped. This isn't me!*

Instead of signing, Amara stomped her feet. Her hands clapped. Her lips pulled in a grimace. She filled her lungs, held that breath, let it shudder out. "It's real," her hands said. Her eyes looked at those hands, moving without her commands. She never watched her own signs. There was no point. But now her eyes stayed glued to her hands as they tumbled over themselves. "It's real it worked I'm *here.*"

"What are you talking about?" Maart asked.

Cilla shuffled closer, but not too close, leaning in with only her head and her still-bare shoulders. She laughed nervously. "How many mushrooms are you on, Amara?"

Amara's head shook, slowly at first, then stronger, enough to send hair slapping against her cheeks. She laughed. The sound was not her own. "No. Not Amara."

What kind of spirit would take control like this? What kind of mage would have her stand here laughing and make her smack her lips?

"I think you're doing something magical," Cilla said slowly. "Something mage-like."

Amara's hands said something else, but with her eyes sliding up to watch Cilla's face, she couldn't see what. Cilla's nostrils flared, and she kept her distance.

Amara concentrated on sensing her hands to identify their movements. The signals didn't come from her, but she could recognize the tug of her muscles, the brush of skin. "—but doesn't know. She never knows," her fingers said.

Amara wanted to scream.

Someone was doing this to her. Someone was pushing and shoving around her muscles. Someone was shutting her out.

"Stop this," Maart said. "Jorn will be back soon. Please stop."

"If you're not Amara," Cilla asked, "are you a spirit? A mage?"

Amara felt her lips stretch. Was she smiling? She never smiled like this. Not with her lips parting, her teeth visible.

"Then who?" Maart shook. Frustration—and fear, too, Amara thought, but she couldn't comfort him, couldn't tell him his fear and anger helped as little as her own.

"I am not a mage. I am—" Amara's hands paused there. The next movements came slowly. "N-OO-L-U-N. S-A-N-D-I-AA-K-OO. The letters aren't the same. We have a separate letter for the d. It's a hard sound, like in Maart, and the k is softer. But this is close. This is how you'd say it."

"Nolan," Cilla repeated, almost a question.

Nolan, Amara repeated to herself. She didn't know the name. How could she not know the name? This person was in her body. This person was in the tips of her fingers and the heat of her belly and the squish-and-pull of her lungs.

She should know the name.

"You're not a mage," Cilla stated. "Why are you possessing her?"

Maart's hands kept rising and moving together as if he wanted to say something, but Cilla had said all there was to say. She looked calm. She was good at that. Even when she was afraid, nervous, she hid it under tight smiles and nods.

This calm was new. Regal.

"Possessing her? No, no, Amara's the mage, not me. I'm just a boy. Amara she pulls me in, she makes me see through her eyes," her hands said. "Her mage powers they do this but she doesn't know it. You have to tell her. You have to explain."

The hands moved too fast. The inflections were wrong, as was the grammar—but not when Nolan wanted his words to work. When he cared enough to slow down.

Amara wanted to shake her head. She wanted to dash away, move backward, as though that would leave Nolan behind in the space where she now stood and leave her free. Her body didn't listen. Her connection to it was severed. Amara was thoughts, nothing more. She couldn't even move that lock of hair out of her eyes.

"So Amara's responsible for doing this?" Cilla asked.

"Yes! She pulled me in for years, since before Jorn took her from the palace I've been in her head, since before the coup. Always in her head. Locked up. She sucks me in every time I close my eyes. She can do more than heal but she never knew."

No. Amara couldn't think beyond that single dim word: no. This was madness. This was beyond believing.

Maart was staring at Amara's hands. Cilla scanned the rest of her. Her eyes dipped to the way Amara's feet stood on the floor, wide and steady, then rose to the eagerness of her hands, and settled on her lips, her eyes. "I've never heard of this happening," Cilla said. "Mages do odd things, but they don't move into each other's bodies."

"They do!" Amara's movements contained too much energy. "Amara does! Normally I can only watch, but now my medicine is changing something. Amara still pulls me in, but now I can . . . I can . . ." Her hands thrust out, then in, pressing to her breastbone. "I can move."

Tears pricked Amara's eyes. Nolan's tears. Not hers. She knew, because if her body was her own, those tears would've shown up minutes ago.

"Where are you from?" Cilla asked, still calm. "Are you responsible for her blackouts?"

"Is she having a blackout now?" Maart asked.

"She must be," the hands said. "That's why you have to tell her."

Yes. The hands. These were someone else's hands, not hers,

not right now. She was not in her own body but in someone else's, deciphering what went on.

That was better. Easier.

"I'm not from here. Before, when Amara blacked out, I took over. I was the one who ran to the carecenter. I didn't know what happened. This time, I wanted to test it. She must be having a blackout. I can't feel her. Normally I can feel her thoughts, pain—everything—but she's blank now."

Not blank! she wanted to shout. I'm here I can see this I can see this! I'm here!

No point. Nolan couldn't hear her.

But he said he could the rest of the time. For years. No, these words on her fingers couldn't be true—she couldn't trap anyone inside her head. Her thoughts were hers. The only things that were hers and no one else's.

"Where are you from?" Cilla repeated. "'Not from here' can mean anywhere. Not from these islands? Not the Dunelands at all? Where, then? The Continent? The Alinean Islands? Eligon? The—"

Amara's head shook. That lock of hair brushed back and forth over her forehead.

"Where?" Something insistent and hard crept into Cilla's voice.

Another laugh that wasn't hers. "I'm not from this world. Not from this . . . planet."

The door opened. Jorn came inside with heavy boots, every step a creak and a cloud of old grain dust.

Abruptly, Amara crumpled. Her muscles sagged, her shoulders drooped, and it was as if those movements finally opened her lungs to her. She drew in air, lifted her head, pumped her lungs full, gasping for more and more and more, in and out, and—was she back? She screwed her hands into fists, curled her toes inside too-hot boots, and felt her exhales turn to near-sobs.

Her body. Hers.

"Shouldn't you be preparing dinner?" Jorn asked Maart.

Maart bounced away as if stung. "Yes. Sorry." He backed up to the food cart. Early winterbugs buzzed around the fish. He waved them off, no longer looking at Amara, not wanting to direct Jorn's attention her way.

Cilla didn't move, though. The skin over her jaw tightened. She must think Amara was still . . . not her. She'd be worried that this Nolan might cause trouble with Jorn.

Nolan. Amara repeated the name, committing it to memory, although she didn't think she could forget it, ever.

She finally brushed that lock of hair away from her forehead. "One of Cilla's brush hairs fell from the stem," she told Jorn. Amara let her hands move slowly, deliberately, the way they hadn't when Nolan directed them. Every sign its place and time. "It could prick her if it slipped inside her winterwear."

"So get behind a grain cart and take off your wear," Jorn told Cilla irritably. "Princess."

"I planned to." All Cilla's reserve seeped away. "I thought, if it was easier for them to check like this . . ."

"It looks clear," Amara said. "But you should make certain."

Cilla turned toward the nearest cart, but her eyes lingered on Amara, long enough for Amara to dip her head. I'm here, she wanted to say. It's me.

Jorn wouldn't respond well to this development. Even the way he regarded Amara now put her on edge, made her want to escape. He knew she was hiding something.

She couldn't let him take her back to Drudo palace as Ruudde had told him to. She didn't want to think about what would happen there. She didn't want to think about anything.

What did Nolan mean, he was in her head?

t worked.

Until Jorn entered and the shock launched Nolan back to himself, he'd pulled it off. He wasn't worth-less. He could move—walk—laugh. He wasn't trapped behind Amara's eyes anymore.

At dinner he was nauseated and jittery, more concerned with picking out Amara's thoughts than anything else. He'd scared her. He'd assumed she'd been gone, but her thoughts now made it clear he'd been wrong. How did that work? How could he sense her normally but not when he steered her body?

Amara was a mess as she worked and ate. Nolan's name cropped up in her thoughts every few seconds, sometimes as signs and sometimes as sounds. The word sounded odd in her mind—the syllables too choppy—but it was his *name*. She'd never thought his name before.

Nolan hardly touched dinner, giving half-there answers and disappearing for too-long blinks that had his parents exchanging knowing looks. *The pills aren't working*, they had to be thinking, and, for once, they were wrong.

After dinner, he found himself scrubbing even the bottom of the dinner plates twice. He kept the dishes low in the sink in case they slid from his hands. The Dunelands startled him too often for him to take risks holding anything fragile.

Scrub, rinse, stack. The water soaked into his fingers. Soap bubbles covered everything, popping open with the scent of lemon.

Nolan hadn't meant to freak out Amara. When she'd first drawn him in, she'd been away from her family and working at the Bedam palace—Drudo palace, now—for only a few months. Nolan had been five; Amara must've been around the same age. The years worked differently there, and so did the days. Amara's were longer by over an hour. It made time hard to calculate.

At first Amara's magic had pulled him in only while he slept, then also when he consciously closed his eyes. Within months they'd reached the here-and-now point of every last blink. He'd never stopped being scared it would progress further. He'd ended up in a coma twice before, when he was nine and thirteen and had given up on fighting to stay in his own body. At some point, he knew it might not matter how much he fought.

He remembered the first time Amara had pulled him in during the day, when he'd hidden in the school bathroom, pressing his eyes shut and suddenly unable to move, suddenly trapped in that other body. In that world people shepherded him—Amara—left and right, teaching her to cut vegetables and sew and carry the horse-fuzz after stable servants sheared Elig horses. Nolan hadn't even been able to wrinkle his nose when she scooped up the manure.

So he understood Amara's fear at being controlled. He shouldn't take over like that. He'd only meant to let her know about him. Still, the thought—oh, the thought of finally balling those hands into fists, or pointing her eyes where he wanted to look . . . Was he supposed to go back to spending half his life trapped? Pretending he wasn't there?

From the living room, Pat shouted, "Nolan! You done? Want to watch a movie?" Some murmurs followed. "Or do you need help washing up?" She sounded less excited now, although Nolan didn't need to hear that to figure out Dad was behind the addendum. He must've made her ask in the first place, too. Pat knew too well what answer to expect.

"Thanks. I've got homework." Actually, Amara had asked Jorn for permission to nap after dinner, and Nolan could use the quiet of her sleep to think.

"You sure? The main actress has huge boobs!" Pat tried nobly not to giggle. Nolan imagined joining them—Dad ribbing Pat while he worked, Pat faking annoyance because she was watching the movie—then a stab of unease from Amara caught his attention. He lowered another glass to the counter and—

—Amara's grip on her topscarf tightened. She stood by her

bedroll, exhausted, unable to convince herself to pull her scarf out of its intricate folds. She wasn't a prude; servants couldn't afford to be. Even if she were, Maart was washing in the creek, and had already seen far more than her shoulders, and Jorn and Cilla sat around the corner, reading. Paper rustled. Amara tried to kill the rage that shot up unbidden. It took them seconds to read those pages—*seconds.*

She still didn't pull off her scarf. It wasn't about modesty. It was about this being . . . hers. Her hands dropped from the scarf's edges. She stepped away from the bedroll, her footfalls quiet without her boots. She felt a sting in her heel, but it passed a second later.

She stopped at a tall window at one end of the building. The world past the glass was so dark that Amara barely saw beyond her own reflection: the ashy shade of her skin, the worn brown of her winterwear, the topscarf in mottled gray and beige.

Nolan studied the sight of her. Amara rarely faced her reflection for long.

She might be his age, but she looked younger. She was slim and hard and hovered on boyish, down to her short lashes and sharp nose. Nolan couldn't think of her as beautiful. Not because of how she looked; if she were anyone else, she'd be pretty enough.

But when she moved her hands, they felt like his. When her stomach rumbled, or when her feet ached, the sensations mingled with his own. Sometimes Amara felt simply like another version of him, a life he led in a world he couldn't touch, and not like a girl for him to fantasize about. They'd never see each other face-to-face.

He'd thought about it, anyway. When she undressed. When she touched herself. When Maart did. He had no way of escaping those images—or the guilt that came with them. He'd learned to live with it.

But now Amara knew about him.

"Are you watching this?" Amara's signs moved so slowly Nolan almost didn't notice them. He felt her hands, though, and saw their mirrored image in the glass. "Is it true? Are you watching this?"

Her hands went up. They yanked at her scarf. Fabric slid past fabric, untangling, unwrapping, until it glided past her shoulders. She tugged the scarf loose and stared at her reflection, at bunched muscles in her shoulders and at eyes squinted nearly shut. At the slight indentation between her breasts visible above the winterwear that hid the rest.

She flung the scarf at the glass. It dropped in a heap. "Are you *always* watching?"

Her hands struck the window, palms *thunking* off, then slammed again, and moved back for a third time, but she stopped there, her arms pulled back and tense. The sound of flicking pages had stopped. Jorn might've heard.

She stood there, shuddering, for too long.

Finally she crouched to gather her scarf. She clasped it so tightly her hands ached from the effort. *Go away*, she thought, angry and broken and so far beyond anything Nolan could name he almost choked on it.

Amara turned. She walked back to her bedroll, stiff with hate. The flutter of pages nearby resumed. She tossed her scarf next to her bed and sank down without taking off her wear. Quietly, with small, restrained signs, she said, "I don't know what I'm doing to keep you here." Then: "Go away."

And something clicked and—

—then the world was black. Nolan's eyes flew open. The first thing he saw: his own water-wrinkled hands. The first thing he smelled: dish soap, sharp lemon.

His eyes shut, turning the world black. They opened again. Shut, open, shut, open, and black every time. Nolan's black, not Amara's black.

He darted away from the sink, sending suds dancing through the air. Of course. Of course! The problem had always been that Amara didn't know she pulled him in. Nolan had thought she'd need a mage's help to kick him out—but she'd just needed to be aware.

She could control it.

Nolan closed his eyes again for good measure, just for a moment, just to revel in the black. He felt dizzy. He wanted to—oh, he could sleep now, sleep without feeling her blanket on her skin and her irises against her eyelids, he could close his eyes and hear only his own breathing, he could—

Nolan turned, almost walking into Dad. "Whoa. Do you need to lie down? I know dinner went badly."

And then Nolan couldn't contain his smile, wide enough to hurt his cheeks. Just like the smile he'd made on Amara's face. Just like the smile he often saw on Pat's and could never imitate.

Surprised, Dad smiled back just as broadly.

"I want to watch that movie," Nolan said.

s Nolan still there?" Maart's hands formed silhouettes in the dark.

Jorn had long ago crawled into his bedroll, snoring like a grunting boar. Amara eyed him cautiously as she signed, "I assume so."

Maart shimmied free from his covers and padded over. She edged away to make room, and he lowered himself beside her, staying on the other side of the blanket. He propped himself up on one elbow. It'd slow his signs, but she welcomed the heat of his body through the thin cover, close enough to reach and kiss. Right now, when he eyed her with nothing but curiosity and concern, his lips curved in a smile, she still cherished the hope that things might go back to the way they were before. Silly jokes, sniping about Jorn. Rolling dice together after tasks. Maart always won.

The hope never lasted. He'd changed. She missed laughing and kissing and futilely beating the walls when Jorn got to be too much to bear. That—that had helped. Now there was talk of Cilla, and of running and standing up to Jorn and other stupid fantasies that'd get them killed. It trickled into every conversation, weighed down every glance, until it was easier to keep Maart at a distance or crush him so closely there was no room for anything else.

*Not now*, she asked him silently. *Not now.*

She couldn't ignore all difficult topics, though.

"About the blackouts . . ." She explained what she'd done, from tracking the mage to leaving her message on the temple, and the corners of Maart's mouth twitched into an almost-smile. "This is not a smiling matter, you know," Amara signed.

"I know." Maart leaned in and kissed her anyway. Once they'd separated, leaving enough space to see each other's signs, he said, "I thought you'd given up."

"No." A smile stirred on her face now, too. "I'm just being smart about it."

She couldn't run yet—not without a plan, not without knowing the truth, not while their tattoos remained, not while it meant leaving Cilla to die—but she saw Maart think, *One step at a time.*

"Tomorrow is market day," she said. "I need you to pretend you're sick, so Jorn will send me."

"Done. Should I start coughing now? Tonight? In the morning?"

She laughed under her breath.

Maart turned more serious, but a different serious than the kind she dreaded. This didn't come with frowning eyebrows or a hard jawline. This came with a relaxed smile, curious eyes. "No more blackouts, though?" he asked.

"A brief one when . . ." They had spelled Nolan's name up to now. She thought for a second, then came up with a sign for him, pushing the tips of three fingers on her left hand into the palm of her right hand, a hard movement, angry. It hurt the tips of her fingers. Maart knew instantly what she meant; she saw it on his face. ". . . when Nolan took over earlier. It must have been an adjustment. I don't think it'll happen again."

She bit her lip as Maart studied her. He looked at her so differently from the way anyone else did. Warmly. Now, though, she knew what he was looking for.

"I hate that I need to learn to control it in the first place," she signed. The confession came easily. This was the Maart she knew and loved. "Jorn won't teach me. I know I'm useless as a mage, but the spirits must smile on me, or I wouldn't heal—"

"You're not useless," Maart interrupted. "Jorn won't teach you magic because then you could fight back or identify his anchors and run. His magic is the only advantage he has over you."

"He's taller, too," she teased.

"I wish I could help." Maart brushed his lips over her forehead.

Amara's own lips parted with wanting, but she pushed Maart's chest, separating them. "You are helping." She hesitated. Maart finally seemed to get what she wanted and what she couldn't yet deal with, and still she had to push him away. "Nolan is watching."

It wouldn't be the first time. That only made it worse. Nights should be just her and Maart. Something Cilla couldn't complicate, something Jorn couldn't beat down. Now there was this Nolan, watching, and feeling—the thought alone nauseated her. "I'm sorry."

"Don't be. This Nolan thing . . . it's pretty screwed up."

"It's only until I can control him," she said, but they both knew that meant nothing if she couldn't find her mage. Maart was older than Amara. If Jorn followed Alinean laws, Maart would complete his duties and be free to leave within a year. Amara had longer to go. And after, when their tattoos were removed and they could walk freely as barenecked servants, they'd have an entire world to discover. What would they mean to each other if not escape?

Amara had chosen to love the Maart of yesterday and today. She couldn't look beyond that.

Maart could—did. Meeting his eyes, Amara knew he'd already chosen every version of her.

For a while they stayed there, nothing but the heat of their skin, the feel of their breaths, their whispered grins as Maart's fingers played across her skin to form newly learned letters. He left too soon, leaving one side of her body cold.

Amara curled up to recapture his heat. Her fingers touched her forehead where he'd kissed her.

Amara checked the airtrain seats for sharp angles, anything Cilla might cut herself on, then stepped aside to allow Cilla and Jorn to sit while she kept an eye on the other passengers.

She'd overlooked two vital things Ruudde had told Jorn: One, that he'd send silver to the Teschel harbor, meaning Jorn ought to pick it up. Two, that Jorn should keep Amara in his sight—and where Amara went, so did Cilla.

Amara's plan looked worse by the minute, but it was all she had.

At least she got to ride an airtrain. She used to love those. Underfoot, she felt the hissing of pipes squishing together air or letting it escape—she couldn't tell which—as the train shook into motion. She looked through narrow, sandblasted windows at the island landscape of hills and heather, but she couldn't enjoy it the way she had in the past.

Amara was still jittery when she stepped onto the board-walk. She wished for the safety of the granary, or that of a city like Bedam, with canals beside her and gentlemansions towering over her and alleyways barely wide enough to shuffle through sideways. Harbor towns like this felt too open, even with market stands lining the street, even overlooked by dunes and squat houses, the colors washed from the sand stuck in every pore. The windows, too, were coated in a layer of beach dirt that must've been brand-new, since yesterday's storm would've washed the glass clean.

The sun hung low in the salt-tinged sky and cast an orange

glow. That sun did nothing to stop the wind from blasting chill into the folds of Amara's topscarf. She ignored it, keeping close to Cilla as she scanned the crowd for her mage. The woman had been sturdy, wide-shouldered, broad-hipped, small-chested, with a bright wrap. Amara saw no trace of her.

Jorn reached into his sidesling for silver. "Amara." She expected instructions to buy kommer leaves or red carrots or thicker topscarves to take them into winter. "Stay here, and stay close. It's too crowded for you to buy anything. You'd have to shout to get anyone's attention." He made for the nearest stall, with dried fruit and imported bugs, then to a stall too blocked by crowds for Amara to see its wares. Raw voices shouted in a dozen dialects of Alinean and Dit and Jélis, and a snatch of Elig Amara recognized but could no longer translate.

"Hey," Cilla whispered, nudging her. "That stand Jorn's at."

When she made no attempt to elaborate, Amara made a questioning noise. If Cilla wanted to talk, Amara was expected to participate. Did Cilla even realize that?

"What does its sign say?" Cilla asked.

Reluctantly, Amara took her eyes off the crowds and craned her neck. The stall had a sign with two lines of cramped, painted handwriting. She recognized the simple Elig figures on the left row, but nothing beyond that. The other row was in Dit. Amara had known since she was a kid which letters made which sounds—mostly—from needing to fingerspell the occasional name, but reading was different. Words were never spelled the way you'd think when you heard them, and there were a dozen ways to write each letter, slanted or blocky, with an extra elaborate slash or one too few. She could make out the first couple of letters on the stall sign, but the next . . . Were those two strokes or one?

Jorn walked toward a stand selling fierce-smelling fish. He looked over at them briefly. Amara's head snapped back. If he'd caught her reading the sign . . . But, no, he kept moving and indicated for them to follow. Amara guided Cilla through the center of the boardwalk, keeping a close eye on spaces to flee to and on people who risked bumping into Cilla.

She sneaked another look at the earlier stall. "Genuine." She kept her hands close to her belly to hide them. People whose ears or voices failed them used signs, too, puffing up their cheeks, sweeping their arms wide, even their lips moving along, but there was no mistaking those signs for the subdued movements of servants. "Eligon?" No, that was the wrong word. "Elig?"

Cilla nodded, encouraging. Amara felt like an experiment, something for Cilla to occupy her time with. But that smile on her face was so, so sincere.

"Furs." Amara's hands fell. She looked away, though she wanted to read the rest of the stall descriptions and see how far she'd come. This was the best time to practice. Real-life scenarios, with Cilla by her side to help if she got stuck. She needed to find the mage, though.

And if she did, Cilla would find out exactly what she was

doing. What she'd heard. She should explain it now and get it out of the way.

Amara's mouth dried. She turned to keep her hands out of Jorn's sight, but the words wouldn't come. *The man who saved your life is working with the man who murdered your family? No.*

Cilla mistook her hesitance for something else. "How are you? After what happened?"

Nolan. After Nolan happened.

"Fine," Amara lied. "May I tell you something?"

"You don't have to ask. That's what I meant to say at the carecenter."

Amara nodded, but knew that couldn't be the end of it.

"I know what you said," Cilla went on, "but why *can't* it be that simple?"

The more Cilla talked this way, the more on edge Amara felt. It was like being lured into a trap. Every part of her screamed, *Unsafe! Unsafe!* and the only way out was to do as she ought. "I shouldn't have said anything. Forgive me."

"Screw my forgiveness! Pretend I'm not the princess. Pretend I'm anyone."

That way would lead to trouble. That way would lead to shouts and punishment. "You're not. You're my better."

In the distance, a ship's horn wailed over the market's noise, that constant hawking, haggling, laughing, chattering, pushing, shouting, crinkling of wrapping paper, clattering of coins, like walls of sound pressing in from every side. Somehow, amid all that, Cilla's laugh—a low, soft sound—rang louder than ever. "The world wants to kill me, Amara. Literally. The world." She pointed at the stones under her feet, and when she looked back at Amara, her eyes shone with admiration. "You've saved my life a hundred times. More. To me, you're my better."

"When we were little, Jorn made us play games together." Amara's hands seemed to move without permission. She shouldn't be telling Cilla this. It would sound accusatory.

But that was what Cilla wanted, wasn't it? Honesty? If she meant what she said, maybe Amara could be disrespectful one more time.

"I remember. I wasn't allowed to play with anyone else."

"One time I won the game. My palace mage conquered your set. You cried, and Jorn pulled me to my feet and slapped me. The next time we played and I was winning, you told me you'd call Jorn. So I lost that game and every one after."

"I—Amara, I—" Panic burned in Cilla's eyes.

Amara hadn't meant to make Cilla feel guilty. Guilt was useless. Guilt made everything about you.

"We were children." Amara's signs softened. The rest of her didn't. Dried leaves scattered over the ground like footsteps, and she lunged around, scanning for prying eyes. A dozen people passed in the space of a breath, but none paid her any mind. Even the green-clad marshal in the distance, tapping her baton against her leg, faced the other way. Still no Dit mage. "What do you think would happen if we fought now?" Amara asked. "People would believe your claim, not mine. If they saw me talking to you so rudely, they'd hit me. They'd be allowed." She stopped before she said something—something else—she regretted.

"I wish . . ." Cilla started, then stopped herself. "Thank you. I'm sorry. I thought we were becoming friends." Cilla stood straighter, more primly, but the clutched hands by her stomach betrayed her as they always did.

"You were too young when you left your palace. You don't know how things work."

"In the carecenter, you said you didn't hate me. Did you mean it?"

Briefly, Amara entertained the thought of speaking the truth. She said nothing.

Nor did she need to. Just then, Jorn signaled for them to follow him. They moved through the market, smelling grilled duck and fruits and sour cheeses and the rich, hot scent of swampcat leather. Stallkeepers' shouts mixed with the buzzing laughter of shoppers and beach workers.

In all that chaos, Cilla only swallowed, then swallowed again, her throat moving uncomfortably.

Maybe this was for the best. If Cilla believed Amara hated her, maybe she'd stop asking things of Amara. She'd stop putting Amara in positions where she had no choice but to obey and to hate both herself and Cilla for it.

A boy appeared, speaking in odd-sounding Alinean. When that got no response, he said in more natural Dit, "Rootstocks?" He raised a rattan basket stacked with roots and leaves and seeds, a heady mix of sweet and mint. "I have kalisse, fennel, ginger, aniseeds—cinnamon sticks? Mint leaves?"

Amara didn't let him continue. She stepped forward, squared her shoulders, and gave a jerk of her head—a simultaneous no and scram!

She rarely saw this kind of pestering. If you pressured customers too much, the market overseers banned you. The Alinean founders had valued good business, and those values lingered. Their love of trading had made them settle in the Dunelands in the first place, the perfect midway point between the Alinean Islands, the Continent, and the Elig south.

The boy might not have learned those lessons yet, but he knew how to take a hint. He sped off, swerving around a vegetable crate, then a firm-looking woman. Amara's lips formed an O.

It was the Dit mage—unmistakably her, from the braids in her curls to the way she stood, legs wide, traditional-looking Dit scarf reaching all the way to her thighs. This time, she wore copper rings in one nostril. The metal sparkled in the late-afternoon sun.

"Y'know, I was worried I'd missed you," the mage said.

Amara stepped closer to Cilla. Her message on the temple had worked. This was her chance, and—she didn't know where to begin. She didn't dare raise her hands and announce herself for what she was.

"Excuse me?" Cilla said warily.

"Listen, I want to talk, as well. I haven't seen anyone like you in a long time. But . . . it's . . . different now, isn't it?"

Amara's fingers itched with unspoken words. She should back out. Turn and run. Jorn would never have to find out.

And she'd never be rid of Nolan.

She pushed her hair aside, cupping her tattoo to hide it from everyone but the mage.

"Amara!" Cilla looked toward Jorn and back, and that half-second glance sent Amara's heart thudding too loudly. She'd defied Jorn before. She'd talked behind his back, she'd sneaked out with Maart, she'd learned to read. But she'd never done anything of this magnitude.

Cilla was right, this was a stupid idea, a stupid, stupid idea, and they couldn't even talk properly—a three-way conversation demanded space and risked more eyes on them—

"All right," the mage said. "I don't suppose you've learned to talk out loud? No? I know a place we can—"

Cilla took over. "No. Someone's watching us. We can't leave. Or be seen talking to you."

With a theatrical sigh, the mage turned to face the nearest stall. She pretended to inspect the fabrics on display, from Dit wraps to intricate Jélisse headscarves. "Alinean girl, can you talk on her behalf?"

"I don't know what to talk about." Irritation crept into Cilla's voice, and Amara signed jerky explanations, about following the mage to the airtrain, the way the mage had seen a presence in Amara that had to mean Nolan. Cilla nodded slowly. She kept facing Amara even when she addressed the woman: "My friend here is a mage. Can you teach her about her magic?"

A laugh escaped the mage. "Depends on how many years she has and how much the spirits like her. She'll need a mentor like the rest of us. How about you tell me how your friend got that tattoo of hers if she's a mage? We never select our own to be servants. We're more useful elsewhere."

"Her magic manifested late." Cilla didn't indulge her further. "You recognized a presence in her, yes? She's been pulling it in without meaning to."

"Call that presence what it is: a spirit. Not many mages have the ability to invite 'em in. I've seen ministers pull it off, but . . . She might've learned to shut the spirit out already, anyway. Its presence was faint yesterday, and I can't detect it at all now."

Nolan was gone? Amara felt a spike of relief that wilted as quickly as it came. She hadn't felt any rush of magic, not a sliver of control. If she didn't know how she'd shut him out, who was to say she wouldn't pull him back in?

"Is this kind of possession common?" Cilla asked, and as they talked, Amara scanned for prying eyes or ears. Voices traveled around corners and through closed doors, and you could never tell who heard. Alineans cut out servants' tongues so they couldn't disturb their betters, and mocked those who stooped to using servant signs, but sometimes, rarely, she wondered if servants weren't better off with those signs.

Then she remembered the servant handler at the palace holding her steady as a palace mage pried open her mouth, and those thoughts turned to ice.

"Not common at all. My mentor on the mainland seeks out people who've been used as vessels, and he's met no more than a dozen. He taught me how to recognize them. It's similar to detecting spells." The mage tested the stitching on a wrap so green it hurt Amara's eyes. "Your friend is a runaway servant, girl. Why should I help her?"

"I thought you were against the ministers."

"I loathe them. Your people did a far better job. That doesn't mean I'm after trouble."

"You *have* to instruct her." Cilla stepped forward to underscore her words.

An eyebrow rose, more curious than anything. "And why's that?"

"You said my people did a—ah!" Her head whipped around. Amara instantly met her eyes out of habit. A second later, she realized Cilla wasn't looking at her. She was looking *past* her.

Amara's head turned. So did the heads of people around her, gasping, backing away at the sight of the abruptly murky sky and lightning slashing down onto—no, that wasn't right.

The lightning slashed up. A stone's throw down the boardwalk, a hair-thin thread of flame snaked from the ground, crackling high and sharp into the sky. The crowd dashed away. A scream tore through the air.

The rope of fire flung itself into a half circle, coiled, then snapped out.

So did the bargaining and haggling. For a moment, the market was silent. Then the air welled up with whispers, questions, the word *magic* in a half dozen languages.

Amara didn't linger on the sight. Her eyes sought out Jorn. He gave a curt jerk of his head—*this has nothing to do with us*—then turned back to the meat stall he'd been negotiating at.

Not everyone was so blasé. "It's that damn jeweler!" the mage said. "I told her to warn people about her honesty spell."

It took a moment for the mage's meaning to dawn on Amara. Mixed magic. She should've known straightaway—something this unnatural couldn't be backlash. Honesty spells enchanted anyone who passed through them, like Jorn's boundary detection. If someone with an existing spell came into contact with one . . .

Determinedly, the mage strode toward where the lightning had been.

"Wait," Cilla said. She reached out but stopped herself at the last moment, letting her hand hover in midair by the mage's topscarf. "Wait! You have to understand."

"Someone is hurt. My oath says to help."

"It wasn't my people who did a good job ruling."

Why would Cilla say . . . Oh.

Around them, people flocked toward the person whose scream had shriveled into high sobs. Others huddled together, shuffled away, or murmured nervously, as if the lightning might strike a second time. And all Amara could do was stare at Cilla dumbly, thinking No, no, don't and, at the same time, She's doing this for me.

The mage barely listened. "Out of my way."

"Not my people. My parents." A whisper of a smile flitted over Cilla's face. "My name is Cilla Annin-Kalhi. Do you know what that means?"

Now, the mage listened. Amara saw recognition dawn in her eyes, saw a hundred expressions appear and fade without settling. She stepped closer. Before Amara realized what she was doing—before Amara could process the threat—the woman slapped Cilla across the cheek.

The slap rang out. Amara's world stopped. Blurred. Shrank to the corner of Cilla's lips where the woman's hand had struck.

"You don't," the mage shouted, "get to use—that—name!"

Amara snapped awake. She threw herself forward with a grunt, shoving the mage into the nearest stall, right into a wrap hanging on display. The stall owner protested, but Amara didn't hear, whirling to face Cilla, who touched her lip and winced. The surrounding skin was already swelling. Cilla's fingers came back dotted with blood. A sharp red line formed. A drop blossomed and rolled down, dangling from the curve of her lower lip.

"Out of all the names of all the dead in this universe," the mage said, "you chose to call a toddler? You had to use her *entire name?*"

"Jorn!" Amara shouted out loud. Forget bystanders realizing what her distorted voice meant. Forget the mage. Forget the magic.

Jorn recognized his name and turned, but he stood too far away to help, trapped by the crowd near the meat stall. The carcasses' dead eyes stared at Amara from across the market. From the alarm on Jorn's face, Amara knew he saw the blood. She pointed at the mage and took Cilla's wrist, pulling her through the market, away from the mage, away from the anxious crowd.

Smooth, hateful cobblestones trembled underneath their feet.

The curse was awake.

15

Nolan's pen tapped the pages of his workbook. He was going over yesterday's physics problems a final time before class. Only a few of the seats were filled, and he could hear streams of students rushing past the door to get to their own classes. Down the hall, some kids were fighting, others cheering.

Nolan double-checked the questions he'd flagged as beyond his reach. Two out of every three.

The totally pathetic thing was that completing even a third of his assignments meant an improvement. Everything was an improvement. He could hold on to his train of thought. He found himself spreading his eyes open in class before realizing he no longer needed to; he could deactivate his phone's alarm, which normally woke him every few hours so he wouldn't stay in Amara's world too long; that morning, he'd woken up disoriented from nothing but the weirdness of his own dreams instead of the jolt of remembering who he was, where he was, that Amara was nothing but a far-off girl in a far-off world.

If she was even that. Maybe the medication worked. Maybe he really had been hallucinating all these years.

"Oh, good!" Sarah Schneider thumped her backpack onto the desk next to Nolan's. "You did those problems. Can I copy them?"

"You probably don't want to." Nolan tried to come up with something else to say, something witty, but nothing came to mind. He didn't have much practice, and, despite his uninterrupted sleep, he was tired. He'd dreamed about the Dunelands, then spent too long staring at the cabinet where he kept his journals. It'd been a real dream, complete with random nudity and Maart showing up in his kitchen and Pat shouting at him—nothing like Amara's dreams or the Dunelands not-really-dreams he'd had as a kid that had evolved into something more. These dreams didn't need to go into the journals.

Nothing needed to go into the journals anymore. What should he even do with them now?

"Oh!" Sarah only now turned to look at him. She must've thought he was someone else. No one ever asked to copy his homework. Mainly because he never did any.

"You can copy my Spanish homework," Nolan offered. "I guarantee that's in good shape."

Sarah laughed, showing off braces that glinted in the stark lighting. "Thanks, I got that from Luisa already. Yeah, yeah, I know, I'm bad." She punctuated that with an angelic batting of her eyelashes.

"I don't . . ." Nolan sucked his cheeks, thinking. He could

do this. Talk to a cute girl. Sometimes he forgot just how clueless he was, though. The way Amara slept with Maart came so easily that Nolan occasionally, sourly, had to remind himself that he was still a virgin.

He'd kissed a girl before, a year ago. Maybe he could do it again sometime. Nothing stopped him. He was like everyone else now. He could date and kiss and a whole lot more—see what sex was like with his own body. He'd probably be decent, having lived the girl's perspective a hundred times already. That had to give him a leg up.

Plus, Sarah was . . . nice, even if she weirded him out. She seemed so young. Not physically, since she was taller and had a lot more going on cleavage-wise than Amara or even Cilla, but just the way she laughed and talked, the way she simultaneously complained and bragged about her part-time job at the fro-yo shop. Last week she and her friends had been late for English class, and she'd been the only one to actually run through the halls despite those tiny heels of hers or her bag bouncing off her hips. Even her brother had lingered with her friends, way too cool to run. Nolan couldn't remember Amara or Cilla ever being that young.

Maybe Sarah wasn't young. Just normal.

"Well, I can't judge you for copying homework," Nolan said, realizing how long he'd been silent.

"No way. Mysterious loner boy cheats on his homework?"

Mysterious loner boy? His eyebrows rose. It didn't sound as if Sarah meant it in a bad way, though. Maybe she was into mysterious loners. "And not just any homework," he said. "I've even copied Luisa's Spanish a couple times. There's no excusing that."

Sarah laughed. "Oh, shit, Luisa never told me that. Seriously? Tell me you were sick."

"Meet-my-lunch sick that time," Nolan lied, half laughing. After yesterday, and given how often he supposedly dozed off in class to check on Amara, it seemed safe to joke about. How was Amara doing? He should close his eyes and—no. She'd kicked him out.

"Well, you can get away with just about anything if you're sick."

Nolan swept his pen at the empty exercises in his physics workbook. "Think Mr. O'Brian will agree?"

"I could cover for you? I can go, 'He was totally hurling, Mr. O! I could hear it all the way from the girls' bathroom!'"

"Take it from an expert. Hurling lets you skip all the tricky assignments."

"Does it?" she said airily. "Well, shit. I oughta try that."

"You should. And we should go out." He didn't even realize he was saying the words until they'd already passed his lips. That . . . might've needed more finesse.

She blinked in surprise. "We should, huh?"

Was that a question or an agreement? "I . . ."

Right on cue, the bell screeched. Mr. O'Brian walked into the classroom.

"Hey. I'll think about it." Sarah flashed Nolan a smile, unzipped her bag, and pulled out her physics book.

His first day without Amara, and he'd already asked out a cute girl. Nolan closed his eyes, reveling in the noise of the classroom instead of that of Amara's world.

Maybe he really could do this.

n a way, Amara supposed Cilla should be grateful for the curse. It must've taken many mages to cast. With that much power, they could've killed Cilla straightaway. It would've been quicker. More effective, too. They'd had one chance to get rid of the princess, and they'd screwed it up.

It would've been easier for everyone if they hadn't.

They couldn't wait for Jorn. Amara kept her hand around Cilla's wrist, ignoring the looks around them as they stormed away, diving between stalls to avoid the crowd. The commotion from the mixed magic served as a good distraction. If they drew too much attention, Jorn would—

Didn't matter. The curse came first.

The cobblestones shifted. Would that be it this time? The stones? Would they twist and groan and batter into her? Would they spread apart and choke her in the earth?

"The cut's small," Cilla said, her voice muffled through her hand. Blocking the blood wouldn't stop the curse, but it might slow it down. "It'll heal fast. At least—at least there's that."

They ran for the market center. One half stood solidly on

the dunes while the other half towered over the beach on high posts; they might find a safe spot underneath. The salt scent of the water was stronger here, mingling with rot and dirt and cold. The market seemed far off and long gone.

The sand shifted as they ran. The dune grass swayed as if carried by a ripple of wind.

The moment they plunged into the chilly shade under the market center, Amara grabbed her knife. She pulled Cilla's hand away to expose her lip. The longer this went on, the more blood Amara would need to make the decoy work.

How could Amara have been stupid enough to think she could trust the mage?

"Do it," Cilla said.

Cilla's cut bled slowly, one drop at a time. Amara would never be able to distract the curse with so little blood. She raised her knife and pressed its point to Cilla's lip. At least the skin there was soft, with no risk of hitting bone or tendons. Amara pressed. Puncture wounds bled less than slashes. They were small, too, which made it easier to block the blood from the air. Cilla held in a grunt.

At the market, the dunes had shielded them from the worst of the wind; they lacked that protection here. A gust blew sand into Amara's eyes and nose. The dune grass rustled by their feet and bent as though touched by an unseen storm, pointing in the wrong direction. So it hadn't been the cobblestones that moved back at the market, Amara realized, but the dune-grass roots underneath, the moss in between. The grass pricked at the legs of Cilla's winterwear, whipping past but not yet through.

Moving away was pointless. The curse would just shift its weapon to the sea or sand.

Amara ran her hand over Cilla's lip, smearing the blood onto her own skin. She pressed it to her hands, to her arms, her exposed throat. Already, the grass was shifting. It tickled at her legs. Amara backed away from Cilla. Her heel hit a half-buried log, and she fell. The ground felt like ice. The sun hadn't touched this sand in years. In her peripheral vision, a sand spider the size of her palm scuttled to safety.

The first blade of grass cut Amara's arm.

Cilla knotted up a corner of her topscarf and pressed it to her face. Once the blood clotted, they could carefully peel away the scarf, making sure they didn't tear open the wound again. Curses followed curses.

All around Amara, the dune grass rustled. She bit back a scream as a blade tore through her wear by her knee. Dune grass was tough and tall, and right now, animated by the spell, the blades felt like just that—blades. Like knives so sharp she almost didn't notice at first when they cut her.

Amara clenched her teeth until it felt like they'd crack. Sticky blood dripped from a dozen cuts. She only needed to wait this out. Cuts were good. Cuts were clean. They healed quickly—no messy bone shards to mend, no skin to regrow over burned flesh—and bled freely, so it never took long to overpower Cilla's blood and leave the curse aimless and dying.

The dune grass was everywhere. It cut deeper, harder. Amara wasn't hiding her face well enough. The points of the grass slashed at the thin skin of her lips, the arch of her throat. She scrunched her eyes shut tightly, so tightly, as blades jabbed her eyelids. Another prick. Amara screamed, but the sound stayed inside her mouth, muffled.

"Amara," Cilla whimpered distantly. "Amara, I'm so sorry, I'm so sorry . . ."

Amara had to choose which parts of herself to shield. Maybe if she pressed her arms to her eyes . . .

Her arms. Why was that first gash still bleeding? Shallow cuts usually healed fast.

She rolled onto her side, her hands pressed to her stomach. Another slash. The edges of the cut stood apart the width of a fingernail. Bright blood sputtered up and dripped over the edges, like water spilling from a sluice. Her mangled legs thrashed, sending stained sand up in clouds. Grass blades dug into her, but more slowly now. Enough of her own blood had spilled to confuse the curse.

But her cuts weren't healing. None of them. The cuts from her lips sent copper spilling into her mouth, sticking to her teeth and the stump of her tongue and the back of her throat.

"What's—what's happening, what's—" Cilla's words crashed into each other.

Amara's arms wrapped around her stomach. Apply pressure. Just as Cilla always did. Apply pressure. But she didn't have enough arms for that. Her stomach bled and her legs bled and her breasts bled and her face bled.

Another voice joined Cilla's. Jorn's. He was running toward them across the dunes, swearing. That was never good, never, ever good.

"Curse ended?" Two words only. Amara tried to answer, but the question was probably meant for Cilla. She should turn her head and make sure, but—

"What's happening? Why—why isn't she—" Cilla said.

The slashing of the dune grass had turned to tickling. That hurt, too. Or maybe everything hurt. Her clothes felt sticky and too warm. Why wasn't she healing? She should focus. Use her magic like a proper mage. But she didn't know what to focus on beyond pressing her hands to her stomach.

Maybe the spirits had stopped favoring her.

Jorn worked his arms underneath her, lifting her up with no effort at all. Her head rolled back. She tried to keep her eyes open. Apparently her eyes bled, too. Everything was red. She blinked as if that would make it stop. Everything just turned redder. Of course. She'd been cleaning blood for years and years and forever. That was how it worked. It spread and thinned, and then you got rid of it, though now it wasn't thinning, so maybe she was doing something wrong.

Jorn would punish her. Or he would let her die. Without her healing, she had no purpose.

"You alive?" he asked, looking down at her. Her legs swung back and forth with every step of Jorn's. He was moving fast, his arms digging into the cuts on her back. They stepped into the sun, higher up now, and the chatter of the market rushed back over her.

She tried to say something, but her hands needed to stay on her stomach. Maybe she could try her lips. They didn't feel right, though. They hurt.

"Where are we going? Can't you heal her?" Cilla sounded distant. Amara couldn't see her. The world was upside down, anyway, and bobbed weirdly, and it was still red.

Did pain really last this long?

"No magic. Her own healing might come back. Do you want to repeat that lightning show?"

"I only meant—"

"Get her topscarf off," Jorn instructed. "Press it to her stomach."

Amara let out a moan. No. Cilla couldn't do that. Cilla needed her hands to compress her own wound, or they'd have to start all over again.

"But—I—" Cilla's voice got louder as she caught up to Jorn.

Jorn swore again. "You can't. Then open the door to that pub. Now!"

Amara could just catch a glimpse of Cilla rushing ahead.

Jorn never let Cilla go ahead alone. Not in places this busy. One bump and she might drop her scarf and then the stones would crush her just like that. That'd happened a couple of months ago, and a year before that, and years before that, and it hurt every time, and Amara's hands and feet always looked weird afterward. Formless. Battered. Like nothing that should be attached to her body.

Drowning was better. It hurt less.

She smelled metal.

"Towels!" Jorn shouted. "Clean towels—sheets—everything!"

Inside was darker, safe, the way she liked it. Sometimes she liked the outside, too, with the beach sand ugly and gray and filled with bugs and dried jellyfish and dirt, and the water just as ugly and just as gray. The diggers made up for all that. Their funny legs and pointy noses. In the north of the Continent, the Jélis had white beaches and blue water but no diggers. Amara had seen paintings. It looked pretty but fake, as if someone had used too much pigment in their paint.

A table pushed into her back. Her legs dangled from the edge. She moaned without wanting to. She was far gone, farther than she'd ever been. Was this what happened when you got hurt? Really hurt? Maybe she'd run out of healing. Poof. Maybe Nolan had screwed with it. Maybe Nolan had broken it. Maybe Nolan had broken her.

She hated him. She didn't know him. But the hate stayed.

"That's runaway palace scum," a deep-voiced man said.

*Palace scum.* That meant he saw her tattoo. The way she lay on the table, her hair was probably pooled under her head. Amara would peel her skin to the bone if the tattoo wouldn't simply return five minutes later.

Sometimes, five ink-free minutes seemed like enough.

"Did she get injured in the magic blow-up?" someone else asked.

"She's not a runaway. We're here on . . . an assignment," Jorn said. "Help her!"

"Hey—you, I'd help," the first man said. He must be talking to Cilla. It didn't matter to Amara, since *you* wasn't *her*, and right now she really needed help. Jorn was pressing on her stomach to keep the deepest wound shut, and she was shivering with cold or pain or something else, and every movement pulled open a different cut. She tried to help Jorn apply pressure to her stomach, but her hands didn't listen.

"You're lying, though," the man went on. "She must've run. Her hair's too long."

He had to be Alinean. Few others would notice her hair, and none would dare call her palace scum. No one else had the money or connections to get away with it. That was what Maart always said.

Maart would be so upset. He would be so upset when he found out.

"I'll pay you!" Jorn shouted. "Get some damned towels!"

"Listen—"

"You listen." Cilla was still here. She'd been so quiet. Amara heard her footsteps on the floor. She stepped into Amara's view. She was hard to see from this angle, and in the dark, and with everything red. Cilla still kept her scarf pressed to the side of her mouth, and she lifted her head higher, her hair falling away from her face. She was pretty like that. Even upside down. Even when red.

"Don't!" Jorn snarled, but he couldn't stop her with his hands pressed to Amara's stomach.

Cilla couldn't do this again. Not after that mage had just— didn't she see the *danger*?

Cilla's free hand went to her scarf. Most of the fabric was already wadded up, so she pulled the rest loose easily. The scarf drooped over her arms, exposing bare shoulders, the beginning swell of her breasts, and that single mark right in the center of her chest. The tattoo's glow pulsed with her heartbeat.

That tattoo was pretty, too. Even when Amara hated it. And she always hated it.

The pub fell silent.

Someone barked an order about getting towels, and the world went away.

17

Pat didn't realize he was there.

Nolan had taken up a quiet spot at the other end of the middle-school gym, leaning on a vaulting horse to watch Pat and her classmates rehearse. They wore their regular clothes and didn't use many props, but when Nolan imagined them in fake hospital gear, with clipboards in their hands, he had to admit the scene might work. Pat was doing a good job. Her biggest problem was waiting for others to finish before she blurted out her lines. No one seemed to mind, though. Their biggest problem seemed to be remembering their lines in the first place.

After twenty minutes, Pat noticed him. She squeaked an apology to her drama teacher and crossed the room. "Nolan! What're you doing here?"

"I was thinking about the movie from last night." Nolan stayed by the vaulting horse. It was weird being back in this gym—though his leg meant he'd never spent much time here to begin with. "That actress was good."

"You just liked her boobs."

"That, too," he said, mainly to get a laugh or cringe out of her. Not that she was wrong. "But her expression when she saw that train explode . . . I was impressed." He nodded slowly, casually. A simple conversation with his sister shouldn't make his heart race like this.

The thing was, they'd never had a simple conversation. Even the times when Amara slept were weighed down by her dreams.

"I know, right?" Pat said. "Did you see what she did with her lips? Just that little quirk at the end—it's so subtle, you know? People online say she was flat, but—" She looked at her classmates and lowered her voice. "What're you doing here?"

"Wanted to see you rehearse."

"Did you walk all the way? It's 108 degrees out!"

"Seemed like a good idea," Nolan said, though his shirt was drenched and he must smell worse than the dressing rooms nearby. "So, you want to be an actress."

"What? No." She paused. "Yes. It's stupid, I know, but—"

"It's not stupid."

"It is," she said heatedly. "Whatever. I want it, anyway." She tilted her head, and it took Nolan a second to realize she was redirecting his attention to the kids at the other end of the gym. "Claudia, over there? She's got a big part, and her cousin is coming over from LA to watch. He's mostly done ads and this one dumb reenactment, but Claud says he just got a part on a CSI-type show. I figure, if he sees me, and I'm good . . . maybe he can give me some advice?"

"Maybe." Nolan tried not to laugh. That'd be one way to

get Pat mad at him real quick. Today, though, not laughing was a real challenge. He was in his own world. When he shut his eyes, he still heard Pat and still smelled the stale sweat of the gym, the old leather of the vaulting horse under his elbows. He straightened out his smile. "Do you still need volunteers?"

"You have time to watch the movie? You're sure?" Nolan asked Mom the next evening, halfway up the stairs. "I'll get the laptop!"

"It's that superhero movie, right?" Mom called. "Super-heroes are cool."

"That's why I downloaded it." He returned to the top of the stairs with the laptop bag around his shoulders and hopped carefully down the steep steps.

This would be his third movie in as many days. He'd spent Tuesday and today doing more than he'd ever thought possible. He was nauseated from the increased dose of medication, yeah, but he'd rehearsed with Pat, who'd learned to get her eyebrows under control; volunteered with her drama teacher; done homework; flirted with Sarah at school—clumsily, though she seemed not to mind—and at the end of the day he still had energy left for TV, swimming, chores.

Maybe he could get superhero comics from the library and see if Mom liked those, too. Maybe he'd finally get to study Nahuatl alongside Dad and Patli; he knew how important

Mexica pride was to Dad and how important it was becoming to Pat. To feel that kind of passion about who you were and weren't . . . Maybe Nolan could learn. Maybe he could understand. God, he wanted to understand.

How had he been able to fill his days all those years, doing nothing at all?

In the kitchen, Mom was wiggling past Dad to grab plates. "Almost done," Dad singsonged at the stove. He stuck a pinkie into the sauce and licked it off. "Very almost."

Mom turned. With her free hand, she reached out and finger-combed Nolan's hair—he could swear she'd lifted that hand before she'd even gotten a good look at him. "Ah, Nolan, you really need to use some gel. Did you run out?" She was seconds away from licking her fingers to improvise. Instead, her hand moved down the side of his face to cup his chin. "I told you we'd get here."

She turned for the living room with a bounce in her step.

Dad leaned against the counter's edge, regarding Nolan appreciatively. "The new dosage really is working, isn't it? You're not having any seizures?"

Nolan aimed for a casual shrug, but the bag around his shoulder—the laptop was a heavy old model that by all rights should've broken down years ago—made it a challenge. "None."

"You happy?"

Nolan's growing smile should say enough. "Yeah. I'm adjusting, but I'm good."

Dad twisted a knob behind him, turning the flame under the saucepan into a tiny blue flicker. "That's what matters. What's on your arm?"

Nolan tilted his lower arm inward. "Just doodles. Hey, I need to set up the movie . . ."

"Sounds good." Suddenly Dad was all business, stirring the sauce around the chicken, sending scents of peanut and sharp chili through the air. Dad rarely cooked like this. Real food took too long and cost too much. Nolan had taken care of the second part, calling Grandma Pérez for advice and using his last remaining birthday money to pick up the necessary items at the corner store, only remembering when he got home that his parents would have too much work to do to cook. They'd taken one look at the freshly stocked fridge, though, and decided to make an exception. Today marked Nolan's third evening and second full day without seizures; they had something to celebrate.

Dad tested the temperature of the tortillas with two fingers. "Oh, this'll be good."

It was, and so was the movie, the four of them nestled on the couch with plates in front of them that they should take to the kitchen and rinse off, but no one did, and no one even opened their mouth to suggest it. By the time the main character's son had a knife to his throat halfway through, Mom was squishing a pillow in her lap, and Pat was leaning forward with the widest grin on her face.

Surreptitiously, Nolan licked his thumb and rubbed at the Dit letters on his arm. In the glow of the television screen, he could see that the ink was already smudging. He'd doodled the letters in history class. He'd just . . . wanted to see if he remembered.

"You're not watching?" Dad nudged him.

Nolan smiled, standing. "I'll be back in a minute. No need to pause."

He headed straight for the bathroom, locked the door, sat on the lid, and slumped sideways to rest his head on the cool wall tiles. He shut his eyes only to find the by-now-familiar black. What was wrong with him? The movie was good, or at least he thought it was; he didn't have much to compare it with.

And the way Mom and Dad had been smiling at him lately—nothing beat that. They'd want to talk about the movie afterward because they so rarely had the chance to watch movies together, and they'd glow even brighter if he joined in. He could nerd out over the acting with Pat or gush over the action scenes, but how was he supposed to care about some actor on that screen? Out there, Amara—maybe Jorn had—

He'd hated her for years. But now, he worried. He missed her.

And the truth was, despite the flurry of activity, he didn't know what to do with himself. Nolan thought of what Dad had said when they'd talked over laundry: What did he want to do? He had so many options now, a hundred options and more. He loved it, he did, he hadn't lied about being happy—

But family nights and cute girls at school and playing big brother and all those things people expected of him paled the second Amara flashed across his thoughts.

He'd thought freedom would be different.

He'd thought he'd care more.

Nolan's eyes burned. If he cried, he'd ruin the movie.

*Amara*, he thought, and—

—pain.

The pain was there, but through a haze of thoughts and images Nolan couldn't identify. He recognized this. Amara was sleeping but not quite dreaming.

So why the pain?

And why was he back? Maybe Amara's magic acted up in her sleep. He should let her be. He couldn't explain the pain, though. It never lasted this long—she should be healing.

Nolan concentrated. He could wake her up, if nothing else. He focused on the center of her belly, the lids of her eyes. Then he opened them. He raised her arms. Bandages were wrapped around them, held together with neat stitches that must've been Maart's doing. Nolan inhaled shallowly and tried to sit. A scream escaped. Something stabbed his—Amara's—belly. He dropped again, panting.

"Amara!" Cilla appeared by his side. He studied her swollen lip, then the ceiling behind her, the walls, the smell of dust and charred wood. They were in the granary. He lay on a bedroll that must be Amara's, though it had been moved. Not far off, near where Maart slept, embers burned in the fire pit. No sign of Jorn.

"Are you OK? Don't move. The cuts might open. Jorn's been using his magic to keep you stable, but he didn't want it mixing with your own healing. We weren't sure when you'd wake up."

Nolan repeated Cilla's words in his mind, as if that might help him understand what had happened.

"You're bleeding again." Cilla winced at the bandages around Amara's stomach. "Jorn took care of most of the cuts, but that one wouldn't heal right. We'll need to wrap it again. Oh, thank the seas. I'm . . . so glad you're . . ." She slowed, then came to a full stop. Her teeth pressed into her lower lip, a thin strip of white on brown. Her next words came steadily: "You're not Amara."

Nolan couldn't sit up, but at least he could move his hands. "How can you tell?"

"The way you look at me is too comfortable. Nolan?"

He nodded.

"Did she pull you in again?"

Nolan tried to sit up a second time, grimacing at the pain that slashed through his stomach and fanned outward, but this time he managed. "Sort of. She pushed me out after last time. Not just out of her body, but her mind, too. That's never happened. I haven't been here at all since the day I took over. I think . . . I think this time I came of my own accord."

"How? Don't move. It's dangerous." Cilla reached for his shoulder to push him down, then paused. Her eyes went to some place past his. Her hand—oddly cool—brushed past his skin, then he felt her fingers on the curve of his ear. "She's healing," Cilla whispered. "There was a cut here. It'd scabbed over. I was just looking at it . . ."

Nolan touched his stomach where he'd felt the wound. He pressed. Minimal pain. He pushed on the other bandages, feeling nothing but the cracking of crusted blood between his skin and the fabric. He scrambled upright. Cilla didn't try to stop him.

He looked down. Cream bandages, some stained red, covered Amara's body. "What happened? Why didn't she heal before?"

"We don't know. She protected me from the curse yesterday morning. It's evening now. It's been a day and a half. Maart spent all that time looking after her. Jorn finally forced him to sleep an hour ago."

"A day and a half? Without healing?" Nolan repeated with rushed signs.

"Until you showed up. She's unconscious. How could she pull you in?"

"Maybe her defenses were down while she slept?" He felt warm, too warm, and it had nothing to do with the embers glowing nearby.

"How long has she been pulling you in?" Cilla's voice sounded harsher than it ever did when she talked to Amara.

"Since we were kids."

"Before she was chosen as a servant?" *Before she had her tongue cut?*

"After."

"When did she start healing?"

"After I first came. I . . . after."

Cilla looked at him flatly. "You appear, she heals. You disappear, she stops healing. Medicine gives you control when she's never had control, ever. Are you sure *you're* not the mage?"

"I think . . ." Nolan said, and he closed his eyes, his hands repeating the signs without him wanting to. "I think. I think. I just wanted to see how she was doing. I was worried. I should go now."

He couldn't be responsible for Amara's healing. He couldn't.

He couldn't be in charge of—

But he'd taken control just now, hadn't he? Cilla was right. Amara was unconscious. She shouldn't be able to pull him in or kick him out. If he could make himself leave now just as easily, then—

—Nolan slid against the bathroom tiles, tumbling to the floor. He flailed, his foot lashing out against the door, his arms stuck between him and the wall. "What—" he gasped.

"You all right in there?" Mom called.

"Yeah, pee carefully!" Pat laughed. She was joking with him more often now. He'd been trying to joke back.

"I'm fine," he said after too long. He pulled himself up by the door handle, unlocked the door, stumbled out. "Keep watching the movie without me."

The amusement faded from their faces.

Was he responsible? If, with those pills, he could travel

back and forth whenever he wanted—if he made Amara heal—maybe she hadn't been the one to kick him out on Monday. He might've simply snapped free on his own. And then, while he was back in his own skin, flirting with Sarah Schneider and finding sites to download films from, Amara had protected Cilla from the curse and almost died.

Because he hadn't been there.

Nolan didn't make it past the top step. He turned and sat, gripping the banister. He stared down the curve of the stairs with hollow eyes. If his presence made her heal . . .

If somehow, all along, he'd pushed himself into her world instead of being pulled . . .

Amara wasn't a mage. She never had been. That was why her healing stuttered and paused: because he kept blinking in and out. Without him, she wouldn't heal at all. She wouldn't have been plucked from the Bedam palace to help Cilla. She'd still be there and she'd be following the caretaker's orders and scooping horse manure and cleaning up after the cooks and sneaking around servant passages and it'd be shit, all of it would be shit and unfair and awful, but she wouldn't be burned and cut and drowned and choked and—

And none of that.

Nolan's hand dropped from the banister. He clutched his hair. The hair Mom obsessed over. He'd been running around blaming Amara for ruining his life while he—while Mom slicked his hair and Dad cooked and Pat freaked out about her play, and he had this cozy little life, and all this time he'd been the one to—

His hand slid down his face, pressing against his mouth. Cool fingers against hot skin.

"Are you having a seizure?" Mom stood at the bottom of the stairs and put her foot on the first step. "You shouldn't sit there. It's dangerous."

"No seizure. I just—I need to be alone for a minute. Keep watching the movie. It's good." He managed a smile, but it wasn't a Mom-smile or any smile she'd recognize.

Nolan didn't know if he recognized it, either.

'm not a mage." Amara stared at her hands as she said that, puzzled. "I'm not a mage."

"Amara, you need to stop—" Cilla cut herself off as Jorn entered. He must've gone to talk to Ruudde again. If Amara died, they'd have to find someone else to protect Cilla. No wonder they'd been worried about the blackouts. They didn't want Nolan to have control. If he chose to go away, Amara was useless.

Was he here right now? She should scratch open her skin and see. If she healed, he was there, snug behind her eyes. If she bled, she was alone.

Jorn stopped in the doorway and looked Amara over flatly. "You're healed."

*And you know why!* Amara said nothing. She nodded.

She was not a mage.

Of course she wasn't a mage. Her healing had never been as solid as other mages'. She'd never done a spell. Never detected any magic. She thought she might have a chance to learn more, finally, but—

She was not a mage.

She was just some unlucky girl. The spirits didn't favor

her. Nolan did. He needed her body in one piece—of course he'd heal her. He'd seemed surprised; she could tell from the way he'd stumbled around in her body, from the way her hands hadn't signed right, but he'd still been the one in control. On some level, he must've known.

Jorn had known, too. All these years.

"Good." Jorn's voice said as little as his face did. "How are you feeling?"

"Better," Amara said. "Hungry. Do we have any rootpatties left? Have you all eaten? We should wake Maart." She signed normally, didn't she? Would Jorn buy it?

"The spirits must've changed their minds." Cilla's smile wavered. "Those cuts on her face started to heal suddenly. She woke up a minute later."

Amara's hairs pricked upright against her bandages. Jorn never looked at Amara this long, and he *never* looked at her while Cilla spoke. You gave the princess your undivided attention.

"What do you think happened?" Jorn pushed the door behind him shut and headed to the table across the room, which was empty aside from some unwashed plates and a water bowl.

"I don't know," Amara said. She tried not to rub her bandages, but they were tight, and the dried blood itched like mad when she signed. "I apologize. I did what I could to—"

"You're back," he stated.

"Yes. I'm back now. It won't happen again." As though she could do anything to stop Nolan.

"Come here," Jorn said. "Both of you."

"Is something wrong?" Cilla asked. She stayed on her chair —Maart's chair—by Amara's bedroll even as Amara climbed to her feet.

"Both of you," Jorn repeated. She saw muscles moving in his jaw, clenching and unclenching, and she knew that look. She wanted to run back and hide under the blankets and press herself against the wall, as far away as possible. She wanted to escape to every last spirit-abandoned nook of the planet.

She didn't want to see that look.

She kept walking toward him. Hollow steps. Trembling hands.

Behind her, she heard Cilla getting up from the chair. Cilla walked more slowly. She could get away with it. Jorn would never punish her. Still, Amara wanted to scream at her to Hurry up and He'll just get angrier and Stop asking questions!

"She saved my life at the market," Cilla said icily.

"You knew you were having blackouts." It wasn't just the muscles in Jorn's face tensing up now, but the ones in his neck, too, and the tendons in his hands as he crushed them into fists. "It wasn't safe for you to be alone with Cilla."

Amara stopped a footlength away. "I'm sorry, I—" she said, but she shouldn't be talking. Her hands still shook. She hated herself for walking over to him when he told her to. Hated herself for apologizing.

"But this isn't about that." Jorn gripped the back of Amara's head. His fist squeezed together bundles of her hair. She yelped. "This is about that mage attacking Cilla. This is about Cilla being stupid enough to show her tattoo after that."

"It was an Alinean pub!" Cilla said. "Amara needed—"

Amara didn't hear the rest. Jorn slammed her facedown into the water bowl. Water splashed out onto her hands as she grabbed the table to steady herself, and then it was up her nose and in her mouth. Her nose slammed into the bottom of the bowl. Something crunched. A mouthful of water went down her lungs. Her fists beat the table.

Her feet kicked at the floor as she tried to yank away, to swing her head free, but Jorn kept her pinned down. His other hand had to be steadying the bowl or she'd be able to move it, and she couldn't breathe. Couldn't breathe. The pain in her nose was fading. Nolan was here. She'd survive, but—she couldn't breathe. She needed to scream or spit or gasp lungfuls of air. She needed to keep her mouth shut. Needed to stop herself from inhaling.

She'd drowned before.

But none of those times had been with Jorn pressing her down and the water only fingerwidths high and she could feel cool air on water-spattered cheeks but couldn't reach and—

Cilla's shriek went through everything—through the bowl and Amara's panic both.

"Keep watching!" Jorn shouted.

Hair tore from Amara's skull as Jorn yanked her back up.

"Breathe," he told her, and she sputtered and gasped and spat out water. Air—air—she needed— "You'll be fine. But Cilla needs to learn. We had the perfect excuse to avoid attention thanks to that idiot jeweler's spell blowing up, and she ruined it."

He shoved Amara back down.

"Stop!" Cilla shouted. "I—I command you to—"

"Do you know how many people saw you? How much trouble we're in?"

Amara beat her hands on the table. She tried to shove it out of the way. Her boots stamped the floor until she lost her balance and her feet skidded away. The bowl rim pushed into her throat. She dangled at the edge of the table, scrambling for footing—

The pressure on the back of her head disappeared. She fell down, the bowl dropping over with the weight of her. The water spilled out. Amara collapsed by the side of the table, onto her side. She spit out water. Gasped for air. She kicked at the floor, trying to get away, under the table, where Jorn couldn't reach her.

Air. What had happened? Was he done?

"Maart!" Cilla shouted. "Don't—"

His bedroll was empty. The noise must've woken him.

Amara pressed her hands flat on the floor to steady herself, breaths surging in and out. Her eyes acted strangely, but she could still see Maart and Jorn. Fighting. Maart was screaming, shapeless noise and nothing more. He threw Jorn into the wall. One fist pulled back.

Jorn muttered a word. The air glowed, and Maart winced,

but it took only a second. Muscles tightened in his arm. The punch hit Jorn square in the nose. Jorn growled, ducking low. He rammed into Maart, shoulder against hipbone, and knocked him onto the floor. He straddled Maart. Two hands gripped his hair. Jorn pulled Maart's head up. Crashed it down.

That ended it.

Just that quickly—just that quietly—Maart stopped moving. Jorn climbed off. He was panting.

Why was Maart not moving? Amara stared.

"Maart?" Cilla made a strangled sound. She dove next to his body, fumbling to press her hand to his throat. Her expression didn't change. Her breaths came shorter. "You. He's. He's."

That was not good.

"I didn't." Jorn leaned against the table. He stood too close. Amara crawled farther against the wall, pressing every part of herself against it. She couldn't hide further. Maybe Jorn couldn't see her from where he stood. "I didn't mean to do that."

Amara was still kicking at the floor to get away. She hugged herself and stared and stared and stared.

"I wanted to stop him," Cilla whispered, and it was like Maart was talking to Amara all over again, sitting across from her in that dimly lit inn room and signing should'ves. He should've fought Jorn. That was what he'd said. He should've fought Jorn to save her.

They buried him.

In the south, in Eligon, people cut holes in the ice and low-ered their dead into the water for the fish to eat. The Elig ate the fish. The fish ate them. That was fair; that was right. They cleaned corpses' houses or melted the surrounding snow, and drowned their dead as soon as they could, keeping their lands pure and the spirits happy.

There was a reason few Elig traveled to the dead-stained north of the Continent and Dunelands.

In the Dit regions of the Continent, they stored their dead in mountain caves. They shut off the entrances with stone. You could walk those trails, see those stones, and remember the dead lifted high above the world. They made exceptions for mages. They lay them on mountain platforms for the sun and the birds. Mages were favored; it was only right their bodies be returned to the spirits for them to use as they pleased.

In the Alinean Islands they had only dangerous volcanoes and no snow. They burned their dead and used the ashes to bless the next-born descendant.

Amara didn't know what the Jélis did with their dead. Or what the people from the northern continents did. She didn't know much about them at all. Maybe she should. Maybe she would like their methods better. Maybe they would be better than sticking Maart into the ground to rot. Worms would eat him or scavengers would dig him up. People would walk over this spot for years to come, not knowing who lay underneath their feet. One day kids would play in these woods and they'd find his ribs and they'd laugh and use them to scare one another, or to spar, or they'd shrug and toss them away and continue their games.

None of that was right.

But: "We bury him," Jorn had said curtly. Blood crusted underneath his nose, where Maart had hit him. Amara thought Maart had done more damage than that. She wished he had. "We're leaving in the morning. A ship is coming to pick us up. Cilla drew too much attention."

No one argued.

Cilla stood to one side because she wasn't allowed near the shovels in case something went wrong. Jorn and Amara worked. They dug deep. They lifted Maart's body in. They put the earth back. Jorn beat the spot with the back of his shovel to make the displaced dirt stand out less, and Amara felt every thump.

"Do you want to say something?" Jorn asked. Then he grunted, "I'll give you a minute."

He leaned against a tree, far enough away that he probably wouldn't be able to recognize Amara's signs if he tried.

He'd catch them if they ran, anyway.

Amara stared at the earth.

Maart had wanted them to run. If she'd said yes—

"I wanted to stop him," Cilla said, urgently now. "I'm sorry. I'm so sorry. I should've helped. I should've . . ."

"You would've gotten hurt," Amara signed. "I know."

"I was scared. I'm sorry," Cilla repeated. She stepped closer. Amara stared at the earth.

"I overheard Jorn the other day." Her hands moved choppily. She could explain it all now. Maart wouldn't have told Cilla anything; he'd have stitched Amara's bandages into place and wished she'd let Cilla's curse take its course. He'd have pressed his lips to her forehead and painted marks on her skin.

Amara stared at the earth.

She'd wanted to mark the grave with stones the Dit way. Jorn hadn't let her. It would take too long to carry in the stones. There were none this deep in the forest, so deep Jorn had lifted the detection spells so Cilla and Amara could pass.

They should've gone deeper.

Maybe this was better. Deeper into the trees would have meant carrying Maart even longer, and she'd have been dirty all over. She couldn't melt herself like the Elig melted snow. Maybe she wouldn't have minded touching him longer. The body was still Maart. He'd still looked like Maart. He'd still had those curls of his, those pretty, long curls. He'd been too pale but he'd still had his freckles. He'd still had his lips. He'd still had his flat nose and his flat eyes and he'd still been beautiful. Amara didn't feel dirty now, and she'd helped carry him out here, pressing his dead body against hers while she could.

If she were really Elig, she'd feel dirty.

"That can't be right," Cilla said once Amara explained about Ruudde and the glass. "Jorn has always protected us. I mean—despite everything he's done, he did protect us." Her voice choked up. "I don't mean . . ."

"Protected you," Amara said distantly.

"I don't know what to . . ."

Amara crouched. She grabbed a twig from between a pair of mushrooms and pressed it to her skin. She pushed and pushed, then yanked the twig away. A dry scratch remained on her arm, surface skin flittering loose. It hurt. The skin turned light. Then it faded.

"Look. He's here." Amara showed her healed skin. "Did you enjoy this burial, Nolan? Anything I can do to improve it? Did you enjoy getting drowned? Did you enjoy—watching Maart—" She shouldn't say his name anymore. You weren't allowed to call the dead. And she was shouting with big gestures that Jorn might see even from so far off. She shouldn't do that, either. She wasn't allowed to be angry. Her fingers fluttered in the air, creating words that weren't even words anymore, until Cilla reached out to still them.

Cilla hadn't had to dig. She'd been able to keep her hands warm in the folds of her scarf.

That was good, because it was the middle of the night and Amara felt chilled to the bone. Her hair was still wet from the water bowl. That didn't help. That didn't help at all.

Amara pressed her face into Cilla's scarf and cried.

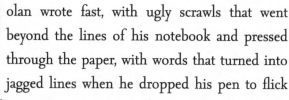

olan wrote fast, with ugly scrawls that went beyond the lines of his notebook and pressed through the paper, with words that turned into jagged lines when he dropped his pen to flick through earlier entries.

This notebook only went back a few weeks. He crouched by his cabinet and pulled out one stack of notebooks after another until he reached the ones at the bottom, pressed flat by the weight of the others. Their paper had yellowed.

He'd started these shortly before turning six. Dr. Campbell had asked him to keep track of what he saw, intrigued by the idea of hallucinations that had continuity, a consistent cast of characters. Those first notebooks were a mix of his own childish handwriting—all slow, careful block letters—and Mom's cursive. She'd helped him back then. He'd continued on his own.

He kept reading. Had he ever opened his eyes wide to wait out Amara's injuries, returning only when she'd already healed? Lord knew he'd tried. He'd never escaped the pain. He'd always figured the same as Amara had: that her magic was erratic.

She didn't have magic.

His fingers traced old letters. The notebooks described the Bedam palace and the royal family. How Amara had sneaked glimpses at the little prince and princesses as she worked. How she'd learned to eat and drink without her tongue. How she'd practiced her signs. How she'd missed her parents.

Once, her parents had watched her from the palace gates. "Don't look," the caretaker had told her. "It'll just be more difficult."

Amara had looked, anyway, letting Nolan see her parents for the first and only time. Their descriptions went on for a full page.

Amara tried sometimes but could no longer remember them. Neither could Nolan. Reading these descriptions, though—about her mother's scarf wrapped sloppily around her shoulders, the way her father's hair had gone gray—the images came back with such vividness, he wondered how he'd ever forgotten.

Her parents had looked sad. He hadn't written that down. He remembered.

He leafed ahead to how Amara had discovered her healing, to the massacre, then to the next notebook, after Jorn had scooped her up and taken her away. He'd showed her the surviving princess, a tiny girl who was just starting to talk in sentences, and Amara had reached out because she'd never been this close . . .

Nolan snapped the notebook shut. Clouds of dust whirled

out. He pored over the others and felt Amara's cheek cut open from ear to lip and woke from the same nightmares of the knifewielder as she did, and he got to know Nicosce, this Alinean stable girl, barely a teenager, all over again. He was taught by her and loved by her and watched her die when the hired mages' arrow hit the wrong person. Then Nicosce wasn't Nicosce anymore, simply *the servant before Maart*, and a narrow Dit-and-Alinean boy with an unfamiliar palace mark took her place.

He became familiar, solid Maart later. Except now Maart wasn't Maart anymore, either.

Nolan sat on his bedroom floor, notebooks piled all around, and stared at the pages in a haze. In that journal, that was when Amara and Maart had first kissed. In the next, they'd gone swimming in the Gray Sea. The water had been freezing and bugs had bitten their feet and they couldn't sign right, and Cilla had watched longingly from the shore, making them awkward and resentful until they got out quicker than planned. That night they sneaked out again. The water was even colder. Jorn hit them when they returned.

Half the things Nolan read, he didn't remember. He'd written it all down painstakingly, then let the details slip from his mind. Now, though, he needed to know.

In that one, they slept together for the first time.

In that one, Maart taught Amara how to cook. She taught him how to scour the rooms for anything that might hurt

Cilla. They watched children skate on frozen city canals. And throughout the other journals, Maart grew more serious, and Amara grew more quiet, and they cracked further each day, and Nolan had sat in this tiny, safe room and watched every minute.

A knock. Nolan made a sound. The door swung open. "Are you really OK?" Dad asked without preamble.

"Sorry if I ruined the movie." Nolan shut a recent journal, where he'd practiced Dit letters.

"No one expected the seizures to stop completely. If you're disappointed, that's all right. If you're feeling guilty . . ." Dad's bushy eyebrows knitted together. "You don't owe us anything."

"I didn't have a seizure." Nolan didn't attempt a smile. He couldn't. "Can I be alone?"

Dad looked at him for too long. Nolan wished he'd leave. Dad hadn't known Maart, and Nolan didn't know what else to say. He already felt bad for telling Dad to leave when he only wanted to help. They all just wanted to help, since they thought he was lonely or shy or insecure, but—it was none of that.

There wasn't any him to feel insecure about.

"Get some rest," Dad said.

Nolan only nodded.

"You OK?" Pat stood in his doorway, gloveless and in her PJs— an overlong shirt with a band he didn't know plastered on the front.

"You should be asleep." Pause. "Yes. Thanks. Mom and Dad already checked." Nolan was sliding his notebooks back into his cabinet one by one. He'd dated them, so it was just a matter of deciphering his old, clunky handwriting to determine the order. "Twice."

"Only twice?" Pat plopped onto his bed, watching his journals like she itched to get her hands on them.

She probably meant it as a joke, but he couldn't deal with it. With her. Not now. "They shouldn't worry so much."

Pat mimicked the vulnerable look they'd been practicing for her play. "*Don't worry about me. I'm just having seizures every two seconds. Woe! Be still, my aching heart!*" She paused to contain a grin. "*But I'm fine. Really. Why are you so worried? I don't understand! BRB, writing angsty poetry.*"

Nolan slapped the cabinet shut and reached for the key.

"*BRB, locking cabinet full of angsty poetry.*" Pat grinned a second time. "You like their attention—admit it."

"I don't," he said tightly.

Pat's laughter finally faded.

They were silent for a moment, and Pat said, sounding awkward, "It's just . . . you go swimming three times a week and they act like it's the Olympics. I snatch up the lead in a play and Dad ruffles my hair. Mom's too busy to volunteer, but she trips all over herself to help with your homework."

"Do you think I like any of that?" Nolan rubbed his face. Could he do this? Forget about Maart, get sucked into his own drama? Live life. Fantasize about Sarah Schneider. Bicker with Pat now that she finally felt comfortable enough to waltz into his room and tease him. Amara's grief didn't have to be his, did it?

"It looks like you do."

Even as screwed up as he was, he saw that this wasn't about him. "Pat, they're just letting you be independent. They don't think you *want* the attention. Why don't you tell them you do?"

"I didn't say that." She looked embarrassed. "That'd be pathetic. And needy. And pathetic. Whatever. It's way late. Mom'll kill you if you don't sleep soon. I just wanted to ask—I had this idea—like, what if I played that ER scene completely flat? On purpose?"

"Sorry." Nolan shook his head. "I . . . tonight's not a good time."

"Tomorrow?"

"Yeah. Maybe."

"You sure you're OK?" She climbed to her feet.

"Absolutely."

"So why not tonight?" When Nolan didn't respond, she said, "You're lying, aren't you?"

He clamped his mouth shut. Anything he said would just hurt her.

When Pat stomped into the hallway, he took his current notebook—the only one he hadn't locked away—and settled in at his desk. He'd be there a while.

he first things Amara saw when she woke were her hands. They said one simple thing: "I'm sorry."

Nolan was back.

Her hands dropped. She tried to fight. It didn't work. Her body slipped from her bedroll. Her hands wrapped her topscarf around her body—and they did every twist and fold right, too, because of course Nolan would've felt her do it countless times. She stood, blinking against the moonlight coming in from the windows. Morning would come within hours.

She knew she needed Nolan—Jorn would discard her if she stopped healing—but did that mean he had to claim her body in the middle of the night? She needed sleep. A few hours to herself before life went on. Quiet and dreams and darkness and nothing at all.

Her feet padded quietly. Pebbles pricked her skin. She thought she'd gotten rid of all those for Cilla's safety, leaving only harmless webs and spiders' egg sacs tucked into shadows.

Nolan didn't steer her gaze toward Maart's bedroll, still messed up and untouched. Amara would've. Her thoughts were there, even if her eyes weren't.

Her hands found a sidesling. Nolan packed a fresh winter-wear, then an extra topscarf. Maart's. She felt the fabric slide through her fingers, its embroidered edges, a clumsily repaired seam, and she wanted to shout. Not with her hands. With her voice. As loud as she could.

Nolan silently stole food and coins. The sidesling went around her waist. Her boots went on last. "You can't stay here," Nolan said once they stood by the exit. Moonlight lit her fingers, slanting in through the windows. "Not after what Jorn did to . . ."

At least he had the decency to stop.

What would she call Maart from now on? What name would settle into her hands and mind? The boy she loved. The boy who hummed. The boy who won every game they played. The boy who teased and laughed and kissed letters onto her skin. The boy whose words she stilled. The boy who didn't understand. The boy who wanted to understand.

The boy who tried to save her. The boy she might've chosen every version of, if she'd had the chance. The boy she failed. The servant who came before . . . whoever came next.

No, she wouldn't use that word. He wouldn't want to be remembered that way. The servant before Maart probably hadn't, either, but Jorn had called her that before Amara had thought of a name of her own. It'd stuck. Whatever else happened, Amara wouldn't do that to Maart.

"I don't want to control you," Nolan said. "I thought I did, but I don't. I didn't know it was all my fault. I promise. I'm sorry."

Her hands signed that—I—pointing at her own chest, but that wasn't right.

"Tell me you'll run." The doors were within reach. "Tell me you'll go on your own."

Nolan was like Maart. They thought everything was simple. They thought Jorn wouldn't find her. That people would help someone who spoke her servant signs. That bartenders wouldn't let her bleed out because of the ink scratched into her neck.

Amara used to wonder why Maart thought they could run. Maybe his palace had been better than hers, his minister friendlier. She'd wondered a hundred times and could think of only one thing: nothing was different, only he couldn't bear to watch her get hurt.

Maybe neither could Nolan. But Maart and Nolan weren't the ones who had their noses cracked on the bottom of a blood-stained bowl. Whatever pain of hers Nolan felt, he had a place to run to. Their guilt made them focus on *now*, on this *can't go on*.

They didn't stop to think about what would come after.

Amara's lips pressed together. Then she realized: her lips. She pursed them again. They obeyed without question. She stared at those doors in front of her. Two seconds. Two seconds, a firm push, and she'd be out in the cold.

She turned and walked back to her bedroll. She set the sidesling carefully on the floor. She leaned over. She untied her boots. She needed to be quick. Jorn might wake. She'd need to put the contents of the sidesling back, too, all the coins and clothes, exactly where Nolan had found them.

Movement to her right made her freeze. Tears pushed behind her eyes. Jorn would kill her. He'd killed Maart, and now he'd think Amara was trying to leave, so he'd kill her, too. She knew how he'd do it. He'd wait between eye blinks, when Nolan wasn't there, and strike quickly.

Her heart seemed to delay every beat, pressing against her ribs until it could take no more and slowly, finally, thumped.

But the movement wasn't Jorn. Cilla crouched by her side. Amara watched her through a haze of unshed tears, then looked at Jorn, who was still asleep. His shape on that roll was big but so quiet. This couldn't be the same person who'd grabbed her hair, who'd collapsed the back of Maart's skull. This Jorn was just a man, sleeping. This might be the Jorn who'd taken over cooking sometimes to experiment with bizarre meals, or who used to call her kid, or who, years ago, had bought them toys when they'd done their jobs well. A Jorn from forever ago.

Amara wanted to check on Maart's bedroll next. She turned to Cilla, instead.

Cilla was signing. She hadn't used signs in weeks. The last time Jorn had seen her do it, he'd shouted at her. She was a princess—she couldn't teach herself these things—she was a disgrace to her family.

She was doing it, anyway, sitting cross-legged on Amara's

bedroll. She must not want Jorn to wake up. Her movements were loose and hesitant, and she spread her fingers in places she shouldn't. Someone like her was only supposed to understand servant signs, not use them. She had her voice, her words, her tongue.

Maart's signs were nimble in comparison. Safe.

"I want to come with you," Cilla was saying.

"I'm not running. I—Jorn can't think I'm running." Amara took off one boot and flexed her toes. She moved on to the other.

"You think I would tell him?" Cilla signed.

"You used to tell him everything. You told him about the blackouts." Amara met Cilla's eyes, too tired for fear. She had all of that saved up for Jorn. Cilla was . . . just Cilla, now.

"I was worried. I'm sorry. I won't tell him. I didn't tell him you contacted the mage, either. On my life. On the names of the dead."

*Maart*, Amara thought.

"I *was* lying the other day." Amara was an idiot for saying this. She no longer cared. "When I said I didn't hate you."

"I . . . thought as much." Cilla breathed deeply. Amara caught a whiff of garlic. Now she knew what Maart had cooked last. When Cilla went on, it was as though Amara had said nothing. "If you're not running, why do you have your boots on? What's in the bag?"

Nolan returned without warning. Her hands halted in opening her other boot, the cord biting at cold fingers.

No, she wanted to tell him. No!

Cilla leaned back. "Nolan."

Was Amara that obvious, that Cilla detected a change in this fraction of a second?

"So . . . running wasn't Amara's idea," Cilla signed.

"You have to tell her to go." Amara felt her expression change but couldn't tell how. She wanted to claw at it. "I won't force her. I'm just giving her the option. Making it easier. Listen. I know her parents' names and what they look like. They lived in Bedam. If we go there, we can find them. They'll have to hide her or return to Eligon, but she'll be safe."

Her parents. Amara had never considered that option. All she remembered were words that weren't Dit, said by voices she couldn't place. The words had to be Elig; the voices had to be her parents'.

How come Nolan knew, and she didn't?

She still couldn't leave. Her parents could be dead or could have moved hundreds of miles away. Jorn would track her. He'd find her. Or maybe Ruudde would, the moment she set foot in Bedam.

She couldn't.

"I'm leaving now," Nolan said. "I'll keep watching in case she needs to heal. Earlier, when she told me to leave, I swear, I didn't know what'd happen."

Cilla's lips pursed. "If we tell you to leave, you leave. And you don't take control unless she asks."

Nolan nodded. He clawed at the blanket of her bedroll—
then her body sagged. She had to remind herself to sit up, to
lift her hands, wake the muscles he'd left unattended.

"I can't go," Amara said. "I can't. I can't. I can't."

"Jorn killed Maart," Cilla signed, and she didn't even seem
ashamed of having that name on her fingers. Amara shut her
eyes too late to miss it.

Maart. Maart. She sang his name in her head, the only
place she could keep it safe. She didn't want to decide on
another name. Not yet.

"We'll go together," Cilla signed. "We'll find your parents."

"Why do you want to come?" Amara knew the answer
before she finished asking.

"He. Killed. Maart." Cilla's eyes hardened.

And, oh, Amara knew Cilla was right, she knew, but part of
her could not help thinking, That's what it took? That's how far
he had to go?

"And he's working with the ministers. Our enemies. You're
the only person I can trust."

"And you need me to survive."

"Yes. And I need you."

It was as though the word hate had never been on Amara's
hands. It changed nothing. She sat there, her fingers on the
edge of her boot. If she stayed, she'd need to remain useful to
Jorn. She'd be stuck with Nolan.

If she ran—she might have a chance. And Maart had

wanted her to. If she'd gone with him before, he might still be alive.

Her hands dropped from her boot. "We'd need to cross Jorn's detection spell."

Cilla's face broke into a smile. Just like that. From hard eyes to that lit-up smile that made Amara love and hate her more at the same time. "We're safe. Jorn never reactivated it. He went straight back inside after . . . He seemed really out of it."

"He'll still track us. He has anchors on us—must be our clothes or boots, or your medicine."

"We'll take the airtrain to the harbor and get out of Jorn's reach before he notices. I don't know how far he can track an anchor. Leaving the island should be enough, shouldn't it?"

Amara couldn't believe she was discussing this.

Cilla's smile faded. "If you don't want to go, don't. You're the one who should decide."

"But you want me to."

"Yes. I want you to."

No, Amara wanted to tell Cilla. No. I don't want to go.

She took her other boot. "We'll find a ship, then. I've already packed money."

"I'll get my things." Cilla bolted for the bag where Jorn kept Cilla's medicine, both the kind that stopped her monthly bleeds and the kind that sped her clotting. She'd need the brush for her teeth, of course, and her clothes, her knee and elbow pads . . .

The smile might have gone, but as Cilla packed, her every movement contained a barely restrained excitement. Was this an adventure to her? She could take the risk of running. She'd get off easily if they were caught. Maybe her only punishment would be watching Amara's.

Amara pulled her boots back on. It didn't matter. She'd made her choice. She felt . . . relieved. It would work or it wouldn't, and either way, all this would come to an end.

She took her knife from her boot and pricked her arm. A drop of blood welled up. She smeared it away, finding the skin underneath whole. "What about you?" she asked Nolan. "Is this just an adventure to you, as well?"

No answer came.

t's not an adventure, Nolan wrote. He'd woken from his millionth nap, sitting uneasily in his desk chair. And it's not about feeling guilty. It's about making it right.

He chugged more knockoff Coke. It was four in the morning. He had school soon. Mom would be furious. Few things were more important to preventing seizures than a regular sleep schedule.

Amara blames me. Prob should. I didn't mean to, but it's still my doing. Should help FIX IT now. Fuck own life. Can't ignore this. My fault. I still don't get what's going on with me but

OK, I <u>think</u> this is what's happening. Nolan underlined the word several times. I'm a mage, or whatever the Earth version is and I can transport my mind into someone else. (Just Amara? Others if I try?) I used to do it without meaning to & now I can control it.

I looked this up: When people blink, something happens w/ our brain, turning on & off diff sections to rest for a split second. So in my case, when brain rests when I blink & sleep, something else happens too. I go to Amara.

So what's in these pills that wasn't in the others? And which part of my brain sends me to Amara? I guess my drs would know, all those weird EEGs from when I was a kid prob show which part of my brain is (in)active when I'm in her mind.

OK, leaves me where??

As long as I take the pills, I can stay out of her mind. So I only need to stick around until she's safe w/parents. Then ??? I take pills the rest of my life & hope I don't focus on Amara too much b/c I'll go by accident? What if she needs to heal? Do I keep checking?

He drained the last drops of his pseudo-Coke can but didn't get up yet to find another. He should've just brought up a full six-pack. And what happens with Cilla? he wrote.

What happens with Amara?

22

The airtrain was nearly empty. It only operated at this hour to take fishers and market workers to the harbor, and many of those had either already left or didn't need to work until sunrise. Cilla and Amara climbed on right as the train was about to leave.

Every second they rode took them farther from Jorn. Amara stared at the passing landscape: the forest where lightning had struck the other airtrain, dunes and farms and heathered hills, gray fields stretching far with nothing but cows, and, near the treelines, a handful of deer. The unnervingly steady drone of the dawnflies' whistling followed the train on its trip.

"Nolan. I'd like to talk to you," Amara signed. She sat at the window, where no one but Cilla could see her hands.

No answer came. Nothing but the train's pneumatic hiss and the dawnflies outside.

"You can take control, can't you? Here's your permission."

She watched her hands intently, spreading them out, turning them. Maybe having someone take over would be a blessing.

Her muscles went rigid, then disappeared from her reach. "Yes," Nolan said. "Sorry. I think I fell asleep. The longer I keep my eyes shut, the more I . . . become you. Yes, we can talk."

Her hands returned to her, as did the rest of her body. She tested her toes and lips and lungs to make sure. "Good," she said. "What do you mean, you *become* me? Explain. Explain everything."

Nolan's movements came more fluidly as time passed. He talked about losing his foot, about never concentrating, about falling into a type of long sleep that he couldn't find the word for in either signs or spelled Dit.

The more Nolan talked, the more Amara knew he meant well. He paused between sentences, allowing for questions and interjections, but never at the right time. She still had to wait for him to allow her to speak. "Enough," she said finally. She amended: "I think I know enough."

She couldn't bring herself to thank him.

Outside, branches scraped the airtrain windows like too-long fingernails. Amara let her hands drop into her lap. They'd slipped so easily from direct signs to rushed ones, from hard words to tentative gestures, that she didn't know what to do with them now. They didn't feel like hers. If Nolan wanted to say something else, he could. She supposed she should be grateful he didn't, but she only felt like washing her hands and all the rest of her, like stripping and wading into the sea to rinse herself clean of him.

Maybe she did care about having control.

"That was a little weird," Cilla breathed. She'd been quiet for most of the conversation, interrupting Nolan only when she needed clarification. "The way you two—all alternating and—" She hunted for the right word. "Weird."

"Yes," Amara said. "It was."

A laugh escaped—hard and joyless—and the sound felt so foreign that for a fraction of a second she thought Nolan had taken over again. He'd made her laugh before. But, no, this was her alone. She hadn't laughed in days, not since Maart . . . and he'd lain beside her and . . .

She needed to keep that memory. All her memories.

Nolan was recalling them alongside her, wasn't he? The laugh faltered, but she didn't want it to die. She looked at dead leaves blowing dizzily past the windows.

"New rule," she said. She felt as if she ought to subdue her movements, to apologize and shuffle out of the way. It wasn't her place to make demands. She squashed that reluctance. "New rule. I can't have you in my head. I can't. Just . . . stay away. Check back in every now and then in case I need your healing, but don't stay." She paused. "Tell me you understand."

Nolan slipped in a moment later. "I understand. But when I'm asleep, I can't go back and forth. Then it will need to be all or nothing. I'm sorry."

He returned her hands.

Have him in her head for hours on hours or risk his being out of her reach when she needed him. Invade her mind or break her body.

"When you're sleeping, stay." Telling someone what to do

didn't feel natural. However terrible her options, though, they were hers, and she would take what she could. "Warn me first. Tell me when you go to sleep and wake up, so I'll know, at least."

Before long, the high masts of ships came into sight. The harbor. "We're here." She stood. Her thigh and elbow felt cool all of a sudden. They'd been pressed against Cilla's in the seat in a way Amara suddenly missed. As long as they sat here, laughter or no laughter, Nolan or no Nolan, she could pretend nothing was wrong. They were simply on a supply trip or moving to another town.

But now they stepped into the briny air, just the two of them without Jorn to clear their path or Maart by her side, and Amara wanted to run back inside the train for the return trip. Jorn might still be asleep at the granary. If they went back now, he'd never need to know they'd left. He'd never need to come after them.

The determination she'd felt on leaving seeped rapidly away. She clung to it, thinking, *Maart.* She could do this.

She *would* do this.

Lamps lit the harbor streets, bathing the cobblestones in pools of warm yellow that made Amara feel too visible. She stepped around the lights, looking for rowdy market boys who weren't paying attention, or holes in the pavement that Cilla might twist an ankle in. The lamps themselves caught her eye, instead: red-and-gold crowns sat atop them, so alien she had to stop and stare. She'd seen etchings of lamps and bridges decorated with crowns before, but the ministers had ordered the crowns snapped off long ago. Some bridges still showed the damage. Amara hadn't known any had survived intact.

Cilla's family got crowns and etchings. Maart got—Maart got drowned in forest earth and she'd never have a chance to choose him—

"Look," Cilla whispered. She put a hand on Amara's sidesling. "Were they here before?"

Amara took a second to calm herself. A slow, hot breath later, she examined the harbor. They'd walked across this same street from the airtrain to the market the other day, but in the dark of predawn, everything looked different. The sea lay beyond the dunes, black as coal, and the harbor mill towered high over the other buildings, determined to catch every breath of wind. Workers walked lightly, trying to wake themselves up. They were mostly Alinean, readying their fishing boats or tugging along carts with covered goods.

But those weren't the people Cilla meant.

Marshals patrolled the docks in padded winterwear and helmets painted leaf-green, the color only visible under gaslight. They'd speak to ship captains, then return to land, talking in low voices and pointing at another group of marshals coming in by horseback.

"Jorn warned them," Amara said. Their way out—gone. Could they run another way?

*Stay*, she told Nolan. She hadn't wanted to need him so quickly.

"Even if Jorn's awake," Cilla said, "he couldn't have called up so many marshals at such short notice. This is because of what I did at the pub. They're looking for me."

Amara nodded, though fear still pinned her feet down. If Jorn hadn't discovered their absence yet, returning to the granary was still an option. She tried to shove it from her mind. This was a trip like any other. Protect Cilla, avoid recognition, keep away from the marshals.

They stayed huddled at the edge of the harbor, outside the reach of the lights, so that people wouldn't spot Amara's signs.

"The rumors can't have spread far. We might be safe once we leave Teschel," Cilla said.

"There's still Jorn. And whoever the ministers might send after us. And the mages . . ." Mages like the knifewielder wanted Cilla dead. No question. But if the ministers wanted her alive—and they had to, based on what Amara had overheard—then who did the knifewielder and other mages work for? The question made Amara's head hurt.

"You're not an optimist, are you?" Cilla let out a low, nervous chuckle.

"We'll need to sneak aboard a ship. They're warning the captains about you." Amara wanted to say more, but someone was headed their way—fast. She reached for her knife. The man might alert the marshals once he saw Cilla. She'd match the description the pub-goers had given, and while there were plenty of Alinean girls in the harbor, few wore topscarves, particularly ones so nice—scarves and winterwears were Dit clothing, unwieldy on boats. Alinean fishers wore sleeved tops and half-skirts over loose trousers.

Amara pressed her knife flat to her ribs, under her topscarf. If she needed to, she'd slash and run. Without looking, she pushed her thumb against the blade. Her skin broke. Seconds later, the cut healed. Good.

The man stopped footlengths away. The light of the nearest lamp caught his face. Though light red in skin, he had the distinct pinched nose bridge and rounded lips of an Alinean, and when he opened his mouth, Amara recognized him straightaway. "I was sure you would've left by now," he said.

The bartender.

Cilla knew him, too. "You helped us!" She seemed not to know what to do with herself. A flicker of a smile crossed her lips before she stood firm again. "Will you do so another time?"

"Without question."

Amara stayed quiet. If not for Cilla, the bartender would have let her die. He didn't even acknowledge her now.

Cilla had the same thought. "If you're loyal to my family, why didn't you help in the first place? Wouldn't you want to aid anyone escaping a minister, servant or not?"

The man swallowed. The knob in his throat rose sharply. "If I'd known—"

"That's not what I asked," Cilla said. A fisher approached, holding a small, furred Elig horse by its reins. It dragged along an empty cart smelling of day-old fish. The bartender waited anxiously to speak until the fisher passed.

"I respect servants for their duty and escaped ones for their common sense, but publicly helping one would be dangerous. If the ministers found out, they'd ruin my business."

"Helping the princess seems even more dangerous."

"The alternative was disobeying my princess's orders."

Cilla nodded. Being demanding came so easily to her. When she spoke, people listened. When she asked, people answered.

"If you'll permit me to help you a second time," the bartender said, "I'm here to see off a friend of mine. She captains a ship that's sailing for the mainland in an hour. She won't betray you, though I can't vouch for passengers and crew."

"We'll have to risk it," Cilla said.

"Are you coming back?" the bartender asked. His eyes gleamed in the gaslight. "Not to the island. To the throne."

Cilla smiled uneasily. "Eventually. The question remains *how*."

"You have a lot of people behind you."

Cilla straightened her back and raised her chin. Amara had

seen Cilla look genuinely regal; this was not it. She faked it well, though. "Show us your friend's ship."

They'd go separately. If the marshals knew about Cilla, they'd also know about the Elig girl with her. If Cilla and Amara traveled side by side, they'd be checked for certain. But under the guise of being crew—there wasn't time to find other clothes, but Cilla had rubbed sand into her scarf to stand out less—they might have a shot at sneaking aboard unnoticed.

The bartender and Amara would board first, with the captain and Cilla following later. She'd have to rely on their loyalty to keep Cilla safe.

Amara didn't like relying on anyone for something this big. She reminded herself not to check on Cilla as she walked alongside the bartender, lugging a sack of supplies. She eyed the marshals instead. Two walked toward the harbor house, which an Alinean girl was just leaving, smoothing her shirt and looking displeased. She was Cilla's age, maybe older. The marshals must've checked her for tattoos.

The harbor air was filled with the scents of fish and salt and wet wood, and no trace of the sun, though the sky was slowly lightening. Their ship was a small fluit moored near the harbor house. The crew loaded crates via pulleys and thick ropes. They'd stop at an island or two, load passengers and cargo, then head for Bedam.

Nearby, a fisher snarled at her crew. Amara jerked at the sound. It wasn't directed at her, but still, she stood out too much. Elig were a rare sight around harbors. She stepped to the right to put the fishing crew between her and the harbor house.

She *meant* to step right. But something glued her feet to the ground.

"Keep moving." The bartender passed her, looking straight ahead.

Amara pulled at her foot again, then another time. She was stuck. Just as she was about to try to call the bartender back, the cobblestones let her go. She tumbled forward. Her kneecaps almost cracked. Her hands broke her fall, and as she hit the ground, something rippled through her—more than just the impact of bony hands on hard stone.

Her hands pulsed. They lit up like the tattoo on Cilla's chest. She tried to climb to her feet before anyone noticed, but it was too late for that—the glow wasn't just in her hands. It shone through the threads of her winterwear and the folds of her scarf, and she had to squint to keep out the light that flared from the rest of her face.

The ground glowed, too, pooling around her feet and running from there in a thin, smooth line to both sides, from the harbor house to the market, forcing anyone who wanted to board the ships to cross it.

The marshals had gotten a mage to circle the area. Her crossing the line had activated a spell.

Mixed magic.

Panic rose in her throat. The line of light flared, turning the solid white of sunlit metal. The light fanned out, and cobblestones cracked all around it, their polished surfaces breaking open. She heard the pop-pop-pop of pebbles launching up and bouncing footlengths away.

Just as quickly, it all died.

Was that it? Was it over? The memory of the lightning at the market bright in her mind, Amara scrambled upright, as if she could escape further effects if she just ran quickly enough—though she couldn't run at all. Her knees throbbed. She cried out the moment she placed her weight on them. They weren't healing. Nolan had left. Right when she needed him. Or—no. The spell she'd crossed must've interacted with his presence. If he didn't count as magic, nothing would. The combination had kicked him out and blown up whatever ward the marshals' mage had put up.

All these years, she'd been scared of crossing wards—and now, all she was left with were screwed-up knees. She might've escaped Jorn years ago and gotten off just as easily. Incongruous laughter bubbled in the back of her throat. If she'd known, maybe—no.

She reeled herself in, locking down her laughter. Running from Jorn didn't mean she could toss out her every last survival instinct. Marshals were headed her way. She gauged the distance between them. Even if her knees healed right this second, she wouldn't be able to escape on time.

"What the—" one marshal shouted as he stumbled over a cracked rock. "I thought the spell was just supposed to bind 'em!"

"You're enchanted?" The bartender kept his voice low.

Amara nodded. The marshals were seconds away. What about Cilla? No sign of her.

"Act sick," he said from the corner of his mouth. He took a firm step toward the approaching marshals. "What's going on? Don't tell me you cast a public spell!"

"Sir, we want to speak to the girl." One marshal, the shortest of the crew, pointed his baton at Amara. She wrapped her hands over her stomach and squirmed as if in pain.

"That girl is my employee," the bartender said, "and what she wants is to go back to the carecenter. Your spell screwed up her healing. She could've died! All of us could've!"

"Sir, we need to—"

"You need to not cast spells willy-nilly where enchanted people risk crossing them! That's such a minister thing to do! Don't you have any consideration for the spirits? For basic safety?" the bartender fumed. "I've seen spells mix before. Do you know what happened? It picked up a house. A house! It rose right up off the foundation. Turned on its side, then crashed to the street. There was a family inside.

"That could've happened here. Or worse! Is this a detection spell? It didn't occur to you that a detection spell needs to check whoever crosses it? That its magic would interact with theirs? I'm not even a mage, and I know that! And the backlash—no, forget it. Let's go, Immer. If we get you to the carecenter now, we might be back before the ship departs."

The bartender played his part well. Many mages took oaths to minimize magic use, but Alinean mages took it further than anyone and suppressed their abilities entirely. They said it was out of respect for the spirits. Alineans also had more mages than anyone else and simply couldn't risk the backlash. Earthquakes and eruptions had already damaged the Alinean Islands enough. They'd tried to institute a similar policy in the Dunelands, which were just as fragile in different ways: low to the ground and close to the water. The policy hadn't taken, though, especially after the ministers took over, and now the sight of magic made most Alineans grit their teeth.

So no one would question the bartender's rant. Amara cringed, anyway. You just—you didn't talk back to your betters. Not to ministers, not to marshals. How hadn't they already whipped out their batons?

At least Amara could pass off her wincing as illness. She took a wobbly step toward the bartender. Her knees stung with sped-up healing, signaling Nolan's return. No matter how much she hated that Nolan was in her mind, she could use his presence. She directed her thoughts at him, telling him what had happened. *Stick around.*

In the distance, a captain blew a whistle and shouted. A fraction of a second later, a collective *no* punctuated the sound of a crate smashing to the stones. The marshals ignored the accident. One grabbed Amara's shoulder. "You match the description of someone we're looking for. Immer, was it?" He watched her mouth.

*Just answer. Easy.*

Past the marshal, she saw movement—people staring at the crashed cargo, others ignoring it and continuing to work, and, more importantly, the ship's captain and Cilla heading toward the boat at a fast clip. Amara stepped back. The harbor spell would react to Cilla's curse; this time, the curse might be the one to go awry instead. She didn't get the chance to warn her. Cilla walked safely past the boundary that had lit up earlier and that now sat on cracked cobblestones as a burned-out, wiggly line of ashes.

At least that was a stroke of luck: Amara must have knocked the spell out completely.

In a deceptively mild voice, another marshal said, "This ward was supposed to check for mages' ink, like a minister's or servant's tattoo." *Or a princess's.* "Is there any reason you're not talking, Immer?"

The bartender tsked impatiently. "Yes. Her stomach. The healers don't know what's wrong with her. Besides, you know

Elig. Pathetic snowhounds. Too dumb to ask for water if their hair's on fire."

"She's not *all* Elig, though." One marshal eyed her hair, her skin. Northerners never realized just how many clans lived in the Elig south—they figured the only *real* Elig had pale hair and pale skin and pale eyes. Not like Amara, dulled down in every aspect. Light enough to be recognizable, too dark to be genuine.

"Just check her neck already," the first marshal snapped, and he stepped forward. Another pair of marshals took off in Cilla's direction, and, oh, how had Amara been so stupid to think they could leave the island so easily?

Amara breathed deeply. *Protect Cilla. A trip like any other.* She lowered one shoulder, letting the bag of supplies the bartender had given her drop. She caught the strap before it crashed to the stones and swung it against the nearest marshal's shins.

His grip on her shoulder faltered. She tore loose and sprinted toward the ships. The marshals' legs were longer, stronger. She heard their boots hit the stones behind her. If she could reach the water, she stood a chance. Either way, the distraction worked. The marshals near Cilla spun back toward Amara. Just a few steps—

A grunt came from behind her. A second later, pain exploded in the back of her head. A baton. Her vision blackened. She went flying to the stones, hitting them chin-first. Her momentum sent her rolling to the edge. Her vision swam, spikes of light stabbing through the dark. She urged her body to roll farther. She felt the edges of the stones in her back— saw the blurred outline of a marshal's glove—and sucked in a breath before dropping over the edge of the dock.

The noise of the world abruptly died. The water drew her in whole, filling her nose and mouth. Just like before. At least this time her body didn't panic. Her head felt like it'd split in two, but the pain ebbed. Nolan was sticking around as he'd said he would.

She waited another second or two, trying to stay calm. She closed off her lungs. She didn't need to breathe. No matter how much her body told her she needed to breathe, she didn't, she couldn't, not yet.

Then she kicked. She'd gotten disoriented, but the harbor wall and the ship's hulls were easy reference points. As she swam, she kept her eyes squinted, the dark of the water obscuring everything beyond a footlength or two. Underneath that ship. Around the pillars of the pier. Avoid the crags of wood. Swim past the anchors. Tear the waterweeds from her face.

Three ships farther, her lungs felt as if they'd pop. She went up for a quick breath. This close to the wall, no one saw her. Shouts came from behind her, where she'd dropped into the water.

She ducked back under. The calm came more easily this time. Her head no longer hurt. No one grabbed fistfuls of hair and forced her still. It was just her. And Nolan.

Amara swam toward the last ship and went to the aft, as far away from the harbor wall as possible. She came up for air a second time. The world rolled back in, voices and shouts, carts racketing along uneven stones, rope fenders thudding against the wood of the docks.

Cilla's whisper-shout cut through all of it. "Amara!" A silhouette ran toward her, just the bobbing of her head along the ship's railing.

Cilla was aboard safely. Amara's distraction had worked. She brought her hands out of the water, relying on her kicking feet to keep her afloat. "You were waiting?" she asked awkwardly.

Cilla leaned over the railing. Even with the sky turning the murky gray of morning, it had to be hard to see Amara in the water. "I'll get rope," Cilla signed back.

"No. They might check the ships for me." Amara tried to make her signs bigger, easier to see in the dark. "I'll cling to the hull. Pull me up when you've left the harbor." The lights on the boat allowed her to see traces of Cilla's face, enough to notice her hesitance.

"Be safe," Cilla signed.

Amara sucked in another breath and dove.

**N**olan!"

Nolan started awake. His chair rolled away from his desk. His arms flailed, knocking his pen to the floor, the notebook dropping facedown after it.

"Are you OK? Are you—" Pat jumped at him, pressing her face into the crook between his shoulder and neck. Her arms squeezed him. Her lips moved against him, mumbling something he couldn't hear. Her face was wet.

Nolan started to sign, then stifled his movements. He was back on Earth. He needed to speak Spanish, English. Anything but servant signs.

"Patli?" he said carefully. He rested one hand on her shoulder but didn't push her off. "What's going on?"

She yanked her head back. Her eyes were red, her face tear-stained. "I was two seconds away from calling 911, you idiot! You wouldn't wake up. I was—I was shouting and—I thought you were having a seizure—"

"No. I was sleeping." He swallowed a lump in his throat. The world dawned on him, both his own and Amara's. Shit. The ship was taking off with her still clinging to the hull. Her head was above water, but waves battered her, seeping into her lungs. He needed to get back.

"Dad's already at work, and Mom's with the Patersons. I didn't know what to do. I thought . . ." Pat ran a hand over her face, now more frustrated than anything. "I pulled your hair! Who doesn't wake up when their hair is pulled?"

"I've been working." He gestured broadly at his desk. He should've seen this coming. It'd been years since he'd stuck around the Dunelands this long. It'd been years since he'd wanted—needed—to as much. He could worry about it later.

"Working?" Pat said. "All night?"

"Seemed like a good idea." He smiled weakly and shut his eyes—

**—and Amara was coughing and her nails scraped the wood, trying to keep hold of that ridge with hands numb from cold, and the water slammed into her—**

"—I need to get back to work," Nolan said.

"Seriously? School starts in half an hour."

"I'm not going." He couldn't let Amara get hurt again.

Pat gaped. "Mom and Dad will kill you."

"I'll tell them I'm sick. Please, Pat. Can you go?"

"You really weren't having a seizure? Mom and Dad are worried about you after last night."

Nolan closed his eyes. He just needed to make sure—

"Stay with me!" Pat smacked his shoulder. Nolan's eyes shot

open, and Pat stood over him, fury in her teary eyes, her fists balled.

"I can't," he gritted out. "You have to go."

"Why? What's going on? Why are you—what's with the—" She pointed at the journals. Her finger shook. "You're scaring me. I'll hit you again if you say you're OK. I will."

"Later. All right?" He propped his elbows on his desk and rested his face in his palms. "I promise I'll explain later. Right now, you need to leave me alone."

He shut his eyes again. This time, Pat let him.

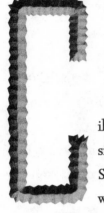

illa smiled broadly as Amara climbed through the sidescuttle. "This is Captain Olym's sitting room. She left spare clothes for us." She gestured at the winterwear draped over a nearby stool. Thick, rich-colored, far too big for Amara, but—oh—dry. Amara's limbs felt so numb she was surprised she'd been able to climb up. "Throw your own clothes overboard in case there's an anchor on them—I did the same. I threw out my other supplies, too. Captain Olym will replace them. Then dry yourself off and come on deck."

"Won't the passengers suspect something?" Amara signed.

"We'll say you were sleeping belowdecks." Cilla held up an off-brown towel. "Do you . . . are you all right?"

The wind blasted through the still-open hatch, cutting Amara straight to the bone. "Just need to dry off." She stepped clumsily forward and took the towel.

"They're waiting for me upstairs. I should . . ." Cilla nodded at the door and went back up.

Amara's first instinct was to wrap the towel around her, soaked clothes and all. One step at a time, though. *You can leave now,* she told Nolan. Even in her mind, her words felt slight. She couldn't make herself thank him.

She pricked her index finger to confirm he'd left. She stuck her head out the sidescuttle to wring the water from her hair, shivered at the wind, and shut the hatch as quickly as she could. Given the smile on Cilla's face, they were safe. Still, Amara rushed through undressing, drying off—the towel was softer and warmer than she could remember any towel being—and slipping into Captain Olym's wear, which was too loose around her chest and waist and everywhere else. She rolled up the pant legs and adjusted the lacing, knotting it in the small of her back and along her thighs and ribs. The boots fit just as awkwardly.

Amara tossed her old clothes out the sidescuttle as instructed and took a look around the cabin. Gaslight illuminated polished hardwood and intricate drapes, which made it look like midnight even with the sun finally rising. The room felt cozy. Safe. A stringed instrument she couldn't name rested in a corner, and fruit in matching colors sat on a square plate twice the size of her head.

This place should not feel safe. Nothing should. This was not just another trip.

She was running away.

She wrapped her arms around her chest. Her eyes fixed on one of the drapes that had been embroidered with a map of the area. Teschel was on the left, shaped like a tadpole, the tail a protective bay. The rest of the map showed the nearby islands and the ever-recognizable shape of the Dunelands mainland— the dagger, as people called it, with the capital Bedam at the tip.

She read the letters slowly, and the names of other mainland towns, and the names of the islands and their cities, too, but reading didn't—couldn't—give her the thrill it had before.

She tried to recall the maps Cilla had shown her over the years. She imagined the lines of the mainland stretching farther east, the Dunelands' dagger growing broader until it bled into the Continent: the Collected Cities, the Ohn and Dit mountains, the State of Jélis, the Andan Kingdom, and a dozen other territories, so much larger than the Dunelands and so far away Amara couldn't comprehend it. And the south—Eligon—was farther still. The maps always colored it white, for the snow.

Amara imagined that same snow crunching underfoot, a hundred days away from Jorn on that island behind her, a hundred days away from the ship swaying under her feet.

If she went on deck, people might ask questions. If she stayed here, people might come find her. If she went on shore, she'd be caught, and if she went back, she'd be caught, and Maart was dead no matter what. She wanted Nolan back in control of her body so she wouldn't have to steer it, since there was nowhere to steer to that didn't make her tremble at the thought.

She swallowed to clear her throat, which felt as if fingers were clenching it shut.

Cilla had asked her onto the deck. Amara clung to that. She left the cabin and went up the stairs, and if the cozy heat downstairs had dulled her, the wind up top woke her up again. She whisked her topscarf higher as cover, wrapping it around the tips of her hair to shield her neck better. She breathed in the salt air, letting it burn away her fears. She was still obeying her princess's orders; she hadn't abandoned her duties.

No one else would see it that way, but it calmed her, regardless.

Captain Olym sat on the deck, talking to a crew member, and she gave Amara a small nod. The captain was a short, round woman, her arms all muscle, her face weathered and lined, her hair cropped to near nothing. The rising sun threw pinkish rays over her face and tinted the air a gray that hovered between yellow and blue, painting the clouds colors Amara couldn't find names for. The cold pricked at her arms, but she didn't mind.

Maybe Cilla had called her up to see this. The view from inside the cabin couldn't compete with something so beautiful.

"Look!" Cilla said.

Amara's eyes stayed fixed on the clouds. "I haven't seen a sunrise from the sea in ages."

"No," Cilla said. She touched Amara's shoulder, turning her around. "Look."

At first, Amara thought Cilla meant for her to see the Teschel harbor in the distance, maybe a ship headed their way. Then she spotted the stretch of beach that made up Teschel's tail, curling at the horizon. Round shapes scampered over the sand in fits and starts, and Amara didn't need to think before signing, "Diggers!"

Her record was seeing three at once, and one of those she hadn't been sure of. Now—oh, she couldn't begin to count the dark shapes dotting the sand. The more she looked, the more diggers she saw, some in the water, others scurrying through the dune grass, visible only by the way the grass swung counter to the wind.

From here, she couldn't see the way their stick-thin legs practically danced over the sand, or the way their pointed snouts would swing left and right in an endless search for bugs, or how they'd slide into the water, legs wide—but she didn't need to. She could imagine.

"Apparently morning is the time to go digger-watching." Cilla beamed.

"You knew I liked them," Amara said. They stood turned toward the beach; as long as she kept her movements minimal, no one on the ship would see her sign. "The servant before— before—told me diggers weigh less than you'd think. That's why their legs are so thin. Their bodies are round, but only because they contain a sack of air that helps them float in the water."

"I'd forgotten that!"

"They breathe in extra before they go into the water and store the air on their backs. If you puncture the skin there, they'll drown."

"That's . . . really sad." Cilla frowned.

Amara fell silent. Her eyes followed the shapes skittering across the beach.

"Just because it's sad doesn't mean you should stop talking." Cilla bumped her shoulder into Amara's.

"I'm sorry," Amara said automatically. "I don't know much else about diggers."

"No, I mean . . ."

Amara knew what she meant.

"Did you only run because I said I wanted you to?" Cilla asked.

Amara didn't know either answer: the real one or the one Cilla wanted. She tried to keep her thoughts on the beach, but the diggers had lost their appeal. She couldn't see them anymore, anyway. The ship moved too fast.

"I meant . . . I thought running was best for you. You can answer me honestly. Except if I have to tell you that, it rather defeats the point, and—" Cilla threw up her hands and laughed feebly.

"Told you it's not that simple," Amara said. Maybe nothing was simple. The world had come close to simple before, doing whatever Cilla and Jorn asked. Now, Amara second-guessed every thought; Cilla probably second-guessed every word. Every formerly innocuous question turned into something more.

Good, Amara thought. Cilla should know that her words meant something.

"You can joke about it?" Cilla said.

"It wasn't a very good joke."

A smile played at Cilla's lips. She looked at the beach, even with the diggers too far to be recognizable. Her hands wrapped around the railing. They looked soft next to the polished wood. "Amara, I know we're not friends, but you're all I have. Jorn is . . . It's complicated."

"Jorn's always protected you." Amara's signs had a hard edge to them. They came choppier, like Nolan's. She wiggled her toes just to make sure she still could. "It's OK to care for him."

It wasn't, but Amara still understood.

"I don't know if I do. I don't *want* to." The wind took Cilla's hair, playing with it, and Amara's first instinct was to smooth it down as she'd done with her own. Cilla had no need to hide her neck, though. "Sometimes he was kind. Sometimes he wasn't. But I wasn't allowed to be alone, and with him, I didn't have to be so *careful.* Maar—he hated me."

No point in denying that.

"I know you hate me, too." Cilla turned briskly. One hand stayed on the railing. The wind brushed her hair into her face in a way that was wild and beautiful and did nothing to hide the uncertainty in her eyes. "I understand. I wanted you to know that: I understand, and I'm sorry. I should've stayed behind."

"If you weren't with me, you'd die. I don't want you to."

"I'm still sorry."

"I know." Before she could change her mind, Amara said, "I just don't know if it changes anything."

Cilla's shoulders squared, as if she was bolstering herself. "I deserve that."

Amara raised her hands to speak, then stilled. She'd never thought about these things. There was no point. But she didn't only *think* about them now, she said them straight to the princess's face, and she wasn't even scared anymore.

It wasn't right. It wasn't comfortable. But it was safe. The thought took her breath away.

"Maybe I was wrong before," she signed. "I don't think I hate you. I hate what you are; I hate what I am, too. We can't change either of those."

"I can. When I'm in power, you'll get everything you want. I'll remove your tattoo. You'll live where you want to. You'll get however much silver you need."

Amara laughed. "I'd want books. I want to read books."

"There's a library in the Bedam palace. You could take every last book in there."

"I'd want to live on the beach. I'd see diggers every morning."

"Yours."

"I'd want to see Eligon."

"I'd arrange it."

It'd be that easy for her, wouldn't it?

Behind them, Captain Olym called orders. The crew adjusted the sails. "I thought you wanted us to be equals," Amara said. She'd depended on Jorn for food, shelter, safety. Being dependent on Cilla, instead—that wasn't freedom.

"But I owe you." Cilla thought. "All right. Tell me what you do need."

Why was Amara laughing again? None of this was funny, but she couldn't help it. The world sank under her feet, and Cilla promised her silver and books and diggers, and she turned them all down. She was turning into Maart. He'd say these same things—or maybe he wouldn't. He might take all that Cilla offered and say he deserved it. He'd be right, too.

"I need . . ." The wind tangled Amara's hair, and the sea stretched out endlessly before her. "I don't know," she said, almost dreamily.

"You're not making this easy." Cilla's laugh was a nervous one.

"I didn't realize a lot of the things you've told me," Amara said. "Like that you had no choice but to spend time with Jorn. Like that we played games together because you weren't allowed to play with anyone else. I grew up thinking *I* wasn't allowed to play with anyone else." She hesitated. "Like that I'm all you have."

"Of course you're all I have." Cilla's hand touched Amara's, sending a jolt through her.

She'd wanted to say something else but was no longer sure what.

Noon had come and gone, and it had taken the sun with it, turning the sky bland and the sea dark, then dangerous. The ship was supposed to arrive in Bedam that afternoon. Instead, it moored at Roerte, a southern mainland town, with Captain Olym repeating apologies a dozen times over. "I can't risk this weather," she told her passengers, standing by the plank that led to the mainland. She was shaking in her drenched shirt but refused to get out of the rain until everyone left the ship. "The Gray Sea is too erratic. Listen: I know Roerte well. I can tell you how to travel to Bedam by land, or I can arrange a stay at an inn. We'll head out tomorrow morning if the weather's improved by then."

A thunderclap punctuated her words.

She didn't say the next part, but Amara saw it written on her face: *Damn the ministers to every last spirit-abandoned corner of this planet.* Storms never came on this suddenly by themselves.

Amara and Cilla made up the rear of the group, not wanting to risk the crush of people. They'd gone by another two islands before mooring here and had picked up at least twenty more passengers. "You two, please come with me," Captain Olym said when they stepped onto the plank. "I won't have you staying at an inn, Princess. I have a farm inland. You'll be my guests."

Within the hour Amara and Cilla were drying off by the crackle of a fireplace. In the dining room, Captain Olym and her father, who managed the farm in her absence, conversed in singsong Alinean.

Cilla was touching her lips where the mage had struck her. A small, healthy crust had formed, but it was in danger of falling off after getting soaked by the rain. The skin underneath might not have healed enough yet.

"I know, I know, I'm being careful," Cilla said on catching Amara's warning look. "It itches, though. I suppose you wouldn't know. Aren't we a pair?"

Amara smiled. As long as she kept smiling, the world couldn't crash down on her. Maart was dead, and she was in an unfamiliar house in an unfamiliar town, with strangers in the next room, yet she could use her signs openly. She hadn't heard Jorn's voice in hours. She wasn't working, and all of that made her feel jittery and so, so strange. She kept hovering between terror and elation and numbness, and she couldn't decide which was safer.

She studied Cilla's lip. "If I find my parents, where will you go?" Amara asked.

"I could find the original royal line on the Alinean Islands. If they know I'm alive, they may help me reclaim my throne."

Cilla knew as well as Amara did that that would never happen. The Alineans had surrendered their claim to the Dunelands years ago. Wars were bad for business. "The Islands are an ocean away," Amara said instead. "How would you survive a trip that long without me?"

No answer.

Amara hid a sigh as she squeezed her scarf and rubbed her wear dry as well as she could. She didn't want to undress in a place so visible. Cilla shouldn't, either. She'd already revealed her shoulders, which was more than royalty ever ought to do publicly.

"What's that noise?" Cilla asked. Amara stopped her movements to listen. The rain beat on the windows, and the wind tore at the unsheathed, tied-down sails of the mill outside, but Cilla couldn't mean that. Through all that noise came voices. Distant laughter.

Amara stepped toward the window. She felt exposed without her scarf, showing bony shoulders and wiry arms and that almost hidden tattoo underneath matted hair, but in this weather no one would be looking in.

Lights shone from a small house across the field.

"Servants," Amara told Cilla, who sat on the carpet and rubbed her toes dry. Their boots stood next to her, heating by the fire.

Sometimes ministers lent servants to help out farmers in need. That kept the farms running, the food production going, and the ministers earned a decent cut. Amara shouldn't have been surprised that Captain Olym had servants. She and her father alone could never handle a farm this size.

Amara stared at the flickering yellow of the servants' windows in a storm-darkened world. The laughter rang out through the rain. The servants were probably enjoying the reprieve from work the storm gave them. They'd be drinking or playing games or telling stories, as she'd seen the older servants at the palace do, or perhaps secretly improving their speech, as some servants managed.

Bedam was the nearest big city, so these servants must have come from there. Their tattoos would match hers. Would they remember her? Would they know Lorres, the caretaker? He'd always looked out for Amara.

She turned just as Cilla was gingerly feeling her cut lip again. Cilla would need protection once they parted ways. Finding other healing mages to help, trustworthy ones, seemed impossible. What Cilla needed was someone like Nolan, some- one to heal her before the curse even took hold.

Was that an option? Those pills of Nolan's had changed so much. If he could travel to another world to possess Amara, couldn't he possess someone else, too?

It would let Amara go free.

Amara pushed herself away from the window. Even if it were an option, it'd be too dangerous. Amara had been lucky to survive when Nolan's presence mixed with the spell at the harbor; combining it with Cilla's curse might kill Cilla in an instant.

Three steps into the room, Amara slowed, then stopped. One hand reached for the bed hatch next to her for support. The movement wasn't hers.

She hadn't felt Nolan take over—she never did. She no longer blacked out or slumped. His mind didn't creep in to shove hers aside. The world went on as usual, except suddenly her breaths seemed out of sync and her body moved in ways she hadn't approved. Invisible strings tugged at her, and she saw only the effects on a dangling puppet and its wooden limbs.

You promised! she shouted in her mind, knowing Nolan wouldn't hear.

He'd caught her thoughts. He must've stepped in at just the wrong moment.

"I'm sorry," Nolan said.

Cilla looked up at the movement. Nolan took two confident steps and crouched in front of her. The drenched carpet cooled Amara's knees. A spark from the fire landed on her hand, but Nolan shook it off. "Amara needs to know you'll be safe," he told Cilla. "How much risk are you willing to take?"

Amara wanted to scream.

Nolan explained Amara's thoughts and the risks involved. Cilla said nothing. Amara saw the same look on Cilla's face she'd seen on Jorn's, that way of scanning Amara for what lay underneath. Jorn had been trying to find Nolan. Cilla was looking for a sign of Amara.

"You and me, huh, Nolan?" Cilla finally said.

"I know you don't care for me—"

"Do it," she said. "Take over."

"Like I said, I don't know if I even can switch bodies. If it does work"—Amara's lips wrangled into a smile that felt nothing like her own—"you'll be the first to know."

He left her.

"Don't." Amara stumbled when her body returned to her,

then lunged toward Cilla. "There are other options. What if we can't find my parents? What if we find another mage? The one at the market—if she'd seen your mark, she would've believed you. We can find others! Ones who heal!"

"If this works," Cilla said, "you won't have to sacrifice yourself anymore. Sometimes . . . sometimes layering magic has only minimal effect. We might not notice anything."

Amara felt Cilla's stare on her lips, her eyebrows, just like before. Their faces were fingerwidths apart, close enough for Amara to taste the heat of Cilla's exhales and see a raindrop dangling from her earlobe. They'd toweled off their faces already; she must've missed a spot.

Cilla smiled wanly. "You two really are different."

Amara leaned back to sit on her haunches. "Don't let him do this. Tell him no. Nolan might listen if you change your mind."

"He shouldn't hijack you like that," Cilla said. "But I like the way his face looks on yours. He looks more relaxed in your body than you ever do."

No, no, why wasn't Cilla listening? If Nolan was trying to make this work right now, as they spoke, Cilla might only have seconds left before the spells mixed.

This could be the end of it.

"Now you look even less relaxed," Cilla remarked. Her voice sounded breathy. Not like her. Everything Cilla did, down to her jokes and laughs, were weighed down by something else. She cared about what she said and did even when she pretended not to. "I don't mean that I like seeing him in you. It's just nice to see Nolan be . . . what you could be." It was Cilla's turn to sit upright. She leaned in. Black hair hung in soaked strands along her cheeks. "I'd like seeing it on you far more."

"Tell him you've changed your mind." Amara's mind spun. Her knees dug into a soggy carpet she could never afford, and across from her Cilla was speaking nonsense, and she might die right now, or in two minutes or two hours or two days, whenever Nolan figured out how to switch bodies. Amara couldn't lose her, too. "Please."

She never said *please*. Even if a servant was allowed to make requests, there was no point.

"The truth is," Cilla said when Amara tried to smile, "I like seeing you no matter what."

And then Cilla's hand was on Amara's shoulder, and her lips on Amara's, and they were hot and full and Amara leaned in before she could stop herself. Her hands found and wrapped around Cilla's hips. She pressed herself closer.

This wasn't like kissing Maart. This was soft and desperate and something Amara had wanted so, so badly even when she'd hated herself for it. Her mind whispered *stop* and *wrong* and *Maart, Maart, Maart*. And *don't do it, Nolan, you can't, don't and let this work and all the pain she caused and you'll hate yourself and it won't last!*

But while it did . . . while the world spun beyond her reach, anyway . . . Their lips kissed and brushed and pulled and nibbled, and they squeezed each other so closely they heated up even the rain trapped between their bodies.

Cilla's tongue tickled her lips. Amara parted them to allow Cilla in. She'd never felt this, never once. Her hands held Cilla tighter. And she might be imagining it—might just be wishing—but Cilla tasted like the fennel seeds Captain Olym had given them to chew on.

Fennel and Cilla.

Amara no longer listened to any of her mind's whispers.

Except she must have, because when Cilla pulled away, Amara was crying. She didn't realize it until the sudden fresh air cooled the tear tracks on her skin.

Cilla touched Amara's cheek. "No," she said. Her hand slid to Amara's shoulder and clumsily gripped her arm. "No, no no no. Please tell me you didn't go along with—that you're not doing this just because I—"

Amara interrupted Cilla by kissing her again. Quick and hot and more.

Interrupting the princess was beyond disrespectful; that would have to be enough of an answer. Any moment Nolan would arrive, to save Cilla or kill her and free Amara either way, and all she wanted was Cilla's fiery, kissed-red lips. She wanted to taste Cilla's tongue. She wanted to taste Cilla's everything while she still could.

The crack of the opening door jolted them apart. They sat there, their breathing heavy, as Captain Olym came in to formally introduce her father.

Fire flickered yellow on the side of Cilla's face, the silk of her arms, the contours of her chest. It made her so damn beautiful that the pulsing of Cilla's tattoo in her center stung Amara all the more.

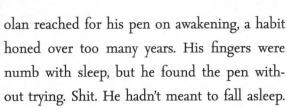

olan reached for his pen on awakening, a habit honed over too many years. His fingers were numb with sleep, but he found the pen without trying. Shit. He hadn't meant to fall asleep. He'd promised to warn Amara first. He'd just been so focused on taking over Cilla, trying, straining, and . . . And now it was close to noon already, and he'd forgotten to close the curtains, making his room sticky with heat. He'd have to plan better. Prevent himself from dozing off accidentally again.

He pushed himself up. His forehead practically stuck to his desk. He bet it'd left all sorts of marks on his skin.

He couldn't find his journal as easily as his pen.

It's not working, he wanted to write, but his pen tip floated in midair, scrawling the letters into nothing. He scanned his desk, then remembered Pat waking him up earlier. He'd knocked his journal off his desk. He rolled his chair back, but the floor was empty, too.

He remembered the notebook falling.

He remembered the damn notebook falling, but it wasn't on the floor, and when he kneeled to check under his bed, it wasn't there, either.

He burst into Pat's room. He knew where she hid her own journal, behind the drawers under her desk, but his wasn't there. He checked under her pillow. Her mattress. Where else? Closet?

Back in his room, he grabbed his cell. *Dont read it*, he texted her. *Pat pls just dont. Im sorry I told you ill explain.* A second text: *Im writing a damn book OK?*

He waited for five full minutes. No response. The cell's clock flashed a sixth minute, reminding him it was almost time for the lunch portion of his medication. He might as well take it now, before something else happened to suck him into the Dunelands and make him forget. He'd need to eat, too, but his appetite had gone missing with his journal.

After the last pill wedged itself down his throat, he paused, eying the carefully laid out evening dose on the corner of his desk. He'd only been able to control Amara after increasing his dosage. If he wanted to possess Cilla . . .

Nolan shouldn't have taken control of Amara the way he had at the fireplace. He'd felt Amara's loathing the second he retreated, and he knew he deserved every bit of it.

He'd just—he'd thought he'd found a way out.

Maybe he still had.

Nolan realized he'd made a mistake roughly around the time Pat came home. He'd cracked open a new journal to write in, snapped awake when he heard the front door unlock, and lurched off his chair. He'd meant to go downstairs to talk to her. He found himself stumbling against the desk, his stomach pounding left and right as if fighting to escape. His balance was shot. He groped his way along the wall. By the time he stepped into the bathroom, his arms gave in, and he slammed to the floor, hipbone landing against a cabinet. He muffled a cry.

He spent the next hour slumped by the toilet. He couldn't breathe right. His vision twisted and dove and climbed. He emptied his stomach and then just felt it spasm and push out painful spikes of air. He couldn't keep his thoughts straight, and he lay dazed, as if stuck in a dream.

Pat came up at one point. Knocked. Nolan managed to push out one word: "Nauseous."

"Should I call Mom?" she asked quietly. Nolan made a sound. He hoped she took it as a no.

Taking control of Cilla still didn't work. He should tell Amara that. He couldn't. Captain Olym had stuck close ever since the kiss, eager to play host to Princess Cilla.

"Sure is nice you can take action now, Nolan," he slurred in Spanish at one point. "Sure is nice. But maybe, just maybe, you should think first." His head lolled the other way. It gave him an excellent view of the toilet plumbing. He drifted into a haze, then woke without being sure he'd ever fallen asleep at all.

Only near dinnertime did he dare push himself up. His head still pounded. His hands shook. His stomach had calmed, though, and he could breathe again, and he vaguely remembered Mom coming home after the worst had passed and checking on him once or twice.

If Mom had seen him earlier, she'd have called Dr. Campbell or even Poison Control or 911. She'd probably have been right to.

"Occasionally, I am kind of an idiot," he murmured, in English again, and dragged himself up. A bruise pulsed on his elbow. With his foot, he nudged open the bathroom door, welcoming the fresh air. The sound of the vacuum cleaner and voices from the TV drifted upward—one of Pat's Michelle Rodriguez movies—and he sat for a minute, calmer now, his head clearer though no less painful.

After a while, Pat's hesitant voice came from downstairs: "Mom? Is he really OK?"

The vacuum cleaner went silent. "He's still getting used to the increased dosage. The side effects should wear off soon."

There was a minute of silence. "Who's Amara? Nolan said that name in his . . . his sleep."

"You should ask Nolan that."

"He's being a jerk about it."

Mom chuckled, sounding tired. "It's his dream. He's allowed."

"So it does mean something?" Pat pressed. "What about Cilla? Jorn? Maart?"

Nolan winced at the last name. Hearing anyone say it was

wrong. The dead couldn't rest if you kept calling on them. But hearing Pat say it, and all those other names, wasn't just wrong but bizarre beyond anything. Even the weirdness of Amara thinking or signing Nolan's name didn't compete. Everything in that world had long since moved past "bizarre"; this world was real life, or at least his crappy imitation. It'd been years since he'd heard Amara's name in his world except in his own whispers.

Pat didn't get the pronunciation right. The r needed to roll deeper in her throat, the a's needed to be more Spanish than English. Slowly, he climbed upright. He hopped to the sink for some water, steadying himself with a still-shaky hand.

"He said all that?" Mom said. "Chatty. I've never heard him talk in his sleep."

"Strange." Pat tried too hard to sound innocent. She hadn't nailed that part of acting yet. Nolan did a better job. No one suspected window dressing.

"Ask him about it, not me, all right?"

Nolan heard Pat thump back into the couch pillows. "I think he's having seizures again," she said then. "This morning it took, like, five minutes to wake him up. He was super weird after."

Mom sighed. "We'll talk to him."

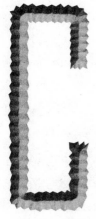

aptain Olym had six servants on the farm, and two of them prepared dinner: roasted duck and spiced patties of roots, carrots, and onions. The servants ate elsewhere. "She stays with me," Cilla had said about Amara.

"Ah," Olym said. "Of course. The others would notice the length of her hair."

"That, too," Cilla said.

As they wolfed down their evening meals, Amara couldn't keep her eyes off Cilla, for so many reasons: to stare at those fennel-tinged lips; because Nolan might still possess her at any moment; because the duck contained bones that might injure her. Amara should've checked. Jorn would've hit her for her negligence.

"You have a lovely farm," Cilla said eventually. "Do you have regular staff? I understand it's unusual to have servants in permanent employment outside of palaces."

The distant sound of the servants across the house buzzed in the background—laughter, the clinking of their plates. Which room were they in? Olym had started to escort Amara there before Cilla stopped her. *I need this one. I like this one. Forget the others.*

"It is. Well, it used to be. Consider it the ministers' approach to problem-solving." Olym smiled wryly.

Amara kept her eyes trained on her plate.

"I used to run the farm with my family and some farm-hands," Olym continued. "I had a partner, two children. My younger daughter is apprenticing with the millwright. My partner and older daughter died in a flood." Bitterness laced every word. "Three floods in ten years in Roerte alone. Two dune fires that lasted for days. And the ministers still claim it's not the fault of their magic."

"I'm sorry for your losses," Cilla said.

"And I for yours. I wouldn't have accepted the ministers' charity normally," Olym said, probably feeling the need to explain, "but after my workers left for Bedam to find a place on trading ships, and after the damage the third flood did to my farm . . .

"My partner came from a sailing family. His mother sold me a ship so I can at least support the farm financially. The work still needs to be done, though. My father helps, but the two of us aren't enough. Ruudde offered magic or servants as aid. Magic! I refused. It'd only cause more floods." Olym took another patty from the central dish.

"I understand." Cilla glanced at Amara with an apology in her eyes.

Acknowledging that look meant accepting or rejecting it, and Amara didn't want to do either. She continued to cut her patties into pieces, smaller and smaller, then mixing them into the sauce to make them easier to eat. She needed Maart here. He should sit beside her, his leg touching hers in understanding, his freckled cheeks scrunching up.

He would be so happy to know she'd run.

"The ministers force us all into situations we don't want to be in." Cilla's voice took on a harsh edge. "I hope to change what I can."

"Even their airtrains cause problems!" Olym said. "The numediks work well—the ministers are smart, I'll give them that—and at least the trains are non-magical, but they scare the wildlife. It's causing all sorts of trouble . . ."

She went into detail, discussing how the trains worked and how they affected deer and boar and undergrowth, beaming at every interested nod of Cilla's, and Amara ate stubbornly on.

The next morning, Olym expected Amara to attend to Cilla's bath while she and her servants worked to repair the storm's damage to the farm. Amara heated bathwater, crouching by lit coals with Cilla hovering over her.

"Do you want other help?" Amara pulled herself up by the tub. If Cilla finished quickly, Amara would have a chance to clean up, as well, before they returned to the ship.

Cilla eyed the tub as if steeling herself. "No. What I want is . . ." A short laugh escaped her. "Actually, I'm afraid to say what I want, because you might give it to me. Why are you pretending nothing happened?"

Amara hesitated. What was it Cilla refused to say she wanted? For Amara to treat Cilla as she'd treated Maart? She hunted for an answer Cilla would accept and ended up settling on, "I didn't kiss you because you wanted me to."

"Then why are you so damn distant?"

"Because what if I anger you?" Amara wanted to turn away, to keep her hands still, but they burst into movement. "I'm not your pet. I'm not different. I'm a servant like all those who don't get to sit at your table. And for a servant, kissing you is dangerous, talking to you is dangerous, and not doing either is dangerous, too. And seeing you unhappy? Like now? That terrifies me. Because it's my fault." She jabbed at herself with angry fingers. She ought to stop talking. She really ought to stop. "That means—that means if you're looking for someone to blame, or if you change your mind—"

"I'm not going to change my mind," Cilla insisted.

"But you could!" No turning back. Her hands moved too fast and jerkily. She was shouting. "You can't dangle an axe over someone's head and promise you won't drop it and then everything is fine!"

Cilla stood by the bathtub. She'd already dropped her topscarf. Her chest was heaving, her nostrils flaring. "I see. You're right." Her mouth opened and shut again. Her eyes gleamed. "I'm sorry about . . . did you want me to do anything about the servants?"

"It's just—you didn't even notice them."

Cilla nodded stiffly.

"I did want to kiss you," Amara said, suddenly deflated.

"But it's not that simple." Cilla echoed Amara's earlier words. "I'm sorry."

Amara's hands stayed by her sides.

"I'm trying." It looked as if Cilla would say more. Instead, she bowed her head and slowly pulled at her winterwear's lacing. Amara whirled toward the window before she saw anything she shouldn't. Her hearing was harder to tune out. Cilla's wear hit the ground with a flutter, and her feet went from padding on smooth tiles to hugging the fox skin by the tub. Next came the clear sloshing of the water.

Amara stared at the curtains in front of her and unwillingly imagined ample skin, muscles and flesh and spine forming glistening dips and creases. Amara wondered what Cilla's skin felt like in the water. If she would smile—cocky or pleased or self-conscious, because Amara loved all those smiles—if Amara turned and leaned in to kiss her again . . . This time, Cilla wouldn't taste like fennel. She'd taste like duck and spiced rootpatties and soapsuds.

Amara quietly shook her head, then pulled the window curtains aside a few fingerwidths to look out at the farm. Yesterday, all she'd seen of the servant house was a few squares of rain-diluted light. Now, in the clear dawn, she saw that the house was bigger than she'd thought, though one corner had sunk into the ground. Servants ran in and out, humming and gesturing animatedly. She should join them in their songs and their work; at least *that*, she knew. They were more her people than the girl in the bathtub behind her. She even recognized the tune two servants were humming, though she hadn't heard it in years.

And, yes, of course, Cilla was trying. Amara ought to be nicer. She ought to apologize. But she didn't know how much of that was what she *wanted* to do and how much of it was what she *should* do. When those two worked in unison, how could she trust herself?

She couldn't sort out what she'd felt for Cilla before, with Jorn's words in her ears and Maart's lips on her forehead, and she couldn't now, either. Not until Maart's death felt real, not in the midst of all this.

It had only been a day.

Amara almost turned when Cilla spoke again. "I know how you feel, you know."

Amara nailed her feet to the ground and studied the silos alongside the barn.

"It scares me just as much when you're angry at me," Cilla said. Water splashed. "It might mean that the next time some-one hits me, you'll stand by and watch. And I know standing by is exactly what I've always done, but I—I don't—" An audible swallow. "I don't want to die."

Amara knew she was right. With Jorn gone, Cilla relied on Amara more than the other way around. It didn't feel like it, though, not with Amara's bones and her mind and her *everything* still telling her that Cilla was in charge and not Amara. Like a stain she couldn't scrub clean.

"And no," Cilla went on, "I didn't kiss you because I rely on you. I kissed you because I *covet* you."

The hunger in her voice heated Amara's skin.

She was still contemplating an answer when her hands moved of their own accord. Nolan. "I didn't want to interrupt—I'm sorry. I didn't know when I'd find you alone again. Listen: N-UU-M-E-DD-I-K-S." Nolan made her spell. "That's not a Dit word, is it?"

Amara waited until he left her. "No," she said, almost relieved at the intrusion. "According to Captain Olym, it's a term the ministers coined to describe the air-pressure system for the airtrains."

"Listen: my language has the same word. P-N-EU-M-A-D-I-K-S. It's pronounced similarly, and it means exactly the same thing. Pressurized air."

Cilla's voice came sharply from behind Amara. "Is he back?"

Amara made a quarter turn so Cilla could see her hands and explanation, but she kept her eyes averted. Water spattered against the sides of the tub as Cilla moved. Amara smelled coals and flower-scented soap. "It's the same word?" she asked. "That can't be a coincidence."

It dawned on Amara at the same time Nolan signed. "I've been thinking about it all night. Numediks"—he had to spell it again; if a sign for the word existed, none of them knew it—"are a recent invention here, right? We knew the concept long before you did. Someone must've brought the technology here. If the ministers coined the term when they built the airtrains, at least one of them is like me. Either they're from your world and visited mine, or they're from my world and brought that knowledge to yours."

Of course Nolan couldn't be the only one.

"I think it's the latter, and I think it's more than just one minister," Nolan continued. "The Dit mage mentioned she'd heard of ministers inviting spirits in. She was wrong about my being a spirit. She might be wrong about them, too. If people like me traveled here, their healing could just be a side effect, nothing to do with the spirits at all."

When she could, Amara nodded slowly. With their healing, people like Nolan would be powerful no matter what, and the possibility of combining that healing with a minister's influence and a mage's magic might be too tempting for them to resist. That magic would be infinite: their healing meant they'd never need to recover from their spells.

"So it is possible to choose bodies?" Cilla asked.

"I don't know," Nolan said before Amara realized he'd

taken over again. "It must be. I need pills to control when I travel. If other people don't have that limitation, who knows what they could do?" He seemed to hesitate. "I thought you ought to know. I'll go now."

Amara flexed her hands, making her skin her own again.

"So what does this mean?" Cilla asked, hesitant.

Amara shut her eyes. She stank of old sweat, and the sun shone brightly as though yesterday's storm had never happened, and the servants hummed on and on as they worked. It made the day taste falsely of summer.

Did this change anything? Whose side were these ministers on?

"I don't know."

Overnight, several of the ship's passengers had chosen to travel by land, but Olym had picked up a handful of new ones in town. The sea didn't calm down until the afternoon, and they were halfway to Bedam when the storm returned so hard and suddenly that there was no chance of it being anything but backlash. Within minutes clouds crept into the sky; by the time the first passenger commented, Captain Olym was herding everyone but crew belowdecks.

*Stay here!* Amara told Nolan, and repeated it until she was sure he got the message.

Waves beat against the hull, splashed up the sides, pushed

in through cracks despite the storm covers over the side-scuttles—although maybe that wasn't the sea but the rain. There was no way to distinguish between them. Amara and Cilla crept into a corner away from the crowd. At least a dozen people huddled by tables and chairs in Captain Olym's sitting room, amid cabinets and gas lamps and that map of the Dunelands' islands against the wall. Amara noted every creak of wood, every time a passenger moved closer.

The companionway opened. They saw a tilted view of the world outside, dark as the night—then lit up with lightning so bright it left them blinded.

"Lights out!" Captain Olym shouted through the cries of the wind. "Backlash might affect them. Last thing we need now's a fire!" A wave rocked the ship sideways. Captain Olym grabbed the doorpost as her feet slipped over wood as slick as oil. Water spilled from the deck down the steps. She slammed the companionway shut.

They had just one crew member belowdecks, an Alinean boy maybe a year older than Amara, who was supposed to keep an eye on the passengers. He stumbled from one corner to the other to extinguish the lamps.

"At least we have enough water to put out a fire, right?" a passenger bellowed.

Nervous laughter broke off when something slammed into the aft wall. People jumped back as though waiting for the wall to burst.

"It's from inside the cargo cabin," the crew member said, an Alinean accent weaved into his words. "Nothing to be scared of."

Cilla crept closer to Amara. They kept cautious eyes on the wall and the passengers.

"Can we make it to shore?" an older woman asked. "Or will we wait it out?"

"That's—um—that's up to the captain."

Amara's eyes were getting used to the dark, allowing her to see the way the boy shot constant, nervous glances at the companionway.

"This is ridiculous!" a different woman said. She had to shout to be heard over the stomping of heavy boots on the deck above, endless sheets of rain, and cracks of thunder so loud Amara jumped every time. "First we have to wait all night and morning, and now this? I should've been in Bedam yesterday afternoon."

"The weather isn't Captain Olym's fault, ma'am." The crew member laughed thinly.

"You know whose fault it is? Mages!" the first, older woman sniped. Her voice turned soft. "Oh, but I'm sure you agree with me, dear. You Alineans are so sensible."

"Politics?" a new voice said. Male, high-pitched. "Let's not."

The older woman sniffed. "It's basic common sense, isn't it? The Alinean Islands are in the best shape they've ever been, and look at us!"

"And you know that because you've been there, yeah?" the high-pitched guy said.

"I have," the crew member said. Thunder rumbled, low and dangerous, and he steadied himself before continuing. "I was raised there."

"Really?" the older woman said. "I didn't think any Alineans were coming here anymore."

Cilla followed the conversation intently and kept so still, it was as though she thought any movement might disturb the ship. Amara reached out to take her fingers.

Cilla started. She looked at their linked hands. A slow smile tugged at her lips.

For a frozen moment between thunderclaps, Amara wished they could just have this. Hands and smiles and kisses, and never thinking beyond.

Without the lamps, the temperature dropped. The wind howled its way inside. The heat in Amara's hand felt good.

The crew member said, "And you're right: the Islands are in fantastic shape."

"How about we discuss something else?" the politics-averse voice from before said. "Let's talk nausea. I suspect that will be relevant very soon."

Laughter. The ship took a sharp swing sideways. Everyone's hands shot out for nearby table legs or lamp holders to steady themselves.

The older woman sniffed. "All the ministers' fault. And the rest of us suffer for it."

"You've gotta be kidding!" the high-pitched guy said. "My mill is doing better than it has in years! I've received personal assistance from the ministers—"

"—when my father's brewery was sabotaged last spring, Della himself came to help—"

"—in the form of magic. Laziness that screws over everyone else!" The crew member was getting into it now.

"So what's the death rate in Alinean hospitals, huh?" The miller scoffed. "Why'd you even come here if your islands are so—"

A deafening slam. The wall creaked and whined. A second slam—wood cracked—and something slid across the floor. The passengers collectively held their breath.

A crate slammed through from the cargo area on the other side of the wall. Cracked panels kept it in their grip, but the damage was done. A set of cabinets dangled from the aft wall by a single corner, unhinged from the blow. Every wave knocking into the ship sent the cabinets swinging left and right. The crate lurched its way into the cabin a bit at a time, loosening the surrounding wood.

Amara jumped to her feet, Cilla's hand still in hers. They ran for the other side of the cabin. Amara pulled Cilla closer. She needed to shield her. This ship, these people, the storm, and the wall—Cilla should never be in a place this dangerous. Never.

Cilla's hand slipped from hers.

Amara spun. The momentum threatened to knock her over, but one leg shot out, steadying herself just in time.

One cabinet flew past, finally knocked free, and smashed against the opposite wall. Amara shouted Cilla's name out loud. The name never worked coming from her mouth, just a mix of useless vowels.

"I'm fine!" Cilla called, and Amara spotted her ducked behind a table. Shards of the cabinet slid across the floor.

"Hurt?" Amara landed in a crouch beside her. At least there was enough light to see her hands.

"No! No, I dove out of the way. I'm fine."

Amara reached to pat her down, check for scrapes Cilla might not notice in the heat of the moment.

"Did you just . . . ?" someone said. Firm steps pounded the floor. Amara turned just in time to see the miller's face. A second later, callused fingers pulled her hair from her scarf. She scooted back. Too late. If he could see her signs, he could see her tattoo, and all she could do was—nothing.

"Amara!" Cilla shouted.

"Don't," Amara said. Too many people in this crowd were loyal to the ministers for Cilla to reveal herself again. Even those who weren't might still want to reap a reward for bringing the princess in. Amara's signs became more urgent. "I know you. Don't!"

"She's a palace servant," the miller said, astonished.

Amara could take her knife from her boot. Olym had given her a new one after she'd tossed out her own. With so many passengers, she might not be able to fight her way out, but she could try. She could slash the miller, make her way up those stairs, dive into the water, and . . . She couldn't tell where she'd end up. She couldn't abandon Cilla to the storm, either.

Amara let the miller drag her to where the other passengers were huddled. Amara's eyes stayed on Cilla. Her mouth formed the word her captured hands no longer could: Don't don't don't.

"Look at the tattoo," someone said. "That's Drudo palace."

"Ruudde, huh? I hear he's generous with rewards."

"How much would she be worth? What about the girl she's with? Check her neck."

"You're disgusting. I want nothing to do with this." The older woman backed away.

Cilla stood and shuffled along the swaying floor. The wall creaked with continued pressure from the crate. Careful, Amara thought.

"If you so much as touch me," Cilla said, "I'll have my grandmother pay you a personal visit. I assure you, you don't want that. Let my friend go."

She said it with so much conviction that even Amara almost believed this grandmother of hers existed, but the miller didn't look impressed. "Fine. You're not a servant, but you're still helping one. I bet Ruudde would love to know that, no matter who your grandmother is."

The crew member checked the companionway. "Let's not get worked up. She's a friend of the captain's."

"This matter goes way beyond this ship. They're criminals."

*What do I do?* Cilla mouthed.

The miller's grip on Amara's arm tightened, leaving her with no way of answering.

om's promised talk didn't come until dinner the next day. Nolan had been focused on three things: staring down Pat, who still hadn't talked to him; scarfing his meal as quickly as possible; and surreptitiously shutting his eyes for too long. Nolan didn't trust the miller—or any of the other passengers—not to hurt Amara. Judging by the way Mom and Dad looked at him, though, he'd failed at the "surreptitious" part.

"Are you feeling better, honey?" Mom asked.

It'd been over a day since he took the extra dose. The headache and drowsiness had stuck, and his eyes still had trouble adjusting. "Much!" he said.

Dad put down his fork. "Tell me the truth. You said the pills were working. Are they?"

"You saw me this week." Nolan smiled, but it was a nervous one. "Of course they work."

"You told us the seizures were gone."

"Well, some," Nolan said, backpedaling. "I mean, it's gonna be hard to stop them all."

"You walked out during that movie. Pat found you practically unconscious yesterday"—Pat ducked her head so her bangs hid her face as Dad said that—"and you spent the rest of the day in the bathroom. You're not even shaving. We called Dr. Campbell. She wants to see you."

"It's just side effects!"

"What your dad's saying is . . ." Mom took Nolan's hand, reminding him of Cilla and Amara belowdecks. He shouldn't be sitting here eating gross canned beans. He should be there, like Amara had asked. He checked back once every few blinks—

**—the last of the wood paneling finally gave way. The crate slid across the floor. The group shouted and scattered, and the crew member yelled, "Through here!"**

**Was Cilla injured? Amara couldn't see her, and she couldn't walk well with her hands tied like this, but surely Cilla would shout. Surely she'd let Amara know—**

"—that," Mom said. "That, right there, is what we mean."

Nolan blinked rapidly. "What? I'm sorry, I . . . I need to go to the bathroom."

"Right this second?" Dad said.

"Yes!" Nolan stumbled upright and turned—

**—Amara caught a glimpse of Cilla being herded into a cabin, patting herself down—**

"—it's all right." Mom took his hand a second time. "We know you want us not to worry."

"The pills are working." Nolan shook his head as if that would make the conversation go away. The way his parents alternated set his hairs on end. Had they rehearsed this intervention? Were they planning to cut off his pills? They couldn't—if he lost the pills—

"This isn't new, Nole," Dad said, finally switching to English. "You always pretend you're doing better than you really are. You skipped school yesterday without telling us."

"I went today."

"Because I drove you. And you left before lunch!"

Mom added, "Mrs. Hannigan said you spent half her class in the bathroom and the other half zoning out. You're hardly sleeping. If the pills work, we'll do anything to make sure you can keep them. You know that. But you shouldn't lie to us about how well you're doing. You're worse than before you started this medication."

"If you're not improving, we're taking you off it." Dad shook his head. "Even with my insurance, we can't afford it."

They weren't cutting him off. Not yet.

"They work," Nolan said. He swallowed. "I promise. They work. I'll do better."

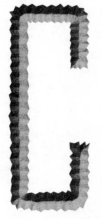aptain Olym did nothing to help Amara. After the storm, an apology flashed in her eyes, and that was that; if anything, she had to be relieved it wasn't Cilla who'd gotten caught. "Oh, please," she'd said to accusations of Cilla helping out Amara, "she's the daughter of a friend of mine, and she's under my protection. She's just a child. Are you really going to put her in front of a minister?"

"Give me one good reason why not," the miller said. He'd bound Amara's hands and found her dagger, which he'd pocketed with a smug smile.

No one met her eyes.

"This is my ship. I could lay claim to the servant as easily as you. Do you realize how tricky rewards get when challenged?" Olym crossed her arms. "Keep the servant, but the other girl stays in my quarters. Anyone care to change my mind?"

They spent the rest of the trip repairing the worst of the damage and treating injuries, including a crew member's broken arm. Throughout, Amara sat tied to a mast, slowly drying in the sun. At one point, the miller freed her hands to ask how long she'd been gone, where she'd been, and why she was dumb enough to go back to Bedam. The answers hovered on the tips of her fingers; the miller was entitled to know and to punish her if she refused to respond.

She spent the journey in silence.

The answer was yes. Yes, Lorres was still the Bedam caretaker.

In theory, the job of caretaker was open to anyone. In practice, caretakers were always barenecked former servants. After completing their service, they'd return to parents they no longer knew, a community they no longer understood, and worry about their friends back at the palace.

So they returned to become caretakers. Taking orders directly from the minister and palace manager, they organized the servant schedules, arranged their educations, acted as a go-between, and looked after them better than anyone else would—because they'd been there.

Lorres had terrified Amara at first. All she'd known of him were narrow fingers prying in her cheeks as he held open her mouth. That memory had faded when she'd gotten to know him—to like him, even. He'd been the only person to look after her.

Now, as he crossed the courtyard toward the gate where Amara, the miller, and the marshal who'd accompanied them from the harbor stood, it took a second for her to recognize him. A fat braid dangled all the way to the middle of his back; in her memory, he'd always worn his hair short. He walked tall, with his shoulders back and head up high, in a way that didn't match Amara's memories, either. He wasn't Elig—or any group she recognized—but she imagined him walking like one, newly arrived in the Dunelands, skulking around like he felt naked. That image fit her memories better.

Lorres opened the gate. "Amara" was the first thing he signed. She hadn't even had time to wonder if he'd remember her. He even knew the sign for her name. "You've been gone a while."

Amara could only nod.

"Would you look at that? She *can* communicate." The miller put his hand on her neck and pulled her hair aside. Amara flinched as he tapped her skin. "Look. I figured you might be interested in getting this one back."

"You'd be right. I expect you want to discuss a reward?"

Lorres switched to spoken words to address the miller, and the sound jarred Amara. He'd so rarely spoken aloud around her, she'd almost forgotten his voice. With practice, many servants could speak at least somewhat intelligibly, but it was forbidden during their service, and few were willing to risk punishment when their signs served them just as well.

It took the miller a moment to decipher Lorres's words. "I wouldn't be opposed." He sounded stiff. Some people were odd about barenecked servants. Instead of treating them with all possible respect, as was proper, they recoiled at the first hand sign or unclear word.

"Your friend can escort you." Lorres nodded at the marshal. "Meanwhile, I'll take this one inside. Would you mind untying her hands?"

The miller's lips pressed together thinly. He did as he was told.

"Thank you," Amara said as she followed Lorres. She rubbed her wrists, though any burns or scrapes from the rope had already healed. Inside the courtyard, she looked around. Too many marshals guarded the palace for her to risk an escape. She'd expected as much.

"No one should tie our hands. Ever." Lorres was back to signing. He shook his head. "I'm glad to see you're alive, Amara."

He didn't say he was glad to see her all right, or back. Her childhood affection for this man was validated in one swift sentence.

She felt stuck in a dream. Every step on the courtyard tiles was a step deeper into a world she knew, with something in the back of her head nagging at her that this isn't right. Things had changed. The gate looked new, she thought, or maybe just freshly polished. Those trees looked younger than they ought to. Maybe the old ones had finally given in and died. The palace itself looked wider. They'd added extra wings—she was sure of that from the discoloration of the stones and paint; at the same time, Amara herself had grown, and the courtyard that used to go on forever now seemed curiously small.

The palace itself wasn't as grand as in her memory, either.

The setting afternoon sun reflected off a million windows and intricate reliefs and colored the pale walls pink. Of the entrance arches, most were shut, leaving only the wide central arch open. Amara craned her neck to see the bell tower. The same silver windvane stood on top. Some of the older servants used to fight over who got to climb up to polish it. The view would be worth the risk. Few Dunelands buildings stood as tall as the palace. Heavy buildings were dangerous in such muddy earth. Fat poles hammered into the ground were all that kept the palace—and the rest of the city—from sinking.

Amara had always wanted to climb up herself, but she hadn't been old enough. Maybe she'd get the chance now.

She was back.

*Back,* her mind sang. *Back.*

She wanted to keep her attention on the gleam of Lorres's braid or on his freckles, but the people crossing the courtyard kept drawing her eye: employees carrying papers and escorting accused criminals, servants working on the yard and lighting the evening's lamps. Their tattoos and the way they signed to one another from afar were unmistakable, but she didn't see many of them. Servants avoided crossing the courtyard. They had their own passages. Amara knew where to look, though; there, one entrance behind the thicket and trees; there, between that stable and shed . . . She saw only flashes, people out one door and in another, carrying bags and jugs that contained food and drinks, cleaning supplies, clothes, repair tools, garbage.

Some servants didn't even reach her hips. Had there always been so many children? There couldn't have been. She remembered being lonely.

"They've done a lot of"—Lorres waffled over the right sign—"recruiting since you left." He must've caught her looking. "And some redecorating. Welcome to Drudo palace."

They passed one entrance and were about to enter another door, one framed by an elaborate arch. Amara halted. She remembered passing underneath that arch. A quiver would run over her skin every time. "Is there still a protective ward here?"

"You remembered. Ruudde had it removed, though."

"You're certain?" She didn't want to explain out here but couldn't take the risk. "I'm enchanted."

He looked surprised, but it didn't show in his signs. "I'm certain. We can take the servants' way in if you prefer, though."

Amara nodded. She remembered that, too; the door was just around the corner, almost indistinguishable from the walls.

She was back. The words repeated themselves over and over in her mind as they walked through the servant passage. Back in Bedam. Back in the palace. Back with Ruudde.

At least she might find answers now. With Cilla roaming Bedam unguarded, though, Amara had a hard time seeing the positives. And what about Amara herself? What would Ruudde do to her?

"Listen," Lorres signed, "I'm putting you in a cell for now. I'll be back to cut your hair. Then I'll alert Ruudde. Normally we wouldn't go so high up, but you've been gone for so long, I suspect he'd want to know." One corner of his lips tilted up. "Not many runaways manage to stay hidden for so long. Someday I'll ask you all about where you've been. And about that enchantment."

*Someday.* Lorres thought Amara was here to stay. That he could cut her hair and expose her tattoo, dress her in palace-issued clothes, and put her with the rest of the servants. She'd cook and clean and build new walls.

Maybe he was right.

"I will ask one thing: did Nicosce take you? You two disappeared at the same time."

"Don't make that sign," Amara said. "She is no longer that. She is the servant who came before . . . before . . ." She didn't know what to call either of them now.

"She's dead?"

Amara thought back to when they'd both worked at the palace. Those memories were blurry, pushed away by more recent memories of the servant teaching Amara about etiquette and cleaning and games, and of her feeding the horses Jorn once traded for. Horses. She'd always been good with horses. "The Alinean stable servant. Yes. She's dead."

"So you did run together." Lorres turned a corner, unlocked a door, and took them through it. The walls turned rougher, darker. Amara didn't recognize this area. It had to be one of the newer parts. Had the servant wing changed, too? Did the palace's main hall still have salt-crystal chandeliers, the finely drawn map of the Alinean Islands on the floor, the seas engraved on the walls? She hadn't thought she'd ever find out.

"Ruudde will have someone punish you. I'll tell him the stable servant took you when you were young, that you're not responsible. It may help." They exited the servant passage into a larger hallway, where the walls looked polished but stayed dark. Lorres stopped in front of a cell that was nothing but three walls and a pot in its center and steel bars too narrow to wedge through. She touched the bars. Cold. She didn't recognize this sort of cell. Another export from Nolan's world? "Not cheerful, I know. Ruudde had them built." Lorres fished a key from his sidesling, opened the door in the bars, and waited for Amara to step in.

"You need to let me go," she said.

He squeezed her shoulder, then pulled his hand back to talk. "I'm sorry. I am. Please don't make me force you inside."

"Do you know how I stayed hidden for so long? I was with a mage." She didn't let him reply. "You worked here before the coup. Do you remember the royal children, the princesses and prince?"

She shouldn't talk about this to someone working directly under a minister, but she saw no other options. While she was trapped here, Cilla was helpless.

Lorres's movements were deliberate. "Of course I remember the children. Amara, I need you to step inside."

"All these years, I've been guarding Princess Cilla." Amara stepped toward Lorres, away from the dank cell.

"Don't use that—"

"Cilla is alive, but she's in danger. She's cursed. She could die without me. You have to let me find her."

"We'll talk about this later," Lorres said with soothing gestures. He must figure she'd been taken from the palace young enough for someone to fill her head with all sorts of lies.

Amara slammed her bare elbow into the wall. "Look," she said as pain flared into the bone. Blood welled up while her skin repaired itself at the edges of the scrape. "This is how I can protect her. I'm a mage." The lie hurt, but the truth was too complicated, and she needed Lorres to listen.

He held her elbow to the light. He cursed. "Mages never select their own as servants."

"They made a mistake." Why was he lingering on this point instead of on Cilla? "Let me leave to find the princess. I have to."

"Amara . . . The younger princess died in the coup. The ministers killed her. They choked her in her bed."

"The ministers lied. Too many people would support Cilla if they knew she survived."

"I saw the princess's body. I burned it, after." Lorres watched her with dark, earnest eyes.

"No," Amara said. "You're wrong. Maybe they replaced her with another child . . ."

"I knew that girl from birth. She had the royal mark on her chest and a mole on her chin. I don't know what the stable servant or that mage you were with told you—I don't know who you think you know—but the younger princess is dead."

Amara's mind stuttered and reeled and ground to a halt.

"Well," a familiar voice said from behind Amara. Ruudde. "This is unfortunate."

Three people stood at the end of the cell wing. Ruudde was in the back, looking older than Amara remembered and draped with more gemstones than ever. A marshal led the group, a short Jélisse man who kept one hand on Cilla's neck and pushed her forward.

Cilla stared at Amara. Her eyes shone wetly. She'd seen their signs.

Cilla wasn't the princess.

29

**H**ow?" Cilla shouted. She gripped the bars of her cell. "Tell me *how*!"

"Maybe later," Ruudde said. "Lorres, thank you for your assistance. You can leave Amara to me. Gacco, keep an eye on the girl. Remember: a single drop of blood . . ."

Nolan stared through Amara's eyes at Cilla in that cell.

"Got it." Gacco adjusted his marshal helmet. Tufts of woolly hair spilled from underneath. He took a spot on the bench opposite Cilla's cell—

—they must've found Cilla at the harbor. Nolan wrote furiously in the new journal. Every word they said. Every name they mentioned. Every odd expression or look of surprise. He needed to stop himself from freaking out, and this was the only tried-and-true way he knew to do so.

So far, he'd confirmed two things: One, Ruudde hadn't wanted them to know the truth about Cilla. Two, Ruudde didn't want her harmed.

At least Cilla hadn't known she wasn't the princess. At least she hadn't lied to Amara. The how of faking the tattoo was easy. Control of the palace meant control of its mages and ink. But why?

Nolan chewed his pen until the plastic cracked—

"—Amara?" Ruudde jerked his head. "Come."

"I know you're working with Jorn!" Cilla shouted. "Tell me what's happening."

"Just keep yourself alive while I talk to your friends, all right?" *Friends.* Plural.

Ruudde gripped Amara's neck the same way Gacco had done to Cilla and shoved her down the hall. Amara saw a flash of Lorres, mid-sign, then he was gone. She tried to keep up with Ruudde's pace even as Cilla shouted behind them. Though not tall, he took firm steps, directing her around the corner of the cell block. In this wing, the floor tiles smoothed, and the walls turned light, like a whole other world.

Leaving Cilla behind.

With his free hand, Ruudde opened the door to a room—a bedroom, it looked like, with an open bed instead of one recessed into the wall. Luxury guest quarters. They hadn't been used in a while. Dust covered the windowsills, cobwebs dangled from the corners, and cocoons clung to the far wall.

Ruudde shut and locked the door. He pulled the storm cover over the window just as Amara was calculating the distance between her and the glass.

"Kid, if you're thinking of escaping—don't. I can heal faster than you, and you've never known the first thing about magic. So sit. Let's talk." Ruudde dropped onto the unmade guest bed and motioned at the single chair in the room.

Amara took a step toward it but made no attempt to sit. "Cilla isn't the princess," she said. Signing the words herself made them feel no more true.

The real Cilla had died in the coup, just as everyone thought. The Cilla Amara knew shouldn't even be using the name.

Which name, then?

"Nope. The girl you know is just a regular girl," Ruudde said. "And it's not you I want to talk to, Amara. Sit the hell down."

"You want to talk to . . ."

"To whoever's in there, yes." Ruudde looked flatly across the room. "You'll only irritate me if you keep me waiting."

Nolan felt Amara's hesitation, her questions; she wondered why he hadn't already taken over. Then she remembered—he wasn't supposed to unless she invited him. *It's all right*, she thought. The distaste that ran through her told Nolan it wasn't. At least not in any way that counted. *Do it.*

Taking over came more easily every time. He simply focused on moving, and Amara's mind faded out of reach.

Ruudde smiled, pleased. "I've waited so long to talk to you. What do I call you?"

"N-OO-L-U-N." He sat in the chair, sending a puff of dust billowing.

"Nolan," Ruudde repeated. He pronounced it correctly, even better than Cilla had. "Where are you from?"

"E-A-R-D," Nolan spelled. The unsurprised look on Ruudde's face confirmed Nolan's suspicions. If Ruudde wasn't from Earth himself, he knew someone who was. "Which world are *you* from?"

Ruudde cocked his head. A beaded lock of hair dropped from behind his ear to dangle by his face. "Apparently you kids know more than you've been letting on. Yes, I'm like you. I enjoy Ruudde's body, but it's not my own."

"Mages don't heal," Nolan said, something between a question and a statement. He itched for a pen to write all this down.

"Well, they *can*, given enough time and energy, but it most certainly causes backlash. For the likes of us, not so much, eh?"

"Are all ministers possessed? How can we travel like this?"

"How do mages receive their power? Spirits?" His tone was mocking. "We're born this way. I suppose we're just special." He propped his elbows onto his knees. "No, not all ministers are 'possessed,' but most are. The others don't have a clue. I found this body a long time ago. Ruudde was already the minister of the greater Bedam area—and a mage. I'd always wanted to try a mage. I already knew I healed every body I was in, but when I started doing heavy spells without paying any kind of physical toll, I realized the possibilities. I located other travelers and found mage bodies for them to use. You know the rest. You know we have power. Magical, political, financial. Name your price."

Nolan let the information sink in. If they could choose which people to possess, they had far more control than he did, medication or no medication. So what could they need him for?

"My price?"

"People want Cilla dead. You know that. And, no, those mages are not working for us. We want to keep Cilla alive—or the girl we call Cilla, anyway—but she's too easy a target if we keep her in a static location like the palace."

Nolan had already suspected the mages who chased Cilla and the possessed ministers weren't allied. But . . . "You were one of those mages to curse her. What changed?"

"Ahh. You think I cursed her, then changed my mind? Interesting theory."

Nolan didn't know what to make of Ruudde's amusement. He'd found Cilla so quickly that he must have been able to trace her. They'd removed all possible anchors; that left only the curse.

"Let's get back to my point: Cilla needs to stay on the run, and she needs to do it with a healer who will keep her safe. I don't know what made Amara come to Bedam, and I don't care. Make her return to Jorn. Bully her, take over permanently, do whatever you like. In return, name your price. Money. Mansions. Truly excellent food. Women, men, whatever the Jélis call those others. As long as you keep Cilla alive, we'll arrange it."

"I'm not taking Amara back to Jorn," Nolan said. "He tortured her."

"That bad?" Ruudde looked as if he genuinely regretted hearing it. "We told him not to . . . Look, we can fix that. He'll be harmless."

"I'm not taking over! It's *her* damn body."

"You seem to feel at home in it, though. It could be yours easily. How long's it been now?" Ruudde raised an eyebrow, then plucked at his topscarf, which was wrapped to dip at his chest and reveal a triangle of olive skin with a glowing tattoo in the center. "I've gotten used to being Ruudde over the years. Some of my colleagues even prefer their new bodies. You might find you like Amara's, too." He gazed at Nolan steadily. "Consider this alternative, Nolan: If you like Amara so much, we'll hurt her. We can hurt Cilla, too. You don't want to know all the things we can do without spilling blood."

The way Ruudde looked at Nolan didn't match his threats. He sounded interested. Open to suggestions.

Nolan tried to see beyond the body to the person in control, just as everyone had done to him and Amara. Ruudde—or whatever his real name was—had controlled this body for over a decade. Had its owner been stuck there all that time? He'd be nothing but trapped thoughts, watching his body paraded around. Executing people. Having sex. Abusing magic and wrecking his country.

And Ruudde wanted Nolan to lock Amara up the same way.

"If you don't cooperate, we'll make do. It'd be easier if you were on our side, though. I don't want to hurt anyone, but I've learned how. Don't make me, will you?"

Nolan shook his head fiercely to chase away Ruudde's words. "Why do you even want Cilla alive? Who are those mages who've been trying to kill her? The knifewielder? Why did Jorn lie about all this?"

"So many questions."

"Why lie about Cilla being the princess? At least tell me her real name."

"That was a neat trick, wasn't it? Great motivation for her to stay protected, out of sight, and *not ask questions*." Ruudde kicked off his boots and dragged his feet onto the bed, sitting cross-legged. "Think, Nolan. What'll it be?"

Nolan couldn't make Amara go back. Even if Jorn changed, she'd still need to distract the curse. She'd still have her every thought listened in on; she'd still be trapped.

Nolan would be trapped, too. Alongside Amara, he'd endure the same pain as before, and this time Jorn wouldn't give him permission to pull back to his own world and write through the hurt. Something might happen to Amara in those few seconds he was gone. Nolan wouldn't be able to bear *not* staying now that he knew, anyway.

Forget the pills; he wouldn't need them anymore.

He let his head dangle, staring at Amara's boots, torn and stained from the storm and seas. He saw her fingernails. They were finally growing back properly.

"She decides," Nolan said.

He drew back—

—and there, at his desk, he wrapped his arms around himself and tried not to vomit. The sun heated his room even through drawn curtains. Sweat sat at his hairline in tiny, hot beads. The air smelled musty.

He couldn't betray Amara. But which option betrayed her more? She had to decide—

—but she didn't.

Amara simply stood from her chair, and Nolan felt her fury fill every part of her. It pushed and pulsed at the edges until it threatened to spill.

"She's not in control, Nolan," Ruudde said. "How many mushrooms are you on? Anything Amara decides, you can overrule. Her, we can control. You're the wild card."

Amara stood mere footlengths in front of him, but Ruudde looked past her, at that boy in another world who ruined everything just by being.

Amara had thought of Cilla that way, once.

"I'll give you some time to consider my offer," Ruudde said. "Let's find a place to keep Amara."

mara got a cell just like Cilla's. They moved in a mattress, a pot, a privacy screen. They cut her hair to her ears in an uneven bob that left her neck cold and bare.

She was a servant.

They spoiled her, though. They escorted her to a bath and gave her clean clothes and brand-new horse-fuzz boots. She got a thick blanket and fresh meals. The servant who brought her lunch looked old, as if he should have been barenecked years ago. Was Ruudde keeping servants even as adults, like the Andans or some Elig clans did?

Of course he was. He had no reason to care about Alinean laws. About any of this world's laws.

Down the hall, Amara heard Cilla receiving the same treatment. For whatever reason, Ruudde wanted Cilla healthy and in one piece, but why spoil Amara? Maybe it was his way of showing good will. Of saying, *If you go back to Jorn, we'll treat you right.*

Only she didn't know if he was saying it to her or to Nolan.

Unlike Cilla, Amara wasn't kept under constant watch.

They'd probably have offered her the guest quarters if not for the risk of escape. As it was, they seemed moments away from gifting her a painting or two to brighten up her cell. They needed her. No, they needed Nolan. Amara was just—a vessel. Something to lug around and damage and repair and then damage all over again. If she broke beyond fixing, no problem. They could replace her.

It was a very convenient arrangement.

Sitting on her mattress after her first lunch, she took the privacy screen, tinted paper drawn over slats, and cracked one of the slats over her knee.

She turned her arm, exposing lighter, fragile skin. She slashed the wood across. It healed. She slashed again. She watched the skin pale, then split and redden, and watched it pull together and fix itself and leave nothing but blood and splinters coating intact skin. She slashed again.

*You can feel this, can't you?*

Slash. Heal.

*Does it hurt? Then go. Go away.*

Slash, heal.

*Your. Damn. Fault. Everything.*

Slash. Slash.

*Get out of my body!*

It didn't heal. She watched the cuts, her arm trembling. Her hand balled into a fist. It hurt. She hadn't realized before. The pain welled up, spread, burned, rooted deep under her skin. The cuts kept bleeding. A steady trickle. She wiped it away and more blood dripped out.

Good.

One day turned into three.

On the first day, the cuts healed within the hour. Amara didn't try again.

On the second day, Jorn arrived on the mainland. He passed her cell on his way to Cilla's and looked almost surprised to see Amara there. He said one thing and one thing only: "Nolan, is it? I tried to warn you."

Amara crawled onto the mattress and waited for Jorn to move out of sight so she could breathe normally again.

She couldn't go back to him.

Down the hall, she heard Jorn talking to Cilla. "Just eat. This helps no one."

On the third day, Ruudde stood in front of Amara's cell and said, "Cilla followed you from the harbor. Did you know that?"

Amara didn't respond.

"I thought she simply wanted your protection, but no. She keeps asking after you. Come."

Jorn already stood in front of Cilla's cell when Amara approached, and the Jélisse marshal—what'd his name been?

Gacco?—sat on the same bench as before. Amara had caught glimpses of him when she stood close enough to her bars and twisted her head just right. He rotated guard duties with a couple of other marshals.

On the other side of the bars, Cilla looked gray. She sat on her mattress, legs crossed and eyes closed. Amara's hands hovered uselessly in the air. She edged away from Jorn, though she had no illusions about Ruudde being any safer. She just couldn't stand being so close. Jorn's breathing was too deep, his skin too warm, his chest so broad she couldn't hide him from her peripheral vision, and when she looked at him, she saw freckles on a flat nose and thought of Maart.

"Amara's here," Jorn barked.

Cilla opened her eyes. The skin underneath them was swollen and dark.

"Your hair," was the first thing Cilla said.

Amara tugged at a lock by her ears. Her fingers ran through it too soon. "My neck is much colder," she signed.

Cilla's eyes dropped to rest on Amara's neck. Cilla had seen her tattoo a million times, but Amara still wanted to turn away or fluff up her topscarf. She felt naked.

"What do they want with me?" Cilla asked. Her voice came close to cracking.

"I don't know." Amara kept her signs low, though it wouldn't hide them from Ruudde or Jorn. "They won't tell me. They want Nolan to keep you alive."

"But first they want you to tell me to eat."

Amara looked at Cilla's soft wrists, at the fullness of her cheeks. She didn't look any thinner yet. Amara wondered how long that would last.

"They sent in Jorn first." Cilla sounded dreamy. "I almost listened to him, too. I guess it's hard to quit lifetime habits."

"You have to eat." It felt like a betrayal. Whatever Ruudde and Jorn wanted, she ought to want the opposite—but looking at Cilla like this, she had no choice.

"Do you know . . ."

"No." Amara swallowed. "I don't know who you are. I don't know why they need you."

"Maybe I'm just that pretty. Do you think that's it?" A hollow laugh.

"I don't want you to die."

"No one does, apparently. Big difference from before, isn't it?" Another laugh. "Maybe I'm not hungry."

"At the farm, you said you didn't want to die."

"I didn't," Cilla said quietly.

"We'll . . . Ruudde wants us to go back to how things were before. We'd have more freedom. We'd have the ministers' support. It'd be easier." Amara couldn't go back. But maybe— maybe if Cilla made the choice for her—

No. That wouldn't be right, either.

"First you run because of me," Cilla said, "then you want to go back because of me."

"I didn't run because of you." Amara wished it were just the two of them, talking like before, but Ruudde and Jorn watched their every movement. They stood close enough for her to smell the sweat on their clothes and hear their every breath, and she felt their eyes on her hands as she spoke. "You simply made my choice easier. I didn't want to leave, but I wanted to stay even less."

"Good." Cilla's smile wavered. "Look where it got us."

"Yeah."

They watched each other from across the length of the cell.

"Which do you want to do less now?" Cilla asked. "Go back? Or stay like this?"

Cilla didn't know about Ruudde's threats. Staying wasn't an option. Sooner or later, Nolan would cave, or Ruudde would run out of patience. "It's not that simple."

"Apparently it never is."

"Eat," Amara said. "I . . . I need you to eat."

Ruudde took her arm and led her back to her cell.

olan couldn't sleep. He couldn't go to school. His parents had been watching him, and he couldn't prove he was getting better, and soon . . . Nolan didn't think they'd fill the rest of the prescription. He'd heard them fight about it. Inside the house his parents usually talked in Spanish, with Dad throwing in what little Nahuatl he knew, and fights were no exception. This time they peppered their shouts with English words, which was how Nolan knew it was serious. They used whatever words came to mind.

Mom said Nolan was getting worse, not better, and that Grandma Pérez said they needed to be tougher on him. Dad said that unless Dr. Campbell agreed the pills were harmful, it was Nolan's opinion that mattered most—if he said he felt better, they couldn't force him to stop.

At the dining table on Friday, Nolan thought they'd agreed with each other. Apparently not.

"What's going on with you?" Pat stood in the doorway to his bedroom. Her eyes spat fire, but the rest of her seemed reserved. The way she used to be around him.

Nolan had been screwed up for most of Pat's life; he didn't

know when she'd first given up on him. He thought this might be the second time.

Pat held out his old notebook. "Explain. You're not writing a book."

"How would you know?" He put the notebook on his desk, next to the new one that lay open in front of him. He'd have to keep the last half of the old notebook empty; if he wrote anything new after already breaking in the other one, he'd mess up the order.

"You don't even *read*," Pat said. "And you would've told Mom and Dad. You know it'd make them happy."

"I'm not writing a book," he agreed.

Pat blinked as if she hadn't expected that answer. "I asked Mom and Dad who Amara and Maart and those others were. They wouldn't tell me."

"Don't—don't say that name." Nolan shook his head. "You know those hallucinations I used to have? Amara was in them."

"So that means you're still having those hallucinations?"

"Yes. That's it."

"But what about the part where you write about how all of a sudden you can change things because of the pills? And where you're talking about, oh, is this a hallucination or isn't it? Your doctors always said the way you acted wasn't right for seizures. And the pain? And walking off at dinner? Stop lying," she pleaded.

"Should I say it's real? You wouldn't believe that."

"No. You need to tell Mom and Dad you're still seeing things." She pointed at the notebook. "It's not healthy. And now you're acting like this and . . . in the journal you wrote . . . I'm worried, OK?"

"Do you think it's real?"

"Of course not." Her pointed finger went from the notebook to him, accusatory. "But I think you think it's real. Don't you?"

And just like that, tears burned in his eyes. His face flushed with heat. As if all of a sudden he couldn't breathe.

"Nolan, I didn't mean—"

He wiped his eyes with his sleeve. It didn't help. "I really—" he said, and gasped in a breath, "I really wish I didn't."

"Didn't believe it's real, you mean?" Pat sounded quieter.

On the Saturday Amara had scratched her arm in that cell, Nolan had shakily tried to make himself breakfast. He'd dropped a cheap jar of peanut butter when the wood tore Amara's skin. He'd screamed and squeezed his arm, whole and uninjured but hurting like hell.

He thought of Ruudde's threats.

"It would be a lot easier if it wasn't real," he whispered—

—and when he closed his eyes the moment Pat left his room, Ruudde was there, standing outside the cell's bars. His arms were crossed, obscuring part of his tattoo, which glowed so fiercely it pulsed.

"Oh, good," Ruudde said. "Talking to Amara can be so exhausting. Why do you bother going home, anyway? I always thought the moment you learned control, you'd either stay on Earth or claim Amara permanently."

If Nolan were in his own body, he'd narrow his eyes, clench his jaw.

Amara did it for him.

"Talk to me, kid."

Amara was waiting for Nolan to take over. She expected him to push her to the back of her mind and step forward. He supposed he deserved that. He'd taken over at the farm in Roerte. He did it whenever he went to sleep or woke up, to warn her, like he'd promised, and he felt her despair every time. He'd felt it two days ago, in the form of wood stabbing her arms.

"This world has magic. It could destroy us if we're not careful . . ." Ruudde extended his hands. Tiny lightning bolts twined between his fingers, creeping up his arms like electricity, and he kept them a fraction of an inch away from his skin, just barely touching, just barely safe. "But it's *magic*. From bedtime stories and fairy tales. What's so good in your own life that you refuse to accept this gift? We could time things better, if you want. If Amara sleeps while you're awake, you'll have both lives."

*It's all right,* Amara thought. *Answer him.*

"How did you keep Cilla alive right after she was cursed?" Nolan asked. He'd keep his movements to a minimum. In and out. The more Ruudde pushed him toward taking over, the less he wanted to. "You discovered Amara by accident, right? You must've seen her in the palace at some point and recognized my presence, or you saw her heal. When you realized she was still in control, not me, you had Jorn take us away.

"The thing is, to realize you needed Amara, you'd need to know about the curse, which meant it activated at least once before you found her. So how did you keep Cilla alive then? She was only a toddler. They injure easily. You either used magic to keep her alive—and you wouldn't have risked that—or you used your own healing."

Ruudde only watched him. Not a flicker of emotion.

"That's what happened, isn't it? One of you smeared her blood on yourself and endured whatever the curse threw at you, and you cowards decided, oh, *that's* not what you came to this world for! *Pain* wasn't part of the deal!"

His signs sped up. "So you find a little healing girl whose tongue you already cut and you hold her down and smear Cilla's blood on her instead, and when she's done screaming, you tell her that's what life will be like from now on."

Nolan lifted his chin. "Am I right?"

Ruudde smiled thinly. "Grow up, kid." He turned to walk away. As he went, he called, "You're running out of time."

Amara was getting used to people passing her cell. Marshals. Servants. Jorn. Ruudde. They glanced at her, checked on Cilla, and tried to talk sense into them both. Amara and Cilla kept their hands still and mouths shut as if waiting for something. Amara didn't know what, though, and suspected Cilla didn't, either.

She spent her days thinking of Maart, mostly.

When Lorres appeared outside her bars on the fourth day and said, "Let's take a walk," Amara allowed herself a flutter of hope. This might be what she'd been waiting for.

"Where?" she asked.

"Central Bedam."

A marshal tied her hand to Lorres's with rope that left barely enough leeway for them to sign. The marshal and a colleague stuck close as they left the palace, one leading, one following, and Amara's hope dimmed step-by-step. Lorres might be an ally, but that didn't mean he'd help her escape.

"I convinced Ruudde you needed some fresh air," Lorres said finally. "I'm worried about you."

They had to pass through a residential neighborhood to

get to the heart of Bedam. The neighborhood had changed since she'd last seen it. The stout houses on either side looked brand-new—the bricks red and white, the shutters deep green, the rooftops gleaming. Even the canal walls were smooth and unbroken. The road they walked on stood out in comparison, the stones cracked and the earth between them freshly stirred, as if the pavement had been hastily removed and put back in.

"Backlash?" Amara asked.

"Right in one. The repairs have been going on for months."

"Cilla needs fresh air, too, you know. More than me."

"The girl is . . ." Lorres hissed air through his teeth as he signed, but in a thoughtful way, not annoyed. "Ruudde wants her in that cell. No exceptions."

They walked in silence. The canals grew wider, the residences taller and more stately, like proper gentlemansions. The scent of canals and the occasional flash of open sewer where workers were still repairing the pavement mixed with that of fish, sharp and penetrating, as fishers carted their haul through town.

"You're not hungry, are you?" Lorres must've noticed her looking. "They're feeding you? They're looking after you?"

"They're treating me fine."

"If you want something to eat . . ." They passed stores closing for the night. A baker was folding his display table, the bread already inside, but he slowed when he saw them pass. Abruptly self-conscious, Amara lowered her hands. She wasn't used to signing in public. She was used to stepping briskly behind Jorn, her head down, her tattoo covered, her hands close.

The baker caught Lorres's eye. He smiled unconvincingly and gestured at his storefront.

"You want anything?" Lorres asked.

Amara shook her head.

"The respect would be better if they meant it, even a little." Lorres passed the baker with a kind nod.

Amara wondered what Maart would've felt when he was finally treated like a bareneck. Annoyed, probably. He always wanted to be left alone. *You and me*, he'd said, *away from them*.

She wished she could've gotten to know that Maart, without their tattoos pushing them together and wedging between them at the same time. She wished she could've gotten to love that Maart.

"They won't tell me what happened." Lorres walked with measured steps, with a certainty rare to servants. "Or what they want of you. Or what's going on with your friend."

"I could tell you what I know," she said, though she didn't think he'd believe her. She wouldn't have, either, if she hadn't seen her own hands dance in front of her. Then there were the marshals—they might not even let her explain. The one in front of them kept looking back, and now he'd stopped walking entirely, watching their conversation.

Lorres kept moving, head held high, ignoring the marshals.

He took a moment to grin appreciatively at a pair of Jélisse performers in a wagon play. "I'd rather you didn't explain. If they don't want me to know . . . well, they're my employers. I do as I'm bid."

Amara understood. Knowing what you weren't supposed to could be dangerous.

Lorres tossed a coin at the performers, although, judging by their costume dyes and their wagon's fine woodwork—had to be Alinean-crafted—they didn't look as if they needed it. They spun across the stage in billowing skirts, their hands outstretched and fingers perfectly pointed, lashing out, parrying blows, avoiding faux stabs with dives and flourishes. Amara took her eyes off them only when Lorres raised his hands again.

"Life at the palace has gotten tougher since you've been gone. I don't know why you're in that cell, but you're years from getting barenecked, and somehow they're not reinstating you as a servant. Do you know how many servants would gladly take your place? What Ruudde wants of you—how bad is it?"

"It's bad," she said quietly.

Lorres turned away from the wagon to face her properly. "Ruudde keeps his promises, and he makes good deals. He's helped me in a lot of ways, Amara."

"It's bad," she repeated.

"If you're a mage, they must want to employ you. Mages can demand respect."

Someone shoved past Amara, and she recoiled at the stench

of beer. "No," she said. "No, I can't, it's not—" A tiny stab of pain. Her unbound hand shot to the side of her head. In the corner of her eye she saw a stone—barely the size of a fingernail—bounce off the pavement and into the canal. Her hand came back from her head flecked with blood.

Across the canal, children laughed and broke into mocking songs. Servants stood out in a neighborhood as posh as this one, where the spiral patterns of waves and clouds in the pavement weren't painted on but were made of actual colored bricks. A shopkeeper stepped outside to reprimand the children, and they fled, their songs echoing in their wake.

Lorres gingerly touched Amara's scalp. "It's healed already," he said out loud, and pulled back. "That's amazing."

"Listen to me." Amara wiped her fingers clean of blood. "It's. Bad."

Lorres's eyes flitted to the marshals as if to check with them.

Amara stepped back. "Ruudde sent you to talk to me." She took another step back, until the rope binding their wrists bit at her skin. "You do as you're bid. Right?"

"Amara, I just don't want you to—"

All around them, the wagon play's audience burst into applause.

"At least when you pried open my mouth, I knew you were doing it on their orders. Take me back." She couldn't sign well with the rope pulled so taut. "I'll start to run. I'll dive into that canal right now. I know the marshals will catch me. I also know Ruudde won't be happy you let it come that far."

"See? Demanding respect already." Lorres smiled, but it wasn't a happy smile.

Amara wished there was even a trace of truth to those words.

"Let's go," Lorres said, and let her lead the way to her cell.

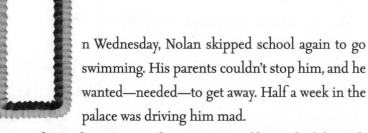

n Wednesday, Nolan skipped school again to go swimming. His parents couldn't stop him, and he wanted—needed—to get away. Half a week in the palace was driving him mad.

The pool was quiet in the morning, and he crashed through the water with even strokes. He stared through his goggles at the starting blocks. By his side, the steps leading out of the pool flashed past. The lifeguards and Dr. Campbell agreed: he had to stick by the pool's edge.

He tapped the wall, turned, kicked harder. They needed to know why the ministers needed Cilla alive. Nolan wanted to do something, move forward, to act now that he finally could—but if anyone could think this through, it should be him. Amara might be the planner, but Nolan had all the time in the world.

Could keeping a fake princess alive to kill her at a later time be a blow to the rebels' morale? No. Too much setup, not enough payoff, and what was the role of the mages tracking her?

Maybe, once the ministers were too old, they'd need some- one new to possess, and a fake princess could take over the

Dunelands without suspicion? No. Lots of ministers, just one girl, and they'd want mage bodies, besides.

Nolan needed to stop thinking about the princess aspect. Ruudde had said that'd only been a ruse to keep Cilla safe and hidden, for whatever reason, and maybe he'd told the truth.

Nolan wasn't used to thinking these things through without his notebook. He'd never been able to focus long enough. Now, despite the blinding lightness of the pool around him, all bleached blue and green, wet skin everywhere he looked, chlorine in his nose—yes, he could focus.

But it got him nowhere.

Start from scratch: if the ministers wanted to protect Cilla so badly, she had to be useful to them. (But how? She spent her days hiding in decrepit granaries.)

Look at it from the other side. Forget keeping her alive. What were the consequences to her death? If she died, the curse ended, and . . .

Nolan paused by the side of the pool. He clung to the edge with one hand. Maybe it wasn't just the curse that would end. There could be a second spell. If Ruudde hadn't been one of the mages to place the curse, and hadn't had an anchor to track—Amara and Cilla had gotten rid of all their clothes and possessions on Olym's boat—how had he found Cilla so quickly? He couldn't have known she was coming, and she would have stayed out of sight. Yet somehow, he'd found her within minutes.

If Ruudde and Jorn had cast a second spell, that could explain how they'd tracked her. It'd explain why they needed to keep her alive—to keep that other spell active. It'd explain why the knifewielder and other mages wanted her dead—not because she was the princess, but to end that other spell. It'd explain something else, too: Amara had always thought those mages had screwed up by casting a curse instead of a death spell. What if they hadn't? What if they'd tried a death spell, and it had mixed with an existing spell, diluting it, warping it?

That worked. All of it worked. Cilla might not matter beyond being a host for their spell. Nolan itched to get out of the pool, dry off, and find his journals, but he made himself slow down. He was still missing one thing. What the hell *was* that second spell?

He wiped some water from his face. At least he had a theory. He ought to tell Amara. He'd been checking in every few minutes—

—and now she was pressing her face to the bars. Cold metal chilled her cheeks. A marshal was running her way, a gaunt woman with skin like birch wood, one of the few Elig Amara had seen in the palace. Keys clattered against the woman's side.

"She hurt herself." The marshal fumbled to get the key into the lock. "You need to get in there—"

—someone's hand was on his shoulder. When Nolan turned, the lifeguard crouched nearby. "Are you all right?" she asked. Stray locks of hair drooped free from her ponytail. The lifeguards all knew about him. His seizures happened too often to take chances. "Do you need your crutches?"

"I'm good. Taking a breather." Nolan offered an automatic smile, but— "Wait. I do need my crutches. Please." While the lifeguard went to get them, Nolan pulled off his goggles and hoisted himself onto the edge—

—heard Cilla's breathing rasp in and out.

Amara bolted after the marshal into Cilla's cell. The walls swayed. Stones were shifting, reaching out. Cilla lay on the cot with her back to the bars. Her topscarf lay on the floor. It tangled under Amara's feet, and she landed by Cilla's mattress in a dive. She grabbed a bare shoulder and turned Cilla onto her back. The red caught her eye first: flecks on Cilla's nails, hands, a line that stretched across her chest. Her tattoo pulsed faintly on both sides of that line.

She'd scratched it open.

Cilla looked up with eyes that were red, too. "Don't," she pleaded—

—Nolan needed to hurry. He unfastened the flipper from his stump. The lifeguard was already there with his crutches, the anti-slip tips still attached. Bringing his prosthesis to the pool was useless; he'd only damage it, and hopping was dangerous as hell on these tiles.

He grabbed the crutches and swung his way to the changing rooms as fast as he could without risking a fall. People pretended not to stare, and he ignored them, because he only needed another second, just a little more—finally he thumped onto a private changing-room bench. His crutches slammed into the door. He buried himself in Amara's world and prayed he wasn't too late—

"—here! Pressure!" Amara kept her signs short and pressed her hands back to the wound to gather more blood, though it was already on her face and arms and even her throat. She had a good view of the wound now, and it wasn't just one scratch—she counted at least half a dozen in every direction, like the starry spikes that surrounded the volcano in Cilla's tattoo. Most of the scratches didn't go deeply enough to draw blood—Cilla's nails were too short for that. She must've gone over the scratch again and again and again.

Amara took Cilla's blood-stained hands, but Cilla shook her head, tried to pull them back. The marshal forced her still, and Amara smeared Cilla's bloody hands clean on the bed's blanket. She couldn't remove all the blood with the stones already eagerly scraping away from the walls or with Cilla fighting like this—and in the names of the dead, she shouldn't be *fighting*!—but she removed the worst of it. It'd have to be enough. *Oh, please, let it be enough.*

Amara wadded up the blanket. She shoved it at the marshal, who pressed it against Cilla's chest and held it there.

Footsteps rang down the hall.

Amara stumbled away from the bed. The smell of copper was in her nose and everywhere else. Normally, she didn't smear the blood on her face. Normally, Cilla's injuries were minor.

A ripple went through the wall. The stones shifted their attention—

—Nolan didn't want to see this. He wanted to feel it even less. His eyes opened with a start. He rolled from the bench before he realized it and grunted as his head hit the wall. The dressing room was well-lit, bright and yellow and safe.

He didn't want to go back—

—he went back and the floor was dragging Amara in. The stones crushed her body bloody and broke her bones and it took too long to end.

Nolan stayed for all of it; she'd heal faster if he did.

By the time the curse faded, Jorn and Gacco had arrived. Amara lay there, her chest rising and falling. Broken ribs stabbed her lungs. She felt them twist, gathering shattered pieces to mend. There were no pauses, no stutters. She healed the way she'd always thought a real mage ought to.

"What do we do with them?" the Elig marshal asked. From where Amara lay, curled up and facing the wall, she could just see everyone huddled near the mattress. The marshal still pressed the blanket to Cilla's chest. She was bloody, too. At first, Nolan thought the blood was Cilla's, but when Amara's gaze lingered, he realized the red lines standing out on the marshal's skin weren't smears but scratches. Cilla had fought her.

She'd given up now, though. Her head lay flat on the pillow, staring at Amara.

"I'm sorry." Cilla barely moved as she spoke. The marshal was still holding her down. "I didn't mean for . . . you weren't supposed to . . ."

"Keep the pressure on." Jorn stepped sideways, blocking Amara's view of Cilla. "How deep were the scratches?"

Amara's head lolled sideways. Watching took too much effort. She couldn't think through the pain. Her jaw repaired itself, bone grinding against bone. The noise echoed in her ears and skull.

Amara drifted out, leaving Nolan alone with the sound of gnashing bones. Injuries like these took a long time to heal, even now that he wasn't blinking back and forth. Vaguely, beyond Jorn's voice, he heard a familiar choked sound. Gacco. Throwing up in the hall.

*This isn't my body,* Nolan told himself. *This isn't my pain.*

It didn't make it hurt any less, but he repeated the words, anyway.

By the time Amara awoke, her bones had mended. Muscles shifted under her skin, following suit. She dragged her arm out from underneath her until both hands rested in the space between her drawn-up knees and head. Her hands were still bloody, the skin and veins damaged, but the tendons and muscles worked.

What was Amara doing? The pain scrambled her thoughts, making them hard for Nolan to pick out.

"Go away," she signed. "Healed enough go away."

Nolan had promised to leave when asked. But—right now, with her body still torn open? Was she thinking clearly?

"Plan," she said. "Go before too late. Plan." She rolled onto her back, letting her arm thump to the side. She wouldn't be able to sign anymore without the others noticing. Jorn and the Elig marshal faced away from her, but Jorn was looking back every now and then, and Gacco had returned as well, his skin a queasy shade of gray-brown.

Nolan drew back.

elp," Amara signed, hoping to catch Gacco's eye. From where she lay on the floor, she saw him slanted and upside down. "Left. He left."

Gacco frowned but didn't move.

Of course. Gacco wouldn't know about Nolan. Amara needed to think. Her mind felt full. Torn in every direction. "Stopped healing. Help," she repeated.

"Hey, Jorn?" Gacco said. "The girl says she stopped healing."

Jorn looked over his shoulder irritably, then back at Cilla, who lay motionless. Amara could just about see him think: *Nolan. That asshole.*

"I can put her in her cell and bring the doctor," Gacco said.

Amara worked up a shudder. She coughed. Blood shot into her mouth and sprayed onto the floor. Must've been left in her lungs. Her hand crept to her chest and pressed on her heart.

She was fine, at least on the inside. Jorn and the marshals only saw the outside, which looked bloody and bruised, with her skin torn and her wear unrecognizable as ever having been clothing. The outside looked as if she could die at any moment. She needed it to. Without the threat of death, Jorn might simply stick her in her cell and wait for Nolan to fix her.

Jorn cursed under his breath. "Take her to the doctor."

"Should I call another marshal to—"

"That'll take too long. She's harmless. Take her!"

Ruudde's voice echoed in Amara's mind: Her, we can control.

Gacco was by Amara's side in two steps. He crouched. One hand went under her knees, the other under her shoulders, the same way Jorn had carried her off the dunes and into the pub so long ago. Back then, she hadn't known Nolan was in control or that he was the one to heal her. She'd thought she was a mage. Maart had been alive. She hadn't run away. And, unlike now, she really had been dying. She'd been panicked and frightened and hurting like hell.

This time, she was angry.

She faked another spasm. She needed Gacco more worried about the possibility of her death than the possibility of her escape.

One thing the old Amara had in common with this one: she still hurt like hell. The injuries she'd asked Nolan to abandon stung and burned and ached. Pain shot through her with every step Gacco took.

Stay away, she thought. Stay away, stay away, stay away.

They arrived at the palace carecenter, which she recognized by scent alone. It lacked the freshness of flowers and polished wood of the rest of the palace. Instead, the room smelled of alcohol, sharp and clean.

Gacco placed her on a table in the center of the room. He was gentle—she'd give him that—supporting her head and adjusting her scarf to cover more of her arms. She looked past him at tables with gleaming bowls and tools. She tensed. She hadn't been here since she was a child, but she had no doubt: they were in the operating room. This was where Lorres had forced open her mouth, where a mage had looked into her eyes and cast a spell and then reached inside and cut her tongue. She'd tasted the blood but not the pain, and even the blood hadn't lasted long. The palace mages had performed that trick a hundred times.

The doctor stopped at her side, blocking her view of the tools. Amara didn't recognize the face that hovered over her. The woman was pretty, though. Older. Wide, green eyes. Jélis, like Gacco—she had the same frizzed hair and curved nose, and most doctors were Jélis, anyway. As the only people without mages, they'd had to find other ways of fixing their sick and injured.

"What in the names of the dead happened to her?" the doctor breathed.

"It . . ." Gacco must've been sworn to secrecy. "Mixed magic. She got banged up in the chaos."

"Mages." Her eyes rolled skyward. "I'll need your help. There, in the corner—light the fire to boil the water. Let me know when it's done."

Amara let her head drop sideways. She identified the exits. The door, the windows.

Before Amara had left to serve at the palace, the kids she'd grown up with had joked about being a servant. They'd sung songs and told horror stories about getting chosen. They held their tongues limp and talked the way they thought servants did. Their parents tsked them and said servants performed a vital duty and needed respect, then went on to ignore real servants on the streets the very same day.

So Amara had known what was coming when Lorres took her into this room. It'd smelled of alcohol even then. She'd looked past the people holding her down at the same windows she saw now. She'd dreamed of escape.

"I'll need to cut away the wear," the doctor muttered, more to herself than Amara. She took a nearby blade. Amara made her knee jerk. Her wear brushed over her injuries, and the next shiver and yelp weren't faked.

The doctor hovered over Amara and brushed aside her hair. "Hang in there. I have something for the pain." Her voice was gentle, lightly accented. She turned away.

Amara considered waiting. Numbing the pain sounded tempting. It might slow her down, though, and with both Gacco and the doctor turned away, this might be her only chance. One hand reached for the nearest table. Her fingers wrapped around the cold metal of a surgical blade. She swung her legs off the bed and landed with a thump that sent pain flaring. No time to linger. Don't look back at Gacco or the doctor. Run. Through the door. Pull it shut.

Run.

She faced the hallway along the side of the courtyard. A window stood open. She climbed through it and spun left. Bloody footprints trailed in her wake. No point in kicking off her boots, since her feet would be no better, but she couldn't afford to leave a trail. As she ran, she sidestepped onto the lawn. The grass might clean off the worst of the blood.

At least the pain seemed to fade with every step. She held the doctor's blade tightly enough to numb her fingers. It wasn't as heavy or familiar as her dagger, but she could still fight with it if necessary.

She heard shouts behind her—Gacco. The sound fired her up, pumping energy to her legs, her lungs. She bolted around the carecenter. She was near the edge of the palace grounds, but escape couldn't be that easy—not with the wall surrounding the grounds. She was in no state to climb quickly enough to escape unseen.

Avoid the wall. She turned left a second time, slipping into a servant passage. Going back indoors was a risk, but so was every choice she made. One evil or another. This hallway at least kept her out of sight. Besides, she'd lived in this palace for a year and dreamed about it for even longer. She thought she'd forgotten, but now, running past, she knew these doors, these halls, these stairs under her feet and these lamp holders on the walls.

People would expect her to go straight for the exit, or at

least stick to the lower floors. She fled into the main building instead. Her topscarf slipped off one shoulder and tangled behind her. Her boots no longer trailed blood, only puddles of mud. That left two problems: a potential anchor and being seen. She'd already passed a handful of servants who'd turned and gawked. Amara had meant to look near death to escape, but now that she had, her appearance worked against her. Nolan was welcome any time now.

She needed to lose the servants. She sped up more stairs and into another passageway that stretched past a dining hall. Memories rose. The hallway existed for servants to enter the dining hall through one of the doors, put down the food or claim the dishes, and disappear just as quickly. They only used the room for special events, so it'd be deserted right now. The hall itself only led to a kitchen and an office or two, so that'd be empty, too.

Except for Lorres, coming her way, holding papers to his chest. He did a double take and promptly dropped the stack. "What happened?" he signed, and bridged the distance in a few steps. He reached out, but stopped himself when Amara dashed back. "You need a doctor. I thought you could heal. How can you even walk like this?"

Could she outrun him? No. But she still had the blade.

"Did Ruudde do this?" Lorres winced as he looked her over.

She strengthened her grip on the blade. Lorres had lied to her. Claimed to be on her side and then . . .

She couldn't do it. She jammed the knife into her boot pocket and turned, stumbling, breaking into a run back the way she came. A shout trailed after her—her name. It came from far enough away that she dared glimpse over her shoulder. Lorres wasn't following.

"I'm sorry," he signed.

Amara slowed. She shouldn't. Gacco would've alerted the other marshals by now, and probably Ruudde and Jorn, as well. The palace would be crawling with people looking for her.

"You're running?" Lorres made no move to approach her. "You said it was bad. I . . . I didn't know it was this bad."

"Yes. I'm running," Amara said. This time the words didn't fill her with fear or uncertainty. Her signs came more decisively as she went on. "I'm running, or they'll do this to me a hundred more times."

"I can't help you find a way out. You know that. Ruudde considers hiring barenecks a risk as it is. If I don't do my job well, whoever he hires next might care about the money and nothing else."

She hadn't counted on help, anyway. "Are you going to stop me?" she asked.

"You must've passed servants on the way here. I'll slow them down." Lorres stepped sideways, allowing her room to flee past him. "Go. Run."

She did.

She ran through the kitchen and blasted out a door on the

other side. At the next intersection, she bent over and wiped a hand down her leg. Her teeth clenched as blood sprayed to the floor. Let them track her here. They'd think she went into one of these hallways.

Instead, she backtracked to the kitchen. Pans were stacked on one side, metal dishes and pots on the other. She crossed to the wide windows that allowed the cooks to vent the air, and she fingered the locks. They gave with no resistance.

Steeling herself, she opened the largest window and climbed onto the ledge. She'd done this sort of thing plenty of times when Jorn signaled her to get Cilla out, but never while injured, and never from a building this high. She was two stories up—and two stories for a building with ceilings as high as this meant three stories on any average building. Her eyes squeezed shut at the wind lashing her too-short hair around her head. Her balance suddenly felt frail. She clung to the wall, numb, and forced her eyes to open to slits.

She breathed deeply. Then she shut the window behind her, careful not to smudge the grease and dirt covering the glass. She hadn't gotten this far just to let fingerprints give her away.

Amara inched sideways on the ledge, concentrating on her steps and not the ground below. She passed the main kitchen window and edged past another one. A couple more steps. A little more. The ledge was slimming now, nothing but stones protruding a fingerwidth or three, but there, in front of her: a dirt-layered, web-covered statue of a merman in a niche. Only the front of his face and the tip of his tail stuck past the wall.

Amara pushed herself closer—there. She grabbed the merman's shoulder and reeled herself in, letting her lungs expel air she hadn't realized they'd been holding. She crept farther into the niche to hide behind the statue. Spiderwebs spread like netting across the merman's face. Shriveled cocoons clung to every cranny—in the corners of the walls, in the space between the statue's hair and neck, the dip between his arms.

Between the height and the recessed niche, she was out of sight while still having a view of the ground below. Carefully, she allowed herself to glance down. Gardens and herb nurseries used to cover this part of the palace grounds, but right now it was deserted, mud and grass and little else. The storms and floods must've hit hard.

Beyond the grounds lay the forest, yellow and red, and beyond that, the dunes and the Gray Sea. On the horizon was a sliver of land. She'd forgotten which island lay so close. Inland, she saw the thin line of the Beedde River and damaged dikes on each side, and more dunes in the distance, and she thought of Cilla—the way she'd shown Amara diggers, the smile on her face so hopeful the memory hurt. The fennel taste of her tongue. Those scratches down her chest, her marred tattoo, and her dark, dead eyes.

Amara couldn't abandon her in that cell, not even knowing her own name. She'd already been desperate enough to hurt herself once.

But Amara didn't know how to free her, and until Nolan came back, she wasn't in a position to try. As she waited, pain dripped steadily back in. Her energy faded, the heat in her veins cooling. Below, she saw two marshals pass, scanning the grounds and the perimeter wall. They didn't notice her. One marshal took a trained wolf into the forest. There had to be enough of Amara's blood left in Cilla's cell for it to have her scent; maybe the wind battering her into the wall was the only thing that kept the wolf from smelling her now.

She shivered in the cold. The air smelled of ocean and forest and old, moist stone. A bug crawled up her leg. She shook her foot to get rid of it, and her teeth clanged together from pain.

Nolan didn't take long to return. For the first time, she welcomed him. She exhaled slowly as Nolan unclotted her bruises, smoothed over the swellings, sewed up her skin. She let it happen and brought him up to speed.

*I'm going to jump, Amara thought. The trees are close enough to make a run for it. No one's expecting me to leave on this side, but if we wait too long, they'll have marshals all around the perimeter.*

*The moment I'm healed from the jump, you need to leave. I don't think Ruudde has a ward around the palace, but if he does, it'll react to you. Tell me you heard this. I have to know if—*

Her head nodded of its own volition.

A second later, her body was her own again. *Thank you*, she thought—finally, quietly—and jumped.

35

The second Nolan returned home from the pool, he retreated to his room and paced, swinging back and forth on his crutches. He rarely used his crutches inside, but he had to keep moving, and pacing didn't work as well when you had to hop.

Amara was running. And if she hadn't been able to reach Bedam safely even with long hair, intact clothes, and Cilla's help, there was no chance at all she could flee it without any of those things.

But Nolan had thought there was no chance of her escaping in the first place. He wasn't sure which surprised him more: that she'd done it or that she'd succeeded.

His door opened. Pat stood in the entrance. He should probably make some kind of irritated comment about her knocking, but—

"So," she said without preamble. "This is where you live. I still don't see the appeal."

Her voice was Pat's, and so was her body. The resemblance ended there. She stood too upright, with her legs spread too wide. He didn't recognize the look in her eyes. Her voice sounded different, flatter, with none of Pat's posturing. The accent didn't fit. He couldn't place it. Something between Pat and . . . something else.

She wasn't acting. This wasn't his sister.

Nolan sat on his bed. His crutches clattered to the ground.

Pat—Ruudde—went on. "You really are just a kid, aren't you? Look, I know it's hard to leave your life behind. I've been there. Your name, your family, gone. But you've seen what that other world can offer. The trade is worth it. And from what I can tell . . ." Ruudde scanned the bedroom skeptically. "You're not leaving all that much."

All of Ruudde's amiability was gone. Amara's escape must've pissed him off.

"You followed me," Nolan said.

Pat rolled her eyes and shoved the door shut. She crossed her arms in the exact same way Ruudde had in front of Amara's cell. "I did. And I didn't need pills to do it, either. If we see someone travel, we can piggyback along. We can hop into any body we see and remember it for later. You didn't know any of that, did you?" Ruudde grinned. "Pills. You're pathetic."

That was why Ruudde had stood in front of the cell the other day. He'd waited for Nolan to arrive so he could establish a link. To Pat.

"I tossed those pills, by the way, before I entered your room. Poof. Down the toilet."

Nolan had a few in his room, but that wouldn't be enough. He'd go back to before. In and out with every blink. No way of communicating. And his parents—how could he explain losing the pills he had left? They'd never purchase new ones now, even if they had the money.

"I wonder how long they'll take to wear off," Pat mused. "Withdrawal might be nasty."

It wasn't right seeing Pat like that, or hearing those words from her mouth. Full of scorn. She was trapped in there. And Nolan knew exactly what that was like. His voice shuddered. "Get out of my sister's body."

Pat's eyes dropped to Nolan's legs. "The boy with no leg and the girl with no tongue. Poetic." Nolan didn't even realize she'd said it in Spanish until she grinned at her own words, as if she'd discovered a new toy to play with.

"Get out of—"

"Ag, shut up. What are you going to do? Hit me?" She laughed. No, *he* laughed. This wasn't Pat. "I never wanted this. I thought if you took control, it would make things easier on both of us. I gave you so much time to think my offer through. And what did you do? You let her run.

"So I changed my mind. We had a good arrangement going with Amara before, and your pills screwed it up. I offered you everything, kid, and that didn't work. So no more excuses. Here's a deadline you can't wiggle out of: turn Amara's bony ass around while you still can. Then your pills will wear off, you'll go back to watching, Amara will go back to protecting Cilla, and everyone stays safe.

"If you don't get Amara back to the palace, I'll make these bodies, your parents and your sister"—Ruudde plucked at Pat's shirt—"kill themselves. Do you have any scissors handy? I can turn off the healing and show you."

"Get—out—of—her—" He couldn't say anything else. His brain screeched to a halt at anything past *he's in her body, he's going to kill her, get him out get him out get him out.*

This room used to be safe. Cramped and messy and hot enough to choke on, but safe.

Ruudde raised Pat's hands in a gesture of false surrender. "I'm going. Meanwhile, you should act smart for once. For fuck's sake. You make this so much harder than it needs to be."

Ruudde gave a last roll of Pat's eyes.

She collapsed to the floor.

36

Amara stole a basket and clothes from a servant house at a nearby dairy farm and dumped her own bloody rags in a pond. Checking the setting sun for directions, she trudged by the side of unpaved roads into the city, boots cracking the autumn leaves. By the time she reached Bedam proper, the chill had taken root in the tip of her nose and every bit of the hand clutching the basket. The skin of her fingers was bone yellow.

She swallowed the pain. Keeping her chin respectfully raised, she crossed slabs bridging narrow, foul-smelling canals, through alleyways, past a stand showcasing exotic Jélisse birds and felines, and stalls offering snacks from places Amara had never heard of. No one stopped her. Servants visited central Bedam for errands daily.

Finally, the harbor noise reached Amara. Shouts, seagulls, horns. The click-clack of cargo horses' hooves on cobblestones. Amara dawdled at the edge of the harbor. Ruudde would've forbidden detection spells to prevent further mixed-magic blowups, but the number of marshals had doubled since her arrival a few days ago.

From a safe distance, alternating hiding behind groups

of people, crates, and warehouses, she squinted at the crates stacked for loading. There were few at this late hour. Most of the crates were marked with their contents or destinations. Amara read the words slowly. Far too slowly. Standing still for that long put her so on edge that every seagull's squawk made her start.

She repeated Cilla's lessons in her head, piecing together slashes and dots until they became letters, then formed words. The biggest trading ships would sail to the Alinean Islands and Eligon, maybe even the Interterran Sea for the State of Jélis on the other side of the Continent, but the smaller ships couldn't go that far. Those had to have Dunelands destinations. None of the crates were labeled ROERTE, though some might stop there on the way. Amara waffled about taking the risk, then spotted another set of crates, already being lifted into a ship: TESCHEL WT WLLW, the letters said.

She hesitated. She'd hoped to find Captain Olym at her farm in Roerte, but the island Teschel might work, too. She could find the bartender who'd helped before.

She memorized the ship—a fluit like Olym's—and its location.

Then she found a quiet spot by the water a few minutes from the harbor and finally put down the basket she'd been clutching. She rapped numb, pale-skinned knuckles on the pavement. She checked for scrapes and saw nothing. Nolan was here. *Do you have time? I'll need you for several hours.*

The thought of cooperating didn't feel as dirty as it had before. Maybe it ought to, but without Nolan, she had no chance of saving Cilla—which she had to try, even if it still felt like a betrayal of Maart or herself or both. She couldn't leave Cilla to Ruudde, and she wouldn't beat herself up for that. The world was bad enough without her help. That one kiss in a storm-soaked world, for all its baggage, was the only good thing to happen to her in a long time.

She remembered what she'd told Cilla: I didn't want to leave. I wanted to stay even less.

The lesser of two evils. That was all Amara could hope for. It'd have to be enough.

Nolan took too long to answer. He was here, though, evidenced by her knuckles gleaming orange in the almost-gone sun, the skin fully healed. Finally, her hands spread out, his doing. "Ruudde visited my world," he said, with slow, deliberate signs. "He threatened my sister."

She stared. Seagulls wailed, circling the harbor.

So much for that flash of optimism. Nolan would abandon her. He would make her walk back to the palace and nod her head to whatever Ruudde said, and she couldn't even blame him for it. If Amara had a family, a way out of this mess, she'd take that chance, too.

The thought of returning to her old life still tore her apart.

"He took my pills. I can't give you long. Find out what you can." Nolan retreated.

Amara stayed in her crouch. She let his words sink in, breathing in cold, salty air and pushing it out again. Nolan was still on her side. He still thought they had a chance. But a chance of what?

She thought about what Nolan had said. *Find out what you can.* If Ruudde wanted Cilla safe so badly, Amara could at least use this limited time to find out *why*.

And that meant returning to Teschel.

Regretfully, Amara looked down at her winterwear and scarf. She couldn't seem to go long without ruining her clothes.

She dove into the water and swam for the ship.

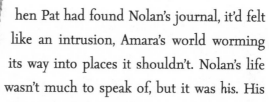

hen Pat had found Nolan's journal, it'd felt like an intrusion, Amara's world worming its way into places it shouldn't. Nolan's life wasn't much to speak of, but it was his. His parents, his sister, his journals, his pool.

This? This was nothing compared to Pat reading his journals.

The lines were crumbling.

Pat downed one glass of water, then another, and set the glass on the kitchen table with a bang. "What're you gonna do?" she asked. Her cheeks were still wet.

"Cross my fingers?" Nolan said feebly. "Amara has a plan. The last thing you read in the journal was—"

"They were escaping the island."

"They succeeded. Partially." He recapped what had happened—Roerte, the palace, Cilla's food strike and worse, Amara's escape. "Pat, I'm sorry. This was never supposed to happen."

"You can't go back to your old life. I knew your seizures sucked, but I—I never knew—I mean, that you had to deal with that kind of pain all the time."

"This wasn't supposed to happen," Nolan repeated.

"I—" She sucked in a rattly breath. "I'm not crying," she said, her voice muffled.

"I didn't say you were." Nolan wanted to offer her another glass of water, a hug, anything to make things better. He wanted to tear even the memory of Ruudde from her body.

"In the journal, you wrote . . . you said . . . 'fuck this life.'"

He'd heard Pat swear before, but in a way that was both off-hand and probing, like she was testing the word on her tongue and seeing if anyone would notice, or like Ruudde, spat in anger. Not like this. Quietly. As if she didn't want to say it at all.

"I didn't mean it," Nolan said. He didn't know if that was a lie. The next part wasn't: "I didn't mean you."

"Never mind. I get it." She didn't sound convinced. "But you can't go back. Not because of me. We'll tie me up or something. Ruudde can't hurt me then." She tried a smirk.

"That's not funny."

"You have some time, right? Before he . . . ?" She went for another sip of water, only to find the glass empty. She rolled her eyes, this time in a way so comfortably Pat instead of Ruudde, so much Farview, Arizona, and not Dunelands, that Nolan wanted to grab her and pull her in safely for the millionth time. He wanted to run.

But running would make no difference to Ruudde. Taking his deal was the smartest plan. The only plan. They'd go back to traveling alongside Jorn and find a way to stop it all from within.

"I'm trying to pretend it's a TV show," Pat said. She probably aimed for casual, but she sounded shaky. "Makes it easier to think about it all. 'Cause if this is real—whoa."

"Whoa," Nolan agreed. In more ways than one.

He'd always believed Amara wasn't a hallucination; he'd needed to in order to function. But on some level, in some corner in the back of his mind, he'd always wondered if his parents and neurologist weren't right. He was epileptic, had hallucinations, end of story.

Unless Pat sitting there all gray-faced and fake-smiling was a hallucination too, though, it was real. Everything Amara had been through—real. Every risk Amara still faced—real.

Ruudde's threat to his family—real.

And he was going to sit here and wait for Amara to risk her life to fix it?

He needed to stop improvising. He needed to think like Amara. He needed a plan. Nolan looked at Pat, determined. "You're a fast reader, right?"

"Look for any encounter with the mages trying to kill Cilla. I know that this book, and this one, I think"—Nolan handed Pat the right journals—"have them attacking. I need to know if they said anything useful. Aside from that, we need to collect physical descriptions. I know there's a tall Alinean woman who uses this hooked knife, an Elig man, and . . . we need all that on a list. Names would be even better."

Pat nodded. She still looked paler than she should. All his urgency probably didn't help her pretend-it's-a-TV-show strategy.

Nolan thought of the last time they'd sat on his bed together, watching a movie on the laptop, laughing at one actor's wooden expressions, trying to turn up the volume beyond what the tinny speakers could handle.

He'd hated that his own life had paled compared to Amara's. It still did. He'd barely even thought about Sarah Schneider's grin since Maart's death, or movies or Nahuatl or school, but this—Pat—Pat mattered.

He wanted a second chance to mock shitty actors with her.

And this might be his only way.

Nolan hadn't really expected to find anything in a journal so far back. Amara's first encounter with the mages trying to kill Cilla—with the knifewielder—had been weeks after she'd left the palace. He checked the book for thoroughness's sake, his fingers trailing over the words.

He'd been six at the time, so he could write, but not fast and not well. Dr. Campbell had been worried he wouldn't keep up with the journal if he had to do it himself, so he and Mom had spent ten minutes together before and after school and once in the evening, wherein he recounted what happened in his hallucinations. He remembered sitting at the kitchen table with his juice, shutting his eyes for seconds at a time so he could describe what he saw. Mom would ask questions: What are these people talking about? What do they look like? What do you think about that? What does Amara think? Are you scared? It's not real, honey. You're safe.

Nolan wondered how she'd felt, looking at her son sipping his drink and talking about a child getting hit in the face for dropping a dinner plate.

Once, Mom asked him to speak Dit. He'd been clunky. She'd looked relieved—at least until he'd raised his hands and formed the fluid motions of servant signs, nothing like what a child would make up.

There wasn't a mage attack in this notebook. Instead, in Mom's rapid cursive, it said: *The same man (Yorn?) who talked to Nolan about how quickly he healed yesterday is back and dragged N out of bed. Yorn cuts him again to see if he'll heal (yes)*

*N looks scared. Ask to describe man: he's Dit(?) and he's not very tall and*

*Dit?*

*N: means he has dark hair. curly and long, like this (elbow) He looks a bit like Dr Zhang from the hospital but only his face, Yorn is darker and really strong!*

Darker like N or like Dad?

N: Like me I think.

Yorn moves him to other bedroom. N didn't want anyone to know he heals. Scared.

Yorn talking to someone outside: minister Ruda(?). N says Amara is confused, waiting at door even though Y said to stay in chair. Scared. They'll punish him (N: "Amara") if they find out.

Yorn: I'm taking Amara. The stable girl, too. We can use them.

Min.: You know what to make of her? If she heals like that (. . .)

Yorn: Does it matter (. . .) And not using it's a waste, Naddi(?)

Min.: Ruda. I told you. Ruda.

Yorn: Come on. Even for . . .

Min.: Even for you. It's hard for all of us. OK?

(. . .) Yorn: Can't leave the girl alone this long. Not safe.

Nolan rarely reread old journals. Amara took up enough of his life already.

He'd skimmed this one as recently as two years ago, though. Nolan hadn't made much of the conversation. Jorn had kept working as a palace mage even after he'd smuggled Cilla to safety, so "borrowing" a healing servant and stable girl from Ruudde for a supposed routine job in central Bedam had been easy. Nolan had thought Ruudde's uncertainty referred to Amara's irregular healing, not Nolan's just-as-irregular presence. More importantly, he hadn't thought anything of Naddi. Amara might've misheard, Nolan might've misspoken, Mom might've misspelled; maybe Ruudde and Jorn had a history and it was an in-joke, a term of endearment, a Continent word Amara wasn't familiar with.

His fingers lingered on the name. *Naddi*. It must be the name of the traveler possessing Ruudde. The traveler must be from Earth. He'd known how to pronounce Nolan's name, and he'd looked utterly unimpressed in Pat's body. This world was familiar to him.

Naddi wasn't a Western name, probably, but Google didn't help Nolan narrow it down. Mom had transliterated the name with a double D, but what if it was *Natty*? It could be short for a dozen things. *Nadi*? Was it a first name, last name? Shortened? Too many options. Nolan had no gender, no location, nothing.

He needed more.

38

Amara spent the night huddled behind the harbor mill in Teschel. She awoke with a chill deep in her bones. With clumsy hands, she pulled off her topscarf, then rewrapped it around her head and neck, mimicking what she'd seen on Jélisse girls. She needed to keep her tattoo hidden. If there were servants on these islands, they worked on farms and had no business wandering around town. She checked her reflection in a stained window, tucked some hair back, and strode toward the boardwalk. There was no market today, which made the street look twice as wide as when she'd been hunting the stalls for a glimpse of the Dit mage.

Still mulling over the information Nolan had shared that night—*Naddi? Two spells on Cilla?*—Amara walked forcefully, though every odd look people gave her made her breathing pause. She stood out too much, but she couldn't slow down. People might recognize her. Between being carried into a bar covered in blood and getting chased by marshals in the harbor only days later, she must've left an impression.

The sweet scents of sugared batter poffs drifted through

the street and made her stomach ache. She pretended not to hear the operator of a lavishly decorated street organ calling at her, or the rattling of his money can, going straight for the market center instead. The last time Amara had seen the pub, she'd been upside down and half dead. She had no idea how to recognize it. She knew the market center, though; from there, Jorn had carried her to the boardwalk, through the market stalls . . . She found the pub on the corner of an alleyway and almost broke into a run in her relief. She yanked at the door. Locked. Teeth gritting, she cupped her hands to see through the glass. Inside, all was black. Not the black of dark furnishings and no light—the black of char, of burned tables and crumbling chairs. The fire hadn't gotten far. The counter was mostly intact, as were the windows, which had even been cleaned.

She knew one thing, though. The pub wouldn't be opening anytime soon.

"Are you looking for Edo?" a voice asked. "The owner?"

Amara turned with a thumping heart. The woman wasn't familiar. Dit, elderly. Slowly, Amara nodded. She repeated the name to herself. Edo.

The woman motioned toward the boardwalk, at a weatherbeaten pub sign extending over the street. "Find him there. Went from serving beer to downing it." She laughed. "That's what you get, huh? I swear, if he didn't have friends in high places, the marshals would've done more than just torch this place. Alinean bastards."

Edo had helped Amara twice. Of course the marshals couldn't let that slide. And now she dared ask for more help?

She nodded a second time, then took off toward the other pub. Good thing she was Elig. People expected them to be quiet. Quiet and frail and distant.

But good at surviving.

Amara found Edo sitting at the bar. He stiffened when he saw her, then slid off his stool and left his drink untouched. "Let's head out, eh?" he said. His breath stank of beer.

They walked to a quiet spot in the dunes where she could sign unnoticed. There were no diggers on the beach this late, just bugs, spiders, terns, sandpipers, and other shorebirds she didn't recognize, scouring the sand with long beaks. Dune grass tickled Amara's hands. It felt almost soft, nothing like the razor grass from before, but she still felt the hairs on her arms prick upright.

"What happened to the princess?" Edo asked urgently.

*She died. As a toddler. Smothered to death.*

"Ruudde has her at the palace. I escaped." Amara paused. "I'm sorry for what happened to your pub."

If Cilla's capture shocked him, he didn't show it. "I knew the risks. What can I do?"

"I need to find mages. Ones not allied with the ministers."

"That's a good number of them. The ministers don't exactly

abide by their oaths." He glowered. "I think I know exactly who you're looking for. She's not far."

Amara crushed a fistful of dune grass. "When can I meet her?"

That afternoon, Amara sat at Edo's dining table and gawked at the woman across from her. Thin braids. Rings in one nostril.

"You're alive," Amara signed.

The Dit mage fingered an odd-looking bracelet. Occasionally, she looked around the room as if admiring the wall drapes or sculptures, but mostly she just seemed to avoid Amara's eyes. "About what happened at the market—I thought I was protecting the princess! I'd never have touched her if I'd known she was telling the truth. Do you understand? You do, don't you?"

"I assumed Jorn—J-O-R-N—had killed you."

"Jorn? Is that the mage who attacked me at the market? No, no, even mages can't get away with killing each other that easily." She seemed to relax now that she saw that Amara didn't plan to push her about the slap. "I got away, but the next day, the marshals tried to arrest me. The ministers or that Jorn must've set them on me. I've been in hiding since then. Edo's been helping me. When he explained what'd happened at his pub, I realized that your friend really was the . . . was Cilla." The mage took pride in that word. Amara tried hard not to avert her eyes at the sting of guilt she felt over making the woman say a dead toddler's name.

The mage prattled on. "I was quite surprised to notice marshals were after me, because mostly they let us mages handle things on our own, you know, but—oh, of course you know. You're a mage yourself. And an escaped servant, to boot. I didn't say it at the market, but that was very brave of you. These ministers, they don't respect the notion behind Alinean servants . . ."

She went on for too long, talking too quickly, and Amara got the odd feeling she was being buttered up. Was this what associating with a princess was like?

The moment there was a pause in the mage's speech, Amara jumped in to sign, "Do you have many contacts? Mages have been working together to kill Cilla. I need to find them."

"Princess Cilla," Edo corrected, returning from his kitchen. He offered them each a small cup of tea.

"Aside from the ministers themselves, who would want to kill her?" Amara went on.

"Certainly not mages! Most us have a deep respect for the Alinean monarchy, you know. Their take on oaths is particularly—well, of course, there are exceptions among even Alinean mages, but . . ."

"These people are definitely mages. I've counted at least a dozen. They cursed Princess Cilla as a toddler and have been tracking her ever since the coup." Amara saw no sign of recognition in the mage's face. Would it help if she explained that Cilla wasn't the princess at all? No—she couldn't risk losing the mage and Edo's help. "I have descriptions, if it helps, and names. Only three." Nolan had overheard the mages shouting at one another years ago. Amara didn't even remember the incident. "One Dit man, short. Shorter than me. His name sounds like K-IE-R-S-T."

The mage sounded out the name and shook her head. "No, no. I can ask around, though."

Amara tried the next name. Chire. It sounded Alinean, though she couldn't be sure, and it didn't matter—the mage shook her head a second time.

Amara hesitated before the final name. "Alinean," she said, "a woman. Tall. Thin. She carries a hooked blade. I-L-A-NN-E."

The mage's face lit up. "Yes! I've heard of Ilanne—here's the sign for her name, by the way. She's near Bedam. Not many Alinean mages are willing to use their magic so freely, you know. She's, ah, one of those exceptions I mentioned. Sometimes I wonder what her oath said, 'cause it's nothing like mine, I can assure you."

Amara swallowed. The image of the knifewielder—no, Ilanne—lanced through her, as it had so often. She didn't want to ask this next question. "Can you help me find her?"

"Anything to help one so dedicated to serving."

I'm not serving, Amara wanted to shout. It's not about that.

"Thank you." She took her teacup in both hands, a good

excuse not to speak further and to banish the image of Ilanne from her mind.

"We need more servants like you. You know, wanting to do the spirits' bidding, put the Alineans back on the throne." The mage winked. "But we've already talked about you and spirits, of course. Did your spirit ever come back?"

Amara sipped her tea, ignoring the question. "The signs of possession you saw in me . . . Did you see those in any of the ministers?"

"Yes, in one, but that was a long time ago. It's probably gone." The mage's brow furrowed. "My mentor said Ruudde has acted as a vessel, too, if you can believe it."

"What about other possessions?" If there were other travelers like Nolan—ones not possessing the ministers—they might give her more information. Having more healers on her side might even help her stop Naddi.

"Oh, I don't know. My mentor rarely spoke to people while their spirit was present, sadly, but the stories they told afterward . . ." The woman's smile stretched as if she was recalling a particularly fond memory. "The spirits touched them with the gift of life. They healed in the snap of a finger. Some of them even communicated—beyond just through the roar of the sea or the spinning of the winds . . ." There was that wistful look again. "The spirits want to try a mortal life, you see. If they're going to help us, they wish to know what it's like to be us."

Amara mentally repeated the words, wading through the

talk of spirits to reach the core truth of the travelers. By now, she doubted spirits used vessels at all—these possessions the mage talked about must all be people like Nolan. "Can I talk to a vessel?"

The mage fingered the handle of her teacup. "I'm not sure where any of them are now. Aside from Ruudde, my mentor hasn't met any vessels since the Alineans held the throne. What we suspect, see"—she leaned in conspiratorially—"is that when the ministers took over, their abuse of magic made the spirits wary. It would explain why the spirits rarely use us as vessels anymore. That's why I wanted to talk to you so badly at the airtrain." She smiled ruefully. "How long did you pull the spirit in for, anyway? Hopefully not so long that it scared you. Some of those people who approached my mentor—they were adults, see, educated adults, and they were petrified afterward."

"How long did it last for them?" Amara frowned. If Ruudde was to be believed, Nolan had the least control of any traveler he knew, and he'd stayed in her body for years without even wanting to.

"The shortest took only minutes. Others, for weeks or even months at a time. Sometimes they left in the middle of conversations. The spirits are, shall we say, fickle."

"And those possessions stopped after the coup?" Amara's signs came slowly.

"As far as I know, yes. We talked to other mages about it, and I'm sure they'd have let us know if they encountered new vessels, but of course . . ." She went off on another tangent, this time about how mages kept in touch, and how often, and the internal politics of it. Throughout, Amara sat numbly in her chair, her fingers hooked in her teacup. Her eyes were on Edo's orange wall drapes.

Before the coup, travelers stuck around for anywhere between minutes and months, sometimes leaving unceremoniously. Why would any traveler leave in the middle of a conversation?

They'd had no control. They came and went randomly.

They couldn't have chosen which body they used, either, because Ruudde—Naddi—had talked of this world and its magic with fire in his eyes. He'd said he'd always wanted to try a mage body.

So why hadn't he found one sooner?

Before the coup: no control.

After the coup: control. The possessions stopped. The travelers chose mage bodies and stayed in them for years.

Something had happened around the time of the coup. Something had changed, giving the travelers control. Something . . . unnatural. Naddi had gone randomly from host to host, and the second he'd landed in Ruudde's mage body, he'd *made* himself and the others stay in their new bodies, using his newfound magic to anchor them to his world . . .

Anchor.

He'd created an *anchor*.

They enchanted someone to be a tracking anchor, letting the travelers continually find their preferred bodies in this world—or a more literal anchor, keeping them rooted to the same place—

Amara didn't even hear the mage's voice anymore. She still stared at Edo's drapes, at images of a volcano erupting and swirling, steaming seas, until her eyes felt so dry she had to remind herself to blink. Nolan was right. Cilla did have two spells on her. That was why she was so special. That was how Ruudde could track her. That was why the ministers needed her safe at all costs. The second she died, the extra spell would end and snap them free from their borrowed bodies.

The spell must've affected Nolan, too. A traveler so weak shouldn't be able to stick around so long. Without Cilla's spell, Nolan might never have traveled here in the first place.

Amara discarded the theories that didn't fit, probed at the ones that might. Of course Ilanne and the other mages would want to kill Cilla, eliminate the anchor. They'd hate travelers more than anything. Controlling their kin, abusing their magic, invading their world.

So the ministers had needed to protect Cilla. They found a palace mage loyal to them, Jorn, and sent him out with the anchor and a pair of servants, armed with lies of princesses and vengeful ministers . . .

Amara sipped her tea. It scalded her tongue and tasted of red carrots and kalisse or fennel. She ordered her thoughts, going slowly.

Why would Jorn help the ministers? He couldn't be a traveler himself. He didn't heal, and, as Nolan had pointed out, travelers were in the Dunelands for money, power, magic. They wouldn't want to spend their lives running around the Dunelands babysitting a fake princess and disciplining her servants.

The ministers might've threatened Jorn's family just like Nolan's. Jorn had an easy way out, though. Letting Cilla die would've gotten rid of the travelers in a second. Perhaps . . . Amara didn't know.

She did know, now more than ever, that she needed to talk to the mages who'd cursed Cilla. If those mages wanted the travelers gone, then they and Amara were on the same side.

"Thank you," Amara said. When Edo and the Dit mage stared at her blankly, she realized she must've interrupted them. Servants were never supposed to interrupt their betters.

She pretended not to notice.

"I need to speak to Ilanne. You said she was in Bedam. Can she meet me near the Bedam palace as soon as possible?"

"The Drudo palace, you mean?" the mage mocked. Then she laughed. "I'll send a message."

rudo.

Naddi and Drudo.

Nolan had spent the night looking through the last of his journals, passing on whatever info he found to Amara. It wasn't much, and nothing like the info she'd passed him. Nolan's mind spun with the thought of Cilla being the only thing keeping him and the other travelers in the Dunelands. If Cilla died, the problem was solved—but that wasn't an option.

Ilanne and Amara would have to find another way.

And they'd have to find it before his pills ran out. He'd decided to lower his doses, stretch the effects for as long as he could, but he already felt odd, warm and restless.

He flicked on an extra light in his room and Googled "Natalie Drudo" coma.

No hits. Nothing without the coma part, either.

Nolan tried Nadir, Nadia, Nadeem, Natalia, Natanie, Nat, Natal, Nate, Nathaniel, Nathan, Natasha, Nadine, going back pages and pages for each search before realizing—of course. The Dit language didn't use separate d and t letters at all. It just used the d everywhere and pronounced it more sharply when it came at the end of a word, like Maart. The people of the Dunelands might be mispronouncing the palace's name en masse based on the spelling.

"Nadir Trudo" coma.

"Nadine Druto" coma.

"Nathan Truto" coma. Then: "Nadia Trudo" coma

Google returned a question. Did you mean: "Nadia Trudeau" coma

The first page to come up when Nolan clicked the link almost made him spit out his third can of imitation Coke.

### TRUDEAU CHARITY FUND
#### Help us keep Nadi alive!

The text accompanied a photo of a twentysomething couple, the man cradling a baby. The woman smiled excitedly at the camera. The photo looked old. Something about the colors made Nolan think it was a scan of a paper photo, not a digital one.

Over ten years ago, our beloved daughter,
sister, and mother, Nadia Trudeau, fell into a
deep coma in her house in Cape Town. Her brain
remains active to this day; doctors all across SA
could find no cause or brain damage and say
she might wake up at any moment.

They told us not to get our hopes up.
How can we not?

Another photo, a portrait, came next. Nadia looked sternly into the camera. She had dark skin, a tall forehead, a mole on one cheek. Wrinkles around her mouth. She looked average, like one of Nolan's teachers or a classmate's mom.

We can no longer afford the medical bills
to keep her on life support. Please help us
fight to keep our Nadi alive. Please give her
a chance to meet her granddaughter.

The website went on for three screens of backstory, accomplishments, photos, memories, EEG scans. Every member of the family told their story. They'd even embedded a YouTube video of Nadi's son and husband recalling memories, and a clip of her newly born granddaughter in Nadi's husband's arms. Schmaltzy music played in the background. The website hadn't been updated in two years, so by now, that baby could probably walk and talk.

Nadi had left behind every person on this website to rule over a world none of them had even heard of. *The trade is worth it,* she'd said. Power did scary things to people. Alinean lore was filled with cautionary tales of mages who let their magic go to their heads and suffered the consequences.

Nolan scrolled to the top of the website and studied the text again. The page didn't say which hospital Nadi was staying in, but he guessed it was close to her family. Cape Town, SA. South Africa. He didn't think it mattered. Even if Nadi had been in the United States, then what? Maybe he could've found a way to sneak into whatever care facility or private home she stayed at. He'd smother her with a pillow, the same way she'd smothered a three-year-old girl in that palace so long ago. He'd shove scissors into her stomach as she'd threatened to do to Pat.

The thoughts nauseated him enough to roll his chair away from the desk and put his head in his hands, which smelled faintly of soap and the ramen noodles he'd brought up to his room earlier. He'd spilled some of the spices.

He tried to hold on to his line of thought. If the choice came down to Nadi or Pat, to Nadi or Amara, Nadi or Cilla . . . Nolan would kill Nadi no matter how much the idea sickened him.

Maybe not. He hoped not. At least he wouldn't find out. Nadi was halfway across the world.

He didn't know which options that left.

"I can't eat breakfast," Pat said.

"Big night coming up, huh?" Nolan asked. The play debuted that evening. He'd almost forgotten.

"I guess. What's your excuse?" Pat flicked on his light and leaned in his doorway, a pose Nolan had gotten used to by now. She was herself again. No trace of Nadi. It'd been a day since her threat—how much longer did they have? "You didn't sleep, did you?"

"Not a bit." The light hurt his eyes, and he grimaced, chugging down his fifth fake Coke.

"Seemed like a good idea?" she said, mimicking the way he'd been saying that lately. Thank God, she could still joke. "You, uh, want to talk about what's going on?"

He considered it. "No. Thanks. How about you? Want to talk about butterflies in your stomach?" Or *about Nadi?*

"Let's not." Pause. "They're more like steamrollers. Oh, man. What if I mess up? There'll be over a hundred people there. A hundred! I've never been in front of that many people before."

"You played that sunflower when you were five."

She laughed. A pang shot through him. Pat seemed so . . . normal. Had she recovered from Nadi's possession so quickly? Or was she just a better actress than either of them knew? "Yeah," Pat said. "I remembered all my lines, too. Go, me. Are you coming to the play?"

"I probably shouldn't. I'm sorry. I want to, but I need to stay with Amara. If I keep closing my eyes during the play . . ."

"Mom would smack you upside the head."

"Yup." Silence fell between them. It wasn't a bad kind of silence. Not a comfortable one, either.

"What's gonna happen to you?" Pat asked. "If . . . things don't work out?"

It was the sort of silence inevitably broken by something awkward.

Nolan rolled his soda can between his hands. Right now, Amara was on the ship back to Bedam, where she'd meet Ilanne. Who knew what'd happen after that? "That's a very good question."

"Is it gonna get an answer?"

He looked up with a tired smile. "You want to rehearse that ER scene one last time?"

"Nah. I'm ready."

Nolan thought back to the last time they'd practiced. With two timelines to account for, it seemed a lot longer ago than it should. "I think so, too."

40

You want us to save the anchor?" Ilanne said. "Give me one reason."

"None of this is her fault," Amara said. "She's been lied to all her life. About everything."

Ilanne leaned against an airtrain stop in Bedam. The sky was slowly lightening at the horizon, but the sun hadn't peeked over the edge yet. A couple of seagulls stood on a nearby stretch of grass, stomping the earth to draw out their morning meal.

Amara had found Ilanne quickly, and Ilanne had confirmed her theories, but none of that mattered if Ilanne wouldn't help. And looking at her now—the sharpness of her face, the slouch of her skinny limbs—she could see the woman wasn't impressed by Amara's answer. She wasn't impressed by anything.

Amara felt the opposite. Every few seconds, her eyes fluttered over Ilanne's clothes, and she wondered where she kept that knife of hers.

We're on the same side, she told herself. After all those childhood nightmares: We're on the same side.

Ilanne went on. "Nor is it the fault of all the people who've died in hurricanes, floods, earthslides, volcanic eruptions . . ."

"We don't even have volcanoes in the Dunelands."

"You think the backlash is restricted to here? Every storm or shake affects the rest of the planet, too. And there's an easy fix."

"I won't help you kill her," Amara said.

"Of course not." Ilanne radiated disgust. "You're one of them. How do you like that body? I don't see why you'd go for a servant. Maybe you just like little Elig girls. Is that it?"

"This is my body!"

"Prove it. I can see your little guest in there right now. Have him take a walk."

"Why? So you can kill me as soon as I stop healing?"

They stood there, fists balled and glaring. In the silence, dawnflies sang their high whistle. Finally, even though all of her screamed to either attack or run, Amara relented. "Listen," she said, "we don't have time for this. They might hurt Cill—"

Ilanne's hands gripped Amara's so hard they hurt. "Don't use that name. You know it's not hers."

Amara tore her hands free. "It's the only one I know."

"Don't call the dead. Ever."

Amara rubbed her wrists where Ilanne had grabbed her. The skin burned. Her jaw set. "Nadi"—Amara had come up with a sign for Nadi's name earlier, one similar to Nolan's sign—"might hurt her. She might hurt my 'guest's' family, too."

"Why should I care?"

"Because we want the same thing. We need the travelers

gone. Right now, we have Nolan's cooperation, but if we take too long . . ." Amara left it there. She didn't want to think about being responsible for Nolan's family, whoever and wherever they were. Once his control ran out, his family was as good as dead. Until then, he could panic at any moment and send Amara running back to the palace without a plan, without a goal beyond *keep my sister alive.*

"And what do you expect us to do?"

"Us?" Amara signed an echo.

"I called other mages the moment I heard your supposed princess was at the palace."

"You won't make it inside without me—"

"We can try. Then we'll kill the anchor and cast a spell to block travelers for good, and our problems are solved."

"Listen!" Amara glared. She wasn't supposed to glare at her betters, not ever. She was supposed to sit meekly and nod when she ought to and follow when she ought to and do everything to please the betters around her.

Even now, part of her told her that. She hated that part of her. And she hated the world for putting it in her. She didn't want to have to wait her turn anymore.

"I'm returning to the palace." Amara kept her signs measured, quick. She had to get through these words without letting Ilanne intimidate her into backing down. "Jorn will make us go on the run again, which means you'll have easier access to Ci—to the girl you cursed. If you give me a tracking anchor and follow us, I'll give you a chance to see the girl away from Jorn. Then you'll do some mage thing to find out who cast the anchor spell—the spell that lets the travelers stay here. We can kill that person instead of her. We'll end the spell that way."

"Whoever cast that anchor spell was possessed by a traveler at the time and is no more guilty than the girl. I'm not going to sacrifice one of mine so your little friend can live."

"And I'm not going to sacrifice her. We could"—Amara bit her lip as she spoke, staring at the seagulls on the grass—"we could make the traveler who cast the anchor spell leave their body. Then, while the mage is back in control, they can reverse the anchor spell."

"And how do you plan to get rid of the traveler?"

Amara went silent. If Nadi had cast the spell, maybe they could trick her into returning to Nolan's world. Nadi would make sure Ruudde's body was guarded during her absence, though.

Ilanne went on. "After this fiasco, I expect the ministers will want the anchor out of the Dunelands. The farther away you and the anchor are from us—from anyone who knows the truth about the travelers and might help you—the safer the travelers are. How do you plan to give us a heads-up when you're sleeping in ancient Dit caves?"

Amara wanted to argue, but Ilanne was right. The ministers would take extra safety precautions now that Amara knew about Cilla.

"And if we put a tracking anchor on you," Ilanne said, not satisfied with dismissing the plan when she could shred it completely, "what makes you think the ministers won't detect and toss it? I won't mix magic by putting it on you instead of your clothes."

"You mixed magic when you cursed Cil—the girl," Amara said. "You're lucky that—"

"Lucky?" Ilanne spat. "The spell only worked on the third try, and even then it was watered down to that useless curse. She should've died on the spot. We lost two mages from the recoil of the first try and another one on the next. We barely stabilized the magic when it went haywire—then spent weeks cleaning up after the backlash. Don't you dare call it luck."

Amara couldn't give up. "I'm offering my help. Any help at all. But only if the anchor lives."

Ilanne watched Amara through thoughtful, narrowed eyes. She answered a long moment later. "You said Nolan could locate Nadi's true body. If we identify which mage cast the anchor spell, can he find that traveler's body, too? Nolan could threaten it in his world."

Amara hesitated. Can you? she thought at Nolan.

In front of her, Ilanne stood tall, wiry-thin, as imposing as she'd ever been. Amara fought the impulse to step back. The last thing she wanted now was to surrender what little control she'd gained. Being away from Cilla and Jorn for so long—longer than ever before—made her feel freer.

It also terrified her. She didn't know what to expect from the rest of the world.

Finally, Nolan returned, saying, "I got lucky finding Nadi, and then only after I got lucky discovering her name. If we can find this mage's true name, and they live in my world, we may stand a shot, but . . ."

"Can you cast a spell to find their body?" Ilanne asked. "This kind of magic ought to be detectable."

"No. We don't have magic in our world."

"Of course you do. You're a traveler. You *are* magic."

"My world doesn't work that way. But I'll do what I can. I— please help. I'm risking my sister's life. Please." Amara barely recognized the desperation in her fingers. No one cared about a servant's pleas. She could only give in or fight harder.

But all Nolan's concern for his family bled into the pleading of Amara's hands. It'd taken her so long to realize he even had a family. A life. What was it like? What was Nolan like? They'd never talked, not really. It had always been this: Nolan would speak. Amara would wait her turn.

She wished they could talk face-to-face instead of this, instead of watching from behind glass as Nolan tried to convince Ilanne this was a risk worth taking.

With a pang, Amara wasn't even sure it was.

Killing Cilla would be the end of it. There would be no more curse to endure. Nolan would stay out of her mind; Amara's body would be her own. The travelers would fade, too, leaving long-possessed mages back in control. The magic abuse would end. All of it would. And Amara needed it to end so damn badly. She no longer wanted anyone to have a hold on her.

But she couldn't kill Cilla.

When Nolan left her, Amara almost didn't realize it. Not until Ilanne said, "This is the only way I can get your help?" and Nolan didn't answer for several long seconds.

It was Amara's turn to decide. She nodded stonily.

"All right. Get me into the palace. I'll need at least a minute with the girl to identify the spell-caster."

"We'll need . . ." Amara thought. The dawnflies sang louder. When Amara glanced up, she realized the sound wasn't dawn-flies at all: it came from the branches drooping over her head, where a dewy spiderweb spanned the length of her arm. In its center, a spider stroked a single thread with alternating legs, drawing in dawnflies using their own steady whistle.

The airtrain approached, hissing and gliding, tuning out the spider's lure and bringing along the scent of rusted metal. Affronted, the seagulls took to the air.

"We need a distraction," Amara finally said. "Two. When are the other mages coming?"

The way out was not to plead. The way out was to fight.

41

**M**om and Dad didn't give a damn what he and Pat had talked about. "Don't be ridiculous," Dad said that evening. "You're going to eat something, and you're going to that play. This is important to her."

"Pat said it was OK." Nolan pushed himself upright too fast, the mattress squeaking underneath him, and he blinked a couple of times to adjust. His head felt light.

"Did you get any rest?" Dad frowned.

Nolan had crawled into bed to be around for the conversation with Ilanne, but he didn't exactly feel rested. "Sort of." He plucked sweaty sheets from his legs. His heart raced. He talked too fast. "I meant to. It probably wasn't enough. I should nap more."

"Nice trick," Mom said. She'd been rushing back and forth through the hallway, talking on the phone to Grandma Pérez, but now stepped into his room. She slipped her phone into her back pocket. "You'll avoid sleeping except when you're expected at your little sister's play?" She jammed a skinny index finger at his wardrobe door. "I'm not picking out clothes for you. If you can't do it yourself within one minute, you'll go to the school in your underwear. Got it?"

It looked as if Mom had finally taken Grandma Pérez's parenting advice. She didn't look happy about it. Her stern expression was just the slightest bit off.

Nolan wanted to argue. "Yes," he said, thinking of her at the Walgreens, thinking of the pills they couldn't afford flushed down the toilet by Nadi.

At least Amara was still OK. She and Ilanne were gathering the other mages, which meant she was relatively safe, but being back in Bedam brought her far too close to Nadi and Jorn for Nolan to feel even the slightest bit comfortable about leaving her alone.

Forty minutes later he trailed after his parents into Pat's middle school, wearing his prosthesis for the first time in days. It itched with sweat.

Out of habit, he smiled teacher-smiles at his old art and social studies teachers, who waited outside the gymnasium, fanning themselves in the evening sun. The heat inside wasn't much better. Had the AC broken down? Was it just him? His heart was still going a hundred miles an hour. He needed his pills.

Without a word, he stripped off his pinstriped shirt, happy to go with only the undershirt. It didn't help against the heat.

Bored-looking kids Pat's age milled around, grumpy at

spending their evening back at school, while parents sat in too-small folding chairs and fiddled with their phones and camcorders. Underneath it all was the stench of old sweat and gym clothes and that muffled, artificial gym smell. Rubber? Vinyl? He didn't know, but the tarp did nothing to hide it—

**—Amara was sitting on dewy grass, absorbing the cool morning sunlight and watching Ilanne hover over a glass pane, the same as when Jorn had talked to Ruudde. Nolan wished he could lend her some of the Arizona heat. She'd probably faint—**

—he had to get out of here. He couldn't be at a damn middle school while going through withdrawal and—and everything going on with Amara.

His phone buzzed in his pocket. He wormed free from the crowd, shuffling toward the stage. The folding chairs gave way to low gym benches, probably reserved for the younger kids. He fished out his phone, which showed a new text from Pat.

*Am backstage. I'm gonna screw this up!!!*

At least that gave Nolan an excuse to move away from the crowd. He nodded at another teacher, though he didn't recognize this one, then at someone else who waved at him. It took him a second to recognize her: Sarah Schneider. Her hair looked different than at school. When she noticed him looking, her waves grew more enthusiastic, and her eyebrows rose in a hopeful question. Was she waving him over to sit with her? She must have a younger sibling in the play, too. Nolan swallowed an expletive at her timing, sped up, and belatedly realized he should've waved back. He moved around the stage taking up a third of the gym and ducked behind a black sheet, then up a small, portable set of stairs.

"You shouldn't be back here," a friend of Pat's—Claudia?—said, blocking his path.

Nolan just showed her his phone.

Claudia read the text and stepped aside with an exaggerated flourish. "Now Pat starts caring?"

The backstage area was cramped, but at least it had a massive fan providing relief. Nolan didn't pause to bask in the breeze, searching for Pat and mumbling apologies to oddly dressed preteens in his path. The one teacher backstage didn't care half as much about his presence as Claudia did. Finally, Nolan spotted Pat near the stage, wearing an ill-fitting white uniform, her hair in an uncharacteristic bun.

"Look," he said. "You rocked those rehearsals. You'll be fine."

"Look," Pat said back. "I found fabric scissors." She held them up. They flashed in the bare bulbs of the lights backstage.

Pat no longer looked nervous.

A girl Nolan didn't know maneuvered past them to get to a stack of hats, and he barely noticed, too rooted to the floor to do anything but stare at the gleaming metal in his sister's gloved hands. She'd lost one of her spikes. But even right before going onstage, even in her white nurse's outfit, Pat stuck with her gloves.

"Amara's on her way back," Nolan whispered.

He couldn't make himself look at Nadi wearing his sister's eyes. He needed to focus on Pat's gloves, her hands, and what they held. The scissors might move if he looked away. Near the scissors, his sister's chest moved with controlled breaths. Too near.

"Amara is back in Bedam," he said. "I'm making her come back already. Please."

The scissors moved a fraction of an inch away from Pat's chest. He saw muscles loosen in her hands. He dared take a breath but couldn't move yet.

"Amara contacted the mages? And you *helped* her?" Pat—Nadi—said. Only then did Nolan's eyes flicker from her hands to her face.

Of course Nadi could dig through Pat's memories when Nolan couldn't even touch Amara's. Nadi must know all about how they'd hunted through the notebooks for clues.

"She's coming back. I promise. I just wanted to know about Cilla—but talking to the mages didn't work and Amara was being stupid and she didn't care about Pat, and—she's coming back. I can still control her. I'm sorry. She's in Bedam! She'll be at the palace by noon. Sooner. Within the hour. I promise!"

Nadi tapped the flat points of the scissors against Pat's shut eyelids. "I know you do."

"Please," Nolan rasped.

"You're sweating a lot, Nolan. You're shaking. Is your control wearing off yet? What do you think will happen if you miss your deadline? Do you think I'll go, Oh, it's not like Nolan can do anything about it anymore, so I might as well forget about that family of his? 'Cause you're wrong." It was as if Nadi was trying to sound like Pat instead of herself now, so much that it raised the hairs on the back of Nolan's neck. "I have a question for you: If you're making Amara turn back, how come you're here with me?"

She ran the scissors lightly along Pat's arm. She pricked, once, in the hollow of her elbow. The scissors were too blunt to poke through. She applied more pressure. The skin turned yellow.

"You might want to hurry back before Amara turns around, hey?"

"I . . . Please don't . . ."

"Go while you can, and your sister will be fine," Nadi said.

"Pat!" Claudia shouted from a couple of feet away, over the heads of a rehearsing set of identically dressed patients. "Mr. Lopez wants to see you! We're starting in five minutes!"

"Be there in a sec!" Nadi shouted. She looked back at Nolan and smiled Pat's toothy grin. "I'll see you soon."

Nolan fought his way through the crowd, his eyes trained on the exit.

"Nolan!" Sarah Schneider said brightly. "I didn't know you—"

Not now, he wanted to say, but the exit called to him, and the words didn't come. He shoved past her, his eyes on that door, his mind back with Pat, and Sarah's voice barely registered.

He'd meant to sneak by his parents. Sarah's interruption had caught their attention, though. "Who was that girl? How's Pat doing?" Mom touched Nolan's shoulder as he passed. "We have seats over there."

"I need to use the bathroom."

"You're going in the wrong direction. Are you having a seizure?"

"No—could you just—give me a minute?"

"Now? Can't you wait until the break?" Some of the lights had gone out. A voice announced that the play was about to begin, and requested that everyone take their seats. A screech of the speakers caused the crowd to collectively wince, then laugh, because they were in a middle-school gym getting ready to watch a middle-school play, and the sun was shining, and they were in such good moods it hurt.

Nolan gripped fistfuls of his hair. He had to bring Amara to the palace. Now. Any moment, Nadi might peek at the crowd and see him lingering next to Mom.

"Nolan, just sit down," Mom said, sounding stern now. "Oh, what are you doing to your hair? It's all messed up now—never mind. Grandma Pérez wanted to talk to you. Did you bring your report card like she asked?"

Anger bubbled up, the same way he'd felt it do so often

in Amara's body. It felt hot. Untamed. He couldn't let it out. Couldn't.

Walgreens, he told himself, but guilt no longer helped.

"It's not like the play is that long," Mom went on. "We'll be home before you know it."

Nolan shook his head, trying to think of a way out, trying to . . . He blinked. The world turned green, like Amara's, and he saw a glimpse of Ilanne's hunched form on the grass.

He hadn't meant to do that. The pills were wearing off.

The headmaster walked onstage to test the microphone.

"Nolan!" Dad leaned toward him from his seat. "Sit down!"

Another blink, another flash of Amara's world, and the second he was back in his own, the words spilled from his lips: "Leave me alone!" Too loud. People were watching. His parents, Grandma Pérez, Sarah. "Just—shut—up! For once!"

The headmaster fell silent. A couple of heads turned.

Mom reached for his arm, but he yanked it away, and with his head spinning and hot, Nolan stalked past the audience, out of the gym, and back into the sun.

Nolan didn't have to announce himself to the palace guards. They took one look, saw the small Elig servant that Ruudde must've told them to be on the lookout for, and restrained his arms.

He let them. The faster Nadi saw that he'd returned, the better. He couldn't let Pat down. He couldn't let the pills wear off.

On Earth, he'd walked straight to the pool—a five-minute walk from Pat's school—and shut himself into a private changing room.

On the way there, he'd seen involuntary glimpses of Amara's world over half a dozen times. Fractions of a second. Snippets of noise.

Just when he'd started to forget what it felt like.

"I hate that it had to come to this, Mr. Santiago," Nadi said. She—and even seeing her in Ruudde's body, it was so easy thinking of Ruudde as a *she*, now that Nolan knew—met Nolan in the courtyard. "I don't like threatening people. It just seems to be the only thing that works."

"You're good at it," Nolan said flatly once the guards released him. If he didn't play the part of the beaten-down victim well enough, Nadi might suspect something.

It wasn't hard. He felt beaten down plenty.

"Do I have to put you in a cell this time?"

"If you want to," Nolan said.

Nadi thumped his shoulder. "You're learning."

They put Nolan in the guest room where he'd talked to Nadi for the first time, around the corner from the cell block. They wanted him close to Cilla.

A handful of dusty books lay on the windowsill. Amara studied them while Nolan lingered in the background. Every time he heard steps that might be Nadi's or Jorn's, he snapped into control. He couldn't let them open the door to see Amara and no one else directing her movements. Amara had asked Nolan to do exactly that, since it'd keep up appearances that he was on Nadi's side, but Nolan sensed her rage and helplessness every time. He could only sign a million apologies that helped her not one bit.

He wanted to go home to check on Pat—

—but he only dared sneak out for a few seconds at a time, standing up from the changing-room bench with shaky legs, taking his phone, deleting the missed calls, checking the texts. There were several, even though no one had followed him from the gym.

The oldest message was Dad's. Nolan read it in between unwanted blinks to Amara's world. *Pat saw you run. She cried onstage. Come back, Nolan.*

Then another one, sent ten minutes later. *Tell us you're all right.*

Five minutes after that, Mom had sent one, too. *Nolan, where are you?? We're not angry. We're worried. Please come back. We'll call Dr. Campbell, OK?*

He texted them that he was safe, then texted Pat, *I'm sorry about the play. And everything. Are you OK?* He wanted to explain what was happening, but his fingers hovered uselessly over the phone. Nadi might take over again and know exactly what he told Pat—

—so he went back. He clung to Amara's world with all his might, from the books in her hands to the storm cover over the window. The pool would close soon, and he couldn't afford to be woken up.

He'd never thought he'd *try* to get sucked in again.

Hours after his arrival at the palace, Nolan heard two short, sharp wails in the distance. The sign Amara and Ilanne had agreed on. The mages were ready to attack.

Nolan knocked on the door, then creaked it open. In the hallway outside his room, an unfamiliar guard looked up from her solitary card game. One hand went to her baton.

"May I talk to Ruudde?" Nolan signed.

"I'll pass on a message. Anything else?"

Nolan shut the door. He counted on Nadi considering him a top priority. He was right: within minutes, Nadi stood in the doorway. "If you or Amara have another brilliant escape plan, don't bother. I've placed a ward around the palace. No one crosses without my knowing about it."

Nolan masked his reaction. Wards would make the mages' job harder. Distracting Nadi just became even more important.

"So, what is it?" She straightened her topscarf. "I do have a job aside from babysitting you, kid."

"Can you explain what we're waiting for? I thought you wanted us gone as soon as possible."

"We're arranging a boat. Storms over the Gray Sea are slowing us down."

Backlash. Or Ilanne buying time to gather the other mages. Judging by the signal from before, she'd been successful. Now

Nolan just needed to keep Nadi busy while the mages infiltrated the palace. He needed to give Ilanne as much time as possible with Cilla.

"Is Cilla all right?" He didn't have to feign his concern.

"Of course she is," Nadi said irritably. "We'd need you if she weren't."

Nolan nodded, and he wondered how those movements came across now. Were they his or Amara's? He'd never controlled her body this long. He didn't know if he was becoming more like himself or more like her. Then—

—then Amara's body sagged. Just for a moment. Just long enough for her breath to be delayed by a half second. Just long enough for Nolan to know he was running out of time.

Their roles were shifting.

When he regained control, his head felt light and the world alien. He grasped at straying thoughts and bundled them together. He had to keep going and keep up his part of the distraction. "Is Cilla eating?" he asked in a burst of signs.

"We're not giving her much choice," Nadi said. "Your pills are fading, aren't they?"

What did "not much choice" mean? A third spell on top of the curse and anchor, massive spells to begin with, was unthinkable. Nadi had to be threatening her. Her favorite weapon.

"May I see her? It'll help her to know Amara's here."

Nadi sighed. "You'll see her when you leave together. But it might help, and it's better to do it while you're still in control."

Nolan followed her to the cells, where Gacco stood guard. How long had it been? Did Gacco know anything beyond "keep the cursed girl alive at all costs"? If Nolan told the guards about Cilla, that could be another way to distract Nadi.

Those thoughts faded once Nolan saw Cilla in her cell. She sat on her mattress, reading a thin book. Her face looked slimmer, her normally round cheeks sunken closer to the bone. Her eyes looked deeper and darker. Her arms had thinned, too, traces of knobs visible around her wrist and elbows.

Nadi had said Cilla was eating. It couldn't be much.

Nolan lost control for another second. It wouldn't be long now.

"You brought her back," Cilla said. The book slid from her hands. Next to Amara, Nadi shot forward, but the book landed safely next to Cilla's feet. "You made a promise." Cilla's voice was weaker than before, but no less accusatory. "You said you wouldn't—"

"Things change." The words nauseated him, but he needed to stall. Jorn always took too long to notice his wards when he was in the inns, drinking his beer and cheering at long-legged dancers, so maybe if Nolan kept Nadi busy enough, she wouldn't notice the mages intruding, either.

"Happy?" Nadi said.

Nolan spun. "You threatened my sister," he said, flat and quick. He didn't say it just for the sake of a distraction. He needed Cilla to see he'd had no choice. He shouldn't care what she thought of him, but he couldn't spend a lifetime in Amara's body and not share her love and hate and more. "Of course I'm not happy. But I'll do what I need to."

"Wonderful." Nadi seemed ready to leave.

"After I saw you that night, I kept reading my journals. I discovered something." He took a deep breath, filling Amara's lungs. "Your family is running out of money. They can't keep up with the medical bills to keep you on life support."

Nadi took a moment to let that sink in. "Nicely played. So you think I'll go back to Earth to try to keep myself alive longer, and then you can—"

"No, no, no." Nolan's hands flapped at the air. "I talked to your family."

"And how did you do that?"

"Nadia Trudeau." It took a long time to spell the name, but Nolan finished it, down to the closest Dit version of the *e-a-u* letters that'd trip up every last person in this palace. He kept his eyes on Nadi.

"There's no way for you to—"

"I talked to your son," Nolan lied. "Jermaine misses you. It's been over a decade since you left."

Expressions flitted over Nadi's face, too faint for Nolan to pin down. Nadi had said this world was worth leaving her family for, but that didn't mean she didn't miss them—or her life. She'd renamed her palace for a reason.

"He lives in Cape Town." A guess. The article never mentioned it. But it meant more to talk about, more names to spell, and every second counted. "He has a daughter. Simona."

"My sister." Nadi still couldn't settle on an expression. She stared at the ground, jaw set, eyes blank. "They were always close. He named her after my sister."

"Simona's two now. She likes"—what did two-year-olds like? The website gave him only so much to work with. Nolan thought back to seeing Pat grow up—"playing with plastic planes." There was no word for *planes* in servant signs or Dit. P-L-EE-N-S, he tried, using the phonetic spelling, and said it out loud as best he could.

Gacco watched, confused and trying not to show it. Nolan glimpsed a key ring on his belt. Once Ilanne arrived, they could make a grab for it.

"Planes," Nadi repeated. The word sounded odd from her mouth. Then, clipped: "Are you threatening them? I swear, if you're threatening them—"

"I'm not!" Nolan stepped back. "I'm not. I just thought you might want to know."

At least Nolan was used to lying through his teeth. Years of *I'm not hallucinating anymore* and *No, this is different from the pain I used to have, these are just seizures* and *Yes, Dad, I'm feeling much better* and *Of course I don't mind, do whatever makes you happy* paid off.

"I wanted to remind you of your original offer." Nolan tried to smile. He was used to that, too. "It's not a threat. It's a bribe. You've seen my life. I couldn't get to South Africa even if I wanted. I just . . . if you could time Amara's sleep so I can get some rest back home, make life a little easier for us . . ."

He felt his control torn away again, felt Amara's body slump. The metal bars of Cilla's cell pressed hard into her back. Amara was hesitantly settling back into her own limbs and mind, her thoughts creeping in at the edges of Nolan's, but he pushed past them, snatched control again, and tried not to flinch at Nadi's scrutiny. She stood, unmoving. Had he made things worse? If he'd screwed up—if he'd endangered Pat even more—but Nolan couldn't grasp the thought. It shattered in his mind the moment he tried to contain it.

"If you have questions, I could talk to your family. Then you can visit Pat, and I'll tell you what they said." He was reaching now, the signs like filth on his hands. If Nadi wanted to talk to her family, she'd do it as herself or as Pat; she didn't need Nolan as a go-between. But it didn't matter. He needed to keep talking. "I'll be your messenger. A trade. OK? Lorres said you made good deals. You're reasonable."

He didn't think she saw his last words. Nadi's head snapped up, and she stared past Nolan at a blank wall.

He recognized the look from Jorn's face. Nadi had detected the mages.

Nolan had bought them a few minutes. But if Nadi figured out he'd been stalling, there was no place for Pat to hide. Nadi could possess her anytime, anywhere. He watched her with burning eyes. *Please, please . . .*

"Gacco. Cell keys." Nadi extended her hand.

Gacco didn't get up from his bench fast enough.

"The *keys!*" she shouted. Gacco tossed them, and Nolan watched them flicker and spin in the gaslight. Nadi snatched them from the air. "Whatever happens, stay here," she said, already backing away. "Get the servant back to the guest room. And guard the girl!" She pointed the keys at Cilla.

"What's going on?" Cilla said with a voice so flat Nolan doubted she expected to be acknowledged, let alone answered.

Nadi was already running down the hall, her boots smacking hard stone, her gemstones clanging together. She'd detected the mages too soon. The cell keys were out of reach. No sign of Ilanne.

Already, things were going wrong.

42

They needed those keys. Ilanne didn't care about freeing Cilla—she could detect the spell-caster's identity with or without bars in the way—but the way Cilla lay there, without her scarf, with bandages extending past her wear, turned Amara's stomach. They had to get her out.

The moment Nadi turned the corner, Nolan let go of Amara's body. Out of choice? Because of the pills? Amara faced Cilla to block her signs from Gacco. "It's a distraction. Pretend—"

Gacco spun her by her shoulder. "Move away from those bars," he warned, as though she could bend the metal with only her hands. For all she knew, he thought she could. He still thought she was a mage. The days when Amara had believed the same thing seemed so far away, she could almost laugh.

Down the hall, Nadi shouted at the marshal who'd been guarding the guest quarters. "Sound the bells. Find the others!"

No one would be guarding Amara's room. Gacco must've realized the same. "Stand over there," he said, motioning at the cell diagonally across from Cilla's.

In the distance, muffled by stone walls, a whistle increased in pitch like some sort of Jélisse firework before sputtering out. A crash followed. Amara could swear she felt vibrations rumble through the ground. The fighting had started.

"What's going on?" Cilla's voice was stronger this time, and she offered Amara a nearly imperceptible nod. She'd seen Amara's warning.

"Do I look like I know?" Gacco thumped back onto the bench. Screams came from the courtyard, followed by another crash. Gacco bolted upright again. The cell wing had no windows. No way to follow what was happening. One hand stayed on his baton, and he looked from left to right as if intruders might burst in at any moment.

They did—but not in the way he expected.

The servant hallway door slammed open. Gacco turned at the sound, baton raised. Ilanne wasn't impressed. She took in the situation, nodded, and raised her arm. Amara leaped aside. A dry crackle sounded. A shimmer—like the air over a fire— swept through the hall toward Gacco. A second later, he skidded back. He crashed into his bench, then slid off and lay still aside from the moving of his chest. Burns blackened the fabric of his scarf. A nasty smell hit Amara's nose.

Not burned flesh, though. Thank the seas.

"Get his keys." Ilanne stalked down the hall. Outside, she'd been intimidating—now, she was downright terrifying. Sharp cheekbones jutted out under blazing eyes. The air around her hand swam and pulsed, ready for another attack. She walked without hesitation, without even a hint of fear. "Which cell is the girl in?"

"Now will you tell me what's happening?" Cilla laughed nervously. The sound died when Ilanne walked into view. Cilla scrambled onto her mattress, backing as far into the wall as possible.

"We're getting you out," Amara said. Then, to Ilanne: "Nadi took the keys."

Cilla stayed on her mattress, shifting her weight to stay balanced. "That's her. It's the knifewielder. What's going on?"

Now wasn't the time to explain. Now was the time to free her and run.

"If we get her out," Amara told Ilanne, "you'll have more time to detect her spell."

Ilanne shifted her attention to the metal bars. She nodded. "You're right. I can open these. Move away." As Amara stepped back, Ilanne pressed her palm against the metal as if testing it. Nothing happened. Her hand moved back, hovering finger-lengths from the lock. The surrounding air gave a single pulse. "Stand farther back. This metal's tough."

Amara moved away. Even then—even then something felt off, something niggling at her, something that whispered wait.

She shouldn't leave Cilla. She should never, ever leave Cilla.

By the time Ilanne's arm stretched through the bars, Amara was already leaping forward.

Too late.

Ilanne locked eyes with Cilla. "I'm sorry," she said.

Cilla made a sound in the back of her throat. The cell lit up white. The air twanged—unevenly, like a plucked string, fading in and out, reverberating, on and on.

Ilanne had betrayed them.

Amara crashed into Ilanne's side. The mage stumbled, then fell sideways, her arm still between the bars. Something snapped. She screamed. Inside the cell, the light flickered like a torch exposed to wind. Cilla dropped to the ground, then Amara's eyes went blind from the brightness. Spots floated into her vision, bright greens with pulsing yellow outlines. She couldn't see beyond a few footlengths away, but there—she could just make out Ilanne, wildly aiming with her unbroken arm. The air in the cell fizzed with magic.

Amara's open palm hit Ilanne's chin, slamming her head into the metal bars. Hard. Ilanne crumpled. The magic snapped out, leaving the cells dark aside from a single lamp that was suddenly no more than a glimmer.

Amara's eyes took forever to readjust. She didn't know whether to focus on Cilla in her cell or Ilanne outside of it, or on the magic and backlash roaring outside the palace walls, or on the marshals who'd surely arrive at any moment.

Cilla won.

Amara shouted her name aloud, sidestepping Ilanne's slumped form. The back of the cell looked even darker now, but in the sudden dead silence of the faded magic, Amara still heard the scrambling of Cilla's feet, her coughing. She was alive.

In Cilla's case, that might mean little.

"I'm fine," Cilla said, coughing again. "She aimed at the ceiling."

"Blood?" Amara's eyes slowly adjusted. Cilla was hunched over on her mattress. Dust billowed in the back of the cell. Chunks of the ceiling lay scattered on the bed and had knocked over Cilla's pot.

"Don't think so." Cilla squinted through the dirt cloud. "Any chance you'll explain what's going on?"

"What's going on is that we're in trouble." Amara swallowed. She'd told Ilanne how to reach the cells via the servant passages. The few servants who'd see her would hesitate to stop her, and with a full-on attack going on outside, it'd take long enough for them to get a minister's attention that Cilla would be long gone by the time they discovered her empty cell.

That'd been the plan, anyway.

Outside came more shouts, searing wails of magic, shattering glass. Once, the walls shook.

"Are those mages outside coming for me?" Cilla's voice sounded neutral. If there was one thing she knew, it was mages trying their damndest to kill her.

"If they have the chance." Amara crouched to check Ilanne's pulse. She should be scared. She'd never killed someone, and she'd never wanted to. Few things upset the spirits—real spirits, not fakes like Nolan—more than murder.

When she felt the soft beat in Ilanne's throat, though, all she could think of was how Ilanne would try to kill Cilla again when she woke. And how easy it'd be for Amara to make sure she wouldn't do either.

That thought *did* scare her.

She looked back at Cilla, with her sharper cheeks and dust-smeared bandages. She seemed nowhere near as desperate as she had a few minutes ago; she stood upright in the center of the wrecked cell, her head high, unbothered by her exposed shoulders.

It had to do with power. Put Cilla in a position where something was happening, where she could take charge, and she thrived.

Take that away, and she broke.

Amara was used to having no power. Her response to a crisis was to plan.

"Ruudde is possessed by a traveler from Nolan's world named N-A-D-I, Nadi," Amara signed. Her gaze flicked to the end of the hall. No marshals yet. Cilla was safe for now—the cell wing was secluded—but Nadi would soon send anyone she could spare from the courtyard.

By now, Amara smelled the faint, distant whiff of fire. Clangs from the bell tower rolled over the palace and grounds. She explained what she and Nolan had discovered as quickly as possible. Whatever else happened, Cilla needed to know the truth.

"We need to get you out." Amara pressed her hand to the cell's lock. Rust crumbled against her skin. "We'll find another mage to detect the spell-caster. Someone we can trust."

Cilla said nothing for several long seconds. Then: "You can still walk away."

Cilla didn't move. Amara wanted to think the rawness of her voice was from the dust in her throat, but she knew better.

"You can pretend you didn't know about the mages' attack. They caught you by surprise, too. Look. You even knocked one out. Ruudde will thank you."

"No. This is our one chance—"

"What happens if you break me out and we run?" Cilla said, looking gray. "They'll keep threatening Nolan's family. He'll give in eventually. He'll possess you and take you back."

"His pills are wearing off. He'll only be able to watch."

"Nadi can still travel to his world. She'll ask where we've run to."

"We have to try!" Amara gripped the cell bars, yanking, pushing, but the metal was embedded so deep in the stone walls it didn't even rattle. "I can't go back to before. I can't. We'll contact other mages. Most don't know you're not—they're loyal to the princess. That Dit mage from Teschel is alive. She'll pin down any spell you ask her to."

"Amara . . ." Cilla looked at her for too many, too valuable seconds.

"You weren't even eating."

"I only wanted them to tell me what was going on."

"You hurt yourself."

"I . . ." Cilla swallowed, as though it stung to see those signs. "It's no use. You can't get me out, anyway."

Amara checked the lock again. The rust made it look deceptively weak. She looked sideways, counting the number of cells between them and the end of the hallway, and—yes. This was a different cell from Cilla's earlier one. That one must've gotten too torn up from the effects of the curse, when the stones had come loose to crush her.

Amara tugged at the bars another time. The walls resisted every fraction of movement. That could change, though the thought of how she'd make that happen dried her throat and made her want to turn and run.

She crouched, feeling Ilanne's clothes, the leather of her boots. Her fingers closed around the handle of a familiar knife. She banished old nightmares and clamped the hooked blade between her upper arm and body to free up her hands. "I can cut you."

"Perfect plan," Cilla said humorlessly.

"I'll take your blood and stay close to the bars." Amara gestured at where the metal punctured stone. "The curse has nothing to work with except the stones or bars. It might give us an opening."

"I don't want you to get hurt again."

"It might be the last time. It'd be worth it." As she said it, the memory of pain sent her heart churning against her ribs.

Cilla stared at Amara with those shiny, narrow eyes, the dark bags underneath setting them off all the more. A smile hovered on her mouth, not quite managing to crease her cheeks, not quite tugging up the corners of her lips. It was enough. "If that's what it takes," she said. She glanced at Ilanne, whose hair splayed out over bare stones. The mage's arm rested awkwardly on her hips, pointing in a direction it shouldn't. Cilla stepped closer to the bars. She moved to the side, where Amara could reach her without Ilanne's body in the way.

Amara breathed deeply. She followed Cilla until they stood close together, only metal bars and shallow breaths between them. The shouts came closer every minute. In a nearby hall, footsteps slammed. Amara took Ilanne's curved blade with one hand and reached for Cilla's lips with the other, her fingers running over the dips and curves and warm skin. She wanted to kiss those lips again. The cut had healed over, leaving a mark that'd fade in time.

Amara's fingers trailed lower, over Cilla's shoulder and down, resting on Cilla's wrist. She pulled it through the bars and pressed the blade to the fragile flesh on the inside of her forearm.

She could still back out.

She could still leave Cilla for the mages to kill.

Part of her wanted to call in Nolan. She was risking his family's life in doing this. Could he even control her anymore? He ought to. He could do exactly what Cilla said. He could step away, claim he had nothing to do with the mages' attack, and point at Ilanne's unconscious body as proof he was on Nadi's side.

That would make it easy for Amara. Not having a choice was always easy. It was always safer. However bad things were, you kept your head down and did as you were told in order to avoid worse.

The world always wanted people like her to believe those lies.

You were never safe as long as you were at someone else's whim.

Amara's eyes met Cilla's, dark and beaten and haunted.

Not having a choice was the worst thing in the world.

Amara pushed the knife down. Nolan didn't stop her. And in that moment, with her enemy's knife in her own hand, a point pressing on Cilla's arm, Cilla's skin familiar against hers, relief sneaked up on her and refused to let go. Because what she'd told Cilla wasn't true. It wasn't that she couldn't go back to her old life; she could. If she went back, she'd hate herself, but it meant survival. It might be worth it or it might not be, and she'd never have to find out because it would never happen. She wasn't going back.

It wasn't because of what Maart wanted, or because of what Cilla asked, or because of what Jorn said. She'd made the choice. It was hers alone. This or nothing.

Blood welled up from Cilla's arm. Amara let the knife clatter to the ground. She reached for the cut. She was almost smiling now, a desperate smile that had her lips trembling, that came with tears burning her eyes.

This or nothing.

Cilla pulled herself loose. She stepped away from the bars.

Amara reached through. Her fingers found only air. Her smile faded, and she shouted, her voice hoarse. Cilla couldn't—why was she—

"Ilanne said she was sorry," Cilla said.

Amara yanked her arms back to sign. "Because she knew she was wrong! You need to—"

Cilla's dull eyes hardened. "No. Because she knew she was right. She felt terrible, and she did it anyway because she knew she had to."

"Come back! We need to—we need to try—" Amara stopped talking. She crouched and took the fallen knife, smearing every drop of Cilla's that still clung to the blade onto her own arm, but it wasn't enough. It didn't compare to the amount of blood on Cilla's arm. And more kept coming, and once the curse hit, there would be more and more—

Cilla went on. "No more Nolan in your head. No more ministers. No more backlash. No more curse. You'll be safe, and his family will be safe, and the Dunelands . . . We won't have to run anymore." A drop of blood trickled down Cilla's arm, changing its path when Cilla reached up to unwind the bandages from her chest, letting the glow from her false, torn-up mark shine through. "I don't know what else to do," she whispered as the rocks in the walls started to shift.

Amara couldn't make signs anymore. Her hands wouldn't listen, and she didn't know what to say if they did. She clawed through the bars. Her muscles stretched so far they hurt, the beams pressing into her shoulder and against the side of her face until she couldn't go any farther. Cilla stood footlengths from even the tips of Amara's fingers. She backed up farther. Stepped onto the cot without looking.

"I'm sorry. For this and for everything else over the years. It wasn't right."

Amara knew it wasn't right, she knew, but it wasn't Cilla's fault, and if she got down from that mattress, if she just—if she just came toward the bars, they could try—fix it—

"You probably shouldn't look." Cilla smiled wanly. "It's not pleasant."

It wasn't.

Cilla's turn to hurt. Amara's turn to watch.

Amara screamed so loudly she didn't recognize her own voice as the first stones wrapped around Cilla. They pulled her into the wall. They pressed her tightly. Stone crunched. Other things did, too. Amara kept screaming. As long as she kept screaming, she couldn't hear Cilla's.

She screamed until footsteps came down the hall, finally, finally, until Jorn's arms circled her and yanked her away from the bars. Metal clinked against metal even through Cilla's cries tearing the air in half. Someone had the keys. Someone opened the cell. Jorn pushed her inside, and Amara stumbled and almost fell.

"Go!" Jorn shouted, but there was no point. No amount of Cilla's blood on Amara's skin would distract the curse this time. There was too much of it, and even more kept coming.

Cilla's scream ended in a choke.

f Nolan took control of Amara, he could take those steps forward so she wouldn't have to; he could reach for Cilla's battered body in the wall and take whatever blood would stick to him.

He couldn't. He was trapped, the way he'd been before he'd ever taken the pills.

At least Pat would be safe with Cilla dead, he thought distantly. At least Nolan would have his life again.

But for now . . . for now, he was here, watching through Amara's eyes fixed on Cilla's broken face, and Nolan could only repeat to himself, *This isn't my body, this isn't my pain, this isn't my world, this isn't my love.*

Stones on each side. Cilla's eyes forced shut. Lips that had kissed Amara's, torn beyond recognition.

*Not my pain not my pain not my pain I don't want to feel this not my pain.*

The hands Cilla had revealed her royal mark with, swallowed by stone. Amara's hands had looked just like that, mangled on the floor in that other cell. Nolan had put them back together. This time he couldn't do a thing. Only watch and wish he wasn't. He'd tried to climb into Cilla's body at Olym's farm, and it hadn't worked, for all his extra pills, for all that he'd focused and wished and concentrated so hard—

It hit him so clearly that the cell went quiet for a full second.

He'd done it all wrong.

Instinct. That was how he'd first controlled Amara. He'd wanted her to run from the mages—urged her on—slid into her mind without realizing it. It was how he'd first left, too. Her pain had cut too deep.

Emotion and instinct. Only with those could he take control.

And now, with Cilla dying and Amara screaming and the palace shivering and crying with magic and the rock still churning . . . This wasn't like sitting in his safe, sunlit room and squeezing his eyes shut to concentrate. This was not a school assignment. This was not a world to chronicle in his notebooks, to distance himself from.

This was real.

*My pain*, Nolan whispered. *Mine.* He couldn't control Amara anymore, but he'd never needed that to make her heal. He only needed to be present. If he could slip into Cilla's body . . . if the pills still offered him control over *that* . . .

He opened himself to Amara's panic until it seared through him so hot and sharp he could no longer separate it from his own.

The air smelled of dust and blood. Cilla wouldn't last much longer. He'd lose her like he'd lost Maart.

That thought did the trick.

Nolan abandoned Amara's panic for Cilla's pain, for blackness, for crunching in his ears, for pressure on every part of his skin. Pushing and breaking and digging in deep. The pain ebbed, flooded back in. At this point, Cilla should have been past the pain. Her nerve endings were destroyed. She was supposed to fade and die.

Instead, her bones snapped into place, broke again from continued pressure, mended themselves a second time. Cuts healed over. Blood drained from places it shouldn't be, slipping back into burst vessels that shuddered deeply under her skin. Muscles braided themselves back together.

Healing would keep Cilla alive, but it wouldn't make the curse stop coming. Too much blood had already spilled, wet and slick.

The stones fell away, anyway. Clattered to the floor and mattress. Nolan followed, falling amid rubble as the stones' grip on him—on Cilla—loosened. He sucked filthy air into punctured, half-healed lungs, dirt clogging up his nose, and knew something was wrong.

The curse wasn't supposed to end, not with so much blood spilled, and Cilla healed, yes, but she did it jaggedly, first on one side and then the other. She felt different from Amara in a way beyond the physical. Something pushed at him, nagged at the edges, tried to get between her and him like a fingernail prying at a seam.

But she was alive. Healing.

Nolan pushed himself up onto all fours. Cilla's body was taller than Amara's, shorter than his, heavier than either of them. His hands on the uneven floor were the deepest brown, his fingers short and broken.

He hurt. But he'd saved her.

Using blurred, newly healed eyes, Nolan sought out Amara. He found her across the cell, lying on her back along with Jorn and the marshals. Debris and dust swept a half circle on the floor, blasted outward—Nolan possessing Cilla must've knocked them all back. Magic on top of magic on top of magic.

Jorn was already climbing to his feet. Nolan glanced over, then—wait—*he glanced over*. He was directing Cilla's body. He had control. Mixing spells either snuffed out magic or amplified it. But for how long?

Jorn shouted at the marshals. He supported himself against the wall, his coughing a distant sound through the ringing in Nolan's ears. Nadi reached the cell and took in the situation without a word. Amara stayed on the floor in a half-sitting position, motionless from her toes to her eyelashes as she stared at Nolan.

He'd seen her in dirtied mirrors, in glass reflections, in still water. Not like this, solid and footlengths away. Face-to-face.

Did she see him, too? Did she recognize him?

Before either of them could talk, the ceiling shook. Nolan's head snapped up. Stone crumbled and dropped. Something rippled through the walls and floors like rings expanding in the water—like the curse. Jorn backed away. So did the marshals. Another lump of rock fell from the ceiling.

Cilla healed fast. Crushed ribs snapped back to their normal positions, pulling lungs with them, sucking in air and dust. Nolan pushed himself up, though his movements wobbled. Pain lanced through his legs. He fell again, to his knees and then sideways off the mattress. Cilla's hands scrambled on the floor, but not because he made them. Was she back in control? He tried to move. Cilla didn't respond.

Nolan still felt those fingernails prying at him, though, wedging him loose. He couldn't let them succeed. Cilla wasn't done healing.

More stone fell from the ceiling. Amara stumbled back, her eyes fixed on Cilla. The marshals were shouting. The metal beams of the cell were twisting loose from the walls. The air itself seemed to quiver.

The anchor, the curse, and Nolan. Too much magic stacked in one body.

A beam lashed around, knocking over a marshal, slamming into Jorn's skull. He crumpled. A perfect triangle of dark shone on his temple, the skin scrunched up on one side. As Nolan watched, it uncoiled, spread out, and started to knit itself back together.

That wasn't right, Jorn couldn't heal—

Nolan's connection with Cilla snapped loose. Suddenly there were thick bars in his vision, and past them, the back of Amara's head, her dust-matted hair.

Pain tore Nolan apart. He looked down, seeing a broken arm and blood on black skin. Ilanne. He'd left Cilla's body, moving into Ilanne's, lying outside the cell—

He snapped free a second time. Pain pulsed through Nolan's head. Whose body was he in now? A marshal's? Jorn's? No, Jorn lay beside him on the floor, no longer healing. The skin on his temple, where the beam had hit, had reattached itself but not yet smoothed over, and the area around the V-shaped cut turned rapidly darker. Jorn blinked slowly. He slurred words Nolan couldn't make out.

How was Cilla? Nolan couldn't see her. A scream distracted him—not the muted shouts from outside the cell block, where the mages were still fighting, and not the marshals as they dove to evade falling stones, but something else, shapeless, unformed. It came from inside the cell. Amara was shouting words she had no tongue to form. She half turned, enough for Nolan to see her claw at her mouth. Her eyes spread, panicked.

It wasn't her. Nolan knew in a heartbeat.

"What's happening—why am I—" a marshal shouted. She was studying her hands, the fingers curling. No, not *her* hands. Few people had their own hands left. Every last spell of Cilla's was tipping sideways. The curse, shredding the walls and agitating the metal; the anchor and Nolan, tearing travelers from their bodies and flinging them into others.

A cell beam caught Nadi in the hip. She screamed and staggered into the cell. She tried to support herself on the walls, but her injured leg gave way, and she slid to the floor. Maybe she wasn't Nadi anymore; maybe this was just Ruudde. He stayed down, hand pressed to his hip.

He wasn't healing, Nolan realized. It *had* to be Ruudde.

Nolan dragged himself to the cell. He had to check on Cilla and Amara. He stepped past Jorn, who was pushing himself to a sitting position against the hallway walls. He stared at his hands. Tears slipped over his cheeks and dangled from the scruff on his chin. He whispered something, nearly lost in the chaos. It had sounded like *mine*.

Nolan slowed. Why would Jorn cry? Or look at his hands like that? He was turning them to see his palms, his stare not shocked or confused but *awed*, and he touched his fingers to his lips, eyes shut, as if savoring the moment.

Nolan stepped toward him—

Saw the world from Cilla's eyes for a flash of a second—

Then another body pulled him in, this one lying on the cold floor. Nolan pried the body's eyes open. A turned-over bench lay by his side. His chest ached, but the pain crept away. He raised his arm. The yellow-brown skin of the Jélis. The green-cuffed sleeves of the marshals. He was possessing Gacco.

Nolan stood. He reached Jorn in two uneven steps, then fell to his knees. "Jorn?" Gacco's lips moved clumsily. Too thick, too wide, too dry. His teeth felt odd, too.

Nolan checked the cut on Jorn's temple. It wasn't healing. This had to be Jorn. A Jorn who was crying and awestruck instead of angry, instead of protecting Cilla from all this chaos . . .

The real Jorn. Maybe for the first time.

Why had they needed Amara, then? Whatever traveler had

controlled Jorn for so long could've distracted the curse for Cilla himself.

A lump formed in Nolan's throat. He knew the answer. He'd shouted it at Nadi: No traveler wanted to deal with the pain that came with guarding Cilla. The traveler must've suppressed the healing all those years, or healed out of sight, wrapping up non-existent wounds, to keep Cilla and Amara in the dark.

"Yes," Jorn said. "Jorn."

"Why would—" Nolan cut himself short when Jorn's head snapped back. His eyes unfocused. The purple started to seep away from the bruise on his temple, the skin knitting up. Within seconds, the healing stopped, and Jorn was himself again.

"We don't have long." Nolan marveled at the taste of Dit in his mouth. It wasn't like reciting sentences at home. Gacco's body knew the words as well as it knew air. "Who cast the anchor spell?"

In his peripheral vision, a marshal stumbled toward them. She extended her arms, fingers straining wide as if to summon magic. The marshal wasn't a mage, though. The air around her hands didn't shift; the magic didn't crackle. It told Nolan who controlled that body, though—Nadi, or the traveler who had possessed Jorn for so long.

And they were trying to attack *Nolan*. In all this chaos, that, not protecting Cilla, was their goal.

Nolan knew enough. He whirled back to face Jorn. "You?" he whispered.

Jorn had cast the anchor spell. They must've wanted him close to Cilla in case she fled. He could track her better than anyone.

Jorn nodded. His eyes looked different. Softer. He swallowed and hesitated in a way the Jorn that Nolan knew hadn't done in years. "I—I know you have to—"

To—what?

Behind Nolan, more stones crashed to the floor. He recoiled, then checked over his shoulder. The possessed guard who'd been coming their way now leaned against the wall. Instead, Amara stalked toward Nolan and Jorn. She picked up Ilanne's hooked blade and moved determinedly around debris and injured bodies, then dove sideways, avoiding another swing of a cell beam.

It wasn't her.

A crack in the cell's ceiling loosened more stones. One crashed onto Nolan's hand and rolled onto the floor. He hissed, but even as his hand healed, he wrapped it around the stone to feel its weight. Heavy. And Nolan's arm—Gacco's—was strong. Nothing but lean muscle.

"Oh," he whispered.

"Do it. Fix it." Jorn's voice was steady. His eyes weren't.

"This isn't what I meant. This isn't . . ." But Nolan's fingers tightened around the stone, rough and cold against his skin. He felt himself pried loose from Gacco's body again, but he latched on, begging for a few more seconds. He needed to stay by Jorn's side just a little longer. Jorn needed to stay himself for just another moment.

He looked at Amara, footlengths away now. She shouted something.

*Nadi*, Nolan thought with odd impassiveness. Something about the way she walked just screamed *Nadi* at him. He smiled anyway. It was still Amara's face, her eyes. She still watched him from somewhere in there. He hoped she saw his smile. He hoped she knew what it meant, because he would never have the chance to explain.

Jorn's tears welled up again, gathering in his eyelashes.

Nolan imagined him burning Amara's hands. Hitting Maart's grave with the back of his shovel. That made it easier.

Not fair, but easier.

Jorn trembled as he spoke. "I don't want to—I'm—I'm s—"

Nolan brought the stone down, right on that purple, fragile bruise.

orn seized and spasmed and then, from one moment to the next, the room's chaos died down and Amara's body was her own again. The cell bars froze in place. Amara stumbled. So did a marshal down the hall; so did Gacco, who stared at the stone in his hand, then at the body he was hunched over. He dropped the stone and scrambled back.

Ruudde—really, truly Ruudde this time—pushed himself to a sitting position. His hands clutched his injured thigh. He looked around the room, blinking, dazed.

Three spells had been too much to handle. Killing Jorn took out two of them—the anchor spell and, by extension, the travelers' presence. The room stopped trembling; the stones became stones again. Amara turned. Ilanne's blade dropped from her hand.

Cilla stood in the center of the room. She had stopped healing.

"They're gone." Amara was the first to say it, signing carefully.

She didn't move again. Neither did anyone else. Ruudde's eyes shone.

Cilla's clothes were drenched in blood, her skin still beaten.

Every part of Amara screamed for her to run over and fix it, take the blood before the curse found Cilla, but she didn't need to.

The world was silent.

And as they collided and their arms wrapped around each other and Cilla's face buried itself in the crook of Amara's neck, and Amara pressed her cheek against Cilla's hair, the world stayed that way.

Ruudde ordered their tattoos removed. Cilla's ought never to have been there. Amara's . . . Amara's was supposed to stay for years to come. Looking at her reflection to see her neck bare felt like cheating, and every palace servant she passed made her cheeks burn in shame.

She'd never dared fantasize about this the way Maart had. Now he was gone and she was left, and she almost wanted to say his name so he'd know she remembered him.

They stayed at the palace for two days to let Cilla recover from her wounds. Ruudde offered to heal her, but Cilla refused. Even with the last traces of her curse removed by the mage who'd cast it in the first place—he'd been on the palace grounds as part of Ilanne's distraction—she didn't want any more magic touching her. She requested a Jélisse doctor. Ruudde obliged.

Amara sat by the side of Cilla's bed. All the beds in the guest rooms were open, not the alcoves she was used to. Those seemed safer. These seemed freer.

She remembered waiting in a room just like this, Nolan hovering in the back of her mind. She hoped he was all right. She hoped his family was safe.

"Are you disappointed?" Amara gestured at Cilla's sternum, hidden by her topscarf.

Cilla sat cross-legged on the bed, bruised-black arms propped on her knees, and mused, "Those few days when I got to be the princess in public . . . part of me enjoyed it. Edo, Olym. People liked me. They finally looked at me like . . . It was finally real."

"I thought as much."

"But, no. I'm not disappointed. I was scared to death of having to rule, anyway."

"You never showed it." Absently, Amara ran a finger over the side of her wrist. It'd gotten scratched by accident. Cilla was right: scabs itched.

"I never wanted you to know. I couldn't even get Jorn to do what I wanted; I would've made a terrible queen. Besides, I would've had to find some guy to have children with, and . . ." Cilla shrugged one shoulder and winced. "It wasn't not being the princess that made me hurt myself. Yes, it was hard, thinking all my life I'm meant for something so big, so important, then having that snatched away, but it was the rest that screwed me up."

She seemed better now. She seemed almost OK. Amara stayed silent, letting Cilla answer the question Amara hadn't wanted to ask.

"When I cut myself, I didn't want to die. I just didn't know what else to do." It looked as if Cilla wanted to keep talking, but she shut her mouth and took a few seconds to work up to her next words. They rushed out all at once. "What do you want to do now?"

Amara remembered what they'd talked about on Captain Olym's ship. Diggers. Books. Silver. Eligon. Her parents.

Amara touched her neck, finding only smooth skin. She had gone from having no choices to having too many. What did you do when life wasn't just choosing the lesser evil? What did you do when you were the only one to decide where to walk, what to say? She didn't know where to start.

Cilla hesitated, then added, "Whatever you do—do you want to do it with me?"

Cilla. That was another choice, wasn't it? Because right now that girl on the bed was smiling, a hopeful, tiny smile that burst with wanting even as Cilla tried so hard to contain it.

Amara rested one hand on the bed to push herself up. She brought her lips to Cilla's.

This time, the kiss was quieter. Sweeter. When they parted, Amara didn't want to sit down again. She wanted to stay here, close, where she could feel Cilla's breath and heat and smiles.

"You're not crying this time," Cilla whispered. "That's an improvement. Does it mean yes?"

Amara crawled onto the bed, next to the warmth of Cilla's legs. "Maybe." She smiled, feeling oddly calm. "You don't know me. You knew a servant who had nothing in this world."

She was still a servant and she always would be. That kind of thing settled into your bones and heart and mind. But every day, she'd move a little farther away from it. Become a little less what people had made her and more what she made herself.

Maybe she needed Cilla to build that person. Or maybe she needed to stay far away.

"I want to know you." Cilla touched Amara's shoulder.

"Me, too," Amara said, which was not an answer, but she kept smiling anyway.

So many choices.

45

**N**olan must've read the notebooks a hundred times.

He had a theory: It wasn't just one traveler who'd possessed Jorn, but all of them. They rotated. Most of the time they reveled in their minister bodies, and one year in every half dozen or so they were on Cilla duty. That was why Jorn went years between drinking and punishments. That was why he'd tell Amara one thing, then another. That was why, two years ago, Nolan's journals had been filled with Jorn calling Amara kid.

All these tiny pieces fit together so well and they helped Nolan not one bit, and they helped Jorn, the real Jorn, even less.

⁓

"What did Jorn say?" Nolan said. He stared at the notebook on the kitchen table in front of him. "Before I hit him, he tried to say something. 'I'm sorry.' Or 'I'm scared.' 'I'm . . .' I don't know."

Pat frowned at him from the living room couch. She slapped the space bar on the laptop to pause whatever movie she was watching. "I don't either, Nole."

"I should know, though." Nolan paused. "I'm not dreaming about him or anything." He'd gone from years of notebooks and empty smiles to killing an innocent man. Took a stone and bashed in his skull. He should have nightmares. He should turn away every time he saw a brick, or wallow in guilt, or something.

He'd spent a lifetime wondering who he was. It couldn't be this. He wasn't a killer.

"Isn't that good? Not dreaming?" Pat sounded more awkward than anything.

She'd had nightmares after Nadi possessed her. So why hadn't Nolan?

"I'm constantly sucking up to Mom and Dad for everything that's happened, and at the same time I'm a murderer. How am I supposed to fit those things together?" He slammed his hand on the table, shoved aside the journal he'd meant to write in. It fell facedown to the floor. He didn't know what to write, anyway. The story was over. He'd left them. He hadn't gotten to say I'm sorry or I hope you have a nice life or I hope this makes up for everything. The journal ended before he'd walked Amara back to the palace.

Pat hissed for him to stay quiet, looking anxiously at the staircase. Mom was asleep upstairs.

"At least you admit you're a suck-up," Pat said once she was satisfied Mom wasn't coming down.

She was trying to make him feel better, but he couldn't

fake his old laughs anymore. "Well, this time, sucking up isn't working."

His parents and Dr. Campbell had blamed his behavior—including going cold turkey on his pills—on side effects. It could've ended a lot worse, Dr. Campbell had said. Nolan's parents still seemed shaken, though. They watched him so carefully, smiled so encouragingly, and tried so hard not to bring up the night of Pat's play that it might've been funny under other circumstances.

"I'm sorry about the play," he said for the tenth time, though it came automatically, and he hoped she didn't notice. "I'll help you rehearse next year. Every year."

"What you did was more important. I get it." Pat finally slapped the laptop shut and dropped it onto the couch cushions. She joined Nolan at the kitchen table. "Do you want to talk about it or whatever?" She tried to look genuine. Her eyebrows contorted weirdly. "Don't look at me like that. I'm being nice."

He'd gambled with Pat's life. It'd worked out, but it'd been an incredible risk. Nolan had placed the life of a far-off girl in a far-off world over his sister's. He'd felt Amara's desperation as keenly as his own, and that didn't make it right, but . . .

Part of him missed that. Feeling what Amara felt. Thinking what she thought. *Fuck this life,* he'd written once. Now it was the only one he had left.

"I don't know who I am when I'm not trying to pretend

everything's OK," he told Pat. There. Straight-up. Words that would've normally gone into a journal or been pushed into a far corner of his mind because he had no right to an identity crisis while Amara went through hell.

Was she still going through hell? He couldn't check. She lived worlds beyond his reach.

"I figured . . . If I was going to be a blank slate, just bouncing off whatever happened to Amara, I might as well keep people around me happy. But I'm not bouncing off anything now. I'm stuck." He jammed a finger at his head.

Right where he'd hit Jorn.

"You're not a blank slate." Pat dropped to the side of her chair, fishing underneath the table for the journal Nolan had dropped. She slapped it in front of him. "I mean, look at this journal. You're way precise. And trying to keep Mom and Dad happy for so long couldn't have been easy. It's something good people do. Not blank slates."

He couldn't find the words to argue.

"And," she said, on a roll now, "remember all your good ideas? You walked half an hour to my school in crazy heat, stayed up all night, you *overdosed*. You're kind of an impulsive idi—um, you're impulsive."

He nodded. Swallowed. "I know." He hesitated, and his next words came like sludge, slow and dark, and he couldn't stop them once he'd started. "I killed Jorn without—I didn't even think about alternatives. And now I don't have nightmares."

Then, in a small voice, he added, "I was so excited when I first got control. And look what I did with it. Look."

And in a whisper: "I thought I was screwed up *before*."

"No. Stop." Pat shook her head wildly. "Stop. It's only been a week and a half. You might still get nightmares later. But they're no good. They suck, Nolan, they suck. Why would you want to feel terrible?"

She'd gone from joking to having tears in her voice.

"I want to *care*," he said.

"You saved me." She palmed her eyes, rubbed them. "You saved them. That's caring."

He looked at Pat and exhaled painful air from his chest. He tried a smile, a real one.

She pushed the notebook his way. "Maybe—maybe you should finish this."

*There's nothing to write,* Nolan wanted to argue.

He'd do it anyway.

*And Cilla and Amara lived happily ever after,* Nolan wrote.

He imagined them fighting, Amara shouting because she could, because she needed to know she could. He imagined her turning away when Cilla needed her, because if she didn't, she'd still be that servant she thought she'd escaped. She wouldn't be able to make sacrifices for Cilla without wondering if it was love or duty that made her do it. She couldn't feel concern without remembering a million times she'd been concerned before, with Jorn looming over her and a curse rattling at the edges.

And when she helped anyway, when she couldn't bear not to because one look at Cilla made her want to press her as close as she could, it would be Cilla's turn to wonder the same things. Because how could she be sure?

They couldn't be equals.

They could love, and Nolan hoped they did, because they had no one else now. But the intensity would fade, and the past would creep back in.

Maybe. He didn't know.

He wrote: *They manage despite everything. Amara asks Ruudde to help with Edo's bar and Olym's farm. She wonders about that boy sometimes who*

No. He wrote: *She misses Maart a lot & places stones on his grave.*

And, the next week: *She works in the palace alongside Lorres, helping servants where she can. Then she fights a revolution and she wins and servants are no more.*

A month after: *She finds her parents and they move to Eligon, and she never sees Cilla again. She finally relearns Elig.*

And: *She and Cilla track Cilla's family on the Alinean Islands, and they travel the world.*

And: Every morning on the beach, she practices her writing and watches for diggers.

And: She is, and stays, her own.

And: I'm going to watch TV with my parents and Pat. She was right: I have nightmares about Jorn now, and about Maart. I'm seeing a therapist. I can't tell the truth but it still helps. I try to help Pat, too.

I'm going to apologize for being a dick to Sarah Schneider and ask her out again. Not just because I can, but because I want to. And I'll find other things to want. I'll listen to music. I could learn to draw, or study acting like Pat.

I don't care about the movies yet, but I care about movie nights, and that's a start.

Nolan put the journal with the others and locked the Dunelands away.

# ACKNOWLEDGMENTS

ndless love to my family, who has offered me nothing but support, and particularly to my mother, for too many reasons to list. (The next one is yours.)

I owe the world to Maggie Lehrman, who fished me out of the depths of the Internet, gave my odd book a chance, and made it a much, much better odd book.

It's been fantastic having Ammi-Joan Paquette's kindness, support, and smarts in my corner during this process.

To both of you: here's to many more!

High fives to the entire EMLA and Amulet Books crews, especially the team responsible for my stunning cover: Vince Natale, Sara Corbett, Chad Beckerman, and Kate Fitch.

I cannot express enough thanks to these wonderful women:

Helen Corcoran: for years of encouragement and brain-storming, and for screaming out loud on the Dublin streets.

Natalie C. Parker: for the all-caps LOVE, which kept me going through months of doubt and rejection, and for pushing me to do better.

Marieke Nijkamp: for all her feedback and twenty-four/seven enthusiasm.

Kim Welchons: for her faith and commiseration, and for long conversations in her car.

My heart bubbles with gratitude for my beta readers: Jodi Meadows, Dawn Metcalf, and Phoebe North for saying in unison: "Your first half needs work!" (and for being right); Alex Bear, for her helpful notes on Nolan's not-actually-epilepsy; Erica Lim, for her insightful comments about Amara's relationships with Maart and Cilla; Julia Rios, for her sound advice regarding the Santiagos; Jessica Silva and Kayla Whaley, for reading at lightning speed; and s.e. smith, for ou smart thoughts on disability.

Thanks also go to Katie Carson, for the word wars; April Helmes, for so kindly answering my questions about amputation and prostheses; Valerie Kemp, for brainstorming; Kalen O'Donnell, for solid advice and publishing gossip; Katey Taylor, for nonstop support over many years; #txrt, for being awesome (and particularly to Carrie Ryan, for her wise advice); and lastly, Anna and Regina, for listening.

You all deserve a snack and drink of your choice just for putting up with me. I salute you.

I also want to thank my stunning blurbers and the good people of the Junior Library Guild for believing in this book.

Strange Horizons magazine and its crew deserve a shout-out for putting "Eight" into the world for Maggie to find.

To everyone who offers their time and energy to discuss—whether via blogs, articles, Twitter, or Tumblr—oppression and marginalization: you've made me a little less clueless over the years, and I'm very, very grateful for that. (It's a work in progress.)

The lovely ladies of Gunning for Awesome—Gemma, Deborah, Michelle, Lori, Amy P., Natalie, Ruth, Amy T., Kim, and Stephanie—and the awesome ladies of the Fourteenery—Livia, Annie, Jessica, Katie, Christa, Kate, Amber, Jenny, Julie, Natalie, Tess, Lindsay, and Robin—and all the OneFour KidLit peeps—I am in no way naming all of you: it's been wonderful sharing this journey together.

To Alisa, Alex, John, Erik, Sarah, Cassie, Jei, Jenni, Jack, Mark, David, Maria, Jeremy, Anne, Nick, Steve, and Alberto; to L. Timmel Duchamp, Minister Faust, Nancy Kress, Margo Lanagan, Paul Park, and Charles Stross; to Neile and Leslie; and to everyone else associated with the workshop . . . thank you. Clarion West 2011: affable mofos for life.

Lastly, a massive hug for the wonderful world of fandom, particularly Suzanne, who led the way, and Diane, Oliver, and all my other RP buds, who nerded out over superpowered teenagers with me and sneakily taught me to write in the process.

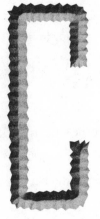orinne Duyvis is a novelist and short story writer. She's a graduate of the Clarion West Writers Workshop and lives in Amsterdam. Visit her online at corinneduyvis.net.